# WIZARD OF
# THE GROVE

The finest in Fantasy and Science Fiction
by TANYA HUFF from DAW Books:

THE SILVERED
\* \* \*

THE ENCHANTMENT EMPORIUM
THE WILD WAYS
THE FUTURE FALLS
\* \* \*

The Confederation Novels:
A CONFEDERATION OF VALOR
Valor's Choice/The Better Part of Valor
THE HEART OF VALOR
VALOR'S TRIAL
THE TRUTH OF VALOR

The Peacekeeper Novels:
AN ANCIENT PEACE
\* \* \*

SMOKE AND SHADOWS
SMOKE AND MIRRORS
SMOKE AND ASHES
\* \* \*

BLOOD PRICE
BLOOD TRAIL
BLOOD LINES
BLOOD PACT
BLOOD DEBT
BLOOD BANK
\* \* \*

THE COMPLETE KEEPER CHRONICLES:
Summon the Keeper/The Second Summoning/Long Hot Summoning
\* \* \*

THE QUARTERS NOVELS, Volume 1:
Sing the Four Quarters/Fifth Quarter
THE QUARTERS NOVELS, Volume 2:
No Quarter/The Quartered Sea
\* \* \*

WIZARD OF THE GROVE
Child of the Grove/The Last Wizard
\* \* \*

OF DARKNESS, LIGHT, AND FIRE
Gate of Darkness, Circle of Light/The Fire's Stone

# WIZARD OF THE GROVE

BOOK ONE

**CHILD OF THE GROVE**

BOOK TWO

**THE LAST WIZARD**

WITHDRAWN

# TANYA HUFF

## DAW BOOKS, INC.

**DONALD A. WOLLHEIM, FOUNDER**

375 Hudson Street, New York, NY 10014

**ELIZABETH R. WOLLHEIM**
**SHEILA E. GILBERT**
**PUBLISHERS**

www.dawbooks.com

First Trade Paperback Printing, March 2016
1  2  3  4  5  6  7  8  9

DAW TRADEMARK REGISTERED
U.S. PAT. AND TM. OFF. AND FOREIGN COUNTRIES
—MARCA REGISTRADA
HECHO EN U.S.A.

PRINTED IN THE U.S.A.

# CHILD OF
# THE GROVE

For my grandmother,

who wouldn't have understood

but would have been proud

of me anyway

# GENESIS

In the Beginning there was Darkness and out of the Darkness came the Mother. From her flesh She formed the Earth. With her tears She filled the seas and lakes and rivers. She walked upon her creation and where She passed grew grasses, trees, and flowers. Her breath became the winds. With her right hand She created all animals that run and swim and fly. With her left hand She created all animals that slither and sting. Her laughter became the song of birds.

When She had walked all the Earth, She sat to rest in a circle of silver birch. As She was lonely, She gave form to the spirit of one of the trees that it might keep her company. And the form was that of a beautiful woman. Her name was Milthra and she was the Eldest of the Elder Races.

When the Mother left the Grove, She gave form also to the other birches that Milthra would never be lonely as She had been. It is said there is form in all trees if the Power is there to call the spirit out.

And as the Mother walked the Earth, She bled four times. From her blood came the other Elder Races, the Centaurs, the Giants, the Dwarves, and the Merfolk. And so She could see what She created, each time She bled She hung a silver light in the night sky.

Then another came out of the Darkness. His name was Chaos and He lay with the Mother and She bore him a son. And the name of the Mother's son was Death. He was very terrible and very beautiful.

As the Elder races were of the Mother's body and blood, they could see Death's beauty but not his terror. Though they could be killed, they did not die; and so they had no fear of him.

Death went to the Mother and begged her to create a people he could rule.

Because She loved him, She did.

But because She loved her newest creations as well, She gave them a gift so they could keep Death in his place. She gave them the power to create. And She gave them a promise that once Death had come to them, they would return to her once more. She called them Humans, but Death called them Mortals which means "to die."

Humans used the Mother's gift to create Gods. They worshiped and made sacrifices in the hope that their Gods could keep Death away. But the powers of the Gods, being Human given, were of no use against the Mother's true son. Soon Humankind abandoned the Gods and learned to face Death. Some even came to see his beauty.

But a God once created cannot be uncreated and so, no longer worshiped, the Gods grew bored. Those given the aspect of men by their creators took to walking the Earth in human form. Eventually, they all lay with mortal women and from those unions the race of Wizards was born.

The Wizards used the powers of the Gods to pervert the Mother's gift and their first act was to turn on their fathers and destroy them. There would be no new Wizards. They formed a great council and for many centuries ruled the creatures of the Earth. Even the Elder Races feared them, for it appeared the Wizards had conquered Death.

Over the years, as their powers grew, so did their corruption. By forcing the breeding of man and animal, they created the Werfolk in a mockery of the Mother's work.

And then the Wizards dared to create something using the very Earth itself. They formed mighty Dragons, giant beasts with command of fire and frost, rulers of the air or seas. But the Earth was the Body of the Mother and the Wizards could not control it. They had created their own destruction.

The Dragons turned on the Wizards and in a battle that changed the shape of the land, slew and devoured their would-be masters. The Dragons that survived returned to the Earth from which they were made.

It is said that, at the end of the Age of Wizards, Death smiled.

# ONE

"M other?"

There was no answer, so the tall young man reached out a slender hand and placed it gently on the bark of the silver birch before him.

"Mother?" he said again.

The tree stirred under his hand, as if, newly awakened, it sighed and stretched. He stepped back and waited. Slowly, very slowly, his mother drew herself out of her tree.

She was tall, with ivory skin, silver hair, and eyes the green of new spring leaves. Her name was Milthra and she was the eldest of the Sisters of the Sacred Grove. She looked barely older than her son.

She opened her arms and he came into them, then she held him at arm's length and smiled.

"You have grown, Rael. You look more like your father every time I see you." He looked so much like his father that her heart ached with the memories. Not for many years had Raen, King of Ardhan, come to the Sacred Grove, and Milthra had to be content with seeing the man she loved in the face of their son. Raen would not come to her for reasons of his own. She could not go to him for a hamadryad dies away from her tree.

She hid a sigh from her too perceptive child and brushed a lock of blue-black hair off his face. "Are you well? Are you happy?"

"I'm both well and happy, Mother." Rael returned her smile, his eyes lit from within by green fires. Immortal eyes in the face of mortal man.

Rael could no longer be content spending whole summers with only his mother, her sisters, and the forest for company—the king's court held more attractions for a young man of seventeen—but when he had time to spare, he spent it at the Grove. It was peaceful there and, unlike his father, his mother had time to listen. No courtiers or supplicants made demands on her, for no one found the circle of birches without her help.

Until Rael's birth the Grove had been legend only. But when the King of Ardhan showed his son to the people in the Great Square outside the palace gates, he named Milthra as the child's mother and placed the Grove firmly in the real world. It was fortunate the king was popular and well-liked, for many disbelieved and not a few muttered of insanity. It was also fortunate that the king was no fool and would not allow the acceptance of his son to rest on his own popularity. He called the six dukes and their households together and had them meet the infant's eyes.

Milthra had walked with the Mother-creator as She rested after birthing the world. A fraction of that glory she passed on to her child.

It was enough.

"My aunts still won't wake to greet me?" Rael asked, sprawled on the velvet grass at the foot of his mother's tree. He dug into his pack for the food he'd cadged from a sympathetic kitchen maid.

Milthra shook her head and accepted a piece of honey cake. She had no need to eat—she drew nourishment from her tree—but did it to please her son as once she had done it to please his father. "It has been a long time since the Mother walked in the forest and we wakened. My sisters are tired and want only to sleep."

Rael looked around at the trees he knew as beautiful women, women who had coddled him, fussed over him, and been as much a part of his childhood as his mother and father. He hadn't seen them since . . . his forehead creased as he tried to remember. Had it really been three years? He stretched out a long arm and tugged on a low-hanging branch from a neighboring tree. Leaves rustled but no hamadryad appeared.

"You're the oldest, can't you wake them."

"Perhaps. But I will not try."

"Why not? Aren't you lonely?" As much as Rael loved the Grove, he'd hate to be the only creature awake in its circle.

"No, for when you are not here I also sleep. My sisters have no ties to the world of men to wake them, that is the only difference between us." If she ever regretted the ties that bound her, or acknowledged that they had brought her more sorrow than joy, it could not be heard in the music of her voice.

Rael scooped up his mother's hands and kissed them. "The only difference?" he teased. "I refuse to listen to such foolishness. What of your beauty? Your grace? Your wisdom? I could continue for hours . . ."

Milthra laughed and Rael laughed with her. He'd always felt his mother laughed too seldom. In later years, Rael would recall that afternoon and her laughter when his spirit needed soothing and the shadows needed lifting from his life. He lay with his head in her lap and told her of the things he'd done since he'd been with her last—well most of the things; she was, after all, his mother—and he even told her of his feelings for the Duke of Belkar's blue-eyed daughter, something he had confided to no one else . . . particularly not the Duke of Belkar's blue-eyed daughter.

But he did not speak of why he had come to the Grove.

All too soon the thick, golden sunlight bathing the Grove began to pale. The shadows grew longer and the breezes grew chill. Rael rose lithely to his feet and extended a hand to the hamadryad. When she stood beside him, he kept her hand clasped tightly in his and stared at the ground, unsure of how to begin.

"I . . . I won't be back for some time."

"There is to be war."

He looked up and saw she gazed sadly at him.

"How did you know?"

"The breezes tell me. Even in sleep I hear them; they say men gather on the western border clutching steel in angry hands."

Rael spread his own hands helplessly. "The King of Melac has a new and powerful counselor and the man plays the king's weaknesses and desires like, like a shepherd plays his pipes. He's driving the king to create an empire. Father says they begin with us because Melac hates my father for something that happened when they were young."

"And my son will go to see they conquer no empire."

"I have to do what I can." He tried to keep the anticipation out of his voice and wasn't entirely successful. This war would be his chance to prove himself. His skill with weapons was his father's heritage, but he moved with a strength and grace no man born of mere mortal could match. In his mind's eye he saw himself a hero, returning from battle not only accepted but adulated by the people he was destined to rule. In his heart, he only hoped he would not disgrace his training.

"And your father?"

His voice was gentle. "The king must ride at the head of his armies."

"Yes." War had brought the young king to her so many years before. He had staggered, lost and wounded, into the Grove, stinking of steel and violence, Lord Death close by his side. Against the advice of her sisters, for the Elder Races did not involve themselves with mortals, she had saved him. Saved him and loved him, and Rael had come of it.

Full dusk was upon them now.

"I must go, Mother."

"Yes." War took her son from her, replaced her loving child with this stern young man, so ready to do violence. If he survived he would be further changed, and who knew if he would return to the Grove where nothing changed at all. She held him. Held him tightly. And then she let him go because it was all she could do.

"Rael?"

He turned; half in, half out of the Grove.

"Tell your father, I am always here."

"He knows, Mother." He waited but she said nothing more. "Mother?"

She shook her head, the brilliant immortal color of her eyes dimmed by a very mortal sorrow. She was the Eldest. She could not beg for the return of her love.

Accustomed to thinking of the hamadryad as his mother, and mothers as always strong, Rael had never noticed before how young Milthra looked, or how frail. He suddenly wanted to protect her, to take her in his arms and tell her everything would be all right, but as he watched she faded and dissolved back into her tree. Only the breezes remained and he had never learned to hear what they said.

Although dark had fallen over Melac, the building of the counselor's tower continued. In the flickering light of torches, long lines of naked and sweating men struggled with block and tackle to lift massive slabs of marble into position. As each slab reached its zenith, a slave was removed from the coffle staked at the work site and placed beneath it. Some screamed, some sobbed, some lay limp and resigned, pushed beyond terror. The slab dropped, then the whole process was repeated for the next. The tower was to be the tallest in the city.

If the men who built it felt anything at all, it was, for the most part, relief that they were not beneath the stones themselves.

This night, as most nights, the king's counselor watched the construction from the wooden dais that gave him an unobstructed view of the work. This night, the king stood beside him, leaning into each death, his tongue protruding slightly, his breathing ragged and quick.

A new slave was unchained; a young man, well formed, who, in spite of lash marks striping his back from neck to knees, fought so viciously that four men were needed to escort him to the stone. He screamed, not in terror but in defiance.

The king started at the sound and actually saw the slave. His eyes widened and he clutched at the blue velvet of his counselor's sleeve.

"That looks to be Lord Elan's son."

"It is."

"But you can't . . ."

"He spoke against me, Majesty, and so spoke against you. To speak against the lawful king is treason. The penalty for treason is death." The golden-haired man smiled and removed the king's hand from his arm. "At least this way his death serves a purpose. Life makes the strongest mortar."

On the stone, Lord Elan's son strained against invisible bonds, muscles standing out in sharp relief. He threw back his head and howled as the slab above him fell.

On the dais, the king swayed and he moaned deep in his throat.


Rael stretched the two-hour ride home from the Grove to nearly four, dismounting to sit for a time in the moonlight. To his left, waited the shadow that was the forest. To his right, a ribbon of brown led to the distant lights of the town that spread like a skirt outside the palace walls. The Lady's Wood. King's Road, King's Town.

His horse nickered and lipped at his hair, more interested in returning to the comfort of stable and stall than in philosophy.

Grasping the gelding's mane, Rael pulled himself to his feet, mounted, and kicked the horse into a trot. He had always known that someday he would be king. He enjoyed the power and privilege, and even the responsibilities, of being prince and heir. But sometimes, in the moonlight, he wished he had a choice.

Hoofs thudded onto packed earth, and Rael turned up the King's Road.

The watch had just called midnight when Rael reached town. Because the King's City was so close to the center of Ardhan, miles from any invading army and surrounded on all sides by loyal subjects of the king, it had no wall. The scattered farms and cottages of the countryside merely moved closer together along the road until they gave way to the houses, shops, and inns of the city. At the Market Square—well lit even at this hour, for when business in booths and stalls shut down, business in taverns and wineshops began—Rael turned, avoiding the light, preferring to remain unseen in the residential neighborhoods where the inhabitants had long since sought their beds. He told himself he avoided the trouble that would arise if anyone recognized the young man tucked deep in the worn cloak as the prince and heir, riding alone, unescorted. He told himself he didn't need his pocket picked, an un-provoked fight, or an escort back to his father.

He had just passed silently through the merchants' quarters and crossed the invisible but nonetheless real line that separated their homes from the only slightly larger ones of the nobles, when the dark and quiet were snatched from around him.

"Bertram, aren't we home yet?"

"Very nearly, sir."

"I'm sure it wasn't this far before."

The whiny, self-indulgent voice belonged to a minor official of the court, one Diven of House Tannic. Rael had endured too many hours of petitions to mistake it, even distorted as it was by drink.

The torchbearer rounded the corner first, followed by an over-dressed man leaning heavily on the arm of his body servant. A City Guard, hired as evening's escort, brought up the rear.

Rael kept his horse walking. With luck they would be too interested in gaining their beds to pay any attention to him.

Luck was busy elsewhere.

"Awk, Bertram! Brigands!"

Bertram looked to the heavens, exasperation visible even to Rael, and patted his master comfortingly on the shoulder. "It's only a single rider, sir."

"Oh. So it is." Any other would have been content to leave it at that. Diven stepped forward, past the torchbearer and directly into Rael's path. Drink made him determined to erase the embarrassment of his fright. "You there, state your business in this neighborhood. Speak up, or I'll call the patrol."

Rael reined in. The torchbearer grinned, obviously looking forward to telling his cronies of how the drunken noble had accosted one of his equally noble neighbors and threatened him with the patrol. Bertram, now up behind his master, was thinking much the same thing, but not with amusement. The guard looked bored.

"Well, boy, do you tell me your business or do I call the patrol? I will, you know, don't think I won't."

Rael wondered how a voice could whine and be shrill at the same time. He had no doubt the idiot would do exactly as he said, and wake the neighborhood doing it. And that would be the end of the dark and quiet, no mere interruption. He sighed, made his smile as friendly as he was able, and pulled back his hood.

"Highness!"

For a moment the smile held them—they began to return it—then the torchlight flared in his eyes.

The guard saluted and all four men began to back away.

Respectfully, and nervously, they backed away.

From the torchbearer and the guard, it was almost understandable for they met the prince and heir for the first time. Bertram also; for all he served in a noble house he was not accustomed to facing royalty so closely and so informally. But Diven of Tannic saw the prince almost daily. And still he backed away.

Rael held the smile until his horse carried him out of the circle of torchlight. Once he would have said something, tried to find the camaraderie his father seemed to share with every man, woman, and child in the kingdom. Once. But all the words had been said and still the people moved away. Not rejecting, not exactly, but not accepting either.

*Let them move if they will,* he told himself wearily, replacing his hood. *I have enough who stand by me.* Then he moved back into the dark and quiet.

At the smaller of the palace gates, he allowed the guard to get a good look at him, and passed unchallenged through the outer wall. Except for a sleepy groom waiting to take his horse, and the men on watch, it appeared the palace slept. It didn't, of course, for within its walls the palace was almost a city in itself and the work needed to keep it running smoothly continued day and night.

He walked quickly across the outer courtyard, slipped in a side door, and began to make his way silently through the maze of stone to the tower where he had his chambers. Once, he froze in shadow and an arguing pair of courtiers passed him by.

At the cross-corridor leading to the king's rooms, Rael noticed the royal standard still posted, the six swords on a field of green hanging limp and still against the wall. His father had not retired for the night. Wide awake himself, Rael turned toward the royal bedchamber, hoping the king would not be too busy to speak with him.

The guards saluted as he approached and moved aside to give him access to the door.

"Is he alone?" asked the prince.

"Aye, sir, he is," replied the senior of the two.

Rael nodded his thanks and pushed the door open.

"Father?"

The king sat at his desk studying a large map, one hand holding down a curling edge, the other buried in his beard.

Rael was thinner than his father, his eyes an unworldly green, but aside from that the resemblance was astounding. Both were handsome men, although neither believed it. They shared the same high forehead over black slashes of brow, the same angular cheeks and proud arch of nose, even the determined set to their jaws and slightly mocking smiles matched. Those who had known the king as a young man said to look at the prince was to look at a piece of the past. The people of Ardhan might wonder at the identity of his mother, and they did, but none could doubt that Rael was the king's son.

Raen looked up as the door opened and his face brightened when he saw who it was.

"Come in, lad," he called. "And shut the damn door before it blows out my lamp."

Rael did as he was bid and approached the desk, collapsing with a boneless, adolescent grace into the sturdy chair across from his father.

"The Western Border?"

The king nodded. "And you'd best get familiar with it yourself. We march as soon as the armies are assembled."

Rael leaned forward to study the map. "You're surely not assembling all six provinces here?" He wondered where they'd put everyone. The six dukes and their households jammed the palace to the rafters during seventh year festivals. The six dukes and their armies . . . !

"No, only Cei and Aliston will come here to Belkar. We'll join with Hale on the march." He traced their route with a callused finger. "Lorn and Riven meet us on the battlefield." His mouth twisted. "And it's to be hoped those two hotheads will concentrate on fighting the enemy instead of each other. I'm thankful you've no rival for your lady's hand."

Rael felt his ears redden.

"You can keep no secrets in this rabbit warren, lad. It's a good match; her father and I both approve. You're lucky I've no need to join you to some foreign princess to tie a treaty."

"Join?" Rael repeated weakly. He'd barely gotten beyond worshiping from a distance and his father spoke of joinings?

The older man laughed. "You're right," he mocked, but kindly, "it's bad luck to talk of joining on the eve of war." He turned again to the map. "And on the eve of war we are; I want the armies on the road in two weeks."

"In two weeks? Father, it can't be done." The Elite, the Palace Guard and the Ducal Guards that made up the standing army, yes, and, he supposed, most City Guards could adapt fast enough, but when Rael thought of the chaos involved in turning farmers and craftsmen into soldiers his head ached.

"It's going to have to be done," the king said shortly. "We have no choice. Melac's moving very fast; he wants those iron mines in Riven badly and has had plans to invade us for years. Though he's a fool if he thinks he's in charge, not that madman he has for a counselor." He looked down at the map and shook his head. "Still, madman or not, he's a brilliant leader. I've never heard of anyone getting an army into the field so quickly." Teeth gleamed for an instant in the lamplight. "If I didn't know all the wizards were dead. . . ."

The wizards had destroyed themselves before there was an Ardhan or a king to rule it. Their dying convulsions had reshaped the face of the world.

"Father! You don't think . . . ?"

"Don't be ridiculous, boy. I was joking." Raen leaned back in his chair and looked fondly at his son. His expression hardened. "You're not wearing your sword."

Rael's hand jerked to his belt and he flushed.

"I saw Mother today, to tell her I wouldn't be back to the Grove for some time. You know how steel upsets her."

"Well, your guards were armed, I hope?"

Rael looked at the cold hearth, the hunting tapestry on the wall, the great canopied bed, everywhere but at his father.

"You took no guards." The king's voice was sharper than Rael's missing sword.

"The guards won't go into the Grove."

"The guards will go where I tell them." And then he thought of Milthra's reaction to heavily armed men tearing up her peace and re-considered. Gods, he missed her. "Well, they can wait with your horse at the edge of the forest, then. They needn't go into the Grove."

An uncomfortable silence fell as both considered another who would not go into the Grove.

"You'll take them with you next time," Raen said finally. "I don't want a dead son."

Rael turned the brilliant green of his eyes on the king. "Who would want to kill me, Father?"

"Balls of Chaos, boy, how should I know?" Raen looked away from the Lady's eyes. "Melac's men. Madmen. You're prince and heir, my only son. When you ride from now on, you ride with guards." King's command, not father's. "I don't care where you're going. I will not lose you."

"Yes, sir." Suddenly, Rael made a decision. He was tired, he decided, of bouncing from the pain of one parent to the pain of the other and tired too of pretending he didn't see that pain because they both so obviously tried to keep it from him. He took his courage in both hands and asked what he'd never dared ask before. "Father? Why don't you go to the Grove?"

Raen stared at the map without seeing it. He remembered ivory and silver and green, green eyes and strong smooth limbs wrapped around him. He remembered a love so deep he could drown in it.

"How did your mother look when you left her this afternoon?" he asked hoarsely.

Rael thought about his last sight of the hamadryad as she merged back into her tree.

"As always, beautiful; but worried and sad."

"And her age?"

"Her age?" He remembered how he'd wanted to protect her. "She seemed very young."

"Now look at me."

"Sir?"

"LOOK AT ME!" Raen stood so suddenly that his chair over-turned. His hands clenched to fists and his voice rose to a roar. "Once my hair was as thick and black as yours. You'll notice that what I have left, and there isn't much, is gray. There was a day I could defeat any man in Ardhan with my bare hands, but no longer. I used to be able to follow the flight of a hawk in the sun. Now I'm lucky if I can see the damned bird at all! I grew this beard to hide the lines of age!" He paused, drew a shuddering breath and his voice fell until it was almost a whisper. "Your mother hasn't changed, but I am growing old. She must not see me like this."

Rael was on his feet as well, staring at his father in astonishment. "You're not old!"

The king's smile was not reflected in his eyes. "Fifty-two years weigh heavily on a man, and your mother is ageless." He raised a hand to stop the next protest. "I appreciate your denials, lad, but I know what I see."

Unfortunately, there was nothing to deny. His father was a mortal man and his mother stood outside of time.

"Mother loves you. It wouldn't matter to her."

"It would matter to me. Let her love me as I was."

Rael ached with the pain in his father's voice that was a twin to the pain in his mother's.

"Father . . ."

"No, Rael." Raen put his hands on his son's shoulders but avoided the leaf-green glow of his eyes. "There is nothing you can do. Go to bed. We have a busy time ahead of us."

"Yes, sir."

*Is he too old for me to hold?* Raen wondered, looking for his child and seeing only a young man.

*Am I too old to be held?* Rael asked the dignity of his seventeen years.

No.

It comforted them both greatly.

*If I can only get him to the Grove,* Rael thought as he left his father's room. *If I can only get him to the Grove, everything will be all right.*

# TWO

"Out of bed, milord. The Duke of Belkar and some of his men rode in last night and your father wants to see you in the small petition room."

Rael buried his head under the pillow as the middle-aged man, who had been his servant/companion since before he could remember, pulled back the heavy curtains and let in the weak early morning light. "Oh, go away, Ivan, it's barely dawn."

"It's an hour past." Strong hands dragged the blankets away with the familiarity of long service. "Get up or you won't have time for a wash and bite before you see the king."

There was time for the wash but not the bite and Rael's stomach complained bitterly as he slipped into the room where the daily business of the kingdom was most often conducted. Raen looked up at the sound, pushed the remnants of his own breakfast across the table, and turned his attention back to the document he studied. More than a little embarrassed, Rael took a chunk of bread and slid into the only vacant chair. The Duke of Belkar smiled at him and the other man, who by his armor could only be one of Belkar's two captains, raised an edge of his lip in what have been either a greeting or a grimace.

Finally the king scrawled his signature at the bottom of the document, set his seal in wax, and gave the paper to the Messenger standing patiently at his elbow. Then he looked up at his son.

"Belkar and I have talked it over and it's been decided that you'll command the Elite."

Rael choked on the bread. The men of the Elite were the best fighters in Ardhan. Every young man who could use a sword dreamed of joining their company. And he was to command them. He suddenly thought of something. "But, sir, the king commands the Elite."

"The king also makes the rules, and I've changed this one. As prince and heir, you must have a command. I thought of creating a company for you out of the Palace Guard. You've trained with them and most of them know you, but the Elite is already a self-contained unit, used to serving under a royal commander." Black brows rose. "Or don't you want to command the Elite?"

"Yes, sir!" *The Elite,* Rael thought.

"As prince and heir," the king continued, a smile twitching at the corners of his mouth, "you'll be obeyed, but I hasten to point out that, training aside, you know little of actual warfare, so defer to the captain."

"Yes, sir." Rael had every intention of deferring to the captain. He'd been terrified of the thickset little man for as long as he could remember.

"Before you head down to the barracks, stop off at the armorers and get fitted for a new helmet, breastplate, and greaves. Your sword's fine."

"Yes, sir."

"Well, get going."

"Yes, sir!"

"He'll be in the thick of the fighting with the Elite," Belkar pointed out as the prince dashed out of the room.

"Aye," agreed the king grimly. "But they'll have to go through the Elite to get to him. It's the safest place I can think of."

"You could order him to remain here," suggested the duke, not at all pleased to have both the king and his only heir in such danger.

"I could, but I'll be damned if I'll chain my son to the walls." Raen smiled ruefully. "And that's what I'd have to do to keep him here."

\* \* \*

By the time Rael arrived at the Elite's training yard, the euphoria was beginning to fade. Though the news of his appointment had obviously preceded him, the Elite weren't yet ready to change their allegiance from captain and king/commander to captain, king, and prince/commander. Every one of them, soldier and servant, politely ignored him as he made his way to the practice ring.

Doan, the captain, perched on the top rail of the fence surrounding the ring, looking like a well-armed gargoyle. He welcomed the prince with a grunt and slapped the rail in invitation, never once taking his eyes off the men training.

Rael climbed up and sat down, a little farther from Doan than was strictly polite. He couldn't help himself; something about the captain put him on edge. It wasn't the man's appearance—although the barrel chest, bandy legs, and habitual scowl made him far from appealing—it was more the feeling of tremendous power just barely under control that he seemed to project. Palace rumor whispered Doan had dwarf blood and Rael believed it. When he looked at the captain through his mother's eyes, he felt the same strong belonging to the land that he felt in the Grove but none of the peace or serenity.

Wood cracked on wood and then wood on bone and then one of the men in the ring was down, blood streaming from a cut on his forehead, his quarterstaff lying useless on the sand beside him.

"Get him out of there," grunted Doan. He turned to the prince and pointed at his sword with a gnarled finger. "The swordmaster says you know how to use that thing."

Rael's back stiffened. He'd never trained with the Elite, for theirs was a very close fraternity, but Doan had seen him work with the Palace Guard often enough to know he could use his sword. And his strength and speed were common knowledge.

"Show me."

As regally as he was able, Rael shrugged and slid off the fence. He drew his sword and tossed his scabbard to one side.

Suddenly, every Elite not on duty surrounded the ring.

Rael looked around at the grinning faces, swallowed nervously, and met the eyes of the captain. They reflected the early morning light in such a way they appeared to glow deeply red. Rael swallowed again and his chin went up. So the new commander had to prove he was worthy, did he? Well, he'd show them.

"Who do I fight?"

A slow smile spread over the guard captain's face. "Me," he said. "Your Highness." And he dropped into the ring.

Doan's attack came so quickly, the fight almost ended before it truly began. To Rael's astonishment, his strength and speed alone were not enough and he was forced to use every bit of skill the swordmaster had drilled into him over the years. The prince was a slender flame tipped with steel. Doan stood solid, each movement deliberate and so slow next to the Lady's son that it seemed he must be cut to shreds. But Rael could not get past his guard, and when their swords met he had to use all of his unworldly strength to block the blow.

Less than three minutes later it was finished.

Doan bent and retrieved Rael's sword. "You'll do," he said as he handed it over. "Commander."

A cheer went up from the surrounding Elite and Rael became aware that a great deal of coin was changing hands. Snatches of conversation drifted back from the dispersing men.

". . . told you he'd get his own in . . ."

". . . expected the captain to beat him to his knees . . ."

". . . four coppers, you jackass, but then I've seen him fight before . . ."

And echoed from more than one direction: "He'll do."

"They'd follow the prince because they had to," Doan grunted as Rael sheathed his sword. "Better you make them want to."

Rael straightened his shoulders. "And how do I make them want to?"

"You've started already." Doan hacked and spit in the sand. "You've proven you can fight."

"But you beat me."

"I know. I beat them, too. But you showed them you could've made the company on your own."

Rael flushed with pleasure. "I could've?"

"Just said so, didn't I?" Doan hooked his thumbs behind his broad leather belt and headed out of the practice ring. "Now if you'll come with me . . ." The pause was barely audible. ". . . Commander, I'll fill you in on your command."


". . . but the strength of the Elite lies in flexibility. We fight on any terrain, on any terms. It all depends on the lay of the land, the enemy, and the Duke of Hale, who runs mostly cavalry. We've fought beside his horsemen before though, and it . . . am I going too fast for you, Commander?"

"Huh?" Rael flushed and dragged himself out of a pleasant daydream where the enemy had been falling back in terrified disorder before his charge. "I'm sorry, Captain. I, I didn't hear."

"Obviously." Doan smiled, an expression that lessened neither his ugliness nor his ferocity. "Drink your ale."

The mug was at his lips before Rael realized he'd followed the order without thinking. As it was there, he drank. *The chain of command definitely needs work,* he thought, putting the empty mug down amid the ruins of lunch. When he looked up, he saw by Doan's expression that the thought had clearly shown on his face. He reddened, then raised his chin and met the captain's eyes squarely. To his surprise, Doan merely nodded in what seemed to be satisfaction.

"Excuse me, Captain, Commander." The Elite First sketched a salute intended to take in both his superior officers. Rael had observed his father with the Elite often enough to realize that the First's apparent disregard for royal rank was, in fact, a form of acceptance and his heart swelled with pride. "The lad's been found. He's waiting in the guardroom."

"Send him in."

"Did you lose someone?" Rael asked as the First left the room.

"Did I lose someone?" Doan's brow furrowed as he turned to stare at the prince. "Did I lose someone?" And then he chuckled, a friendly sound so at odds with his appearance that it was Rael's turn to stare. He was still chuckling when the lad in question entered the room.

The young man, in the full uniform of the Palace Guard, was the prince's age or possibly a year or two older. He carried his helmet on his hip but, as his pale hair was damp, he'd probably just removed it. He had a strong face with high cheekbones, a thin-lipped mouth, and deep-set, light blue eyes. The glint on his upper lip may or may not have been the beginning of a mustache. He stood self-consciously at parade rest, his eyes regulation front and center, his gaze locked on a spot some three feet above Doan's head. Every achingly correct inch of him fairly trembled to know why he'd been called into such exalted presence—the exalted presence obviously being the captain of the Elite and not the prince and heir.

Rael wondered what the guardsman had done to bring him to the notice of the Elite Captain. There were no openings in the company. And besides, he was too young.

"Rutgar, Hovan's son, from Cei." Doan had stopped chuckling.

"Yes, sir." It wasn't a question but it seemed to need a response.

"Joined your Duke's Guard at fifteen and moved to the Palace Guard last year."

"Yes, sir."

"You're moving again." He pointed with his chin across the table. "The commander needs an armsman. You're it."

"Sir?" This from both young men. It was enough to drag the young guard's eyes off the wall. They studied one another for a heartbeat and then Rutgar went back to looking at nothing and the prince turned to Doan.

"But I've already got a servant."

"I didn't say he was to be your servant. He's your armsman. The men fight in pairs, live in pairs, the officers can't. He'll take care of your armor and your horse—trust me, you won't have time—and guard your back if it needs guarding." Red-brown eyes raked over the newly appointed armsman. "He's young but," he added pointedly, "so are you. You can learn together. Anyway, he'd have made the company himself before this war's over."

A small explosion of air escaped from the pressed line of Rutgar's mouth.

"Did you say something, Armsman?"

"No, Captain."

"Good. Get outfitted. Meet us on the reviewing square in half an hour."

"Yes, sir." Only the gleam in his eye showed the young man's emotion as he wheeled and exited the room.

Rael shook his head and his brow furrowed.

"Problems, Commander?"

"It just happened so fast . . ." Rael squared his shoulders. "What if I wanted someone else as my armsman?"

Earth-colored eyebrows rose. "Do you?"

"Well, no, it's just . . ."

"A good commander should have faith in his officers." The tone was not quite sarcastic. "Now, if you're ready, Commander, we'll review the troops."

The men of Belkar, farmers and herdsmen for the most part, began to gather outside the city. Soon they were joined by the fishermen of Cei and the shepherds of Aliston. Most of these men were skilled with a quarterstaff or spear and some were fine archers, but very few of them could use a sword. In less than two weeks, they had to be an army. It would have been impossible had they not wanted to be an army so badly. Raen was a good king, more importantly he was a popular king, but they wouldn't be fighting for him. They'd be fighting for their land.

"Riven and Lorn know the mountains and they take care of border raids every winter," Raen said, jabbing at the map with a dagger. "They'll do. We can count on Hale to supply cavalry out of those crazy horsemen of his." He sucked his teeth and looked grim. "They say Melac can field tens of thousands of trained soldiers."

"Impossible," scoffed Cei. "Mere rumor."

But none of the men in the room looked very happy.

The palace bulged with the three dukes and their retinues, officers and couriers, clerks and servants, until it resembled an anthill more than a royal residence.

Rael was up at dawn and in bed long past dark but still there weren't enough hours in the day.

He had training.

"You just removed the ears from your horse, Commander. Try it again and swing wider."

He had fittings for new armor in the plain, cold steel of the Elite.

"Stop squirming, Highness."

"You're tickling."

"I assure you, Highness, it's unintentional."

He had Royal Obligations.

"But I don't want to have dinner with the dukes, Ivan. Why can't I eat with my men?"

"You eat with the dukes, milord," Ivan finished fastening the red velvet jacket and stepped back to view his handiwork, "because your father commands your presence." He picked the gold belt off the bed and slung it artfully around the prince's hips. "And because, milord," he continued, firmly removing Rael's hands when he tried to hitch the belt higher, "it is good policy for you to get to know the dukes."

"I know the dukes." Rael held out a foot so Ivan could force it into a tight red leather boot. "Aliston will pay attention only to his food and perhaps grunt once or twice if Father addresses him directly. Cei will worry out loud and continuously. And Belkar . . ." A violent shove almost tore the second boot from Ivan's hands. "I haven't anything to say to Belkar." Belkar's daughter had been left at home.

"Then the dukes must get to know you, milord."

"They know me, Ivan." His voice was suddenly bleak and his eyes flared. "And only Belkar looks at me."

The older man met the brilliance of the prince's gaze without fear. "Someday they will see you, milord. And when they do, they will stop looking away."

Rael let the green burn brighter. "And what will they see," he asked softly.

Ivan smiled. "All that you are. All that you can be. All that you are not."

The unearthly fires were abruptly banked.

"You're talking in riddles again, Ivan." Grumbling, Rael went to have his dinner with the dukes.

He had new people to know.

"What I don't understand," he asked as Rutgar unbuckled his practice breastplate, "is why it's such an honor to be an armsman." The armor came free and he took a deep breath; the morning's maneuvers had been particularly strenuous as the Elite honed itself for the battles to come. "I mean, you were moving up in the Palace Guard and now," he shrugged himself free of the padded undertunic, "now, you're just a well-armed servant." He winced. "Uh, no offense, Rutgar."

"None taken, Commander." The armsman bent so Rael could reach his buckles in turn. "Perhaps you haven't noticed, but all the officers of the Elite were armsmen once. It is, after all, the best position to observe and learn in. Only the best are chosen to be armsmen."

Rael's jaw dropped and the corners of Rutgar's mouth twitched.

"If you'll sit down, Commander, I'll get those greaves."

And still the day to day governing of the land must go on.

"Your Highness, please inform your father that unless something is done soon, the water situation in the camps will become desperate."

"Prince Rael, I must have more men if I am to make all the arrows ordered by the king."

"Young sir, a moment of your time. The men of the camps have been tearing the town apart and I can't get near the king."

"Rael! Haven't you got something to do?"

"Yes, Father, but . . ."

"Then do it, lad!"

"Yes, sir."

There could be no letting up of the pressure, no thought of taking more time to prepare. Not only was there an invasion to meet, but so many men in so little space would become a serious problem if the army lingered too long.

Although it seemed as if he'd done enough work for two years, only two short weeks later Rael heard his father tell the dukes and the captains that they would march with the dawn.

"And tonight, milord?" inquired a captain, one of Aliston's by his badge.

"Tonight," replied the king, hitching up his broad leather belt to get at an elusive itch, "I will ride amongst the men."

"They'll be glad to see you, Sire."

"I certainly hope so. Would you like to ride with me, son?" he asked, turning to Rael.

"Me, sir?" Rael felt as if he hadn't been out of the palace in months.

"Yes, you. If I have another son in this room I haven't been told."

One of the captains snickered and Rael felt himself turning pink. "Yes, sir, I'd like to go with you."

When the king and the heir rode out that evening, they wore plain armor and took only two of the Palace Guard, but everyone in the camp knew the iron-haired warrior and the young man with the fire-green eyes.

Rael drank in the sights and sounds and smells: the kraken pennant of Cei, blood red against the gray of evening; two men cursing genially as they diced; sweat and leather and steel. Here was a different world from those he had known—the forest and the court—cruder, less disciplined, more rawly sensual.

Raen watched the tall young man riding beside him with pride, and some amusement, as his son tried to take in everything without appearing to notice anything at all. He submerged the thought that in war young men die and he buried the fear that this one he loved so dearly could be taken from him.

The men were in good spirits and some called out to the riders as they passed. They had a long march ahead with Lord Death waiting at the end of it and a soldier, even a temporary soldier, makes merry when he can. Many of the sentiments were not those normally heard in the presence of the king and the heir to the throne. A grizzled archer bellowed out a riddle so coarse that the prince blushed, but the King roared with laughter and gave back the answer.

"Aye, the king knows his women," slurred a loud voice from the crowd. "Pity he can't find a real one to get a son on."

Raen stopped laughing. Silence fell. So complete a silence it was possible to hear the soft whistle of the horses' breath. He held up a hand to stop the Guard from riding forward, and watched his son. He remembered how Milthra had handed him the squalling, naked babe, the love in her eyes lighting up the whole Grove. When Rael looked up, he nodded.

A pulse beat in Rael's throat like a wild thing held prisoner, but it was the only movement visible. His eyes flamed and one by one, not even aware they did it, men stepped aside until a massive soldier stood alone.

Silently, Rael swung off his horse. Slowly and deliberately, as if afraid a sudden movement would release the emotions held rigidly in check, he moved to stand before the man. He felt his mother's heritage well up within him. The strength of the tree. The strength to withstand wind and storm. The strength to root into bedrock and hold on. His blood sang and his eyes blazed. And his fists clenched, for he was also his father's son.

"You have no right to speak of my mother."

His voice was so soft it might have been the passing breeze that spoke.

Swaying unsteadily on tree-trunk legs, either too foolish or too befuddled by wine to see the threat in the slim young man who faced him, the soldier narrowed his eyes belligerently. "Your mother," he slurred, "was likely a common street whore who spread . . ."

In the stillness, the sound of Rael's fist striking the other's jaw rang out like a thunderclap. The soldier's head snapped back, he hung for a moment on the night, and then crumpled to the ground.

Still outwardly emotionless, Rael remounted. He ignored the blood running down his fingers from where the skin had split over a knuckle. Only the trembling of his hand as he took up the reins betrayed that he felt anything at all.

"His neck's broken," said the old archer looking up from the body. "He's dead."

"Then bury him," said the king. And they rode in silence back to the palace where they went to their separate rooms and spent the rest of the night staring sleeplessly in the direction of the forest.

The Grove was silver and shadow in the moonlight. Clothed in night, its beauty became sharp edges and satin blackness, drawing away from the world of mortals to that of an older time. Within the circle of birches, no nightbirds called, no animals, large or small, stalked prey or were stalked in turn, no breeze wandered to disturb the listening quiet of the trees.

One moment the Grove waited empty and still, the next Doan, the Captain of the Elite, stood before the eldest of the trees and said: "All right, you called. I'm here."

The tree murmured in protest as Milthra pulled herself from its heart.

At the sight of her face, Doan winced. "You know."

"The breezes told me when it was done," Milthra admitted, the clear chimes of her voice flattened with worry. "But they have not returned again and I must know what is said of my son."

Doan shoved his thumbs behind his belt and paced about the Grove, breaking the moonlight into Doan-sized patterns. He had done little since he'd heard the news but listen for reaction to the deed. He knew this summons would come. "Those who saw," his rough burr broke the silence of the Grove at last, "say the man deserved it. Not death perhaps, but the blow at least. Fortunately, the man was not well liked. Most admire the prince for standing up for you himself when he could've hidden behind the Guard. Many are impressed by his strength and are anxious to see it on the battlefield. But," his fingers drummed on the leather around his waist, "there are those for whom it only marks his difference, and difference is always distrusted. And in everyone's mind, although for the most part it remains unasked, is the question, 'If he kills so easily now, when he is king, how can any of us be safe?'" He met Milthra's eyes and smiled grimly. "It would've been simpler for all concerned, Lady, had you loved a woodcutter or a farmer and not a king."

"So you have said before, old friend, but I could no more have refused that love than I could refuse to breathe; I am sorry for the burden it places on my son." She sighed and, behind her, her tree swayed in sympathy. "Even you, who are fully of the Elder Races, are accepted in the mortal world more easily than Rael."

Doan shrugged. "I play a part. And even if I convinced them of what I truly am . . ." He spread his hands. "Dwarves brought mortals fire and taught them to build; helped them to rebuild after the destruction of the wizards. We showed them a number of ways to cheat Lord Death. We've never been either revered or feared."

"And I am both?"

"They don't know you, Lady."

Milthra shook her hair over her face and wept behind its silver curtain.

Anger and pity rose in the dwarf's breast. Anger that she who was Eldest and most beautiful should be reduced to weeping over mortal man. Pity for much the same reason. He reached out a hand and Milthra pressed her cheek into it. Then she stepped back to the safety of her tree and he held only a tear that ran down his palm. It slowed, stopped, flared suddenly, then darkened to an emerald that held all the greens of the Grove in its depths. He slipped it in his belt pouch and bowed to the silver birch before him.

"I will continue to watch him, Eldest," and his eyes glowed deeply red, "both for your sake and his. But remember, not all the Dwarves from the Mother's blood could keep Lord Death away if he comes to claim his own and, your life mingled within or no, your son is as mortal as his father. Perhaps you should save some tears for that."

And then the Grove was empty, save for the silver of moonlight, the blackness of night, and the sound of the Eldest weeping for her child.

# THREE

Rael swore as sweat rolled into his eyes and he blinked furiously to ease the burning. He used his shield to smash aside the vicious hooked blade of a Melac spearman and in the same move swung his sword around, over, and down onto the man's arms. The meaty thunk of metal through flesh and bone was absorbed by the sounds of battle. Beneath him, his horse struck out with steel-edged hoofs, giving Rael time to yank free his blade, turn, and open the face of the man who threatened on his right. He tightened his legs and the warhorse leaped forward. Another Melacian went down, gurgling blood, his ribs a mass of splintered bone.

Then there was nothing in front of them but a rock-strewn slope, and the stallion stretched into a canter. They thundered up the hill, wheeled at the crest, and looked down over the valley. The warhorse stopped so suddenly at Rael's command that the prince rocked in the saddle. After four passes across the valley, cutting their way through the enemy position, the animal knew that this was his chance to rest and he stood, sides heaving, while Rael, no less winded, lifted his visor to better suck in great lungfuls of air. Beside and behind him, other members of the Elite did the same.

The valley held a seething mass of men and weapons and dead and dying. Hale's horsemen, more lightly armored than the Elite, darted in and out of the melee, sabers red and dripping. The space was too enclosed for their speed and maneuverability to be totally effective, but they stung the flanks of the enemy like gadflies. The ducal guards of

Belkar, Cei, and Aliston fought in clumps, lending their strength and skill when they could to the farmers, fishermen, and herdsmen who fought beside them but too used to fighting as units to do more than slow the slaughter of the common folk. Over it all, crows and other carrion birds rode the updrafts, waiting for nightfall and their time in the valley.

Safely out of it for the moment, Rael was conscious of the noise in a way he hadn't had time to be while he fought. It filled the bowl of the valley, the deep-voiced defiance of thousands of men and the slam and clatter of thousands of weapons, with eddies of greater noise where the fighting was fiercest, and every now and then a scream piercing through the din like torchlight through smoke.

From here, Rael mused, the Ardhan and Melacian dying sounded very much alike.

From a distance, as though he wandered through someone else's mind, he considered the absence of terror and disgust and shame—at what he'd seen and what he'd done. His ability to feel had gone as numb as his nose; he'd long since stopped noticing the omnipresent stench of blood and guts and sweat. His brain had apparently decided to concentrate on the essentials, survival and command, and let all else wait until later. *"Much later,"* he prayed, remembering how he'd felt during the butchery of the first charge. *"Please, much later."*

"Over there, look!"

Down the line, one of the Elite called and pointed and the men raised a ragged cheer as a flight from Belkar's archers collapsed an advancing enemy line. Although the rest of the Elite saw the arrows as smudges against the sky and could tell only by their direction which side fired and which died, with his mother's eyes, Rael watched each double-barbed arrow land, diving deep to burrow through armor and into the soft meat beneath. He tried not to flinch. It wouldn't look good.

"Cristof lost his horse, Commander, but he got out on his Half's stirrup. And we've got two cut reins from those damned hooked blades."

Rael started as the First broke through his thoughts and, glad for an excuse to stop watching the carnage, he turned to face the officer.

"Keep the Halves together." That much, at least, he knew he had to do. The Elite fought in pairs; each man a Half and each man's Half closer to him than mere comrade or friend. It was not a commitment all chosen for the Elite were willing to make and those men who weren't stayed in the Guard, but it was a part of why the Elite fought so fiercely; each Half *knew* another's life depended on his skill. "Have Cristof's Half give his reins to repair the two reins cut. Then the Pair can head back, get outfitted again and rejoin us on the far side of the valley after the next pass."

"Very good, sir." The standard response sounded like praise. An unorthodox solution, perhaps, but it kept together three Pairs who would have otherwise been split. The First moved away and began barking orders. The company's respite was nearly over.

"Yes, Commander, very good." It seemed Doan's surly chestnut could move as silently as its rider. One moment the space to Rael's left stood empty, the next the captain filled it, perched—given the length of Doan's legs, there could be no other word for it—on his horse beside him. "These cross valley charges of yours seem to be working as well. You were right, the enemy does find it demoralizing to have us thunder down and through the middle of their position."

Rael searched the captain's words for sarcasm and found, not praise, exactly, but acknowledgment of success. He was almost too tired to be pleased.

"You hurt?" Rutgar moved his horse closer to Rael's right and nodded at the blood that clotted and congealed down the prince's leg.

Rael looked down and shrugged. "Not mine." He turned and studied his armsman. "How about you?"

Rutgar touched a dent in the side of his helmet with his shield hand and grinned. "My ears'll ring for a while, but I'm all right. Who'd have thought they'd throw rocks?"

A quick glance around showed the Elite to be ready. Rael, prince and commander, slammed his visor down with the edge of his sword, touched his heels to his horse, and led the Elite on another slash of destruction through the foe.

The command tent was hot, smoky and entirely too full of sweaty, tired men; three dukes and Aliston's heir, for the Duke of Aliston was too old to travel so far and far too old to fight, eleven captains, the king, and the prince, all with the smell of battle clinging to them. Sweet candles had been lit, but the odor of blood and death refused to be defeated by jasmine and spice. Rael gritted his teeth and hoped his nose would go numb to this as well.

"We have to keep him in the valley where his position works against the number of men he's throwing against us." The king jabbed at the map with his dagger. "If he forces us out to the Tage Plateau, he'll be able to expand his front beyond our ability to contain him. He's got the manpower to flank us easily."

"I hardly think easily, Sire." Hale played with one beaded end of his mustache. "More room to maneuver could work to our advantage as well."

"Well, I don't think every horse in your province could stop the number of men Melac is putting into the field." Cei dabbed at his dripping nose with a square of cotton. "You can't herd men like cattle, you know."

Hale raised both brows in a barely polite expression. "Oh? Can't I?"

"Gentlemen." Raen's voice developed an edge. "It's a moot point what Hale's horsemen can or cannot do because I have no intention of allowing Melac out of the valley even if he dumps every able body in his kingdom on us."

"Which he seems to be doing," Belkar added dryly.

"Yes . . . well . . ." Raen directed their attention back to the map. "I think we can all see why he chose this pass. The Melac side may be difficult to maneuver through, but it opens so smoothly into Ardhan that once the valley's gained it's damned difficult for us to defend against him."

Belkar scratched at a bandage wrapped around his knuckles and shook his head. "And unfortunately this madman cares little how many men he wastes getting to our side of the mountains."

"Fortunately for us," Hale corrected smoothly. "The enemy arrives to fight us exhausted from fighting the mountains. It gives us a small edge against his superior numbers."

Cei sniffed and rubbed at his nose. His already lachrymose disposition had not been improved by a reaction to the plant life of the area. "What I don't understand is how a whole army got so close before we knew where it was going. What I want to know is, why weren't Riven and Lorn watching their borders?"

"They were. Only by their vigilance did we manage to arrive in time to contain Melac where we have. It would've gone a lot worse with us if the Dukes of Riven and Lorn had not been watching their borders. And it would go a lot worse for us now if they and their men were not out in the mountains making sure that this is the only breach Melac makes."

Cei hunched his bony shoulders under the lash of the king's voice.

"What amazes me," Hale, cool and slightly amused, defused the rising tension, "is how they ever managed to agree that the attack would come here. They can't even agree whose province this valley is in." He stretched out long legs, still in stained riding leathers. "I suppose if we win, they'll both claim it."

Belkar nodded. "And if we lose, neither will want it."

Many of the men chuckled and even Cei managed a smile. The young Dukes of Riven and Lorn were cousins, born less than two days apart. They had ascended to their Seats within a year of each other and were alike right down to their taste in women and tinder-dry tempers. Tempers that had flared lately over a woman they both had a taste for.

Rael breathed a quiet prayer of thanks that neither duke was present. In reminding the company of their constant, albeit generally affectionate, bickering, Hale had averted a potentially bad situation. For all his wildman posturings—and the barbaric affectation of his beaded mustache—Hale was a born diplomat. The prince hoped that someday he'd be half that smooth.

"I don't think we've any more to discuss." Raen leaned forward. "We've had a long day, gentlemen, and we all need some sleep. It'll be more of the same tomorrow."

The dukes and captains bowed and left, breaking into smaller groups outside the command tent as they headed back to their men. Finally, only Rael remained.

The king stood and put his arm around his son's shoulders as they walked to the open flap.

"I was proud of you today, son. You fought well."

Rael flushed. "I did no more than any man, sir."

Raen smiled. "Yes, well, I was proud of them all."

They ducked out of the tent together and stood breathing deeply, clearing their lungs of candle smoke and their minds momentarily of battle plans. Two of the Palace Guard stepped forward to escort the king to his tent. Raen turned and cupped his son's face between his hands.

"And what did you think of your first day's battle?" he asked quietly.

Rael looked past the numbness that had mercifully continued even after the fighting had finished. "I hated it."

"Good." Raen kissed his child on the forehead—yes, still his child in spite of size and age and armor—and allowed the Guard to lead him away.

In the tent he shared with his armsman, Rael stood while Ivan stripped him and sponged off the worst of the battle.

The old servant muttered to himself as he sponged, for purple and green bruises began to show against the clean skin. He wanted to scold but couldn't for fear of waking Rutgar, who already slept, one arm flung up against the light. He turned down the blanket, trimmed the lamp, and would have suggested he pour wine had the prince not dismissed him. Still muttering, he gathered up the day's clothes and left.

Rael threw himself on his pallet and stared up at the canvas above his head.

"Hey." Rutgar had risen up on one elbow. "You okay?"

Rael turned so he could see his armsman. "I thought you were asleep."

Rutgar shrugged and grinned. "Nah, who could sleep with all that serving going on."

Both young men turned their gaze on the outer chamber where Ivan still puttered about, then Rael leaned back and sighed. "Rutgar, you've fought before, haven't you?"

"Yes, Commander, at the Tantac raids two summers ago."

"How did you feel?"

Rutgar studied the prince's profile. There was a tightness to it that had not been there before. "How do you feel now?" he asked instead of answering.

"Numb. I don't feel anything."

The armsman nodded. "That's how I felt," he said and chewed his lip at the memories. "Numb."

Rael sighed again. "I don't think I like it, this not feeling."

"Don't worry," Rutgar's voice was caught in the battles of two summers past, "it wears off." He reached up and pinched out the lamp. "Good night, Highness."

The man should have been dead. With every beat of his heart more of his life pumped out the gaping hole in his chest, but still he advanced. His lips drew back in a rictus grin, blackened, rotted and fell away. The flesh of his face writhed with maggots, whole chunks dropping off to expose the yellow skull beneath.

Rael gagged on the stench and tried to back away, but his feet seemed rooted to the ground. He struggled to lift his leg, looked down, and saw that skeletal hands rising out of the earth held him firmly in place. Blackened nails dug into his ankles and anchored themselves by driving deep into his bones.

Still the Melacian spearman advanced, a shambling corpse hardly more than an arm's reach away.

The smell clotted into solid matter in Rael's nose and throat and he gasped for air.

He waved his sword at the monstrosity before him and found to his horror that the blade had become a strip of birch bark torn from the living surface of his mother's tree. The bark bled and called his name.

He forced enough air into his lungs to scream.

"Highness! Commander! Rael!"

Rutgar's face hung above him and Rutgar's hands were on his shoulders and nothing was coming at him out of the darkness.

Rutgar's mouth twisted in sympathy. "I told you, it wears off," he said gently.

"I was dreaming . . ."

The armsman nodded. "I know. I had nightmares for months after the Tantac raids." He sat back on his heels. "Still do occasionally."

Rael released his grip on his blankets and lightly touched the back of Rutgar's hand. Warm. Living. "Thank you for waking me."

Rutgar smiled, a warmer expression than his usual one-sided grin. "I'm here to guard your back, Commander. It's just a part of the service."

His commander managed a weak smile in return.

"It won't always be this awful," Rutgar reassured him, returning to his own pallet. "Too bad in a way. If the horror of wars stayed with us, maybe we'd stop having them."

"Maybe," Rael agreed. And lay for a long time listening to the quiet breathing from across the tent.

So ended the Ardhan army's first day in the valley.

He had flung himself off his horse when his Half went down, not knowing he was already too late to help, and now he was trapped. The Elite were the best and he had no doubt that one man at a time he could cut his way back to the Ardhan lines. But the enemy didn't face him one man at a time, or even two or three, there were a dozen at least. And he was surrounded. Through the bars of his visor he saw the last of his comrades break free of the battle and ride up the slope of the valley. He raised his sword in a fast salute and prepared to die.

"Commander! Nicoli is . . ."

"I see him." The muscles in Rael's legs trembled as he forced them away from his horse's sides, forced them away from giving the order that would send the Elite charging down to rescue their fallen comrade.

"Commander, we can . . ."

"No." And although he didn't have to explain, he continued. "We couldn't reach him in time. And I will not risk more lives to save a corpse. They'd know where we're heading and be waiting for us." A murmur ran down the line as his words were passed and a mutter ran back. Rael felt their eyes on him, but he sat straight in his saddle, clenched his jaw, and kept his gaze on Nicoli as he fell.

That night, after the day's slaughter had ended, Rael sat in the dark on his pallet seeing again the two broken suits of armor that had been retrieved from the battlefield with the other bodies. Nicoli's lips had been drawn back in a snarl. His Half had merely looked surprised.

He froze when Rutgar entered the tent and protested weakly when the armsman lit the lantern hanging from the center pole.

Rutgar made no mention of the tear tracks that marked the prince's face or of what had happened that afternoon. He merely folded long legs, sat down beside his commander, and wordlessly held out the wineskin he carried.

Rael looked at it for a moment, as if unsure of what it was or what he was to do with it, then he took it, tilted back his head and filled his mouth.

His tongue curled up, his throat spasmed, and he barely prevented himself from spraying the mouthful of wine across the tent.

"What is this stuff?" he demanded, coughing and choking.

Rutgar rescued the wineskin and took a long pull. "It's what the men drink. A little rough for the royal palate perhaps, but . . ." He offered it again.

Rael took it, shrugged, and drank, this time managing to relax his throat enough to swallow. He drank again, then returned it. "You may end up protecting my back from my own men," he said at last, staring into the flickering lamplight and rubbing his palms across his cheeks.

"They're soldiers. Any one of them would've made the same decision."

The wineskin made another pass.

"But they didn't make it. I did."

"You're the commander. It was your decision to make."

Rael reached for the wineskin. "Yes."

"They understand that."

"But they would've preferred a rescue."

"Yes."

Rael drank again. "Mother-creator, but this stuff is awful."

"It is," Rutgar agreed. "But it does what it has to."

And they drank in silence until it was gone.

So ended the Ardhan army's second day in the valley.


"Commander, over there!"

"I see them."

The Elite had gained the valley's edge but had left a Pair behind in the battle. As one man, they turned their gaze on Rael. The day before, a Pair had died.

This day Rael looked and smiled. "One squad," he called to the First beside him, pulled his stallion's head around and charged back down the path he'd just cut. This Pair was close enough and one was still mounted; this Pair, he could save. At the edge of his vision he saw the armored head of Rutgar's bay and close behind he heard the thunder of a dozen heavy horses.

The Melacian position, barely recovered from the last pass, crumbled before them.

Rael rammed the point of his lance through an enemy visor, rode it free, and reached the lost Pair. The downed man, Payter, was pinned beneath his horse. There was only one way to get him out. Rael kicked his feet clear of the stirrups and dropped to the ground.

Rutgar and Payter's Half stayed close while the squad began to circle their position, forming a living barricade against the Melacians.

The pike that had killed Payter's horse still stuck from its chest. It had reared and come down on the point, driving it deep into its own heart, then it had dropped like a stone, giving its rider no time to get free. His legs were trapped beneath the double weight of horse and armor.

"Leave me, Commander," he gasped, "and take my idiot Half with you. You can't free me."

Rael's brows rose and Hale would've recognized the tone as he said, "Oh? Can't I?" He squatted, shoved his hands beneath the horse, and lifted. His gauntlets slid free. The weight he'd intended to throw under the horse shifted, and he sat suddenly, nearly doing more damage to Payter in the process. Cursing under his breath, he yanked off the offending gloves and shoved them under Payter's unresisting hands. This couldn't take too long or the Melacian archers would begin to make their presence felt. He squatted again and gripped the still warm body under shoulder and haunch. Then he stiffened his back and straightened his legs.

Slowly the horse lifted a foot, then two feet off the ground.

"Can you get out?" Rael grunted, his knees braced under the saddle.

"Uh . . . yes, Commander . . ."

"Then do it, damnit!"

"Yes, Commander!" The man crabbed backward on hands and elbows.

When Payter's feet came clear, Rael stepped back and the horse crashed to the ground. He grabbed his gauntlets, grabbed the man by the shoulders, and flung him up and over the pommel of his Half's saddle, hoping his armor would cushion the blow. Using the dead horse as a mounting block, and completely disregarding the weight of his own armor—although something in his muscles said he'd pay for all this later, mythic parentage or not—Rael launched himself into his own saddle, set his lance, and screamed: "Back!"

The circling Elite formed a wedge, pointed their heads toward the rest of the company, and began the fight back. Rael and Rutgar bracketed the rescued Pair and readied to move out.

*I've done it!* Rael crowed. He beat away a spear that came a bit too close. *Nothing can stop us now!*

Suddenly Rutgar threw up his shield and an arrow ricocheted off the rim. "Cover!"

One of the Melacian longbowmen had found a bit of unoccupied high ground. He stood, safely out of range of return fire, but close enough to Rael and his men to be able to choose his targets with care.

From a standing start it would take a moment or two to fight their way clear and get moving. During that moment they might as well have targets painted over their hearts.

"Why, you . . ." Rael's jaw went out and his eyes blazed behind his visor. In a single fluid motion, he stood in his stirrups, twisted, and flung his lance at the bowman.

It seemed that both armies watched it fly, and watched it land, point buried a foot in the earth and the Melacian bowman hanging off the end.

The squad was virtually unopposed as they rode back to join their company.

Doan met Rael at the top of the hill. "You seem to have taken the heart out of them, Commander."

Rael turned to look and, sure enough, the Melacians were leaving the field, forming shield lines and retreating with the Ardhan army harrowing them every foot of the way.

"A bit showy." Although Doan's tone was dry, he couldn't stop his lips from twitching back into a smirk. "But definitely effective."

So ended the Ardhan army's third day in the valley.


"It took them a while," Doan nudged the prince and pointed, "but they've finally learned. They've moved their pikemen out of squares and down both sides of the valley. We try to charge into that and we'll skewer ourselves."

Rael raised a hand to shade his eyes and Rutgar, who was forcing a new strap through a buckle, growled low in his throat. "If you don't mind, Commander . . ."

"Sorry." Rael lowered his arm and squinted instead. "I guess we'll just have to try something else."

Doan and the armsman exchanged questioning glances.

"It looks as though we've made them nervous," the prince continued. "They seem to be placing a barricade of pikemen between their bowmen and the Ardhan lancers."

"They are." Doan's eyes were as good as Rael's and he could shade them against the early morning sun.

"The trouble is, the Melacians aren't in possession of a rather important piece of information." Rael turned to face his companions.

"And that is?" Rutgar sighed, pulling Rael back into position by the recalcitrant strap.

"The Ardhan lancers are bowmen as well." The commander of the Elite looked down at his captain. "The strength of the Elite lies in flexibility."

Doan's jaw dropped. He recognized his own words to Rael on the day the prince took command. He stared at the Melacian lines, then said: "We ride at them in ranks of three, fire, wheel, and repeat. Between the dust and the ranks of pikemen blocking their sight, they'll never hit a moving target."

"And they'll never expect it," Rutgar added. "As far as they know . . ."

". . . we have no mounted archers," Doan finished. "And when we break the line, Hale's horsemen can lead the foot soldiers through. It just might work."

"Might?" Rael grinned in a way that made him look very much like his father. "Of course it'll work. Captain, inform the Firsts. Have the Elite form up in three ranks. Today, we're archers."

Doan's salute was faultless. "Very good, Commander." He spun on his heel and marched off to pass the commander's orders to the officers of the Elite.

Rael turned back to stare at the distant line of the enemy. "Well?" he asked Rutgar. "What do you think?"

"I think," muttered his armsman, finally cinching tight the buckle.

"That you're getting a bit cocky." He looked up and smiled. "Commander."

The commander grinned and slammed an elbow into his armsman's side with a sound of clashing kettle drums. "You're just jealous. I tell you, it'll work."

It worked.

At the end of the fourth day, the Ardhan army still held the valley.


The fifth day, by throwing lives in a seemingly endless parade onto the Ardhan weapons, by making a path on their dead and dying, by washing away the Ardhan barricades with a river of blood, the Melacian army left the valley and moved the war onto the Tage Plateau.

# FOUR

Deep in the shadow of the mountains, the armies of Ardhan and Melac slept, but eastward, in the camp that attended Melac's king, it was dawn.

"Still four bloody hours from the front!" The cavalry officer dropped the hoof she'd picked up and straightened with a groan. "Shopkeepers and peasants are moving up into battle and here we stick, guarding the rear."

"Guarding the king," her companion reminded her with a jut of his chin toward the starburst pennant hanging limply from the center pole of the largest pavilion. His raised eyebrow reminded her that although the nearest of the King's Guard appeared to be out of earshot, things didn't necessarily work that way anymore.

She grimaced but dropped her voice. "We could serve the king better by fighting."

"We serve the king best by doing as we're told."

"Right." She peered over her horse's withers and added: "They're moving out the troops."

Across the camp, a double line of foot soldiers began the march that would take them to the battlefield.

"You know, I've never seen conscripts so willing to meet Lord Death."

"Lord Death is preferable to what they'll meet if they stay behind."

And both pairs of eyes turned again to the largest pavilion.

"Still, they're only peasants."

He grunted in agreement and raised a hand to block the sun. "Isn't that Lord Elan?"

Even at that distance the lord's stocky figure was unmistakable as he entered the tent.

"Maybe he's going to plead our cause with the king."

"Right."

The looks exchanged said very clearly that both knew it was not, nor had it been for some time, the king who was in charge.

"Still," she bent to lift another hoof, "after losing three wars in as many years, I'd follow Chaos himself if it meant we could win one."

"We have taken the valley, Sire, and the battle has moved to the open area beyond."

"Good." The reply came not from the king, but from the man who sat by his side. Red-gold curls fell in silken coils about his face as he inclined his head and repeated the words to the wasted body that slumped on the throne.

Slowly, his movements a series of tiny jerks, the King of Melac raised his head. Eyes, sunk deep over axe-blade cheekbones, opened. "Good," he echoed, then fell silent once again.

The king's counselor looked regally down at the kneeling lord. "Was that all?"

"Sire," the elderly man came as close to turning his back on the counselor as was safe, "you must send the cavalry on ahead."

The king ignored him. The king's counselor did not.

"Must send the cavalry? Do you dictate to your sovereign? Would you leave him unprotected?"

"Sire, you are still on the Melacian side of the border. Still four hours' hard ride from the battle. Your Guard can protect you. Without the cavalry, every foot the army advances is piled high with the bodies of the dead."

"If the cavalry consists of such doughty fighters, able to turn the battle by their mere presence, should they not remain here to guard against assassination?" Slender hands spread, the tracery of gold hair on their backs glittering in the torchlight. "Or do you mean to deny His Majesty protection by the best?"

"Sire, I don't . . ."

"Or perhaps you don't feel His Majesty is worth protecting?"

"Sire, of course I . . ."

"Then why do you deny him the cavalry?"

"Sire, I can only repeat that without the cavalry on the field, we cannot win."

"But we are winning, are we not?"

"Are we?" the lord snapped, turning at last to glare at the man beside his king. "We gain the ground, but is it winning when three out of every five men we send into the field die?"

Red-gold brows rose. "But what better death is there, than to die for your king? There will always be more men and they go willingly to fight."

"Willingly? They're driven!"

"Really? By what?"

"You know very well by what, you . . ."

"Are you about to criticize me, Lord Elan?" His voice was as soft as the velvet that fell in sapphire folds from his shoulders, and rather more deadly than the dagger that hung at his waist.

For an instant, for just an instant, Lord Elan's jaw went out and the hatred that bubbled and seethed below the surface showed on his face. For an instant. Then the flesh sagged, the gray returned, and his eyes dropped. "No," he whispered.

"No, what?"

The hand that rested on Lord Elan's knee quivered. "No, milord."

The counselor smiled. Lord Elan could always be counted on for a few moments of amusing bravado. That was why he still lived. The cavalry *was* needed at the front, but there was no need to rush, not when the delay kept the old lord so frustrated and entertaining. In the meantime, what difference did it make if a few more peasants died. "The cavalry stays here . . ." He paused and his smile grew mocking. ". . . to protect the king."

As though animated by the sound of his title, the king suddenly pulled himself erect, satin robes rustling like dead leaves. He leaned forward, pinning Lord Elan with his fevered gaze. "How many?"

"Sire?"

Bony fingers crabbed along the broad wooden arms of the throne. "How many have died?"

Hope flared in the old lord's face and he leaned forward as well. If the king could be made to care . . . "Hundreds, Sire, thousands even."

"Thousands . . ." He sank back into the cushions, his expression almost beatific. "Thousands. And they all died for me."

"All for you," the king's counselor agreed, and only Lord Elan heard the laughter in his voice.

"There are just too damned many of them!" Rutgar pulled off his helm and slicked back his dripping hair. "They've no need to kill us, we'll die of exhaustion killing them."

Rael snorted and dropped down beside his armsman on the felled tree that served as bench, table, and occasionally surgery. "At least it's over for today." He dropped his own helm and began to worry at the straps of his greaves. After a moment, Rutgar slapped away his hands and began to work at them himself.

"They'll jam if you twist them like that," he muttered, "and I'll be the one who replaces the straps if we have to cut you free."

"Highness."

Rael looked up and managed a weary smile. "My Lord Belkar."

"I thought I should warn you that as prince and heir, you'll be taking the council tonight."

"I'll what?" Rael pulled his leg from Rutgar's grasp and stood. "Has something happened to Father?"

"Your father," Belkar paused, and his voice became decidedly acerbic, "the king, has ridden out with a patrol to prevent us being flanked by the enemy."

"Father has?"

"Yes."

"But that's crazy."

"So I told him, Highness."

"The king can't just go riding off with patrols in the dead of night! Did he take his Guard?"

"I believe some members of his Guard rode with the patrol, yes."

"What if he gets killed out there, miles from anywhere?"

"I asked him that question myself."

"And he said?"

"He was tired of strategy and tactics."

"That's it?"

Belkar's lips twitched. "Except for some personal and unsavory comments about nursemaiding directed at myself, yes, that was it."

"Oh, that's just great." Rael stepped past Belkar. Stopped. Returned. And threw himself back down on the tree. He had a sudden vision of what his father's reaction would be if he took the Elite out after him. "Just great," he repeated and thrust his leg back into Rutgar's reach.


*Now this is more like it,* Raen thought, lips pulled back from his teeth, his eyes shining beneath his plain iron helm. He lifted his sword and flicked the point left. The nearest member of the patrol, a shadow against the broken shadows of the forest, nodded and passed it on, then the line moved forward.

They could hear the Melacians coming toward them—had been able to hear them for some time.

*Ten, maybe twenty yards and we'll be right on top of them.* Raen ducked under a low branch and hoped his men were not advancing with the same amount of noise as the Melacians.

The Ardhan line advanced, three feet, four, then a bellow of astonishment filled the night, closely followed by the clash of steel on steel. While the Melacians dealt with the idea of an enemy patrol where no patrol should be, the Ardhans overcame their own surprise and attacked.

*How in Chaos did they get so close!* Raen blocked a spear with his shield, slashed low to take another man in the knees and dodged a blow that would have removed his head had it connected. He slid around a tree, taking an instant to ram his shield edge into the downed man's throat, and bellowed the Ardhan war-cry. The rest of the Ardhan patrol picked it up and the woods rang. Dark-adapted eyes could tell friend from foe, armor differed enough that the silhouettes were unmistakable, but there was no sense taking chances. Besides, the King of Ardhan preferred a noisy fight.

*So I'm old.* Raen grinned as a Melacian fell, screaming at his feet. *But I haven't lost it yet.*

The flash of blue light at his gut attracted his attention seconds before the pain hit. He glanced down to see a spear point, glowing eerily sapphire, pressed up against his breastplate just under his navel. Time slowed as the point, and the light, poked through the steel plate and into his belly. He grunted, the pain so intense it closed his throat, preventing a scream, and his sword dropped from spasming fingers.

The head of the spearman hit the ground beside his sword, still wearing the astonished expression with which it had greeted the blue light.

"Sire!"

As the spear was snatched away the pain lessened, becoming more a normal agony. His back braced against a tree, Raen managed to stay standing and find his voice. He tried to sound reassuring, but the words came out a powerless husking whisper. "Not as bad as it looks." His probing fingers discovered this was the truth. His breastplate was holed but the wound beneath it was through skin and muscle only, nothing vital. He dragged his cloak forward, ripped off a strip a handspan wide and shoved the ball of fabric up under his armor.

"Sire, your breastplate . . ."

"Was obviously badly forged." He bent and retrieved his sword, teeth gritted against the wave of dizziness. "Well, come on." He forced his treacherous voice closer to normality. "There're more of them out here."

"But Sire . . ."

Raen's eyes did not glow with the power of other worlds, as did his son's, but the worldly power they held was quite sufficient.

"Yes, Sire. I'll re-form the patrol."


The surgeon stepped from the king's tent, wiping her hands on a towel.

"His Majesty," she said to Rael and the Duke of Belkar, "is not a young man."

Rael winced.

"He is also," she continued, "an idiot. Had he returned directly to camp when this happened, he would have been up and bashing heads this morning. As it is, he's going to spend a good long time in bed."

"He's not going to like that," Rael pointed out.

The surgeon glared at the prince. "Too bad," she said, and pushed past him back to the infirmary.

Belkar and Rael watched her go, her back ramrod straight and un-compromising.

The duke shook his head, managing to be both admiring and irri-tated at the same time. "She'll fight Lord Death every foot of the way and if he wins, she'll spit in his face. I almost pity him." He draped his arm around Rael's shoulders and pushed him toward the tent. "Don't worry, lad, Glinna's the best surgeon with the army. If your father was in any immediate danger, she never would've left him."

"But his breastplate . . ."

"Flawed. And it still absorbed most of the blow. You might be able to pop a spear through unflawed steel like it was paper, but that's be-yond the rest of us poor mortals." His tone was light and reassuring, but he carefully kept Rael from seeing his face. There had been nothing wrong with the breastplate except for the hole punched through it . . . as though the steel had been paper.

\*       \*       \*

Rain during the first three days on the Tage Plateau kept fighting inter-
mittent and casualties light. The fourth day the sun shone and the killing began again. The strength of the Elite fell from fifty-five to forty
men. The Duke of Cei lost half his Guard but the remainder held. The
Duke of Belkar lost twenty archers when their position was overrun.
The Duke of Hale lost his life.

"Then who is Hale now?" Rutgar asked, his fingers digging the tension out of the prince's shoulders.

Rael rolled a blue glass bead between his thumb and forefinger.
He'd found it near where Hale had fallen. He couldn't imagine the
duke with an unbeaded mustache. He couldn't imagine the duke dead.
"The eldest son, just ten this summer. I think his name was Etgar."

"Was Etgar?"

"It's Hale now."

The Melacians died by the hundreds, but more continued to come
through the pass.


"Father, are you sure you should be out of bed?"

Raen glared at his son. "I'll not lie in bed, while my people die."

"It won't help them if you die as well."

The king put his foot in the stirrup and pulled himself up into the
saddle. "I have no intention of dying," he growled and turned his warhorse toward the battle.

At the end of the day, the edge of the king's surcoat was stained
with blood and he had to be lifted down from his horse.

"I'm fine," he protested as two of the Palace Guard placed him gently
on a litter. "I'm just a little stiff."

"Father!" Rael pushed through the gathered crowd and flung himself to his knees, desperately catching up his father's hand in his.

"I'm fine," the king insisted. He managed a weak smile, but his face
was gray and slick with sweat.

Rael looked up at Belkar, his whole body begging the duke to say it
would be all right. Belkar shrugged.

"The king is down," ran the whisper through the ranks. "The king is dying." Weapons, tools, meals, lay forgotten as the army fell silent and waited for news.

"Get out of my way." Glinna's voice, impatient and commanding, pushed apart the silence and split the circle surrounding the litter. The surgeon strode through the break and glared down at the king. Her mouth pursed and her eyebrows lowered. "I told you so," was all she said, but there were several lectures worth of meaning in the words.

A wave of near hysterical giggles rippled outward. The king would live. No one used that tone on a dying man.

Glinna looked up at the sound. "Don't you lot have something to do?" The crowd melted away and she shifted her gaze to stare pointedly at the prince. He stared back, the green of his eyes growing both deeper and brighter. She raised one eyebrow. "Very pretty, Highness. Now get up off your knees so we can move your father inside."

Rael sighed as he scrambled out of the way. *It's not fair,* he thought. *When I want people to be impressed, they never are.*

As the litter moved away, Glinna slipped her hand under the bloody surcoat.

"Madam!" Raen gasped, his eyes wide, pain mixed equally with surprise. "Try to remember, I am your king."

"And if you want to remain my king," the surgeon told him dryly, lifting the tent flap and standing aside to allow the litter to pass, "or anyone else's king, for that matter, you'll do as I say." The flap fell behind them.

"She's got a terrific way with her patients," Rael muttered and started back to where he'd left Rutgar holding his horse.

The Duke of Belkar fell into step beside him. "Think of it as an incentive to stay in one piece, Highness."

"What do you mean?"

Belkar's voice quivered on the edge of laughter. "If you're injured, she'll be taking care of you as well."

Rael shuddered.

*        *        *

The sun rose high over the mountains, turning arms and armor to a burnished gold, but the Melacians remained in their camp at the valley's edge. Rael, Doan, and the remaining dukes gathered on the highest bit of ground they held; little more than a hillock but enough to give them a clear line of sight. Not that it did them much good.

"Even I can see they're still in camp, Prince Rael." Cei blew his nose vigorously. "What we need to know is why."

Rael squinted, trying to bring the tiny figures of the enemy closer by force of will. Finally he shook his head and gave up. "Something's upset them, they're scurrying around like headless chickens. The only thing I can say for certain is that, for now, they show no interest in us."

"Then we attack. Ride in and grind the scum into the mountain."

With the Duke of Hale's death, and the heir only a child, command of his forces had gone to Allonger, the senior of his two captains, a vicious fighter, a man of quick and explosive temper, who was also the dead duke's uncle. Most of his conversation since he took command had centered on revenge.

"Too risky," Doan grunted. "They hold the high ground. It's got to be a trap."

"Then we wait?" Aliston's heir suggested.

"We wait," Rael agreed. Allonger opened his mouth to speak but snapped it shut again as the prince continued. "It's a pity we can't get scouts close enough to nose out what's going on, but there's no cover and I'd never order a man to commit that kind of suicide."

Belkar hid a snicker behind a cough. Doan became very interested in the space between his horse's ears. Cei and Aliston's heir, safely out of line of sight, exchanged amused glances. Rael looked steadily at Hale's captain.

Allonger glared at the prince, well aware he'd been neatly outmaneuvered. A very long moment passed in silence. "Oh, all right," he said at last. His voice was gruff, but the edges of his mustache trembled as he tried not to smile. "We wait." He inclined his head, adding respectfully and without a trace of sarcasm, "Your Highness."

They waited all that day, thanking the Mother-creator for the rest, and wondering what kept the Melacian army in camp. Not until the sun began to set did they find out.

"Highness!" The Messenger darted into Rael's tent, glanced quickly around and headed for the inner room.

Ivan snagged her sleeve and dragged her to a stop. "And just where do you think you're going, young woman? You can't just run in here like you owned the place, this is . . ."

"Let her go, Ivan." Rael ducked through the inner flap and smiled down at the Messenger, who twitched her sleeve free and ducked her head in a shallow bow.

"It's the Dukes Riven and Lorn, Highness. They're in the command tent. Milord Belkar asks you to attend them at once."

Lorn was not in the command tent when Rael reached it moments later, but Riven sat, head buried in his hands, at the center of a milling crowd of the dukes and their captains. Voices were hushed and shoulders tense and every eye on Riven.

"They blocked the pass, Commander; Riven, Lorn, and their men." Doan fell in at the prince's side as he crossed the tent. "They drove wooden wedges into cracks in the rock then poured water over them until they swelled and slid a couple of tons of rock into a canyon just the other side of the border." His voice was frankly admiring. "Couldn't have done it better if they'd had a company of dwarves."

"Most of the men in these parts are miners, they know what they're doing. Where's Lorn?"

Doan paused before answering, weighing the words to use. "They took him to the infirmary," he said at last, his tone carefully neutral.

Just then Riven looked up. His dark hair hung in a tangled mass down his back, his face was pale and streaked with dirt, his nails were broken and his fingers were scraped raw. Blood stained his hands and clothes; much more blood than his own wounds could account for.

"He wanted to die, but I brought him back. I couldn't leave him out there." His throat convulsed and the sound that emerged quavered halfway between a choke and a sob.

Belkar, who stood close by Riven's side, looked up and shook his head at Rael's silent question. "I don't know, lad, that's all he'll say."

Rael dropped to the bench, took a goblet of wine from a hovering servant, and shoved it into the Duke of Riven's hands. "Drink," he commanded.

Riven sipped, coughed, then drained the goblet.

"Now, tell me," Rael prodded gently. "What happened?"

Once, twice, Riven opened his mouth but no sound came out. The third time the words spilled free. "I, I was on the other side of the canyon. They said, his men said, one of his captains was standing too close to the edge when the rock began to fall. He tried to save him. They both went over." Riven's eyes went dark with memories and tears began to cut new channels through the dirt. "I got to him as fast as I could. He wanted me to kill him."

Startled, Rael looked up at Belkar.

"His legs were crushed," the duke said softly.

"I couldn't kill him." Riven turned to Rael for support. "I couldn't. I dug him out. I brought him back."

Rael had no idea of what to say or what to do. He reached out a tentative hand and touched the grieving man lightly on the shoulder.

Riven drew a shuddering breath. "I couldn't kill him." Then he threw himself to the floor and began to smash his fists into the canvas leaving scarlet smears, his blood and Lora's mixed together.

"He carried Lorn every step of the way himself," Doan said later as he stood with Rael looking toward the enemy camp. "The men with them say that he wouldn't let anyone help. And during every lucid moment, Lorn begged Riven to kill him. When begging didn't work, he tried curses."

"Will he live?"

"Probably. But he'll never walk again. Myself, I'm more worried about young Riven."

Rael remembered Seven Day Festivals, when the boys who'd grown up to be Riven and Lorn had come to the palace with their families. They were only five years older than the prince. He'd watched them running and playing and fighting as a single unit. He'd envied them their closeness.

Doan shoved his hands deep behind his belt. "It won't mean much to them now, but the two of them have ended the war. With supply lines cut, no cavalry, no new troops, and no line to their king, the Melacians will have to surrender. It's the only logical thing to do."

Rael pushed away visions of falling rock and two boys who would never run together again, and brought himself back to the present. "How did the King of Melac think he could command from four hours behind the lines?"

"He may have sent up the occasional order," Doan grunted, "but the real commanders are out there on the field."

Over the Melacian camp a cold blue fight suddenly flickered and then darkness claimed the night again.

"Sheet-lightning?" Rael wondered aloud.

"Maybe."

Just for a moment the captain's eyes flared brilliantly red. Rael blinked and the moment was gone. He had the feeling Doan knew more than he was willing to tell, but after one glance at the rigid set of his jaw, Rael decided not to ask. Now that the war was over, there would be plenty of time for questions.

In the morning, the Melacians' expected surrender turned into an all-out attack.

"This is crazy!" Rutgar yelled, tossing aside the splintered remains of his lance and drawing his sword. "They can't possibly hope to win."

"Don't tell me!" Rael bellowed back, in the breathing space they'd cut for themselves. "Tell them!"

Rutgar stood in his stirrups. "You guys are crazy! You can't possibly hope to win!"

Rael laughed and bashed his armsman lightly on the shield. "Feel better?"

Behind his visor, Rutgar's teeth gleamed and he laughed as well. "Yeah, I do!"

When the Elite charged, crashing through the screaming chaos the enemy pikeline had become, the Melacians swarmed about them, rats turning on the terrier. The horses' legs were soon red to the hocks. Weapons dripped and armor ran with gore.

"I don't believe this," Rael muttered as the press of bodies, the dead, the dying, and the living behind them, slowed the charge and forced the Pairs apart. He roared the retreat, ripping his throat raw with the sound. All around, he heard the call repeated. And then he heard the scream. Behind him.

He twisted in his saddle.

Rutgar.

His shield arm hung limp and blood ran down the armor, pouring from his fingers in a ruby stream. His sword wove dizzying patterns of steel, trying to protect his wounded side, but he was tiring, and there were too many attacking.

"No!" Practically lifting the animal onto its hindquarters, Rael yanked his horse around, cutting and chopping like a madman the entire time. The Melacians surrounding him began to fall back. If they were crazy, he was crazier. If they welcomed Lord Death, he'd happily send them Death's way. But Rutgar was not going to die.

Three horse lengths apart.

Rutgar faltered. A sword drove through the seam between breast and back.

Two.

Hands stretched up to pull the swaying armsman down from the saddle.

Too far away to help, Rael saw the terror on Rutgar's face; saw Rutgar's hand reach and close on nothing; heard, as though there wasn't another sound on the battlefield, Rutgar call his name.

It was Doan who kept him from vaulting out of his saddle, Doan who steered him back to the Ardhan lines when he would have ridden into the heart of the Melacian army and tried to cut it out, and it was Doan who held him while he wept.

Later, in the command tent, he glared out at the assembled men and said, "Enough."

"Granted," Cei agreed. "But what can we do?"

"We take out their commanders, tonight."

"Tonight?"

The raw emotion on Rael's face choked off the babble of questions before it truly began. "Doan."

The Captain of the Elite stepped forward.

"The Elite will follow where you lead, commander."

"Will you follow him into Lord Death's embrace?" Cei sniffed. "Because without a moon, that's right where you'll be going."

Although Cei stood almost two feet taller, Doan managed to look down on him as he repeated, "The Elite will follow where he leads."

"Cei's right," Belkar said gently. "Without a moon, that valley will be pitch black."

"Then they won't expect an attack. The lack of a moon can work to our advantage as well, giving us cover and a better chance of success." Rael ground out the words, the lack of expression in stark contrast to the pain that twisted his face.

Belkar sighed. He wished, not for the first time, Glinna had allowed Raen to attend. A king and father could command where others could only advise. "I want to end this as much as you do, Highness, believe me, but men cannot see in darkness."

"If the Elite will follow," Rael lifted his head and green fires blazed in his eyes, "then darkness will not stop us."

# FIVE

It was raining the next morning when Rael came to his father's tent. He stood for a moment and stared blindly at the wet canvas, letting the water cut channels into the red-brown mud that caked his armor. The lines etched into the pale skin about his mouth and the purple bruises beneath his eyes, eyes in which the green fires had all but died, bore eloquent testimony to the night's work. He had never looked less like his mother.

The Guard before the entrance saluted and stood aside but Glinna, standing guard within the canvas walls, could not be so easily passed. She folded her arms on her chest and blocked the way.

"The king finally sleeps. Anything you have to say can wait."

"I have news of the war."

"No doubt," she said dryly. "But I don't care if the war is over, you may not wake him."

"The war is over."

Her eyes widened. She looked down at the dried blood that stained his sword hilt, so thick in places that it filled the hollows in the ornate scrollwork, then she stepped aside.

"Don't allow him to become excited," she cautioned as Rael passed. "If he opens the wound again . . ." Her words trailed off, but the meaning was clear.

When Raen had left his bed and reopened the wound, it had infected, swelling and putrefying. From a serious although hardly fatal injury, it had grown to be dangerously life threatening. Glinna, however, refused to admit defeat, draining, cleaning, cauterizing, and pouring potion after potion down the king's throat. Three times she forced Lord Death away, and in the end she won; the king lived. But under the scented smoke that eddied around the inner room, the smell of rot remained.

"Less than a week," thought Rael, looking down at his father, "how could he change so much in less than a week?"

As the war had aged Rael, the wound had aged Raen. Flesh hung from his bones as if it belonged to another man, and the lines of his face were now furrows. Not even the most loving son could deny that the king had grown old.

Rael dashed a tear away with an impatient hand. *You will not mourn him while he still lives,* he told himself fiercely. *He needs you to be strong.* He dragged a chair over to the bed and perched on its edge. "Father?" Reaching out a slender hand, he placed it gently on the sleeping man's chest. The steady rise and fall seemed to reassure him. He sat quietly for a moment then called again.

With a sound that was half question, half moan, the king woke, blinked, and focused slowly on Rael's face.

"Father, the war is over."

"You have the battle commanders." It wasn't a question. Late in the night, Belkar had told him what Rael planned to do, indeed, was doing, for the prince had ordered the duke not to speak until he and the Elite were well on their way. "You did the right thing. The only thing. I wouldn't have stopped you." The boy had needed an outlet for his grief. The war had needed to be ended. That both had been accomplished at once, and with a plan only the prince commander himself could carry out, would further consolidate said commander's position with the army. That said commander was his son, and the plan placed him in mortal danger, had given Raen a sleepless night. "Did they surrender?"

"Not quite." Rael leaned forward and propped a pillow behind his father's head. "We torched their camp, destroyed half their army, and still had to knock a tent down on the commanders to get them to quit."

"Prisoners."

"Besides the seven commanders, about eight hundred; at least half of them wounded."

Raen brought up a skeletal hand to stroke his beard. "Hmmm, not many." His eyes unfocused as he considered the best course of action. "The men are rabble without the leaders. Strip them of their arms and have them taken back across the border."

"But, Father, the pass is blocked."

"Oh," Raen looked momentarily confused. Had he known that? Memories of the last few days were soft edged and smoke-filled; he remembered pain clearly but not much else.

"And they don't want to go back."

"Are you sure."

"Very sure." Rael shrugged wearily. "But I don't know why."

"Well, I've a pretty good idea," Raen snorted, suddenly more energetic as he came across something he thought he understood. "They lost. Melac and that idiot who advises him aren't likely to be very welcoming."

"Father, about that counselor . . ."

"An ambitious upstart," the king dismissed their unknown enemy with a choppy wave of his hand. "I'm not surprised someone like him showed up to grab power. Melac was always weak. We'll keep the border guarded and have nothing more to do with either of them."

Rael was not convinced. From things he'd overheard in the last few hours, he suspected Melac's counselor would remain a threat. But that was for the future to deal with; here and now he had other worries. "So what do we do with the prisoners?"

"Divide them up and scatter them amongst the dukes." The crease between the king's eyes deepened as he remembered the mass graves that held the flower of Ardhan's youth. "We'll all be a little shorthanded for a while. I'm sure they can find ways to put them to use. If they truly don't want to go home, they can begin to work off the lives they owe us."

"And the battle commander and his officers?"

The king sighed. "Well, they *can't* go home. Melac can always get more spear-carriers and crow-fodder, but returning his officers would be asking to do this all over again. Have them take the standard oath about laying down arms and ever after cleaving to the soil of the land they invaded."

"They won't." Rael sighed as well, and rubbed a grimy hand across the bridge of his nose. "They say they've taken blood oaths to fight for Melac and the Empire until death."

"Empire!" Raen snarled and tried to sit up. "What Empire?"

Rael pushed him gently back. "The one we were supposed to be the first part of. They're fanatics, Father. When we took away their weapons they attacked with bare hands. We practically had to bury them in chains before they stopped. They fought like men possessed." He paused and his eyes narrowed in memory. "Or men in mortal terror."

"They'll have to die."

"Father!"

"How many men did you kill last night?" Raen asked gently.

"I told you, we torched the camp. It's likely hundreds died."

Raen held his son's eyes with his own. "No. How many did you kill? Yourself?"

Rael yanked his gaze away and stared at the carpet. "I don't know. Eighteen. Twenty maybe. I lost count."

"And Rutgar's still dead."

The terror; the reaching hand; his name screamed.

"Yes."

"It didn't bring him back, so the killing is over."

Rael lifted his head and green embers stirred. He'd fought last night blinded by anger and pain and with every life he sent to Lord Death the anger bled away until there was only the pain. "Yes," he said. "There's been enough."

"Unless those seven die, the war isn't over and we've won nothing. Rutgar died for nothing. The men you killed last night died for nothing." Raen lifted a hand and touched his son's arm. "A king has no conscience, lad, he gives it to his people."

"That's garbage, Father, and you know it. The people do what you say."

Raen let his hand fall back onto the blanket. "Then do as I say, Rael, and carry out my command."

Rael searched the stern, closed face on the pillow for his father but saw only the king. He stood so quickly his chair tipped and fell and he almost kicked it out of the way as he spun and headed for the door.

"Rael."

He paused but didn't turn.

"Last night you let your anger define the thin line between justice and murder; a king never has that luxury."

"A lesson, Father?"

"If you wish, and here's another. You'd rather I gave this task to one of the dukes, but the king must be willing to carry out the king's justice. As I am not able, you must stand in for me."

"I don't think I'm ready to be king."

Raen's teeth flashed white amid the dusky gray of his beard and the lines of his face lifted with the smile. "Good."

Doan was waiting when Rael left the king's tent. The night's work had added a limp and several new scars to the Elite Captain's inelegant appearance. He fell into step beside the younger man.

"You were right," Rael said at last.

Doan kept silent. He appeared to be watching the rain drip off the edge of his helmet.

"We're to divide the men amongst the dukes, but the commander and his captains die. I'm to see that it gets taken care of."

Doan merely pulled his cloak tighter to stop the rain from running down his neck.

Rael's laughter sounded a great deal like choking. "Life would certainly be a lot easier if my father was a woodsman or a farmer."

The captain grunted, there being little he could say to his own words.

"If it must be done, then let's do it now."

"I'll call for volunteers, Commander." As Rael's head jerked around to face him, he added. "You must only be present, Highness. You don't strike the blows yourself. And it's not a job you can command a man to do."

By the time the Guard was formed, the rain had stopped. The sun came out, and seven men died.

And the war was over.

"At least I never enjoyed it, Mother," Rael whispered as the breeze lifted his hair from his forehead and blood soaked into the ground at his feet. "At least I never enjoyed it."

The fire reached the grimy foot of the elderly woman tied to the stake and began to lick daintily at the blistering skin.

"'Ware the child," she screamed in a mad voice raw with much shrieking. "'Ware the creation of Lord Death's children."

"Lord Death's children?" Lord Elan half turned, enough so he could see the king's counselor but not so much that he must look at the king. That pain at least he would spare himself. "What does she mean, Lord Death's children?"

The golden-haired man lounged back in his chair and sighed. "The race of Man was created for Lord Death's benefit. Thus Man," he inclined his head toward the stake with chilling courtesy, "and Woman also, are Death's children."

"It burns! Brilliance within! Brilliance without!" And then not even madness was enough to overcome the effects of the flames. The old woman sagged against the ropes and prophesied no more.

The king shifted on his throne, hips rotating with each spasm of the body on the pyre.

"She wasn't very clear," Lord Elan grunted.

Full lips molded themselves into a smile. "She was clear enough earlier and more than willing to repeat the entire prophecy as often as I chose to listen." Even the most obscure prophet could be convinced to find clarity and while there was no real need in this instance, the convincing had filled a few otherwise tedious hours.

"Then what does it mean?" The old lord sounded tired. The greasy smoke stung his eyes and coated his throat. He hated executions, even the most necessary, and had attended this one only because he'd vowed that the king would spend as little time alone with his counselor as possible. Others of the nobility, those who had not died with the army—he saw their faces wide-eyed in the firelight—seemed to be taking their idea of pleasure from what pleasured their liege. He gritted his teeth and glanced quickly at the king.

He was beginning to lose interest now that the body had stopped moving.

The voice of the king's counselor was closer to content than it had been in years. He lifted his face to let the evening breeze cool skin flushed by the heat. "It means, Lord Elan, that I have something to look forward to."

"But we're going back to Ardhan."

"No."

"But . . ." Lord Elan jerked as sapphire eyes caught his and held. A thin rope of drool fell from one corner of suddenly slack lips. He jerked again as he was released and would have fallen had he not clung, panting, to the arm of the king's throne.

"I said no," the counselor repeated quietly. He stared past the pyre, out over the remains of the army. So clever of him to have kept the cavalry back; they would replace the officers killed and, well, one could always get more peasants. *South and east*, he thought. *I will create an Empire to the south and east, giving Ardhan enough time to fulfill the prophecy.* Glancing down at the smoldering pile of meat and bone, he rubbed long fingers against the silk covering his thighs. "Well," he purred in a voice barely audible over the sizzle and crackle of burning fat, "almost enough time."


The army returned triumphant to the city, although the king did not ride proudly at its head but was carried on a litter. Rael, with the Elite behind him, led the army home.

The war quickly became a thing of the past. Men went back to holdings and fields, battle armor was polished and put away, and Rael received a most unexpected welcome home from the Duke of Belkar's blue-eyed daughter—who had supposedly ridden to the palace to meet her father. Rael was pleasantly surprised to find that blue eyes held depths as well as green and that the eyes of mortal women also glowed.

The king did not recover.

Glinna now slept in the room next to the royal bedchambers, when she slept at all. The infection had returned and spread, and now the king's whole lower body strained against its increasingly heated covering of skin. She did what she could but finally, no longer able to deny what training and common sense told her, she admitted defeat.

"His life is now in the hands of Lord Death," she told the prince. "I can do nothing more."

"My father doesn't believe in Lord Death," said Rael bitterly.

"Well, Lord Death believes in him," replied the surgeon and left Rael alone with his thoughts and his dying father.

But Lord Death, never predictable, stayed his hand and the king did not die; although he didn't exactly live. Affairs of state were left in the hands of the council and royal decisions increasingly fell to the prince, for the king tired easily and Glinna demanded he rest.

"Why have a council," she snapped, prying dispatches from his hand and shoving them at an embarrassed Belkar, "if you don't use it?"

Raen raged against the weakness that held him to his bed, and the raging left him weaker still, until he was only a shadow of the man he had been.

"I am no longer a man."

"You're more of a man than anyone in the kingdom," Rael told him, his eyes filling with tears he refused to shed.

The king laughed humorlessly and stared down at his wasted body. "That doesn't say much for the other men in the kingdom."

The king was dying and everyone knew it. Already a funereal hush hung over the land. The dukes, down to crippled Lorn and ten-year-old Hale, gathered in the King's City, waiting. Rael went numbly about the task of learning to rule. He knew he should go to the Grove and tell his mother that the mortal man she loved lay dying, but he couldn't. He just couldn't. He told himself that Milthra, being who and what she was, probably already knew. That didn't help very much.

One morning, in the quiet hours just past dawn, some five weeks after the war had ended, the Duke of Belkar came to the king. The two men shared an age, but the man on the bed made the other seem obscenely healthy.

Belkar looked down at his liege and his friend and wondered where to begin. Raen spoke before he got the chance, anger turning the words to edged steel.

"It would have been so much easier had Lord Death collected me on the battlefield. Then those I love would not have had to watch me die by inches. And I would not have had to watch their pain as they watched me."

"Raen, I'm sorry, I . . ."

"No." The word was faint but still very much a king's command. "It is I who should be sorry. You didn't need that on top of everything else. I was feeling sorry for myself and you bore the brunt of it." His face twisted in a skeletal caricature of a smile. "Forgive me?"

Belkar nodded, not trusting his voice, although what he thought to hide when tears ran unheeded down his face, he had no idea.

"So," Raen's voice became as light as he was still capable of making it. "To what do I owe your presence so early in the day?"

More than anything in his life, the duke wanted to follow Raen's lead, to try to banish the darkness for just a little while, but he was desperately afraid there was no time for even that small amount of comfort. "The people talk."

"They always have. Death, taxes, and the people talking, the three things you can count on." Raen shifted into a different but no more comfortable position. "Sit down, Belkar, and tell me what they say."

Belkar sat, spread his hands, and stared at their backs. It was easier than meeting the king's eyes. "They're speaking against the prince, saying he isn't human."

"They always knew that; I told them who his mother was when I declared him my heir."

"To most of them, the Lady is something to fear. The Elder Races have never been friendly to man. People fear and distrust her power and they fear and distrust her power in him."

"He proved himself in the war."

"Yes, but the war is over. And . . ." Belkar sighed. ". . . he proved himself different."

"He won the war!"

"He used his mother's power to do it. Half of the talkers see the danger in that alone. The other half wonder why he waited so long to use it and ask what game he played."

Tendons in Raen's neck stood out as he ground his teeth. "And those titled vultures who circle about my deathbed?"

"The dukes," Belkar reminded him gently, "have the right to see the crown passed." Raen dipped his head a barely perceivable amount, as much of an apology as he was willing to make. Belkar continued: "They worry about his mother as well, and the effect her blood will have on the way he rules."

"They've never worried before."

"He's never been so close to being king before."

Raen squinted up at his oldest friend. "They remember that soldier? The one my son killed?"

Belkar nodded.

"And what do they say about me?" The king's eyes held a dangerous glint.

"They say you don't heal because he bewitched you as his mother did."

"And what do you believe?"

"I," Belkar pointed out, "have met his mother." Once, many years before, the duke had gone with Raen to the Grove. He still held the memory of the hamadryad like a jewel in his heart. Occasionally, he held it up to the light to rejoice in its beauty.

"Then," said the king, "you shall stand with me when I speak to the people."

Belkar shot a startled glance at the surgeon, sure she would not allow such a thing.

Glinna shrugged.

"He is dying. Let it at least be where and how he chooses."

Raen smiled, his first real smile in weeks. "An honest woman, Belkar. Every dying man should have one." And then the smile slipped and his eyes looked into the future. "At least the Elite will stand by him. We've seen to that, he and I."

"They'd follow him into the bedchamber of Lord Death," Belkar agreed. "But would you throw your country into civil war if people decide he is not to have the crown?"

"He is my son and my heir. Five generations ago my house was chosen to rule. We gave our name to the land. He was trained to rule and there is no one else."

"If you'd only had more children . . ."

"He would still be eldest and my heir."

The two men locked eyes. Belkar's gaze dropped first.

"I know. I will support him and do what I can, but the people will make up their own minds."

"Then I'll just have to convince them. Now," he waved the duke over to his desk, "write me a proclamation and see that the criers get it immediately. I want everyone, from the lowest beggar to all six dukes, in the People's Square by noon." His voice grew quieter and he sank back on his pillows, exhausted. "I must ensure the succession for my son."

*And how can you do that when such little speech as you've had with me nearly kills you,* Belkar wondered. But all he said aloud was: "Shall I have the prince sent to you?"

"Not now. Let him have this morning to himself. Send him at noon."

Noon.

The people gathered in the Square.

Rael entered his father's chamber slowly, his heart so heavy it sat like a lump of coal in his chest. This would be good-bye, he knew it. It took a moment to penetrate his grief, but instead of his father lying wasted on the bed he saw the king being dressed in royal purple. Even the crown, massive and ugly, stood close at hand.

He grabbed Glinna's arm and dragged her out of the milling crowd of servants.

"What's going on? Is he better?"

"No. If anything, he's worse." The surgeon's tone made it quite clear that she took the king's condition as a personal affront. "But he insists on speaking to the people."

"Why?"

"The people say they won't have you as king."

"I don't care what the people say."

"He does."

Rael studied his father standing supported between two burly footmen as a valet pushed his feet into boots. Raen's skin was gray and his eyes had sunk deep in indigo shadows. The column of his throat stood out in a bas-relief of ridges and hollows. "Will he survive it?"

"No."

"And you're just letting him die?!"

"Yes." She held up a hand and stopped Rael's next words. "Before you say anything, consider this: he is still the man he was. Would you have that man die in bed?"

Rael released her arm and shook his head. His father might have no fear of Lord Death, but he would refuse to meet the Mother-creator's true son lying helpless in bed.

"I thought not. Now, go to him. He needs you."

Dressed, the king reached for the crown, but his hands shook so they couldn't grasp it. Rael's hands covered his. Together they lifted it from the table.

"A crown," said Raen as it settled on his brow, "is a heavy burden." He grinned a death's head grin as he struggled to straighten his neck under the weight. "There's more than a little truth in these old cliches."

"Yes, Father."

"I'm going to see that this burden goes to you. Perhaps I'm doing you no favor." He sighed. "A king has no conscience, my son, he gives it to the people."

"I will remember, Father."

Raen snorted. "They're not likely to let you forget."

Attendants moved the king to a litter and carried him through the halls of the palace, Rael keeping pace alongside. Although they tried, it was not always possible to keep the litter even and once, when it jerked on a stair, Raen bit back a pained cry. Choking back a cry of his own, Rael reached out a hand and his father's wasted fingers closed gratefully around it.

Belkar, in the formal, ornate robes of a Duke of Ardhan, stood by the Great Door.

"My liege." He knelt and kissed the shadow of a hand stretched out to him.

"Just help me off this thing," Raen snapped. Friendship could weaken him now as easily as pain and he still had much to do. "I'm not dead yet!"

The king had not stood unassisted since he had been carried off the battlefield for the second time, but when he was on his feet he shook off the supporting hands of his son and his friend.

"This I must do alone," he said through gritted teeth. "Let it begin, Belkar."

Belkar shook his head at the prince's pleading look, a look that said as loudly as if Rael had spoken, *You can't let him do it alone!*, and gave the signal. Trumpets called and the great doors swung open.

The People's Square was full and overflowing with the entire population of King's City and, as commanded, all six dukes. They represented only a small percentage of the population of Ardhan, but they would spread the news and by the end of the week, the whole country would know. And then the people would judge.

Raen did not call up deep reserves of hidden strength so that he walked proudly, shoulders back and head erect to the edge of the dais—he had no reserves to call. He tottered that twenty feet, sweat running and lips snarling against the pain. One foot went in front of the other by strength of will alone.

The people saw what it cost him and began to cheer. First those near the dais and then the noise moved back through the crowd until the walls shook with it and Raen felt it through the stones under his feet. He stopped and raised his hands for silence, but the crowd refused to quiet until he swayed and collapsed.

"Father!"

Rael, Belkar, and the king's attendants rushed forward, all expecting the worst, but the king still clutched at life.

"Get me on the litter," he rasped, "and raise it so I can see and be seen. I must say what I have come to say."

"Father, it isn't important, I . . ."

"This isn't just for you. I will not have my country torn by civil war!"

With gentle hands, Rael lifted his father and laid him carefully on the litter. Some of the crowd hissed at this show of his strength—wasted or not, the king was a large man still—but Rael didn't care. His only thought was for the man he loved who lay dying.

Two of the attendants hoisted one end of the litter to their shoulders. Raen stared out at the Square from the dark hollows his eyes had become.

"I am still your king!" he cried in a voice surprisingly strong.

The people cheered.

"This," he continued, taking Rael's hand, "is my son."

Only a few cheered. Most muttered sullenly and one, a weaver, apparently the chosen spokesman, twisted his cap in his hands and called out: "We don't doubt you are his father, Sire, but we have concerns about his mother."

"You know who his mother is."

The weaver squirmed and reddened but he persisted. "And that's the problem, Sire. He isn't human and who's to say with you gone that he won't turn on us. You can't trust the Elder Races, they've never had what you'd call good will toward man. If he should take after his mother . . ."

"If you knew his mother," Belkar's voice rang out over the muttering that signified agreement with the weaver's words, "you wouldn't . . ."

His last words vanished under the noise that rose from the far side of the Square. There was no need to strain to see the cause of the commotion, for Milthra's silver head shone like a star amongst suddenly drab browns and reds and yellows.

"The Lady," ran the awed whisper as the crowd parted before her. "The Lady of the Grove." Those who had lost their ability to believe in the wondrous found it again. Those who had doubted, couldn't remember why. A young woman reached out and let a lock of the Lady's shining hair caress her fingers and then stood gazing at her hand in amazement as if it belonged to another. Peace walked with the Lady and the smell of a sun-warmed forest grove filled the air.

She looked neither to the left nor the right as she approached the palace, her eyes never moved from the man on the litter or the youth standing beside him. At the steps of the dais she paused, as if gathering strength—the fragrance of the forest became stronger and a breeze danced through her hair—then she lifted her skirts in her hand and climbed the steps.

With a strangled cry, Rael threw himself into her arms. She held him to her heart for a moment, stroking his hair, and then gently pushed him away. Green eyes gazed into green.

Rael wondered how he could ever have thought of his mother as young. He saw wisdom, understanding, compassion to a degree most mortal minds could not accept, let alone achieve, resting in the depths of her eyes. She had walked with the Mother-creator at the beginning of the world. She had seen the creation of man. And she loved him. Rael felt her love wrap around him, a warmth, a protection he would always wear.

Milthra saw that her son would make a fine king. His heart sang with courage and pride and his eyes were filled with hope. He might stumble and fall, but he would try, and no mother could ask more. She had no regrets.

The people in the Square saw only the Lady of the Grove and the young man she claimed as her son, but it was enough. The unworldliness of their future king turned from a thing to be feared to one to be treasured. Not one of them realized what Milthra had done in leaving the Grove.

"Mother," Rael's voice grew heavy with a new anguish, "you've left your tree."

"I have left my tree." She touched his cheek softly. "How could I live when my love died? My sisters sleep and someday a child of your children's children will wake them, but my day is done."

She kissed him and turned to the king.

Raen looked up at her with such a mixture of longing and pain that those in the crowd who saw it, wept.

"Why have you come?" he cried.

"You would not come to me, beloved, so I have come to you."

"Then you will die."

"Yes. But what is my life without you?" She tried a smile, but it faltered and the brilliant green of her eyes dimmed for an instant as they filled and overflowed. Her hands were caught in his, fingers too tightly woven to be parted, so she let the tears drop where they would.

They fell almost slowly, taking form and beauty in the air, and then lay shimmering like jewels on his breast. Instead of drying in the sunlight, they caught it, bound it, and gave it back. Their light grew and grew until everyone save Raen and Milthra covered their eyes. Even Rael stepped back and shielded himself from the glory.

When eyes could see again, an old and dying king no longer lay on the dais. In his place was a young man with hair of jet and smooth golden skin over corded muscle.

"The king," sighed the crowd. "His youth has returned."

Rael's eyes widened, joy beginning to surface, but Milthra shook her head.

"It is an appearance only, my child," she said. "Death is the true son of the Mother and not even I can stop him." And then she looked beyond Rael, to the young man who stood in his shadow. The young man that only she, of all the hundreds in the Square, could see.

Under the weight of her regard, Lord Death bowed his head and when he raised it again said softly: "I would spare you both if my nature allowed it, Eldest."

Raen looked down at his body and raised his hands to his face.

"It's true!" His voice throbbed with passion. "I'm a man again. I am as I was in my prime!" He held out his arms and Milthra lay down beside him, her head pillowed on his chest.

"As you always were to me, beloved, and as you always will be now."

He kissed her once, softly, and then together they died.

The silence was so complete, the crowd so quiet and still, that the sunlight bathing the bodies in golden luminescence could almost be heard. From the distance, from the forest, came the sound of thunder.

Belkar stepped forward and three times opened his mouth to speak. Finally, his voice got past his grief and filled the Square.

"The king is dead!"

And then he dropped on one knee before the tall young man with eyes the green of new spring leaves.

"Long live the king!"


Rael buried his mother and father in the Sacred Grove under the remains of his mother's tree. It had been hit by lightning and then consumed by fire until only a charred stump remained. Not one of the other trees, or even so much as a blade of grass, had been touched.

"This stump shall be your headstone," he said softly, patting the last bit of earth into place. "And I will see that none disturb your rest."

*"I won't cry for them"* he had told Belkar, *"for they're together at last and even in death that is no cause for grief."*

As the young king left the Grove, he thought he heard women's voices, lamenting, soft with sorrow, but when he turned, he saw only the wind moving through the circle of trees and leaves falling to cover the grave.

# INTERLUDE ONE

Rael joined with the Duke of Belkar's blue-eyed daughter and their years together were filled with love and laughter and children. He never found the common touch that had so endeared his father to the people, but he ruled well and was always after remembered as just.

For all the years of Rael's reign, Doan, the Captain of the Elite, stood by his side. His unaging presence became a part of the king: two arms, two legs, and the captain. And when he buried his sword in Rael's grave and vanished from mortal lands, that too was accepted with no surprise. It could not be imagined he would serve another.

The death of the Eldest became the subject of a thousand songs and in her honor, or perhaps to save her sisters from a like fate, Rael, as his first act as Lord of Ardhan, forbade all mortals entry to the Grove, swearing those who knew its direction to oaths of secrecy. Over forty years later, when his son took the throne, time had erased the reality of both the Lady and the circle of silver birch and left only the songs.


The dwarf stepped back from the sapling and nodded once. "Just like you said."

The great black centaur that stood beside him returned the nod, although both kept their eyes on the tiny tree. Around them, the Sacred Grove was silent and still. No leaf rustled, for no breeze dared to intrude.

"Can They hope to succeed?" the centaur asked at last.

Doan shrugged. "I don't see why not. This," he waved a hand about the Grove, "is the oldest magic in the world and They've woven themselves into it. Sacrificed Themselves to do it. They've succeeded, C'Tal, that tree holds a life as real as any in this place. But after . . ."

"So much rests on the Mother's youngest children." C'Tal folded his arms across his massive chest, the black beard flowing like silk over them. "And the Mother's youngest children have never been strong."

"Strong enough to begin this mess," Doan snorted. His gaze dropped to the lichen covered mound the young birch grew from, all that remained of Milthra's tree. "Strong enough to draw out the Eldest and take her from us."

"True," murmured the centaur and the trees around them stirred and moaned. "But you must never forget, she chose her path."

"Forget!" Doan whirled and his eyes blazed red, not with power but pain. "As if I could!" He turned again to the sapling. "I could end this, here and now." He grabbed a tender leaf and ripped it free. The small tree shuddered. "They've risked it all on this one toss, and if I destroy Their vessel it's over."

"Perhaps for us as well."

Doan's arched eyebrows invited C'Tal to continue.

"He has no checks on his power this time. Who is to say when he is done with the mortals he will not turn at last to the Elder Races?"

"So *that's* why you finally stuck your noses in." Doan's laugh was bitter. "Fear."

"Unlike other races, we do not become involved in that which does not concern the centaurs." C'Tal's voice remained calm, but the points of his ears lay back against his head and for an instant great slabs of teeth showed startlingly white against the black of his beard. "Nor, given the evidence, is it unreasonable for us to fear what he may do and wish to stop him."

Doan looked thoughtful. He rubbed another leaf between thumb and forefinger, but this time the action was almost a caress. "I could end it now," he murmured, his voice unusually gentle.

"But you will not." A huge black hand reached down and engulfed the dwarf's shoulder.

"No." He pulled himself out of the other's grasp and stood flexing the shoulder the centaur had held. "And you needn't snap bones to convince me either," he added peevishly. "For the little of her that's woven here and greater part of her yet to come, I'll let Them try to right the wrong Their brothers did."

"You must do more than that." C'Tal ignored both glare and clenched fists and continued. "As you infer, They cannot protect themselves now; if you can destroy Them, so too could another. Until the seed is sown, They must have a protector."

"Go on." Doan's voice was the rasp of moving rock.

C'Tal looked surprised. "You have been protector once before."

"And I don't choose to be again. I am needed in the caverns."

"Your brothers can guard what the caverns hold. You are needed here."

"No." A muscle jumped in his cheek; the Lady lost to love, her son to Mortal time and he could protect them from neither. "Do it yourself." Moving jerkily, stamping indentations into the velvet grass, Doan pushed past the centaur and out of the Grove.

C'Tal stood quietly, an ebony monument, framed by green and gold. He did not appear distressed by the refusal of his chosen guardian. He merely waited.

"All right." The pain was safely masked by irritation. "But only until the seed is sown. I've raised one child and I don't care to repeat it."

"Until the seed is sown," C'Tal agreed as Doan stomped back and stood snarling down at the tree. "Then we will return to the mortals' ranges . . ."

"Big of you," Doan interjected sarcastically.

". . . and as we did with the others, we will instruct the child."

"Yeah? Well, get it right this time."

It was C'Tal's turn to glare, but all he said was: "We shall."

"If there is a child."

"You think the Eldest's line will not be able to accomplish what they must to fulfill the prophecy?"

The dwarf threw his hands in the air, then, catching sight of C'Tal's face, he closed his mouth on the cutting remark that had risen to his tongue. The centaur was truly worried. "You want my opinion?"

"Yes."

Doan remembered. He'd been standing in the Square, with the rest of the Elite when Milthra had given herself to Death so many years before. He would never, for the eternity he might yet live, forget the look on her face.

"The Mother gave each of the Elders one role to play in the lives of her youngest."

"She did," agreed C'Tal.

"Dwarves guard. Centaurs teach. But the Eldest . . ."

The sapling's roots were deep in the remains of Milthra's tree, deep in the earth where Milthra and her beloved had been returned to the arms of the Mother.

". . . but the Eldest loved. And the Youngest were strong enough to bear that. In my opinion They have not sacrificed in vain. The weapon will be forged. There will be a chance to defeat the ancient enemy and maybe, just maybe, we'll have peace for a time."

The centaur sighed and once again the great hand closed on the dwarf's shoulder.

"Thank you," said C'Tal, and almost the trees around echoed him. Then, with the uncanny speed of his kind, the centaur was gone.

For a moment, Doan stood quietly, looking down at the miniature silver birch, considering the life within it. The moment passed, his face fell back into its accustomed scowl, and he kicked at a nodding buttercup.

"Seeds, bah! They need a gardener not a guardian."

# SIX

"Tayer, we're lost. We'll never find our way back."

"Oh, do be quiet, Hanna. I'm trying to think."

"But what about bandits? We could be killed. Or worse!" The girl's voice rose to a piercing wail.

"Hanna!" Tayer turned in her saddle and glared at her cousin. "There are no bandits in the Lady's Wood. And if you'll just be quiet for a moment, we may be able to hear the horns and find our way back to the hunt."

Hanna sniffed but stopped wailing. All her life she'd followed the older, stronger-willed girl and now habit conquered fear.

"If we could only see the sun," Tayer mused, standing in her stirrups and squinting up into the thick summer foliage, "at least then we'd know which way we were heading." But the sky was overcast and what showed through the leaves was a uniform gray.

"It'll probably rain."

"Oh, Hanna!" Tayer's laugh lightened the wood's darkness for a moment, and it almost seemed the birds fell silent to hear. Songs without number had been written about the laugh of the Princess of Ardhan. Every bard in the kingdom, and not a few from outside, had tried to immortalize the sound. They'd never quite managed it. As had been said more than once, the sound, although beautiful beyond compare, was nothing really without the princess. Strands of gold wove through the thick chestnut of her hair, flecks of gold brightened the soft brown of her eyes, and a sprinkle of gold danced across the cream of her cheeks. She was the youngest of the three children of the king, the only daughter, and the image of her dead mother. The king counted her amongst the treasures of his kingdom.

Hanna's pale, delicate beauty had always been overshadowed by her cousin's—what chance had a violet against a rose, even one just barely budded—but she appeared content living in the light of reflected glory.

The four generations since the death of Milthra and Raen had wiped out all overt physical resemblances to the hamadryad in the Royal House of Ardhan, but nevertheless differences remained. When Rael, at sixty-four, took his mother's road and followed his beloved into death, he had looked like a man of less than forty. His son was seventy-five when he finally married and one hundred and thirty-five when he died. The blood of the Eldest could not keep Lord Death away indefinitely, but it certainly delayed his coming.

In those four generations, the Lady's Wood had become just another forest, distinguished only in that Royal Law forbade the cutting of any living tree within its boundaries. In this generation, it had become the favorite hunting ground of the Court.

A bird with snowy white plumage, startling against the deep green of the forest's summer canopy, had separated Tayer and Hanna from the rest of the hunt. Tayer had thought it so unusual, and so beautiful, she rode off after it to get a better look; Hanna trailing, as always, along behind. When the bird disappeared, seemingly between one tree and the next, they were in a part of the forest completely unfamiliar to them and hopelessly lost.

A certain heaviness in the air, a waiting stillness, said Hanna's fear of rain was not wholly brought about by depression. The horses' ears lay flat and the animals had to be urged down the trail. Heavy underbrush clutched at the girls' clothing and the horses' legs with sharp, damp fingers. No birds sang and even the leaves hung still. The sounds of the horses' hoofs on the forest floor were muffled and indistinct.

Silence shrouded the forest.

Thunder shattered the air.

The horses went wild. Hanna screamed and dropped her reins, but Tayer hung grimly on and fought to control her plunging mount.

For what seemed like hours, Tayer's world collapsed to the space between her horse's ears, the reins cutting into her fingers, and the saddle trying to escape from between her legs. Finally the mare stood, trembling but calm, and Tayer turned to check on her cousin.

She wasn't there. She wasn't anywhere in sight.

A trail of broken branches and crushed underbrush showed the direction Hanna's horse had taken in its panicked flight and Tayer thought she could hear, very faintly, her name being called in desperation. Over and over.

Concern and anger chased each other across Tayer's face as she stared at the destruction. Finally, she sighed and swung out of the saddle to better guide the mare around on the narrow trail. She dearly loved Hanna but sometimes wished the girl would learn to cope on her own. It never occurred to her that she dominated Hanna's life so thoroughly there was rarely anything, besides Tayer, for Hanna to cope with.

"She rides as well as I do," Tayer muttered to Dancer, the mare, maneuvering until they could get off the trail at the same place. "There's no need for this." She remounted and urged the horse forward.

Dancer picked her way delicately along the line of destroyed underbrush, avoiding the spiky ends of broken branches. Tayer kept her eyes on the forest ahead, hoping for a view of her cousin's pale blue jacket amid the greens and browns.

The second crack of thunder was, if possible, louder than the first. This time Dancer would not be controlled and she took off on a panic-stricken flight of her own. Tayer could only try to keep her seat and pray the horse wouldn't stumble and fall. A branch whipped her across the face and her eyes filled with tears.

When she could see again, it was too late to avoid the heavy limb hanging low in the path of the frightened animal. Tayer had only a brief glimpse of bark and moss and leaves and then the branch swept

her from the saddle. Gasping for breath, and more frightened than
she'd ever been in her life, she was miraculously unhurt by the blow
and would have walked away only badly bruised had the trees not been
so close together where she fell. She screamed as a stub of wood
slammed needle-sharp into her shoulder and then the back of her head
came down on a protruding root, almost as hard in its gnarled age as
stone. For a while, she knew no more.

Drifting in the gray mists just this side of unconsciousness, Tayer
felt strong arms lift her effortlessly and cradle her against something
that smelled of leather and earth. She giggled weakly, for although she
was securely held, the tip of each foot dipped to touch the ground with
every step her rescuer took and it struck her as funny that one so strong
could be so short. She tried to open her eyes, but the lids refused to
obey. Her head lolled back against the stranger's shoulder and the gray
turned black.

When the darkness lifted for the second time, she felt herself upon
the softest of beds where gentle hands cleaned and treated her throbbing shoulder. These were not the hands that had carried her; she was
sure of it although she had no idea of how she knew. Beneath these
hands her body trembled and it seemed she had waited all her life for
their touch. She gave herself up to the golden glow they wrapped about
her, but the reality of her injuries could not be denied for long and pain
pulled her from that sanctuary.

As she became aware of the ache in her shoulder and the fire that
burned in her head, she also became aware of an arm across her back
raising her lips to touch the edge of something wet and cool.

"Drink," said someone softly, and she did, never even considering
questioning the voice.

The cup held only water, but drinking it she thought she had never
tasted water before. It was like drinking light, or liquid crystal, and it
washed all the pain away.

The sound and smell of the forest was around her still but, rather
than feeling the terror her recent experience should have demanded,
she had never felt so safe. It reminded her of being very young and held

securely in the circle of her mother's arms. As her head was gently lowered, Tayer opened her eyes.

Sunlight slanted down through the leaves of the tree that towered above her. She struggled to her elbows—helped by that same arm across her back, which withdrew as she steadied—and looked around.

She lay in a clearing ringed with silver birch in their full summer glory and filled with soft golden light. Either the storm had ended or it had never penetrated the circle. The stillness here was peaceful, not ominous. Thick grass covered the ground where she rested—soft and springy and unlike any she had ever seen before.

And he who went with the voice . . .

Never had Tayer seen a man so beautiful. His hair fell to his shoulders in a white so pure it surrounded his head with a nimbus of light. His skin was the color of old copper and his body was so well proportioned he seemed more an artist's conception than a real man. And his eyes . . . Tayer caught her breath when she met his eyes. It looked as if the sunlight poured through them as it did through the leaves of the birch above her and she felt herself sinking into the glory of the other world they showed.

She could have stayed within those eyes forever, but her arms gave out and she collapsed to the grass, the spell broken.

"You are weak," he said, stroking her forehead. "Rest."

Tayer felt his touch resonate through her body. Her soul sang, a harp string he had played upon, only she did not, as yet, understand the song.

"Who are you?" she sighed as her eyes closed.

"I am Varkell," came the answer. "I am a part of the Grove."

She wanted to ask if she would see him again, but her mind felt wrapped in amber and she couldn't get her voice to work. The last thing she saw was a compassionate smile and then she slept.

When she awoke, she was in her bed in the palace.

"But you believe me."

"Of course I believe you." Hanna adjusted her sling and settled more comfortably amongst the pillows on the lounge. "It's exactly the sort of thing that would happen to you." The faintest shade of resentment colored her voice and she punched at an overstuffed pink square with her good arm. "Like something out of a fairy tale."

Tayer turned from the window, where she'd been straining her eyes to see the distant line of trees, and smiled dreamily. "That's exactly what it was like. Like something out of a fairy tale."

Hanna sighed. The healer, a man of undeniable skill but little imagination, had explained that the silver-haired man with the leaf-green eyes was probably a hallucination caused by the bump on her cousin's head. He'd also said that the scar puckering the smooth curve of Tayer's shoulder was an old wound, long healed. Hanna hadn't argued, because it wasn't her way, but she knew there had been no scar when they rode out for the day's hunt. And if the part about the wounded shoulder was true, she saw no reason to doubt the rest.

"Maybe he was a woodsman," she said in her most matter-of-fact tone, knowing full well that no woodsman would dare to venture so far into the Lady's Wood.

"He said he was a part of the Grove," Tayer declared, soft lips curving at the memory.

"But no one has been to the Sacred Grove for years, not since the Lady died. No one even knows where it is! And I should think," Hanna added, remembering long hours of lessons, "that if a priest tended the Grove, the Scholars would've told us."

"There were birch trees all around, and green and gold sunlight, and the music of the wind in the leaves."

Hanna gazed at her cousin in astonishment. Tayer was staring into space, her eyes focused on something Hanna couldn't see, her head cocked to hear a song Hanna couldn't hear.

"He was so beautiful." Tayer's voice caressed the words. Her hand reached out to stroke a cheek that wasn't there. "He looked into me."

"The Lady was very beautiful," Hanna said thoughtfully, trying to bring Tayer's experience into line with what they'd been taught about the Grove, "and tall, with silver hair and green eyes and her sisters were the same. Maybe it was one of the other hamadryads who tended you. Are you sure it was a man?"

Tayer's eyes lost their dreamy look and gained a mischievous sparkle.

"Oh, I'm very sure," she said, standing and shaking out the red velvet folds of her skirt. "He was naked. I can't stand to be inside any longer, I'm going for a walk in the garden."

"Naked! You never mentioned that before!"

The princess turned in the doorway and ran a finger up and down the vines carved around the frame. "Would you have mentioned to your father and brothers that the man who found you unconscious in the woods was naked? Besides, it didn't seem important at the time." Then she laughed and was gone.

"Well, it would have been important to me," Hanna muttered at her cousin's departing back.

"What would've been important to you, little one?" asked Mikhail, entering the room through the other door.

"The man Tayer met in the woods was naked."

"The hallucination?"

Hanna got to her feet. "I don't think she was seeing things," she said with a conviction that was quite unlike her.

Mikhail took his sister firmly by the shoulders and sat her back down. "Tell me about it," he commanded.

As he listened, Mikhail paced. He was fair, like Hanna, but where she was the pale gold and blue of early morning he was the tawny gold and violet of a sunset. Like all the children of the Royal House, he was tall, for height was one of the Lady's gifts, but where Hanna and his cousins were sapling-slender he had the bulk of an ancient oak. Although generations removed and thinned by marriage, the power of the tree was still his. Coupled with his massive frame, this heritage gave him the strength to create legends. His black sword was dwarf-crafted, the only such blade in the kingdom, and the tale of how he won it was sure to be told any time men gathered and ale flowed. Mikhail found the tales an embarrassment and would retreat, ears burning, from any praise. As he told Tayer's brothers, "It's no great feat to split a man in half with one mighty blow when you're twice his size with the strength of the Lady and a magic sword to boot." As the only warrior in the royal family, both by choice and inclination, Mikhail commanded the Elite.

He moved restlessly from window to window as Hanna told him of the scar and of all she and Tayer had discussed that morning. From the way he twisted and crushed his heavy leather belt, Hanna could tell he wasn't pleased with Tayer's strange experience.

"Has there ever been a man in the Sacred Grove, Mikhail?"

"Not that I ever heard of, only the Lady and her sisters. And the Lady is dead and her sisters are asleep."

Hanna sighed and shook her head. "So if it was a man, Tayer must have been seeing things." And if those were the kind of visions a bump on the head caused, she would be more inclined to fall off her own horse in the future. The visions caused by a broken arm were tedious in comparison. "Still, we could've been in the right part of the forest."

"By King's Law," Mikhail reminded her, "no one has been to the Grove since the Lady died." He raised a foot to kick a delicately carved footstool out of his way, thought better of it and stepped around. "Not even those of us who bear her blood know its location."

"But we all know it's in there," Hanna insisted. "We all know it isn't just a story."

"Aye." Mikhail stopped his pacing and stood at the window where Tayer had stood earlier, his gaze also trying to pierce the dark line of trees. "But I've hunted all over that area, been through the forest and to the Great Lake on the other side, and I've never found the Grove."

"Perhaps it didn't want to be found."

"Perhaps."

"Do you think Tayer was seeing things?"

He turned from the window and looked down at his sister. His face was troubled.

"No."

And they both remembered the scar. The healer had insisted that Tayer had carried the mark since childhood, but they knew better.

"Where is she now?"

"She went for a walk in the gardens."

Hanna watched her brother's departing back with concern. He thought no one suspected, but she knew him too well to be fooled. There were times when his love shone from his eyes like a beacon and Hanna wondered how Tayer had not been blinded by the intensity of the light.

Tayer, used to being adored, had never noticed.


On his way to the garden, Mikhail considered all that Hanna had said. Tayer was vain and willful, he was not the sort to let love blind him to another's faults, but she had never been a liar. She'd never even had to resort to the small lies children use to make themselves important; from the day of her birth she'd been the darling of the court. If Tayer said she saw a naked man in Lady's Wood, then that's exactly what she saw.

But why did she not want her father and brothers to know? He could think of only one reason.

He scowled and growled low in his throat, so frightening a young servant hurrying by on some errand of her own, that she dropped the tray she carried and pressed herself against the wall one fist in her mouth to stop a shriek.

Mikhail stared at her in astonishment, then, realizing that her terror was directed at him, blushed and bent to retrieve her tray.

"You mustn't mind me," he said, wincing inwardly as the girl continued to stare at him with wide eyes.

"No, milord?" She gave a tiny, jerky bow as she took back her tray.

"No. I was thinking of something else and didn't even know you were there." He smiled down at her, the last of his anger fading behind his embarrassment.

She tried a tentative smile in return. "As you say, milord."

It suddenly occurred to him that he had no idea of which garden Tayer had gone to and there were at least half a dozen scattered about the palace. "You, uh, haven't seen the princess, have you?"

Although Hanna was equally *a* princess, *the* princess could only refer to Tayer.

"Yes, milord. I saw her enter the small walled garden behind the new archives in the south wing."

"Thank you." Mikhail smiled again and headed toward the maze of corridors that would take him to the recently added south wing.

The servant stood for a moment, watching him go, her expression remarkably similar to that Mikhail's sister had worn moments before. The emotional entanglements of royalty were not her concern, but the look on his face when he mentioned the princess sent shivers down her spine. She sighed and went on her way, wishing that someday, someone, would look at her like that.

Mikhail stepped into the late afternoon sunlight of the garden and the color drained from his face. Tayer lay crumpled on the path, pale skin made paler by the deep crimson pool of her skirts. He dove across the tiny courtyard and threw himself to his knees by her side, a trembling hand reaching out to touch the smooth column of her throat. Beneath his fingers, her life throbbed fast but sure.

"You called, milord?"

"No, I . . ." Mikhail looked up at the gray-robed Scholar. The noise he'd made as he moved had not been a call exactly, but. . . . "Uh, I mean yes, I called. Get a healer. The princess has fainted."

"In bed for a week? But I feel fine!"

"Of course you do, Princess, which is why you were taking a nap in the roses."

"I just fainted."

"Precisely my point." The healer motioned for the maid to close the heavy brocade curtains and, with the room darkened, waved a candle before Tayer's face. "Follow the light with your eyes, please."

"The Lord Chamberlain's wife faints all the time and she doesn't have to stay in bed."

"Just with your eyes, Princess. Don't turn your head. The Lord Chamberlain's wife is a weak, foolish woman who thinks fainting makes her interesting. *You* have received a nasty blow to the head. Not the same thing at all." He blew out the candle. "In bed for a week. No riding for a month."

"A month?"

"A fall from a garden bench is one thing, a fall from a horse is something else entirely. It is, if you recall, what got you into this mess in the first place."

"Oh, please, you can't mean it." Tayer looked up at him through her lashes, her lower lip beginning to quiver. Women less beautiful than Tayer had destroyed whole countries with that look. The healer, however, was more concerned with the way her pupils were dilating as the maid threw back the curtains and flooded the room with light.

"Of course, I mean it," he said, apparently satisfied for he turned to go. "I always say what I mean. No riding for a month."

Tayer pleaded, pouted, and petitioned her father, but the verdict stayed the same: visits around town in a litter were permitted but riding was not.

One could not go to the forest in a litter.

Used to being active, the princess was unbearable as an invalid. With riding denied her, there just wasn't that much that she could do. She had little interest in statecraft and the public duties of the third child of the Royal House were few and far between.

"If I have to set one more stupid tapestry stitch, I shall scream!" Tayer leaped to her feet and darted about the room, almost bouncing from the walls. "There must be something else I can do."

Hanna sighed and bent to retrieve the skeins of silk now widely scattered and hopelessly tangled.

"I know," the princess dropped back into her chair in a most unprincesslike manner, "I shall garden."

*       *       *

"Tayer, what are you doing?"

Tayer glared up at her brothers and jabbed her ivory handled trowel into the damp earth. "Even you two should be able to figure that out. I'm planting roses."

Davan pursed his lips. "They'll never grow there; not enough light. Why don't you leave gardening to the gardeners and do something you're capable of?"

She threw the trowel at him. Then, just to be sure he knew she was truly annoyed, followed it with the tray of seedlings.

Eyrik laughed.

She stood and dumped the contents of her watering pot over his head.


Only Hanna noticed how often Tayer went to the one window in the palace where the dark line of the forest could be seen in the distance.

No one heard her call out his name in her sleep.

Hanna bore the brunt of Tayer's dissatisfaction. She was expected; not only by Tayer but by everyone else in the palace, to keep her cousin entertained and cheerful. She not only suffered from Tayer's moods but from the accusations that she could have done something to prevent them.

"I love Tayer," she sighed to Mikhail one evening, "but there have been times lately when I haven't liked her very much."

"How can you say that?" Mikhail protested. "You've always been like sisters. You should be glad you can help her."

"There are times," Hanna said sharply as she hurried down the hall in answer to an imperious summons from the invalid, "when I don't like you very much either."

Mikhail stood and stared in astonishment as Hanna slammed the door to Tayer's room behind her. "What did I say?"

When the month finally ended, a great picnic was arranged in celebration of Tayer's official return to health. The king allowed Tayer to convince him that such a picnic could only be held in the lee of the Lady's Wood. Officially, because the shade beneath the trees would be welcome in the heat of the afternoon. Actually, because, unlike the healer, the king was not immune to his daughter looking up through her eyelashes and quivering her lower lip. He knew his weakness, however, and he was grateful she wanted such an insignificant thing.

If any of the court considered a two-hour ride for a picnic a little extreme, they kept silent. As the king had allowed himself to be convinced, so did the court. And if truth be told, after the last four weeks, the court was as glad Tayer was mobile as Tayer was herself.

A large and merry company set out from the palace in the early morning. In the midst of the crowd, the laughter, and the sunshine it was easy to miss seeing that Tayer's gaiety had a brittle edge and that Mikhail smiled grimly if at all. Hanna noticed, but, as usual, no one noticed Hanna.

Mikhail didn't know who, or what, Tayer had seen in the forest that day but he knew that whether spirit, demon, or mortal man, it had bewitched her. He had no doubt she would try to lose herself in the woods that afternoon and attempt to find the creature. Silently he vowed, and swore on his sword, that he would not take his eyes off her until she was safely back in the palace and far away from the naked man with silver hair and green fire in his eyes.

Keeping an eye on Tayer turned out to be difficult; she flitted from person to person like a nervous butterfly. Mikhail's efforts were further hampered by the duties expected of him as a Prince of the Realm. It wasn't easy being charming, witty, and vigilant all at once.

When the sun was at its zenith and its warmth—combined with a large and excellent lunch, sent on its way with several gallons of good wine—was putting many of the party to sleep, he noticed Tayer disappearing amongst the trees. With a curse, he leaped to his feet and, paying no attention to the drowsy protests rising from those about him, ran after her.

The forest seemed unnaturally still. Not a leaf rustled, not a bird

sang, and although Mikhail was barely thirty feet from the meadow—
and could, in fact, still see brightly colored robes and gay pennants—
not a sound from that direction could he hear. Motes of dust danced
in rays of sunlight, but they danced alone. There was no trace of
Tayer.

Loosening his sword in its sheath, Mikhail bent to study the ground.
Very faintly, for the moss and leaves were already shifting to fill the
track, he saw the print of his cousin's foot. And then another. The trail
shifted, and twitched, almost as if it had a mind of its own, but Mikhail
was one of the best trackers in Ardhan and this was no ordinary hunt.
Soon he was running, his eyes never leaving the ground.

He didn't see the root that tripped him. He would've sworn there
was no root there. It came as a great surprise to find himself suddenly
stretched full length upon the forest floor, the wind knocked out of
him and his chin digging a trench in the sod. He lay there for a moment
catching his breath, and then for another moment strangely unwilling
to rise. The silence and sunlight washed over him in green-gold waves.

The forest had welcomed Tayer. The moment she stepped beneath the
trees the force which had pulled her this way and that, keeping her on
the knife's edge between fear and longing, disappeared. Only the longing remained and a gentle tugging which directed her feet.

As she walked deeper into the Lady's Wood, on paths she had no
doubt were created just for her, a breeze came out of the stillness, caressed her bare arms and ran unseen fingers through her hair. When
the path disappeared, she unquestioningly followed the breeze. It drew
her through a ring of silver birch and then left on errands of its own.

Tayer had never seen a more beautiful place. The sunlight poured
down into the clearing like liquid gold. It had a tangible presence in the
air and spilled out of the buttercups scattered in the thick grass. As
Tayer stepped into the center of the circle, she felt the light fill her, like
rich wine in a crystal goblet. The birches that surrounded her, all but
one majestically old, glowed with their own inner light.

"You have come."

From the one tree still straight and smooth he stepped, and for Tayer the light in the clearing dimmed in the glory of the light that flowed from him. He was just as Tayer remembered.

She stepped forward to meet him, hands outstretched and trembling.

"You were not a dream," she said softly, thankfully. "You were not a dream."

And Varkell, who was a part of the Grove, with silver hair and eyes that held an unworldly green light, looked very human as he drew her into his arms.

"Nor were you."

She'd left Varkell's side only because he'd told her she must, but every part of Tayer's body still sang with his presence. Even outside the Grove, there was a lushness in the air, a glory in the ordinary things; in trees and shrubs and moss.

*New words,* she decided, *will have to be created to describe how I feel.*

"Princess."

Any other day, the ugly little man perched on the fallen tree would have sent her screaming for her guards but today, today he couldn't possibly be a threat. She paused and fearlessly met the glow of his eyes. Her nose wrinkled as the fires damped down to an unusual shade of red-brown.

"Do I know you?" she asked, struggling to hold the teasing edge of a memory.

He spread rough hands and scowled. "Is it likely?"

"No," Tayer admitted. He was obviously not a member of the court and she knew few others, but still there lingered the thought that she had met him before.

"If you go past that big pine, Princess, you'll find your cousin. Perhaps you should gather him up as you go."

"Thank you." She smiled and followed his pointing finger, barely

five steps beyond him before the lingering radiance she moved in drove
the meeting from her mind.

"Not yet," Doan snorted, watching the slender figure disappear,
"but soon."

Struggling through the green and gold wrapped about him, Mikhail first
became aware of bird song—second of a woman's laughter more beautiful than the song. He opened his eyes to see Tayer standing over him.

"You've picked a strange place for a nap, Cousin," she said, extend-
ing a hand to help him up. "Did the ladies of the court prove too much
for you?"

"I didn't choose the place," Mikhail replied, rubbing his eyes and
glaring about him suspiciously. The forest, so still before, had come
alive with sound. The sunlight no longer fell heavy and somber but
slanted through the trees at a rakish angle.

"The time . . ."

"It's late afternoon. Come," she tucked her hand in his, "we'd best
get back if we don't want to be left behind. Listen, they're blowing the
horns for us."

Mikhail listened and in the distance he heard the king's horn.

"I don't understand," he began, looking down at Tayer as they
started to walk, and then he stopped and grabbed her shoulders. "Your
clothes! They were red and brown this morning!"

Both tunic and pants were now a pale green with golden trim.

Tayer smoothed the cloth over her hips and smiled. "He made this
for me, out of new leaves and sunshine."

She had never looked so beautiful, nor, Mikhail realized, so complete. Her eyes shone and there was a gentleness about her that had not
been there before. She looked as if a great artist had taken the unfin-
ished canvas of her and made it into a masterpiece.

A little overwhelmed, and not sure he liked the change, Mikhail
allowed her to lead him from the forest. He didn't mention the clothes
again and neither did she. No one else noticed, although their absence

provided food for the palace gossip mill and evoked more than a few thoughtful glances from the king.

Over the next few weeks Tayer sang around the palace. Nothing could dampen her good spirits. Rumor had it that she was in love. Rumor didn't know the half of it.

One afternoon, when Mikhail was on duty, for even in peace the Elite still trained and its commander was expected to attend, the ladies of the court went to the forest for wildflowers. They returned that evening so heavily laden, those who had remained behind laughingly accused them of having stripped the Lady's Wood of blossoms.

Tayer brought back only a single buttercup that glowed with an inner light. A light that endured until Mikhail ground the delicate flower under his heel.

Hanna was at first pleased with the change in her cousin—Tayer had never been less demanding nor more affectionate—but as the weeks passed her pleasure dimmed. Tayer made it clear she no longer needed anyone but the creature of light she carried in her heart. With no real position in the palace beyond that of Tayer's companion, Hanna found herself completely unneeded and even longed for the days when Tayer had blithely ordered her life. More than ever, she felt mousy and insignificant beside her cousin. Whether this was due to the new depth and gentleness in Tayer's manner or the sudden mature light of her beauty, Hanna was not sure, but she found she didn't like it.

# SEVEN

As the glorious summer drew to an end, a shadow fell on the kingdom. Word came from Riven and Lorn on the western border that Melac's raids had begun again.

"Why do they bother!" roared the king, slamming down his fist and causing the Messenger who'd brought the news to flinch and wonder if she was supposed to know.

"It's fairly obvious, isn't it, Father?" Davan, the heir to the throne, steepled his fingers in an unconscious imitation of his father's habit. "Melac's armies have gotten so large, the Empire's conquest is moving so fast, that there's no one left to grow food and they must raid us for supplies."

"That's exactly what they want us to think," said Mikhail shortly, turning away from a detailed map of the west to face his cousin.

Davan snorted. "Are you still on about that?"

The king, who had been asking a purely rhetorical question brought on by frustration, raised bushy eyebrows at the discussion between his son and his nephew.

"They raid to gather information," Mikhail insisted, "not grain and cattle. Those men are soldiers, not brigands. Our land, our people, our way of fighting, is being studied."

"Studied?" Davan scoffed. "What for? Melac's armies move south and west; the emperor has no intention of attacking us. He tried that once, remember, back in the Lady's time, and was soundly trounced."

Mikhail shrugged. "We are being studied," he insisted, wondering why he seemed to be the only one in the country who could see it. "Melac is waiting for something."

"For what?"

"I wish I knew. Sire," Mikhail turned to the king, "every year we drive the raiders back, but every year we lose young men and women to Lord Death before their time. The western border is like an open wound that bleeds with the lives of our people."

"Eloquent," muttered Davan.

Mikhail ignored him and once again made the plea he'd made yearly since taking up arms. "Melac's Empire stretches far to the southwest, but it is directed still from the towers of the old capital, not three days' march from our western border. Let me raise the country, Sire. I'll destroy the head of the Empire and see that Melac never bleeds us again."

And, as every year, the king denied the petition.

"If Melac ever turns all of its armies against us, we stand no chance; Ardhan as a country would be wiped from the memory of man. These raids are a small price to pay for the survival of our nation. Someday, Melac will have to be dealt with, but there will be no war in this land while I am king."

*By the time you're not king, there'll be no men left to fight,* Mikhail thought bitterly. He knew Davan held the same beliefs as his uncle; there would be no war when Davan was king either. It looked as if the wound on the border would bleed for generations more.

"I understand how you feel, Mikhail," the king said kindly, and he thought he did for his brother and brother's wife, Mikhail's parents, had died in a border raid. "I will not risk war, but I do have plans to strengthen our defense."

Mikhail choked back a final plea, bowed to his liege and left the room. It would, he knew, do no good to argue further. In years of trying he'd convinced neither king nor heir of what appeared so obvious to him. Both had a blind spot concerning Melac that he'd never been able to breach. He could only cause as much damage to the enemy as possible with the relatively few men they'd given him and hope, when war finally came, Ardhan would not be taken totally by surprise.

Leaving his feet to find their own way to the training yards, the Commander of the Elite wrapped himself in battle plans and troop deployments and almost missed seeing Tayer sitting with the Duke of Belkar's wife in a sunny corner of one of the small gardens.

Almost.

All thought of battle, of war, of Melac, vanished. It had been days, he realized, since he'd seen her and only the Mother-creator knew how long it would be until he saw her again. He stopped and stared, imprinting her on his mind; the sunlight dancing through the gold in her hair, her lips slightly curving, the soft swell of her breasts beneath ivory silk. This would be a vision to carry him through the long days and nights ahead.

Tayer, oblivious, continued dangling a blossom over the chubby face of Belkar's infant heir. Lady Belkar, perhaps feeling the weight of Mikhail's gaze, looked up, started, smiled, and beckoned him closer.

"Milord Mikhail," she greeted him graciously when he approached. "I'd thought you on the border by now."

"Soon, milady." He bowed over her hand. "Tomorrow."

"Tomorrow. . . . We'll miss not having you about the court." She peered sideways at her companion, her tone carefully neutral. "Won't we, Tayer?"

Slowly, Tayer raised her head and Mikhail's heart gave a sudden lurch. He gritted his teeth and forced a friendly smile through the longing.

"Oh, yes," she said, "it'll be . . . different . . . around here without Mikhail."

Different. He could only hope she'd even notice he was gone. Then a sudden flush of jealousy caused his hands to curl into fists—she'd notice all right, for without his watching, who would stop her from riding off to be with . . . Him? The thing she'd met in the Grove. The creature that had bewitched her. The thought had occurred to Tayer as well; he'd grown up with her, he knew the speculative expression she now wore.

Lady Belkar looked from one to the other and felt like shaking them both. Mikhail stood staring down at Tayer, longing, pain, and anger mixed in about equal proportions on his face. Tayer sat staring off into the distance, longing and things harder to pin down mixed on hers. Not being privy to either's thoughts, Lady Belkar jumped to entirely the wrong conclusion on everything save what Mikhail longed for, and that had been an open secret about the court for almost a year. The tension thickened and she wondered if she should speak, then the baby on her lap suddenly howled and the moment was lost.

"Oh, dear, he's wet." Murmuring soothing sounds into the baby's hair, she stood, and placing her free hand on the rigid muscles of Mikhail's arm said: "Perhaps you would walk me from the garden, milord?"

With an effort, Mikhail drew his eyes from Tayer and managed a jerky nod.

At the edge of the garden, they paused and looked back.

"You should speak to her, Mikhail," Lady Belkar said softly. "You simply cannot go on like this. Neither of you can."

"Speak to her of what?" He was amazed how steady his voice sounded. Surely the turmoil that seethed beneath the surface should show more.

Lady Belkar sighed. "Speak to her of how you feel. Tell her you love her." At his sudden startled expression, she added. "Everyone knows."

"Everyone?" he asked.

She smiled at his tone of stunned disbelief and reached up to pat him lightly on the cheek. "Everyone except Tayer." Then, under the prompting screams of her son, she left.

Mikhail looked again at the distant figure of his cousin, his love, his brows drawn together as he considered how he felt. Perhaps it was time for him to speak.

But he didn't. And the next morning he left for the western border.

Over the last few weeks of summer, and the early weeks of fall, Tayer almost daily answered the call from the Grove. The summons beat in her blood, day and night, and left unanswered too long it grew until it filled her every moment and she thought she would go crazy with need. When she was missed, all assumed she was with Hanna. Hanna, for reasons of her own, kept silent.

The day Mikhail returned, with a limp and a new resolution in his heart, Tayer was not in the palace. Although the need to ride after her beat at his thoughts—and he had no doubt of where she could be found—his duties kept him tied to his men and his reports.

But he was in the stableyard when she rode in.

He opened his mouth to tell her, the words cut and polished over long nights alone in his tent when she was the only thing on his mind, in his dreams. Then he saw her face and the words shattered. He had seen that expression too many times in his mirror to mistake it now. Tayer was a woman very deeply in love. He had waited too long.

He should leave, he knew, hide somewhere and lick his wounds. He hadn't thought he could be in so much pain and still live. But he stayed. Whether to hurt her in return or hurt himself further, he wasn't sure.

"Where are your guards," he growled as she swung from the saddle.

"The guards rode with you."

"Well then, servants," he snapped. "You know you're not to ride out alone."

"I can take care of myself," Tayer sighed. "Please, get out of my way." She pushed past him and led Dancer into the stable. A groom came forward, took one look over her shoulder at the glowering prince, and retreated with the mare as quickly as he was able. Tayer sighed again and slowly turned.

Mikhail noticed that in the two months he'd been gone, Tayer's face had lost all memory of childhood. Its beauty was startling; the curve of her cheek was a song, but sorrow lay close to the surface and the sparkle in her eyes had been replaced by the reflected glow of another world. With one hand he held her shoulder in an iron grasp and with the other he lifted a red-gold leaf from her hair.

"So, it's not all happiness in the Sacred Grove," he snarled, and crushed the leaf to powder.

Tayer met his gaze and he flinched before the radiance.

"No," she said. "It is not."

The pain in her voice hit Mikhail like a bucket of cold water, washing his anger away and leaving him trembling. He released her shoulder and took an unsteady step back. He wanted to take her in his arms and comfort her, but he feared her reaction. He didn't think he could stand it if she pushed him away.

"I'm sorry," he said finally.

She touched his cheek gently as she passed.

"So am I."

He watched her walk away and could think of no reason to follow.

The next morning, a great shouting in the courtyard dragged Mikhail up from an uneasy sleep. Briefly he wondered why he felt so rotten, then he remembered: he'd lost Tayer, lost any hope of her ever returning his love, and had tried to forget in every tavern in the city. The memories of the taverns were dim, but the memory of the pain was still sharp and clear. Holding his throbbing head, he stumbled to the window to see what all the noise was about. From the pennants and the livery, the seething mass of men, women and horses appeared to be a Royal Envoy from Halda, a small country that shared borders with both Ardhan and Melac. As Mikhail watched, the Lord Chamberlain appeared, ushered the men and women ceremoniously inside, and had the horses removed to the stables.

"They arranged it while you were away."

Mikhail turned. Hanna had come into the room and now perched on the edge of his bed.

"Arranged what?" he demanded, pouring some wine to clear the fog from his head.

Hanna looked down at her entwined fingers.

"Tayer's joining."

"What!" Mikhail threw the goblet to the floor, dove across the room, and yanked his sister to her feet.

"Tayer's joining," Hanna repeated with remarkable calm, considering that she had just been shaken vigorously. "The king has arranged for her to marry the Crown Prince of Halda."

"But why?"

"For mutual support against Melac obviously. The crown prince has no sisters and Tayer is the only daughter the king has."

"Why so quickly? These arrangements usually take months. Or years."

Hanna looked pityingly up at her brother. "The king has seen the way you look at Tayer. This is a very important state joining and he wants it done before she has a chance to fall in love with you. And she has been acting rather strangely of late."

Mikhail suddenly remembered the king speaking of plans to strengthen Ardhan's defense. This, then, was what he had meant.

"What does Tayer say about it?"

"I doubt she was asked. Princesses are expected to go along with this sort of thing as part of their duty to the kingdom. Besides, what could she say; I can't join with Halda because I'm in love with a hallucination?"

"No." Mikhail set his jaw and dropped Hanna back onto the bed. "I won't allow it." He dug his breeches out of a pile of discarded clothes and yanked them on. "I won't allow it." He couldn't believe he'd almost given up without a fight. It wasn't over yet, of that he was suddenly certain.

"There's not much you can do," Hanna said quietly. "And Tayer's gone. I just came from her room."

Tayer had ridden out before dawn according to the stable boy, but he had no idea of which way she'd gone.

"Beggin' your pardon, sir," he apologized to Mikhail, "but I ain't the one to be stoppin' the princess if'n she wants to go, and I ain't the one to be keepin' watch of where she went."

Mikhail knew exactly where Tayer was and he knew if he didn't catch her before she entered the forest he'd probably never be able to find her. *To the Grove,* pounded the hoofs of his galloping horse. *To the Grove,* pounded his heart. *To the Grove.*

When he reached the Lady's Wood, Dancer stood grazing in the long grass of the meadow, but Tayer was nowhere in sight.

Leaving his horse with the mare, Mikhail drew his sword and

stepped beneath the trees. He was no longer truly in control of what he did. A force he couldn't explain drove him and he only knew that he had to find Tayer.

He began to run, crashing through the underbrush, using his sword to clear a path. All logic, all woodcraft, left him.

Sword first and panting, he stumbled into the Sacred Grove.

The birches wore their autumn dress of old gold and bronze, their leaves whirling free, carried and caressed by the breeze. In the midst of this erotic dance, stood a couple in a close embrace. The woman was Tayer. The man . . . Aware of the intruder, they turned in each other's arms to face him.

Mikhail didn't see the hand extended toward him, nor the welcoming smile. All he saw was Tayer gazing up into the leaf-green eyes of the creature who held her. Throwing aside his sword, he charged.

The two men were matched in height, but Mikhail was heavier and fighting from the depths of his pain. The suddenness of his attack allowed him to get his hands around Varkell's throat and the muscles of his arms bulged as he tried to snap the other's neck. This thing had taken Tayer from him.

Pushing Tayer to safety, Varkell swept Mikhail's feet out from under him and they crashed to the ground.

The fall and his own weight broke Mikhail's hold, but he quickly gained another. From a distance, a saner part of his mind cried out that this would solve nothing, but he couldn't, wouldn't stop. Varkell made no attempt to return the attack, merely defending himself against Mikhail's assaults. A blocking elbow hit Mikhail in the mouth and his lip, caught between tooth and bone, split. As he jerked his head free, six drops of blood arced away—where they landed, the grass died. They thrashed about the clearing, tearing great gouges out of the velvet sod, first gold head on top, then silver.

Finally Varkell gained the top and kept it. Mikhail looked up and fell into, the other world that burned in Varkell's eyes. Seeing what Tayer loved, and loving it himself, in spite of himself, he turned his head and closed his eyes in defeat. Tears seeped out through his lashes and left glistening trails down his cheeks. There was nothing left but the pain. There would never be anything but the pain.

"I yield," he said softly. "You have won."

Varkell stood, but Mikhail didn't move. He wasn't sure he could. He knew he didn't want to. The peace of the Grove, too deep to be shattered by the battle just ended, began to lap at the edges of his soul.

"Mikhail." The voice was a summons impossible to deny. "Look at me."

Mikhail opened his eyes. He saw, standing before him, a tall young man with silver-white hair and leaf-green eyes. The other-worldliness was gone.

"No, never gone." Sorrow clouded the words. "Just pushed aside for a time so we can talk."

"Who are you?" Mikhail asked, getting slowly to his feet. "What are you?"

Varkell pointed to the young birch in the circle of ancient trees.

"In that spot, amidst the roots of a tree long gone, were buried the bodies of a hamadryad and the mortal man she loved. Out of their love came the Royal House of Ardhan. Out of their bodies and the roots of the holy tree grew the tree you see here. I came from the tree."

"Are you a god?"

"No, only a messenger."

Varkell turned and smiled sadly at Tayer. His eyes blazed as she came into his arms. "And, may the Mother help us all, the message has been delivered."

The look he then turned on Mikhail was far removed from mortal understanding, but a greater part of it held the full weight of pain Tayer had only reflected.

"She carries my child, Mikhail. This is the last time I shall see her."

"It burns, Cousin," Tayer said softly, "this brightness within and brightness without. I can no longer bear them both."

Mikhail stared at them. He felt large and stupid. "What can I do?" he asked, knowing he would do whatever they wanted but not knowing what he could possibly do that would help.

"The joining planned for Tayer must not happen. You must join with her yourself."

"She doesn't love me."

"No, she doesn't." Varkell could not lie. "But when I am gone, she will."

Mikhail looked at Tayer and then within himself. The flame of love he had carried for so long still burned, perhaps now more brightly than ever. Tayer had been chosen for glory; he could love that as well. He nodded and held out his arms.

Walking like one in a dream, Tayer came to him and rested her head against his chest with a sigh. Holding her gently, as if afraid she would break, Mikhail bent and laid his face upon her hair. When he looked up, they were alone in the Grove.

On the ride back to the palace, Mikhail pondered how much to tell the king. In the end, he decided not to mention the Grove. He'd not have believed it himself without proof. As everyone seemed to know of his love for Tayer, Mikhail felt his best chance lay in convincing the king that Tayer cared for him in return, hoping the older man's love for his daughter and his desire to see her happy would cause him to call off the arranged joining.

He glanced at Tayer riding serenely beside him. It could only help that she was so obviously a woman in love.

Hanna met them in the stableyard.

"He's been asking for you both," she told them. "You'd better hurry. He's waiting in the small audience room."

Mikhail took Tayer's hand and together they went into the palace, Hanna trailing along behind. Heads turned as they passed and the halls filled with rumor. Tayer, listening to the song of another world, didn't hear. Mikhail set his jaw and pretended not to.

"Sire, I have to speak with you."

The king looked at his nephew and then at his daughter.

"Yes," he said dryly. "I should say you do."

His Majesty had not been impressed when Tayer's absence had been discovered and he was less impressed when she showed up five hours later with Mikhail. What must the envoy from Halda be thinking?

"Sire, your daughter and I wish to be joined."

Keeping his face carefully noncommittal—he'd been afraid something like this would happen since the first time he'd seen the light in Mikhail's eyes—the king sat down and peered over steepled fingers at Tayer. "Is that what you wish, child?"

"Yes, Father."

"This talk of your joining is a little sudden, is it not?"

"If I'd known you were arranging a joining, Sire, I would've spoken sooner, but I was away on the border . . ."

"Defending the country. You grew up in my household, Mikhail, I know your worth. However, nothing prevented Tayer from speaking when I made her aware of my plans." Although he'd carefully kept Mikhail from finding out, he'd made sure Tayer had no objections before he sent the Messenger to Halda.

Mikhail held his breath and sent a short prayer to the Mother that Tayer remained enough in the world to lie.

"I was unsure of my feelings, Father," she hesitated then looked almost shyly up at Mikhail. "It wasn't until I saw him on his return that I knew."

Mikhail smiled at her and gently squeezed her hand. It seemed very small in his and very cold. Then he gave his attention again to the king.

"If Tayer joins with Halda," the older man said thoughtfully, "Ardhan gains a valuable ally. What does the country gain if she joins with you?"

"The country would gain less, it's true, but you would have comfort in the knowledge that your daughter was happy. Sire."

The king raised a bushy eyebrow.

"And you don't believe she will be happy in Halda."

"No, Sire." Mikhail met his gaze steadily. "If she joins with the Crown Prince of Halda, it will be a joining without love."

"Do you love her?"

"Oh, yes, Sire! With all my heart!"

Only a fool would doubt the sincerity of Mikhail's response. The king was no fool.

"Tayer?"

For the first time since she had entered the room, for the first time in many months, Tayer looked at her father directly. He drew in his breath sharply under the full impact of her eyes. He couldn't question the love they held—he couldn't know the love was not for Mikhail.

"If love is the way of it," and he wondered how he could've been so blind to think that Tayer had no more than a sibling's affection for her cousin, "you have my blessing. I will do what I can about Halda."

"I will join with him, Sire."

"What?" The king spun around, Mikhail stared at his sister in astonishment, and even Tayer rejoined the world long enough to look surprised.

Hanna got up from the stool where she'd been sitting and stepped forward.

"Hanna, child, I didn't know you were there."

Hanna smiled strangely. "Yes, Sire, I know."

"What's this you've said?"

"I am willing to join with the Crown Prince of Halda. If he approves, you'll still have an ally and Tayer will be happy." The Mother forbid, said her eyes, that Tayer should be unhappy.

"That's a very noble sacrifice you're making for your cousin," the king began kindly, wishing that either Hanna's mother or his beloved queen still lived. "And we are all touched that you're willing to put her happiness ahead of yours but . . ."

"I'm not doing it for her," Hanna explained, wanting someone to understand, just this once. "I'm doing it for me."

"To go away from your family, to join with a man you've never met." Mikhail took a step toward his sister, his hands spread in puzzlement. "What is there in that for you?"

"A place of my own," Hanna answered softly, turning to face him. "Where I am not overlooked. Where I am myself, not Tayer's cousin or Mikhail's sister or the king's niece. You and Tayer have each other, why can't this be for me? All my life I've been the second princess; I'd like to be first for a change."

The king's heavy brows drew in over his nose and he studied his niece as if seeing her for the first time. "We never knew you felt this way . . ."

"That," said Hanna, "is part of the problem. Please, Uncle."

And the king nodded.

"If Halda agrees . . ."

A Messenger was sent and Halda agreed. One unknown princess would do as well as another in the opinion of the crown prince, who had little interest in being joined at all. At the end of a week of state festivities, a proxy joining was held on the dais of the People's Square. Hanna managed to look regal in the ridiculous clothing demanded by the occasion and gave her responses in a strong, clear voice that carried to the meanest viewpoint at the back of the Square.

"I still don't understand why you have to do this," Mikhail said, as attendants carried her back into the palace and the Great Doors closed.

"If you'd understood," Hanna told him sharply, removing the cumbersome headdress, "I wouldn't have had to do it."

Mikhail looked to Tayer for support, but she only smiled sadly and shook her head. With the light she carried had come understanding, but it was far too late to start making amends.

The next day, Hanna left to live with a husband she had never met and, although Mikhail and Tayer both watched until she rode out of sight, she never once looked back.

Tayer and Mikhail were joined by the king in a quiet ceremony; a ceremony they both considered to be unnecessary. In their hearts, they knew they had been joined that day in the Grove. Tayer's condition soon became obvious and her father was delighted.

"The Mother has blessed this union," he declared, so enchanted by the idea of a grandchild he ignored the unusual aspects of the pregnancy.

For the most part the rest of the court took their cue from the king. Tayer was insulated from gossip and Mikhail heard little of it, for only a fool would speak in Mikhail's presence, but what he heard caused him great uneasiness.

"Tayer?"

With a visible effort, Tayer brought herself back from the light. She smiled at Mikhail, who knelt at her feet, and gently touched the tumbled mane of his hair.

"Tayer," he hesitated, considered what he was asking and found, with no little surprise, that the question was painless. To think of Tayer with another man would have torn him to pieces, but to think of her with Varkell brought only a renewed sense of wonder. "Tayer, the child you carry, when did you conceive?"

"A month after you left for the border."

Mikhail cursed beneath his breath and Tayer looked at him in puzzlement.

"What's wrong?" she asked.

"When the child is born, the court will know it isn't mine. Your time will be either a month too early or a month too late." Convincing the court, and her father, that he'd impregnated her before leaving would've been bad enough but nothing compared to what was likely to happen. A royal child was meticulously examined and then presented to the people, making an eight-month lie impossible to sustain. He didn't want to think of what Tayer would go through then.

"Don't worry." She took one of his hands and placed it on the gentle swelling of her stomach. "It has been taken care of."

And suddenly, Mikhail felt that it had.

Tayer's pregnancy was not an easy one. Throughout the long winter, as the child grew within her, she seemed to fade. Cheekbones cut angles into her face and her hands became thin and frail, almost transparent. She gave all her strength, all her life, to the child. Her eyes still shone as bright, or brighter, but few could meet the unearthly beauty of her gaze. Mikhail, looking beyond the beauty to the glory that consumed her, was himself consumed with worry for his young wife.

Winter finally ended. The grip of ice and cold released and the first greens of spring began to appear. The time came when, by Mikhail's count, Tayer should deliver; and then it passed. Taken care of, yes, but Mikhail worried that Tayer would not be able to bear the burden much longer. Every day he carried her out to the gardens, but it did little good, for every day she grew weaker. At long last, on a cloudless summer afternoon, the pains began.

The midwives expected trouble. The princess' hips were narrow and she wasn't strong. The birth, they feared, would rip her apart.

"And if it comes to it," sighed the younger as they scrubbed their hands, "who do we save, the mother or the child?"

"Both," came the reply and the voice held conviction that even Lord Death would have hesitated to challenge.

When everything was ready, they let Mikhail into the room. He sat by the bed and held Tayer's limp hand in his. Her grip tightened and she whimpered. He doubted she knew he was there. He'd never felt so helpless.

"Isn't there anything I can do?"

"Give her what strength you can, milord," said one of the women, laying a cool cloth on Tayer's brow. "This isn't going to be easy."

But the babe had other ideas. As if wanting to make up for all the trouble that had gone before, she slid effortlessly into the world and greeted the day with a hearty bellow.

"A girl, milord, milady. A fine, healthy girl."

Mikhail looked at the bloody, wrinkled bundle at Tayer's breast and touched a tiny cheek with one massive finger.

"She's beautiful," he whispered.

A breeze came through the window, bringing with it the scent of trees and forest loam. It gently fanned the mother and child.

"We shall call her Crystal," Tayer said, looking down at her tiny daughter, "For the light shines through her."

When Tayer raised exhausted eyes to Mikhail's face, his heart sang with joy for though the other world had left her they still shone with light . . . only now, at last, as Varkell had promised, the light was for him.

\*        \*        \*

Seated on a moss-covered log, just outside the Sacred Grove, Doan waited. The seed had been planted and nurtured. All that remained of Varkell was the tree and the child. The tree was an empty vessel. The child had her own guardian in Mikhail. One last thing and he could return to the caverns.

"So, little gardener, your job is done."

Doan's eyes narrowed as the speaker sat down beside him. The sapphire robes should have looked ridiculously out of place in the depths of the Lady's Wood; as it was, the Wood looked out of place about the robes. Doan suppressed the urge to move away. "I felt your presence," he growled. "I waited. You're too late."

Slender fingers ran through red-gold curls and the full lips curved. "But I came to talk to you."

"Why?" the dwarf demanded.

One wickedly arched brow rose. "Why to thank you for being such a sturdy guardian, of course."

Doan hooked his thumbs behind his belt and glared. "I guarded against you, not for you."

"But I never had any intention of interfering." He stretched out long legs and settled himself more comfortably against a protruding branch. "I'm a game player, always have been. Your *seedling* is likely to be the last worthy game I'll be able to play."

"Last game?"

"Don't get your hopes up, little man. She can't defeat me, although I won't begin until she thinks she has a chance."

"You'll stay away from the child?"

"I just said so, didn't I?"

"You lie."

"Yes," he agreed, "I do."

Doan could not decide if this amiable admission was general or specific so he left it. It was enough that the enemy saw only the most obvious scenario, that his vanity blinded him to possibilities other than outright confrontation. "Was that all you wanted to say?" he demanded after the silence stretched to uncomfortable lengths.

"That you've been more than useless here? Yes."

"You came all this way just to annoy me?"

He smiled lazily. "Basically. It's a hobby of mine, annoying people."

A twitch. Another. Then Doan threw back his head and laughed. He couldn't help himself. It was, after all, a hobby of his as well. When his eyes stopped streaming, he was alone on the log.

*I almost liked him,* he realized, wiping moisture from his cheeks. *Mother-creator help you child; he is more dangerous than we thought.*

# INTERLUDE TWO

Tayer's baby grew into a child, not outwardly different from other children. She learned to walk early, and then to run. Soon, the entire court, the Palace Guard, the Elite, and a small army of servants were watching out for her as she frequently appeared in places she had no right to be, her harassed parents and nurses often with no idea of where she'd got to. She learned to talk late, but when at last she did, she spoke in full sentences; never resorting to baby prattle, and never hesitant about expressing her opinion. Green eyes wide and oddly mature, she backed many an adult away from their views.

She was pampered and much indulged and proved without doubt that a child cannot be spoiled by too much love.

For ten years she grew as other children did. And if she moved a little faster, threw herself into childhood with an almost desperate enthusiasm, involved herself in everything she did with a thoroughness and single-minded purpose, it was easy for the adults surrounding her to miss seeing. Or seeing, misunderstand.

Toward the end of her tenth year she quieted and began to spend long hours with Tayer in the gardens, leaning against her mother's knees. She went to Mikhail's office off the training-yards and stood, cheek pressed to his shoulder, watching as he worked. At odd times she stood, head cocked, as though she listened to words carried on the wind.

Two days after her eleventh birthday, the centaur came, appearing suddenly in the garden where Tayer and Mikhail sat with their daughter.

"Crystal." His voice was the rumble of a thousand galloping hoofs. "I have come for you."

Slowly, Crystal pulled herself from Tayer's nerveless fingers, and walked forward until she stood within the shadow of the massive creature. Then she turned and faced her parents.

Whatever protests they might have made washed away in the flood of radiance from her eyes. For the first time in eleven years, they were forced to confront who her father had been; not the mortal man who'd loved and raised her but an enchanted being of power and light. Still, Mikhail might have found the strength to deny it had the child not raised her eyes to his. Once before he had looked into the other world they showed and that time, as this, he'd admitted defeat. His angry questions choked off and became a pained nod.

Tayer dropped to her knees and held wide her arms. Crystal hesitated a moment then ran to her mother's embrace. The light poured from them both and Mikhail, refusing to look away, was temporarily blinded by it. Then his arms were full of a warm bundle smelling of sunshine and hidden forest groves and the apricot she'd been eating . . . had it been there moments before?

"Don't worry, Papa," breathed a quiet voice against his cheek. "I shall take the pony you gave me for my birthday, and I shall remember you, and he shall help me not to be lonely."

Then his arms were empty and when he could see again, Crystal sat perched on the broad back of the centaur. As the creature turned, the sunlight flashed on a single tear running silver down the gentle curve of her face, and then they were gone.

Tayer, who had been brave for her daughter's sake, shuddered and turned to face her husband.

"You knew," he realized suddenly. "You knew that someday this would happen."

She nodded and her tears scattered to fall like dew upon the roses. "I carried that light beneath my heart," she said. "I am sorry, my love, but I could never forget she was her father's daughter."

Mikhail wordlessly opened his arms, much as Tayer had done, and Tayer, much as Crystal had done, ran into them.

He stroked her hair, marveling at the strength it must have taken to hold such pain within herself for so many years.

"What shall we tell your father?" he asked at last. "The king and the court will have to know something."

"We will tell them the truth. The truth from the beginning."

"Will he believe us?"

"It doesn't matter," Tayer cried, her fingers digging desperately into Mikhail's arms. "She's gone."

Doan pulled his hood closer around his face and glowered up through the rain at C'Tal. "This'd better be important," he warned.

The centaur nodded, hair and beard a solid wet mass on shoulders and chest. "It is," he said. "Else we would not have felt it necessary to call you. You are aware that it is raining?"

"No," Doan snarled. "I hadn't noticed."

C'Tal looked confused. "You had not noticed? But . . ."

"Of course I'd noticed, you overeducated carthorse." He scanned the area, stomped to a nearby boulder, climbed to the top and sat with an audible squelch from sodden clothes. This put him eye to eye with the centaur. "I'm cold, I'm wet and I'm fast losing what little patience I have. Get to the point."

"It is raining." C'Tal held up a massive hand as Doan's eyes began to glow red. "Please, hear what I have to say. The rain is, as you have said, the point. It has rained here for eight days now. The child is causing it."

Both Doan's eyebrows rose until they disappeared beneath the edge of his hood. He held out one gnarled hand, palm up, then brought the captured water to his lips. "I'm impressed," he said at last. "How?"

The centaur absently scraped at the rock with a front hoof. "She is not even aware that she is doing it. But," he added, anticipating Doan's next question, "we are aware and we are sure it is her doing."

"Just what exactly did she do?"

"Eight days ago, her pony died and in her grief she wept."

A slow smile spread over Doan's face. "And the world weeps with her. Sympathetic magic."

"So we feel also. But she has stopped weeping and the world has not. As this is not something we taught her to do, we are not able to teach her to undo it. This is not something any of the others were ever capable of."

"Well, they weren't a very sympathetic lot, were they?"

Great corded muscles stood out along C'Tal's shoulders and arms and his voice was ice as he replied: "We only teach. We are not responsible for what is done with our teachings."

Doan slowly rose to his feet and the two ancient powers stood immobile, gazes locked. With a shudder that ran down the length of his body, C'Tal broke away, his head and shoulders slowly bending under the weight of an impossible burden.

"We are not responsible for what is done with our teachings," he repeated, his voice so low it sounded like the distant rumble of thunder. "We cannot be responsible for the actions of any thinking being. But this time . . ." His head came up and his mighty shoulders squared. "This time we teach where the responsibilities lie." He snorted, an amazingly horselike sound. "We are no longer so blind as to think the Mother's Youngest will know this on their own."

Doan stood a moment longer, then he nodded, once, and abruptly sat. "Which brings us back to the rain. Have you tried to comfort her?"

C'Tal backed up a step, his tail flicking from side to side in short, jerky arcs. "We are not . . ." he began. "That is, we do not ever . . . it is not in us to . . ."

A *centaur at a loss for words*, Doan thought, the corners of his mouth twitching slightly despite the circumstances. *Now that's something you don't see every day.* Aloud he said, "Let her go home, C'Tal."

"But her learning has barely begun!"

"Not forever, you idiot; just let her visit."

"If that is all you can offer, you may return to your caverns. We hone a weapon and time is short."

"Try to remember that weapon is still a little girl. No, wait!" Doan chopped through whatever C'Tal was trying to say with that staccato command. "You asked for my advice, now listen to it. Responsibility isn't enough. She'll never know compassion if she isn't shown it, nor love either. If you can't give that to her, take her to someone who can."

"Emotion is . . ."

"Emotion caused this." Doan gestured up at the glowering gray sky. "Remember? She's tapped into something here the Enemy doesn't have. I don't know how, maybe it's her parentage, the Mother knows that's strange enough, but if she's to be the key to the Enemy's Doom she'll need all the help she can get. Don't cut her off from this. It may save her life. It may save all our lives."

C'Tal appeared to be thinking it over. More rain gathered in his hair and beard and began to stream over his motionless body.

"It is possible that you are correct," he said at last, spun on one hind leg, and galloped away.

"You're welcome!" Doan snarled as C'Tal's glistening black haunches disappeared into the distance. A centaur at full gallop moved too fast for the eye to follow. "I don't envy that child her next few years with those pompous nags," he muttered, climbing down off the boulder. He scowled as he realized he was wet through, then he smiled suddenly. "Nor," he declared vindictively, heading for home, "do I envy those overblown horse's asses their next few years with her." He snorted. "They'll remember this rain with fondness if she ever gets mad."

# EIGHT

One moment, all was peace and stillness in the Sacred Grove. The next, the muffled boom of a distant explosion sent Tayer into the sanctuary of Mikhail's arms. The sound had barely died when there came another. And then another.

In the quiet after the third blast, the birches of the Grove shuddered and swayed, although no wind moved through them.

"Balls of Chaos," Mikhail swore softly, holding Tayer safe against his chest. "What was that?"

"The beginning of war," replied a clear, young voice. "And possibly the end of Ardhan."

"What . . ." Mikhail's hand went to his side, groping for his absent sword. Not since his first visit, seventeen years before, had he carried a sword into the Sacred Grove. Not until this instant had he missed it.

But Tayer pulled herself from Mikhail's grasp and stepped forward eagerly, scanning the circle of trees.

"Crystal?" she called.

The young woman who stepped out from between the birches seemed to have also stepped out of legend. Although barely more than a girl, she stood as tall as Mikhail, sapling slender, and graceful in a way unseen since the Eldest died and her sisters disappeared from mortal sight. Her hair was a white so pure it shone silver and her eyes were the green of new spring leaves flecked lightly with gold.

She was dressed for travel, breeches, tunic, and riding boots all in black, and she looked like a shadow defying the soft sunlight of the Grove.

"Crystal," Tayer said again and held open her arms.

Crystal went eagerly to the embrace, resting her cheek on her mother's head with a weary sigh. She had come a very long way in the last few days and she had a disagreeable duty still to perform. This temporary haven was welcome.

Tayer broke away first. She pushed her daughter out to arm's length and looked her up and down. "Black becomes you," she said at last with a smile. "But what are you doing home? Have they given you a holiday?"

"No, Mother. My time with the centaurs is done. They sent me to help."

"Help what, child?" Mikhail asked.

Crystal looked over at her stepfather, her face grim enough to wipe away his smile of greeting. "From the time of the Eldest, through the raids we have fought every harvest, we . . ." She waved a long-fingered hand. ". . . Ardhan, has been part of a most deadly game, put through our paces by Kraydak, the wizard who has controlled the throne of Melac for the last four hundred years."

"Wizard," Mikhail grunted, his brows drawing into a golden vee as he considered it. "That would," he muttered to his memories, "explain a great deal."

Tayer shook her head. "You must be mistaken, child. The wizards are all long dead."

"No, not all. Two remain. The sounds you heard were Kraydak's work." Crystal paused and took a deep breath, the rest was difficult to say. "We must go back to town at once. The palace and everyone in it has been destroyed. We three are the only survivors of the Royal House of Ardhan. Mother, you are now queen."

The distant cry of a bird was the only noise as shock, anger, sorrow—a cacophony of emotion—roared through the Grove. But no disbelief. No denial. The truth in Crystal's voice was stronger than those.

"Everyone?" Tayer asked at last, her eyes wide, her voice trembling.

"Yes, Mother. Everyone."

Mikhail looked out at Crystal through the numbness that thankfully seemed to be cushioning the despair. "You were in the Grove seconds after the sound died. How can you know what happened?"

"The centaurs foresaw Kraydak's attack. As I could do nothing to stop it, they sent me here to you." She looked earnestly at her parents. "Although I'd have tried if there'd been time . . ."

"You could do nothing to stop it?" Mikhail interrupted, a dawning light of understanding showing on his face. "What could you possibly have done?"

Crystal backed up a step, laced her fingers together, and stared down into the pattern.

"I," she said softly, "am the other wizard."

When Tayer, Mikhail, and Crystal brought their lathered horses to a stop in the People's Square, they were instantly surrounded by terrified men and women. Hands clutched and pulled at their clothing and the horses' harnesses. Voices wailed, sobbed, and cried out in despair. Tayer and Mikhail sat like statues in the midst of chaos and stared in shock at the smoldering pile of rubble that had been the palace. Even Crystal, who had known what they would face, sat silent and disbelieving.

The blow had been well aimed. The outbuildings—the stables, the barracks, the servants' quarters—had not been touched. The old palace wall, with its seven new arches opening the palace up to the people, still stood. Only the palace itself had been destroyed. The great hulking stone edifice that had squatted ugly and supreme in the center of King's City was no more. It looked as if a giant had lifted his massive fist and squashed it flat.

A score of people—those of the Guard who had not been in the building at the time of the attack, as well as nobles, servants, and townsfolk—crawled over the wreckage. In several places, small groups marked another body being lifted clear. On the pile of debris that had once been the West Tower, a girl, no more than ten or twelve years old, crouched and rocked a broken, bloody body in her arms. The body had been so badly crushed it was impossible to tell at a distance if it was male or female, mother or father. The girl's face was wet with blood from pressing her lips against her grisly burden. Her eyes were wide with shock, staring ahead at nothing. She wailed, a thin high cry, sorrow and fear mixed together. It rose and fell to the cadence of her rocking.

On the very edge of the Square, atop the rubble of what had been the sunroom wall, four bodies lay. Around them stood a Guard of Honor. The guards' arms were red to the elbow and their uniforms were spattered with blood. Dull crimson stains marked the sheets, that covered, but did not hide, the identities of the four dead.

When Tayer's anguished eyes Tested on what lay guarded there, she moaned softly and tried to swing off her horse. The mob clung to her in desperation, and she retreated, trapped. Mikhail peeled his hand from the pommel of his sword—it had gone there in a truly useless gesture of defiance when he first saw the destruction—and reached for Tayer's reins, his intention clear. If the crowd would not let them dismount, then he would force a way through on horseback.

Crystal laid her hand on his arm and, when he turned to look at her, shook her head. She dropped her own reins, took a deep breath, and sang.

If the song had words, no one afterward remembered them. It was more a song of feelings. It was reassurance, security, hope. It was the song a mother hums to her child as she tucks it in at night. It was powerful, universal, calming.

One by one, the crowd quieted as the song poured over them. Some began to weep bitterly, but the panic stilled. Even the young girl stopped wailing and turned to stare at Crystal with wounded eyes.

Crystal's gaze swept the crowd, resting briefly on each mourner. Not until all who needed it had drawn strength from the green fire of her eyes did she stop singing. The breezes carried the melody for a few seconds more, then they too were still.

Mikhail swung down to the pavement, the creaking of his saddle leather sounding unnaturally loud. He held up his arms to Tayer. She collapsed into them, paused for an instant in the security of his embrace, then, keeping a tight grip on his hand, started the long walk to the edge of the Square. The people parted to let them through.

When she reached the bodies, Tayer knelt and lifted the edge of the sheet. They were all there: her father, the King, Davan and Eyrik, her brothers, and Savell, Davan's pregnant wife. She brushed a lock of hair out of Savell's eyes and gently lowered the fabric, wiping her bloody hand on her skirt.

"Majesty?" a merchant asked quietly, his words falling into the silence like stones into water. "What are we to do?"

Tayer looked up at her daughter, but Crystal had banked the fire in her eyes and had no answer. She looked at Mikhail but he merely shook his head. The message was clear. Tayer was now queen. The choice must be hers.

The queen searched for her voice and forced it past her grief. To her surprise it neither quavered nor shook although it was husky with the tears that streamed down her face.

"We will bury our dead and we will prepare for war."

War. Of all those in the Square, only Crystal did not recoil from the word. Her eye had been caught by the glint of sunlight on red-gold curls and she stared in horrified fascination at the man beneath them who stood at the edge of the crowd. It wasn't his beauty she marked, nor that his sapphire robes were clean and unstained by blood or grime. It was the fact that in the full light of the afternoon sun, he cast no shadow.

Aware of the scrutiny, he smiled up at her, raised one hand in a mocking salute, and faded slowly away. The breeze carried the sound of his laughter.


"Crystal?"

She turned slowly from the window. The voice was not one she knew, but the face hovered on the edge of memory. She searched until she found a name to fit it.

"Bryon?"

The tall, dark-haired young man flashed a dazzling smile and made an elegant leg. "At your command."

Crystal stared in amazement.

"Bryon?" she repeated.

Bryon gracefully straightened up.

"Ah," he said. "I see you're puzzled. After all, it's been six years, how could you be expected to recognize me?" He leaned closer. "I'll let you in on the secret." His lips hovered at the edge of her ear and his breath was a warm breeze on her cheek. "I've gotten taller."

Crystal backed away.

"So have you." Bryon nodded solemnly, but his gray eyes danced. It didn't seem to bother him that the startlingly lovely creature his old playmate had grown into had a slight advantage in height.

Crystal—who had almost ceased to think of time, for the centaurs having all of eternity never bothered with it—was suddenly aware of just how long those six years had been. This was the grubby companion of her childhood? This handsome courtier with the disarming smile who was planting warm kisses on the palm of her hand . . . who was planting warm kisses on the palm of her hand? She snatched her hand away.

"Bryon!"

"Crystal!" He mimicked her tone exactly, then threw a brotherly arm about her shoulders and propelled her down the hall. "Come on. They want you in my father's library."

His father was the Duke of Belkar. The House of Belkar was cousin to the Royal House through Meredith who had joined with Rael, the son of the Lady of the Grove. The current duke had opened his townhouse to what was left of the court.

"So," said Bryon conversationally as they walked toward the library, "I hear you're a wizard."

Crystal, preoccupied with analyzing the peculiar warmth radiating out from where Bryon's arm lay across her shoulders, merely mumbled an affirmative.

"Well," he continued, apparently undismayed both by her lack of response and by the knowledge of the slaughter the ancient wizards had caused, "I suppose everyone needs a hobby."

That penetrated. She twisted lithely out of his grasp and turned to face him. *People will be wary of you,* the centaurs had said. *They will treat you with caution and respect. Some will even be frightened.* They'd never mentioned that some would be amused.

"Hobby? I have powers you couldn't even imagine and you call it a hobby? Don't you realize what I am?" She regretted the outburst the moment the words left her mouth, her voice sounding shrill and childish. Sounding, in fact, like the voice of a child overreacting to being teased. Bryon had always been able to get that response; that, at least, the six years apart hadn't changed.

But Bryon, secure in his victory, only smiled and held the library door open for her. "You're late," he said.

*It's difficult to impress someone who tied your braids to a pigsty when you were seven,* Crystal reflected as she went into the room.

The library was large and Crystal was surprised by the number of books and scrolls it contained. The duke, a grizzled old fighter, had not stuck in her childhood memory of him as much of a reader. Tayer sat behind a massive table covered over with a map of Ardhan and the surrounding territory, trying to make sense of what Mikhail and the Duke of Belkar were saying. This was no easy task as the two men contradicted each other loudly and often, pulling the map back and forth while trying to make their point. Crystal felt sorry for her mother, caught in the middle of something she had no hope of controlling.

The only son and heir of the Duke of Riven leaned on the mantelpiece, staring into the ashes of an old fire. Deep circles bracketed his eyes and he plucked nervously at the hilt of his dagger with one fineboned hand. He had lost his mother and his younger sister in the destruction of the palace and it looked as if he would now lose his father to grief.

The Court Treasurer, one pudgy hand smoothing the burgundy velvet of his robe as though he soothed a cat, argued quietly with the Captain of the Palace Guard. They were the only two ranking members of the palace staff left alive. A gray-robed Scholar stood to one side, listening. He had been with Belkar's household only a few weeks, but as none of the Scholars advising the royal family had survived the destruction of the palace, the duke had asked him to attend.

The captain noticed Crystal first, and fell silent. One by one, all heads turned toward her. Even young Riven looked up from his sorrow. The room grew so still that a breeze could be heard dancing through the linden tree outside the window. The silence extended and became awkward.

Finally, Bryon, who had followed Crystal into the room, cleared his throat.

"I have brought the princess as you requested, sir."

The princess. Much easier to deal with than the wizard. The tension in the room eased and the duke came around the table to take Crystal's hands.

"It's good to see you again, child," he said. "Though one could wish it were under better circumstances." He leaned back slightly to look her full in the face although he carefully avoided meeting her eyes. It couldn't hurt to be careful around wizards, even if you had dandled this one on your knee when she was a baby. "You've grown some since we last met."

"That was six years ago, sir. I was eleven."

"Ah, yes." He dropped her hands. "Well, now, your father tells me you know something of what attacked us. We've got to have details if we're to fight this thing, eh?"

Crystal glanced at Mikhail. Her father . . . As one of the six dukes, Belkar had to know the truth of her parentage. Whether he refused to acknowledge it out of disbelief or from respect for Mikhail she wasn't sure, nor did she care for she refused to acknowledge it herself. Mikhail was the father of her heart, all the father she would ever want. She met his eyes. He dropped one lid in a slow wink and, just for that instant, the tasks yet ahead did not seem so impossible.

"Now then," the duke continued, "what's this you've got to tell us about Melac?"

Crystal discarded the princess with relief. The wizard answered.

"We aren't fighting Melac. We never have been."

"Could've sworn it was a Melacian put a spear through my leg when I rode with the Elite," muttered the Captain of the Guard.

"Perhaps. But he was a tool in another's hands. The Wizard Kraydak has ruled Melac since before the Lady died." In Ardhan, there was, and always would be, only one Lady.

The room erupted into a flurry of questions and exclamations of disbelief. Even young Riven was momentarily shaken from his stupor. Only Crystal and the Scholar remained silent.

When order had been restored, Mikhail turned to the gray-robed man. "You didn't seem surprised to hear that," he said suspiciously. "You knew about Kraydak? About this wizard?"

The Scholar shook his head. He was as tall as the members of the Royal House, who were taller than most of their subjects, and was thin and wiry, his dark hair streaked with gray.

"No, milord, I knew nothing, but there have been rumors of how the Kings of Melac have a counselor who never dies and through him a weak and struggling nation became an empire. Although there have been no great magics that only a wizard could perform, Melac's armies have had entirely too much help from the elements for it to have been coincidental. The Scholars have studied the ancient wizards . . ." His face twisted suddenly. "After all, they nearly sent the whole world to Lord Death. Of them all, only Kraydak had the power to survive the Doom." He shrugged. "But I know nothing. Scholars have not been welcomed in Melac or her conquered countries for years."

"Nonsense," broke in the duke. "Why, I myself was in Melac not more than a year ago to try to hammer out some sort of treaty and there were plenty of Scholars about then, they certainly looked welcome . . . flitting around like shadows . . . noses in everybody's business . . . gave me the creeps." He suddenly remembered who he was talking to. "No offense, Lapus."

Lapus smiled thinly. "None taken, sir." Then the smile vanished. The Scholar's voice deepened and passion marred its smooth composure. "The gray-robed ones you saw were not Scholars whatever they called themselves. A Scholar has no master but knowledge and lets nothing, and no one, stand in the way of the search for Truth."

Crystal studied the Scholar thoughtfully as he spoke. He was nothing like the genial teachers she and Bryon had shared as children. His intensity when he spoke of knowledge as the only master was almost fanatical. He reminded her very much of the centaurs. She missed her old teachers, and the feeling of certainty they radiated.

"I am old for lessons," she began as Lapus finished speaking, "but I have been with the Elders for so long I know little about the ways of Man." Her eyes, the muted green-gold of sunlight through leaves, locked onto his. "Will you teach me?"

Trapped in the quiet depths of her eyes, Lapus couldn't have said no had he wanted to. A pulse began to throb in his temple. With an effort, he bowed his head and forced his gaze to the tile floor.

"Yes, milady," was all he said.

Crystal nodded once and turned away. The exchange had disturbed her as much as it obviously had Lapus, for all that had looked out of the Scholar's eyes when she held them with her own was the reflection of a tall young woman with ivory skin and silver hair. She wasn't supposed to see herself in another's eyes, her power looked through to their heart.

The duke cleared his throat and indicated the map on the table. "Lessons will have to wait, child, now we need plans for war."

"Wage it any way you like," the wizard told him curtly.

"Crystal . . ." Tayer said warningly, aghast at her daughter's rudeness.

Crystal sighed. She would have to straighten some things out with her mother. "I will have no involvement in the fighting," she explained.

Tayer looked at her in puzzlement. "But Crystal, you said we were fighting a wizard."

"I beg your pardon if I've confused you, Mother, but I am fighting the wizard. You fight only his armies."

"Amounts to the same thing, doesn't it?" snorted the Captain of the Guard. "The wizard . . . his armies?"

"No, it doesn't."

"Well, what about that mess on the hill then? If that's not fighting a wizard, what is?"

"You didn't fight him though, did you?"

The captain remembered the three mighty and invisible blows that had reduced the palace to rubble. He'd been standing thirty feet away and yet had not been touched, although the sound nearly deafened him. His ears still rang with it. He remembered the stream of blood trickling out from under the crushed stone and how it had lapped daintily against his boot. His ruddy face paled and he shook his head. "No, I didn't. But I would've," he growled, "could I have got my hands on him."

"If you'd got your hands on him, you'd be dead." Crystal moved to the window and lifted her face to the sun. She drank in the warmth and light, saving it up against the darkness to come. She didn't want to be the world's savior . . . she didn't have a choice. Then she sighed and turned back to the gray despair that filled the library.

"The Scholar was right. Only Kraydak survived the holocaust and it took almost all of his great power to do it. He had his life but not much else. He was also afraid that the Doom which took the other wizards might still claim him so, defenseless, he hid. And he stayed hidden for over a thousand years, rebuilding his strength and gradually coming to realize that he had escaped completely. None of the shadows that lurked in dark corners were waiting to claim him.

"When he emerged; he found that people had changed. Having been free of the tyranny of the wizards for generations, they were not likely to bow down to the lone survivor and he was still weak enough to be killed if the mortals were determined enough. Kraydak took another road to the power he craved; he offered his services to the weakest king he could find. Not as a wizard, but as a counselor and a friend. He played on the king's weaknesses, on his yearning for power. He took the king to his tower and offered him the world. The king took the offer and from that day to this he and his heirs have been figure-heads, for the power of Melac is in Kraydak's hands.

"Armies moved out, always attacking where the defenders were weakest, protected by the knowledge that should they begin to fail, fire, flood, or some other seemingly natural disaster would come to their aid. Perhaps they lost a few battles, but they won all the wars. Melac became an Empire.

"Young men and women began to disappear into Kraydak's tower. Those who spoke of resistance or rebellion were visited in the night. The ones who lived went mad; most died."

"We share a border with Melac," the duke interrupted. "Why weren't we one of the first attacked?"

"We were. The battle that killed the Lady's love was the beginning of Kraydak's push for an Empire. Fortunately for Ardhan, he forgot to take the mountains into account and his neophyte army had to fight the terrain before they met the enemy. He was new to mortal warfare, and so he lost. He hasn't returned for two reasons. Once he got his people moving south and east, the way of least resistance, momentum kept them moving away from us. The second reason concerns a proph-ecy, that in Ardhan would be born the last of the wizards and his pos-sible defeat."

"I always felt Melac was waiting for something," Mikhail said qui-etly from where he stood at Tayer's back. "If you studied the border raids, it was the only thing that made sense."

Crystal nodded. "Kraydak was waiting for me."

"Well, that makes no sense," fumed the duke. "If he knew you were coming and you could defeat him, he should've taken the country to keep you from being born."

"He was bored."

"He was what?"

"Bored. Everything came too easily, there were no challenges, so he watched and waited and when he thought I would give him a good fight—but not one he felt he would lose—he let me know he knew I was here."

Crystal stepped back and directed the duke's gaze out the window. Not far away people still moved amid the ruins.

"He destroyed the palace to tell me that the game has begun."

Nyle, the young Lord of Riven, looked up. His eyes were rimmed in red and the whites were murky from lack of sleep. A piece of chestnut hair hung lank across his forehead. His lips curled back from his teeth and he glared at Crystal from under heavy lids.

"My mother and sister are dead," he snarled, "and you think it's a game?"

"Kraydak thinks it's a game," Crystal corrected him gently although her expression remained stern. "I have never been more serious. Much of my family died in the palace as well."

"He wouldn't even be here but for you! He would've left us alone!"

"Perhaps."

"Then it's your fault; your fault my mother is dead and my father is dying." He jerked away from the fireplace and turned toward her. "Your fault!"

"NYLE!"

Mikhail's bass roar blasted some of the glaze from the young man's eyes. He stopped and drew a long shuddering breath.

"Milord?"

"Go see to your father," Mikhail commanded kindly. "He needs you by him."

Nyle nodded slowly and began to leave the room, his shoulders bowed under his load of grief. At the door, he paused, and the face he turned to Crystal was damp with tears. "Your fault," he whispered once more, and then he left.

"I would watch that young man," Lapus said softly. "If he truly believes that the princess is responsible for the death of his family, he may try to harm her."

Crystal looked at the Scholar and just a flicker of her power showed deep in her eyes.

"He couldn't."

Mikhail stared at the closed door for a moment and then turned to

Crystal. He made his voice as impersonal as he could and hoped she would understand it was the prince who spoke and not her father. "I have to ask this—would it make a difference if you left?"

Crystal understood, she'd asked herself that same question. She shook her head and motes of light danced in her silver hair. "No. If I left, he would destroy Ardhan piece by piece until I came back to fight."

The captain's scarred forehead had been furrowed for some time. Finally figuring out just what he didn't understand, he spoke.

"If this Kraydak never meant to go after us until now, why the raids every year?"

"He was studying us," Crystal explained. "Studying our land and the way we fight. He wants a challenge not a rout."

"Sounds like he's got all the angles covered," muttered the duke. "And this is the man we have to beat . . ."

"No," Crystal corrected again, almost severely. "This is the man I have to beat."

"Can you?" Tayer's voice was heavy with fear, fear for her country, fear for her daughter.

Crystal heard. She looked out the window and watched something, someone perhaps, being lifted from the wreckage. The salvation of her people settled more firmly on her shoulders and she braced herself against the weight.

"I hope so." And then, with a nod to her parents, she left the room.

Bryon stood aside to let her leave, then glanced up at his father. Go with her, said the duke's expression, she shouldn't be alone.

As this agreed perfectly with Bryon's desire, he bowed to the queen and followed.

# NINE

Tayer would have no coronation, no robes of gold, and no great feast where the six dukes of Ardhan would come to pay homage to their new queen. She would go on no tour of the six provinces to acquaint herself with her realm. The huge and ugly State Crown was buried deep in the rubble that had been the palace. The dukes would give homage when they met on the battlefield. She would tour only the provinces the army must cross to meet Kraydak's attack. The queen rode at the head of her armies.

"How can you be so sure," Mikhail demanded, "that the attack will come at the Tage Plateau? What about the Northern Pass into Lorn? They've tried there before."

"And found it wanting," Crystal replied, a breeze fanning her hair. "Kraydak's armies will come to the Tage Plateau. That far he has let me see his plans."

"Has let you see his plans? What in the name of the Mother for?"

"It's my guess he's anxious for the battle and doesn't want me to miss it," Crystal said dryly. "He'll keep telling me enough to ensure we're in the right place at the right time." Then she left, taking the breeze with her.

Mikhail looked at Tayer who was plotting the route from Belkar through Hale and up into the mountains. The duke's library had become war room, throne room, and petition room for the new queen.

"How does she know?" Mikhail muttered.

Tayer looked up at him and forced a smile. "I doubt we'd like to know, my love. I doubt she found out in a manner befitting a princess and the heir to the throne." The smile vanished and she shook her head. "I can't deny what she is, Mikhail. I've tried never to do that, but she must acknowledge my heritage now as well as her father's and I'm afraid the two will not mix."

"Why not?"

"The rules are too different." She tried to remember how it felt to rest safe within the light, offering no resistance, but it had been too many years. Her memories of the Grove, of Varkell, of carrying his light beneath her breast were muted by distance and blocked by her responsibilities to her people. She scrubbed a fine-boned hand over her eyes. "Never mind, I'll speak to her." She considered the map again. "The War Horns go out today. Aliston can meet us at Hale's Seat, but I suppose Cei and Lorn had best meet us at the battleground."

Mikhail stared down at his wife. He knew she had a core of strength that seldom showed to those who knew her less well than he, but that strength had been sorely tested over the last few days and he wished he could do more to ease her burdens. "You do that like an old campaigner," he said at last, because he had to say something.

"I was trained to be queen." Tayer sighed. "Although with two older brothers it didn't seem likely I'd ever have to use the training." Her eyes misted and her voice dropped to a whisper as she remembered. "And I'd give anything not to have this chance."

Mikhail laid his hands on her slender shoulders and squeezed gently.

"I'm all right," Tayer told him, only a tiny catch in her voice betraying her sorrow. "But now Crystal must be trained as I was. The succession must be secure, especially as we ride to war."

A vision of his beloved hacked to pieces by enemy swords caused Mikhail to close his eyes in pain. But if Tayer could prepare for the possibility so calmly, could he do any less? He twisted the topic away from the battlefield.

"She won't like it. She didn't like the maid you insisted she have, said a wizard doesn't need a maid."

"A wizard may not, but a princess does."

Mikhail smiled as he spoke. "Considering some of the outfits she's expected to wear, I don't see how she can do without one."

"There are a lot worse things than maids facing her. Although she should've consulted with us first, I'm glad she asked that Scholar to help her. I very much doubt her schooling over the last few years included economics, local histories, diplomacy, protocol," she paused, "and the making of war and the sending out of War Horns."

They were back to the battlefield.

"Is there no place for Riven in your plans?" Mikhail asked, suddenly recalling the distribution of War Horns she'd mentioned earlier.

All remaining light left Tayer's voice.

"Riven is set upon joining his wife and child. He forgets he still has one child left living to grieve and goes running back to the arms of the Mother. He doesn't hear the tears of his son or the pleading of his friends. He just lies there, waiting for Lord Death to claim him." She reached for Mikhail's hand and laid her cheek against his side.

His other hand came around and gently stroked her hair. "This should never have been set on you," he said softly. "Your life shouldn't be death and destruction but sunshine and birdsong and the laughter of children."

"Do you regret not having children, Mikhail?" They had long ago given up hope.

Mikhail remembered a tiny girl-child who had clamored to be lifted to his shoulders; her delight at the white pony on her fifth birthday; the day she and Bryon had locked themselves in the dungeon and the entire palace staff had searched for twelve hours before they were found.

"I always felt I had one. In fact, the way Bryon was constantly underfoot, I often thought I had two." And he remembered the silver tear that had fallen the day the centaur came and took her away. She'd looked back only once and the tear had shone like a star on her cheek. Now she had returned. "I always felt I had one," he repeated sadly.

A knock on the door boomed through the silence that had fallen as they both considered their daughter and what she had become.

Tayer released Mikhail's hand and he moved to stand behind her, a solid wall against her back.

"Enter."

The door swung open and the Captain of the Guard marched into the room, followed by two of his soldiers supporting a man between them. The man appeared to have been badly beaten, then kicked into a corner and forgotten for some time. His lips were cracked and bleeding, his eyes swollen shut, and his skin showed purple and black with bruises through his ripped and blood stained clothes.

"Who is he?" asked Tayer as the soldiers dragged him forward.

"This pitiful remnant," declared the captain, drawing himself up before the table, "is the only survivor of the palace."

"What!"

"That's right, Majesty. This scum, who beat his own brother to death and was sentenced to die by your father the king—may he rest in the arms of the Mother—survived when everyone else was crushed to a bloody pulp. I've brought him to you for resentencing."

"Release him."

"Right, I'll . . ." The captain froze, in the act of turning away. "What?"

"Release him."

"But, Majesty, he's a convicted killer!"

"He is alive! Too many others are dead and too many others will die. Take him out of here," commanded the queen, "and release him!"


The Duke of Belkar's late wife had loved flowers and to please her he had extensive gardens planted around all of their residences. After her death, he'd found great comfort in them and often said that in the gardens she still lived.

The garden at the townhouse was not very large, but it was exceptionally beautiful. Crystal—clad now in a style befitting a princess, a gown of palest green with a silver net loosely confining her hair—had found in it much the same peace the duke found; problems could be temporarily forgotten and demands for the impossible momentarily ignored. She let the healing balm of the spring flowers and delicate lace-work of the flowering trees wash over her.

"May I join you?"

Lost in thought, she hadn't heard Bryon approach. Still not quite back, she opened her eyes.

Bryon had been thinking of her as a part of the garden, a rare and beautiful flower with silver petals and the scent of sun-warmed flesh. But when she opened her eyes, the garden disappeared and he was sinking into green fire. Sinking joyfully into green fire. Sinking ecstatically into green fire. Wanting it to consume him.

"Oh, Bryon, I'm sorry!"

He blinked once, twice, and was suddenly looking into a pair of concerned green eyes.

"I was thinking . . . I didn't know you'd be looking at me so directly."

"What else would I be looking at?" he muttered a little peevishly, but added in a more normal voice when he saw how distressed she appeared: "It's nothing to worry about, I'm all right."

Crystal drew him down beside her on the bench and searched his face anxiously. If he wasn't all right, she'd never forgive herself. After a moment, satisfied that what he said was true, she sighed and turned away.

*"You must never forget,"* the centaurs had told her time after time, *"that you have the potential to be as great a danger as Kraydak himself."*

Bryon watched the effect of the sigh on Crystal's profile and the sparkle came back into his eyes. She was the most magnificent woman he had ever seen and he had every intention of presuming on their childhood friendship. He took her hand gently between the two of his and carefully, as if it were a timid bird he must not startle, began to stroke it.

"What were you thinking of?" he asked softly.

"About my time with the centaurs."

"Were you very lonely?"

"At first, but there was so much to learn in so little time. And there were always the breezes."

"I can't imagine a breeze being much company."

"That's because you don't know how to listen to them. They hear everything and they love to gossip." She almost smiled as she looked back at her younger self. "I even gave them names and made up faces for them. There was one that seemed to take a special interest in me, I called him Barrett. Although the centaurs didn't approve—they felt my reality was wide enough without adding to it—I imagined him with black hair and gray eyes. He's still my good friend."

"He?"

She turned to face Bryon . . . and his black hair and gray eyes. She snatched her hand away and felt her cheeks grow hot, not wholly as a result of the afternoon sun.

"What makes you think I was lonely?" she asked, smoothing the already perfect folds of her skirt.

"For one thing," and his smile caused two deep dimples to appear, "you used to laugh all the time, but I haven't heard you laugh once since you've been home."

"There's not much to laugh about, is there?"

"No." The dimples retreated. "I guess there isn't." But Bryon knew that wasn't all of it. It was as if Crystal's purpose left no room for anything else. Had she given up her humanity when she took up her powers? He looked forward to finding out.

A chill breeze wrapped around them both. Crystal caressed it with long fingers, her head to one side, listening.

"I have to go." She stood suddenly. "The old Duke of Riven is dead."

Bryon hesitated barely a moment and then he rose as well. "I'll go with you," he said, but it was too late. Crystal had used his hesitation to move quickly toward the house. He followed, but a gust of wind snapped a thorny branch into his path and he lost all hope of catching her when he had to stop and unsnag his breeches.

"Well, Barrett," he muttered, watching the swing of Crystal's departing hips, "I guess it's between you and me." He didn't quite hear the breeze chuckle as it sped away.

The War Horns went out that afternoon; north to Aliston, south to Cei, west to Hale, and northwest to Lorn. As well as the horns, each Messenger carried a scroll sealed with the queen's signet. The Horn was a part of the ancient bond between the dukes and the High Court. The scroll carried the plans for war.

The Messengers of Ardhan were chosen from the finest young men and women in the kingdom. The four that carried the War Horns were the best of an exceptional group. They were highly trained, highly motivated, healthy, intelligent, and totally helpless should Kraydak decide to prevent them from reaching their destinations.

"I will be watching," Crystal assured them, meeting each of their eyes in turn and allowing them each a glimpse of the light. "If you should be attacked, I will be there to protect you."

And no one questioned the value of that protection save Crystal herself.

The new Duke of Riven also rode out that afternoon. He carried his own War Horn but, instead of a scroll, he had the bodies of his father and sister. His mother's body had not been found.

It was two weeks' hard ride from King's City to Riven; burdened with the heavy wagon the trip would take almost a month. Long before Riven could be reached, the dead would be beyond the point where the living could travel with them. If he wished to take his father and his sister home, the new duke had no choice but to accept the wizard's help.

"They would not be dead but for you," he said as she stepped back from the task, "and now they will not return to the body of the Mother because of you."

"When they are placed in Riven's soil, the Mother will take them back," Crystal told him, trying to forget the feel of dead flesh beneath her fingers. "Remember, had Kraydak not been waiting for me, Lord Death would have taken them much sooner than he did."

They locked eyes and although Crystal carefully kept her power masked (*"The people of Ardhan must respect you as well as fear you if they are to be any use in battle,"* the centaurs had cautioned her. *"It is not advisable to keep reminding them that you are their only hope for a future."*), young Riven looked away first. With a grunted "Perhaps," he threw himself on his horse and began the long ride home. The War Horn of Riven hung from his saddle, but even when swearing allegiance to the queen, he had not said if he would sound it.

That night, long after most of the townspeople had gone to their beds and the sounds of the Guards had faded toward the outskirts of the town, a solitary figure appeared in the ruins of the People's Square. In the silver light of the moon her hair seemed to burn, each strand alive with cold fire. When she dropped the cloak from her shoulders, her naked body ignited as well until she seemed a slender silver flame.

She cupped her hands and lifted them to the moon. White light filled them until it overflowed down her arms then, throwing her arms wide apart, she scattered the light over the rubble . . . and called.

The call was lower than anything that should have come from a human throat. It was deep and insistent and commanding.

On the third call, the earth answered.

The paving stones began to vibrate as a note too low to be heard sang up from the ground. The broken pieces of the palace began to shift and pitch. Waves rippled through them as if they were water, not stone.

The silver figure stepped forward and stood for a moment, not on the stones but on the air above them. Then she began to dance. She moved slowly at first, outlining the perimeter—for everywhere her feet had been there lay a silver tracery—but as the earth's call began to rise, still unheard though felt at temple and wrist, the dance began to move more quickly until she was indeed a silver flame in the moonlight.

As the pattern was completed, the song beat so quickly it seemed it must escape. As the last line was closed, it stopped. The pattern sank into the earth and all the dogs of the town began to howl at once.

Shutters slammed back. Sleepy voices demanded explanations and called at curs to be quiet. Had anyone looked toward the palace they would have seen, not a silver dancer who moved like flame, but a silver birch that lifted lacy branches to the moonlight and swayed in a gentle wind.

The dogs quieted at last, and the town returned to sleep. The dancer descended to the street, picked up her cloak, and disappeared in the shadows.

The next morning, twenty-six sheep grazed in the meadow that had erased the scars of the palace.

# TEN

"My mother will ride at the head of the army," Crystal remarked thoughtfully to Lapus as they threaded their way through the twisting hallways of the duke's house. Although rain denied them the garden, Crystal was too restless to sit still. "But all I hear talk of is men. The men will do this, the men will do that . . . don't the women fight?"

"Some, but not many."

"Why not?"

"Someone must see to the day to day running of the land."

"But why the women?" Crystal was puzzled. "The centaurs always said that the men were in charge."

"In charge of what?"

"Well . . . the country."

"And who does that leave in charge of the men?"

Silver brows rose. "The women?"

"Who sees that the men get fed, and clothed, and to council on time? Who teaches them to love, when to be strong, and when to be weak? Who sees that the race continues? Some say that the Mother created women in her image and then created men to give them something to do."

"Lapus, you're a traitor to your sex!" Her tone was almost teasing. She had somehow managed to keep her whole purpose for existing at a little distance over the last few days of waiting ("*Always remember that you were conceived solely for the destruction of Kraydak.*") although it was never far from her thoughts.

Lapus stiffened at the word traitor. "I am true only to Truth, milady, and although it is true that men and women are equal in the eyes
of the Mother, it is equally true that they are not the same. It does no
honor to men that they are better able to facilitate the arrival of Lord
Death. Perhaps because a woman better understands how difficult it is
to create a life, she becomes less willing to take one. Most of the surgeons and healers that ride with the army are women."

Crystal dropped into a window seat and stared pensively at her slip-
pered feet. "It appears," she said, "that I not only have much to learn
about being a princess, but someone had better teach me to be a woman
as well." She looked up at Lapus and smiled. "Do you think you could
make a woman of me, Scholar?"

The smile was his undoing. For a change, there was nothing of the
other world in Crystal's expression, unless it was the innocent beauty
of that smile. Lapus swallowed twice and shoved his hands deep in his
sleeves to hide their trembling. He opened his mouth to speak, but all
he could get out was one word.

"No," he said. And fled.

Crystal stared at his fleeing back in astonishment. "Did I say something wrong?"

The rain on the window had no idea.

She was still trying to figure out the Scholar's strange behavior
when Bryon sauntered by a few moments later.

"What's up?" he asked as he threw himself down beside her, one
arm draped negligently behind her shoulders.

"Lapus doesn't want to make me a woman."

A dangerous glint surfaced in Bryon's eyes and his expression hardened. "He doesn't what?" he asked, his voice stony.

"I think," said Crystal seriously, making an honest effort to get to
the root of the question, "that it's a philosophical problem."

Bryon's face relaxed as he realized that Crystal had no idea of the
double meaning of what she'd said. Such innocence was rare around
the court, he wasn't used to it. He shook his head and took himself
sternly to task for even momentarily allowing himself to consider that

Crystal and that skinny Scholar with no looks and less personality would . . .

"Forget philosophy, Crystal." He brushed a strand of hair from her cheek and made his voice a caress. "In my eyes you're a woman already."

She turned from his touch, not understanding why she felt cheated when his hand dropped. She suddenly didn't feel like pursuing the question further, for a strong suspicion said Bryon had a great deal to do with her recent restlessness.

"They tell me you'll be leaving soon."

"Within the hour. Father is sending me around the province to help rally the men."

"Will you be back?"

"No, I'll join the army in Hale. Will you miss me?"

"Of course, I'll miss you," Crystal said more snappishly than she'd intended. "You're my friend."

"Ah, friend," Bryon's eyes twinkled. "A sad word that, when you're hoping for more."

"More?"

His arm tightened around her shoulders and drew her close. With his other hand he cupped her chin and gently forced her head up. Taking an incredible chance, he held her eyes with his, but the green fires were banked and he saw only a reflection of himself.

Confused, Crystal tried to straighten out the mess Bryon was making of her emotions. She had spent the last six years with the centaurs learning to be a wizard while Bryon, growing from good-looking boy to handsome young man, had been getting an education of a different sort. Centaurs, being immortal, have no love, lust, or desire. Crystal might be able to move mountains, call up demons, and—hopefully—destroy the enemies of her people, but in this area she was totally unskilled. She didn't understand her reactions and she didn't like the feeling that things were out of her control.

She also didn't want Bryon to stop. Whatever it turned out he was doing . . .

She didn't understand that either.

Bryon had no intention of stopping: Their faces were inches apart and her breath moved against his mouth like a warm breeze. He drank in the feel of her, the smell of her, the touch of her.

"Your horse is ready, sir."

Crystal jumped back, trying to ignore that briefest touch of his lips on hers. Bryon, realizing the moment had been irrevocably shattered, grinned up at his father's footman and got jauntily to his feet.

"Look for me in Hale," he said and, planting a kiss on her palm, was gone.

Crystal stared down at her hand, the soft pressure of his mouth still clinging to the skin.

"We were children together," she said to the empty passageway. "He treats me like a whole person, not as just a wizard or a princess. He is my friend." But she sat until dusk hid her in shadow, considering it.


The Horn carriers had been on their way for three days when Kraydak moved against them. While the truncated court sat at dinner, all the windows in the hall crashed open. The winds roared around the room, causing the lamps and candles to sputter and flicker and the men and women of the court to grab at everything not fastened down.

Crystal leaped to her feet and called the winds to order. They flew to her side and buffeted her about in their embrace. One at a time, she gentled them, heard their messages, and then sent them back out into the night.

When the last of the winds had left, Crystal looked up to see the court regarding her with awe—all except the Duke of Belkar who was dusting off a crusty roll which had been blown to the floor.

"What is it, child?" Mikhail asked, his heart wrung by the expression on his stepdaughter's face. All the recently developed signs of humanity had fled and the wizard looked bleak and cold.

"Kraydak is marshaling great power. He will strike at the Messengers tonight."

"Now?" asked Tayer. "During dinner?"

Humanity returned for an instant and Crystal raised a silver eyebrow in her mother's direction.

"But you haven't even finished your soup. You can't just run out in the middle of dinner. What will people think? No . . ." Tayer blushed suddenly and dropped her head in her hands. "I'm sorry. Do what you have to."

"Is there anything we can do to help?" Mikhail asked, laying a warm hand on the shoulder of his distraught wife.

"No." Crystal shook her head. "What I do tonight, I must do alone. But first thing in the morning, someone had better check . . ."

Tayer seemed to draw strength from Mikhail's touch. "You can stop him," she said firmly, raising her head and looking her daughter in the eye. "You can stop him."

"I can only try, Mother." She'd dreaded the thought of this night and now it had come. The first test. And what hope was there for the future should she fail? She forced herself to walk calmly from the room.

As the door closed behind her the buzz of conversation began again, almost as if it had been switched on by her leaving.

Tayer rose to follow. Mikhail gently guided her back into her seat.

"I could at least walk her to her room," Tayer protested, but without pulling away.

"I don't think she wants you to." He could offer little comfort in a room filled with their subjects so he merely held tightly to her hands. "You said she could stop him, now believe it."

Tayer sighed. "I feel," she said suddenly, "like a chicken trying to mother a duck, frantically trying to keep my child out of the water."

Crystal took the steps to her tower room two at a time. She yanked open the door, flung herself into the room, and rocked to a halt at the sight of her maid.

"Is dinner over so soon, milady?" the girl asked, stepping forward. Then she saw the expression on Crystal's face, and her own paled.

*"Anna, child, this will not be an easy job,"* the queen herself had said, *"but the princess must be made aware of her position. No matter what she does, stay with her."* Wanting nothing more than to retreat from the light that blazed in the princess' eyes, Anna swallowed once and clung to duty. "Shall . . . shall I take your hair down now?"

Startled, Crystal's hand flew to her hair, then she shook herself, as though to free the wizard from the entanglements of the princess. "You must go," she said, moving away from the door. "I have work to do."

Anna stood her ground. "I'm sorry, milady, but your mother, the queen . . ."

"Is not here."

". . . gave me very precise instructions," the maid finished, obviously intending to obey them to the letter.

"She instructed you to serve me?"

"Yes, milady."

"You can serve me best by leaving."

"I don't think, milady . . ."

Muttering beneath her breath in a language that had not been spoken for centuries, Crystal abandoned her attempt to be reasonable, shoved the frightened but determined servant out into the hall, threatened her with a dire fate should she return before dawn, and slammed the door on her protests.

Then she paused. Why hadn't she reinforced her commands with power? The small fraction needed to control the girl would not have been missed from the night's work and the result would have been much faster than arguing. In the back of her mind, where usually only the centaurs spoke, the memory of her mother's voice spanned the years, instructing a tiny girl-child in the rights of those who served. Uneasily, she slammed the lesson back into the past. She must be only wizard now; divided, she could not hope to win.

With a wave of her hand, the lamps went out and a light flared near the center of the room. A small copper brazier cradled a green flame which danced and beckoned.

The winds raced round the tower and the sounds they made as they wove about each other all said, "Hurry!"

Crystal moved forward and her elaborate dress dropped to the floor with a rustle of silk. She stepped free and into the plain white gown that had risen to meet her. Pins showered to the floor as her hair danced out of complicated braids and flowed down her back. Another two steps brought her to the brazier, but as she was about to sit, she paused, turned, and threw a fine web of power across the door. She didn't trust her mother, and certain others, to stay away. Tucking the gown between her legs, she sank to the floor.

"Hurry!" wailed the winds.

She wiped sweaty palms on her thighs. She had to be in four places at once and she had to defeat a man who had been honing his powers for several dozen lifetimes while she'd had only six short years.

Finally, she looked into the flame.

The first Messenger woke to a sudden weight on his chest. He opened his eyes and the largest crow he'd ever seen cocked its head, dug its talons into his leather vest, and glared at him balefully with a yellow eye. For a moment he thought he was dreaming and then one of those talons ripped through to his chest. The pain was real.

With a startled cry, he flung himself to the side as the wicked beak stabbed for his eyes.

His movement dislodged the bird and with strong beats of its wings it took to the air. The Messenger almost gagged on the carnal odors carried on the down-draft. He'd rolled away from his sword and the bird nearly took off his hand when he tried to reach for it. His fire had turned to embers and so, when he saw it, did his hopes of driving the creature away with flame.

The bird dove again and again and the Messenger soon bled from a number of small wounds. Only by blocking with a saddlebag had he managed to keep it from anything vital. He knew his luck, and the saddlebag, couldn't hold out much longer. He was winded, fighting for each breath, and the pain and loss of blood were weakening him.

The creature seemed to be taking a malicious delight in his torment.

And then it happened as he knew it would. He faltered, his guard dropped, and the bird moved in for the kill.

He braced himself for the blow, but it never came. A great white body hurtled into him, throwing him to the ground. The crow shrieked in rage, the first sound it had made, and turned to face the intruder.

Both Messenger and bird stared in astonishment at the great white owl that paced the ground between them. Its talons were over six inches long and its wing-span covered more than ten feet. It looked the young man up and down and then, satisfied with what it saw, it launched itself at the crow, its eyes burning with green fires.

The crow was large and its evil purpose strong, but it knew when it was defeated. There was only one thing left—escape.

With long, powerful strokes of its mighty wings, the owl took to the air and quickly climbed above its fleeing prey. Then, with talons extended and gleaming in the moonlight, it folded back its wings and struck.

The two birds hit the ground with an audible thud. Holding the crow securely under one massive foot, the owl bent its head to feed.


A persistent tickle disturbed the sleep of the second Messenger. Tiny balls were being rolled across his face. No matter how many he batted away, more kept coming. Finally he dragged himself up out of slumber to deal with it.

To find the tiny balls were trickles of dirt and the ground below him was giving way. He was sinking, being swallowed by the earth!

Successfully fighting panic, he got his hands beneath him and tried to sit up. The movement made him sink faster. He tried to lift his legs and found he couldn't.

He lay in a Messenger-shaped trench, one foot, two feet, four feet, six feet deep, flat on his back and looking up at the stars. He did the only thing left to do—he stopped fighting the panic and screamed.

And then the walls fell in.

The earth rolled quickly down to cover him. The bonds that had held him were gone, but that did little good as the world sat on his chest, crushing the breath out of him. Worst of all, he could no longer scream.

His lungs were crying out for air and stars were exploding behind his eyes when he felt the movement at his back. A hundred tiny fingers touched him and moved on. He remembered all the small and slimy things that lived in dirt and began to tremble with terror. Was being buried alive not enough?

He felt a firmer touch.

And then another.

Something grabbed at him and held.

The earth rolled back and he was lifted, gasping and choking, into the night air. He finally came to rest cradled high off the ground in the branches of a full grown silver birch.

The third Messenger was caught in a dream. She was running. At first the way was easy and she covered the ground in long loping strides, but then the path began to climb and her pace slowed. Soon she had to use her hands to scrabble up and over mounds of rock strewn across a shattered hillside.

It was then she became aware that she was being chased. And her pursuers were moving much faster than she.

In the shifting shadows of night, the long, broken path to the top of the hill was doubly treacherous. A misstep, a fall, could mean death.

Not far behind her, something bayed. A dog . . . or worse.

One torturous step at a time, she struggled toward the summit. Her hands and knees became cut and abraded by the sharp edges of rock and her feet were bruised by the shifting masses of stone. Her thighs trembled as she forced them to carry her over one more ledge. And one more.

She was almost to the summit when the baying began in earnest. They were on the scent, her scent, and now the chase would truly begin. With desperate haste she covered the last few yards, but not without cost, for a rock which had seemed solid rolled suddenly and crushed her hand. Whimpering with pain, she pried up the rock and dragged the damaged hand free, leaving an ugly smear of blood on the stone.

Her mangled hand tucked in her belt, she crested the hill and turned, breathing heavily, to look back the way she had come.

Half a dozen animals—possibly dogs, but she doubted it—long-legged and lean with narrow heads and glowing eyes, were just reaching the bottom of the hill. Not very far behind them rode a red-cloaked man on a pale horse. Lord Death, true son of the Mother, the Huntsman who escorted the unwilling dead back to Her arms.

The Messenger knew a terrible fear. She wasn't dead. Why did Death hunt her?

The beasts started up the hill.

She turned and ran. In the distance was a dark line of trees. If she could make the forest, she might stand a chance. She ran as she'd never run before, ran until the soles of her boots were worn through and she left a bloody trail of footprints behind her. Until the stitch in her side was a pain too great to breathe through. Until the bitter iron taste of blood filled her mouth. Sweat ran into her eyes and her wounds and they burned.

Behind, but getting rapidly closer, came the baying of the Huntsman's hounds.

She kept her eyes locked on the trees ahead, but she knew she wouldn't make it. The echoing hoofbeats of a steel-shod horse sounded above the cries of the beasts.

And then, over the pounding of her life in her ears, she heard another sound. Hoofbeats, but unshod and from the right. She risked a glance over her shoulder.

Gaining quickly, but only marginally closer than the hounds, came a white unicorn with silver hoofs and horn. Its nostrils were flared and its eyes flashed green fire.

Her eyes drawn from the path, the Messenger stumbled and fell. As she got to her feet, the unicorn reached her side.

"Get on!" it commanded.

"Wha . . ."

"GET ON!" A flashing hoof neatly crushed the skull of the fore-most hound.

The messenger grabbed a handful of silky mane and dragged her-self awkwardly up on the broad back. She was barely seated when the unicorn leaped forward, out of the range of the rest of the pack, and landed galloping. The trees which had seemed so far away were reached in seconds. She closed her eyes and held on tightly as her mystical mount wove among them without losing speed or breaking stride. Suddenly a thought struck her, almost causing her to lose her balance.

"I'm not a virgin!" she wailed.

"That's hardly my fault," the unicorn muttered in reply . . . or it might have just been the wind of their passing.

Abruptly they were out of the trees and then, horrifyingly, they were out of ground. A horse could not have stopped in time, but the unicorn reared and managed to halt on the edge of the cliff. They both looked down.

Many miles below, clouds scuttled about like sheep, herded by a wind they were too far away to feel. They could not see the ground. About thirty feet out from the edge, perched on a marble pillar that tapered into the depths, was the home of the Duke of Aliston, the Mes-senger's destination.

The unicorn backed away from the edge. "Hang on," it warned. Powerful muscles bunched and it launched itself forward.

And screamed shrilly as razor sharp teeth tore into a hind leg.

They landed safely, although three legged, and turned to face back over the gap. The pale horse stood at the precipice, the hounds winding about its legs. With a toss of his head, the rider dropped his hood. His red-gold hair shone dully in the moonlight but his blue eyes and smile blazed as he lifted his hand in salute.

The Messenger awoke to find herself staring up at familiar stars
with a crushed hand and the knowledge that had she died in the dream,
she would be dead indeed.


A cold and driving rain woke the fourth Messenger. He'd camped in a
small hollow on a treeless plain and had no protection from the wet.
Huddled miserably in his bedroll, he wondered where the storm had
come from for it had been a clear, moonlit night when he'd gone to
sleep.

The rain fell harder. Soon he was soaked and shaking uncontrollably. It was far, far too cold for a spring night so close to summer. The
rain seemed to leech the warmth from his body. He'd lost all feeling in
his hands and feet when the wind began to blow. It whipped the sheets
of rain viciously about, giving him blessed moments of dryness. Its
touch carried the promise of golden sunshine and summer's warmth
and the scent of trees, and grass, and forest loam.

Up above, the massive black storm clouds were losing their battle
with the winds. They were thinning, being forced apart. Here and
there, through sections grown tattered, a star could be seen.

Finally, the rain stopped and the young man lifted his dripping face
to the sky. The last thing he saw was the dazzling blue of the lightning
bolt as it arced down from the clouds. He didn't see those clouds break
up and drift away as harmless vapor. Nor did he see the moon come
out and bathe the land in silver light. He was dead.

For a time he lay as he had fallen, one arm flung up to stop the blow,
his clothes gently steaming from the heat; then the ground beneath him
began to crumble away as he was welcomed back into the body of the
Mother. Gently, the earth enfolded him and covered him against the
cold. Soon, all that could be seen was a grass-free patch of dirt.

Moments later the patch began to tremble, clots of earth danced
and tumbled about. No less majestic than the moon itself, a birch tree
rose to mark the young man's grave. Its trunk was a silver headstone
and its leaves sang dirges with the wind. From out of the cloudless sky

swooped a giant white owl. It plucked the War Horn from the Messenger's gear and headed north to Lorn.

At dawn, Tayer and Mikhail met Lapus at Crystal's door.

"Majesties," he said, bowing himself out of their way. "My anxiety for the princess made it impossible for me to sleep. If I can be of assistance . . ."

"Stay if you wish, Scholar," Tayer replied, worry making her voice sharp. "Mikhail, open the door."

Mikhail, who had seen Lapus trying to open the door without success as they approached, shot the Scholar a suspicious glance when the latch lifted easily in his hand.

"Oh, Crystal!" Tayer rushed forward and clasped the limp body of her daughter in her arms. "Mikhail, she's been hurt."

A rust red patch of dried blood stained the white gown and pasted it to Crystal's left calf.

Mikhail knelt, eased the fabric away, and inspected the wound. New pink skin had already formed over what appeared to be an ugly bite.

"It's not bad." But he carefully did not let Tayer see the damage, for it certainly looked as if it had been bad, whether it was now or not. "It's already nearly healed."

Crystal's eyes fluttered and opened; the green so washed out that they appeared a pale gold. She gazed around, unsure of where she rested.

"Mother?" Her voice quavered, sounding very tired and very young.

"I'm here." Tayer stroked the silver hair back from Crystal's face and with a little cry Crystal buried her head against the warm security of her mother's breast. She could take no comfort in duty and responsibility for she had failed.

"I couldn't save the last one, Mother. I was spread too thin. I wasn't strong enough. He died and I couldn't stop it." She sounded very close to tears.

"Hush," Tayer softly kissed the top of Crystal's head. "I'm sure you did your best."

"My best wasn't good enough." She closed her eyes and the face of the fourth Messenger looked back at her from the inside of her lids. Later perhaps she would mourn him, but now she was frightened. Kraydak had allowed her only a glimpse of his power, but that glimpse let her know she would have been unable to save any of the Messengers had he truly wanted all four dead. He'd been playing with her. If she was her world's only hope, then it appeared they had no hope at all. Just for that moment, she wished she'd not been so thoroughly trained and could give up before she had to face him again.

"So one War Horn will not be delivered." Lapus kept his voice carefully neutral.

Crystal's eyes opened and a green ember stirred in their depths as she glared up at the Scholar. "All the War Horns will be delivered," she told him, struggling to rise. "That, at least, I did." She put out a hand to steady herself and knocked over the copper brazier. Soft gray ash fell to the floor.

Mikhail offered his arm and Crystal pulled herself to her feet. She staggered and only Tayer's grasp about her waist prevented her from falling.

"You'll feel better after a little breakfast," Tayer reassured her.

Crystal brushed several black feathers off the front of her gown. "No, thank you, Mother, I've eaten."


In the old capital of Melac, now the heart of a cruel and corrupt Empire, a blue light flashed from the top of the highest tower and the folk who saw it quailed. Within the upper chamber, Kraydak sat and considered the night's work, hands steepled beneath his chin and blue eyes thoughtful.

"This wizard-child is not as powerful as I feared she might be," he said at last to the ancient skull that sat on the table before him.

The skull, once a king, made no reply.

"Neither," he added, rubbing a finger over the yellow bone, "is she an unworthy foe." She had used only as much power as she needed to defeat him except . . . At the end he had given her a glimpse of what he could do. She had not met it in kind although he was as certain, as only five thousand years of existence could make a man, that she held more power than she'd let him see.

"Perhaps she is wise." He smiled, his teeth very white even in the red-gold glow that lit the room. "The longer she holds my interest, the longer I will let her live."

On an afternoon when the sunlight spread over the circle of trees like a golden blanket and the breezes brought the promise of summer, Tayer and Mikhail said farewell to the Sacred Grove.

They stood quietly, letting the peace of the Grove wipe away the darkness that had wrapped about them these last few weeks and touch them with a gentle healing. They had no need to speak, words were so clumsy when a look, a smile, or a touch could say all that was necessary.

As the shadows started to lengthen, they clasped hands and headed back to the horses and the war.

# ELEVEN

In the days when wizards were common and not yet too powerful, the War Horns of Ardhan had been enchanted. They weren't the War Horns of Ardhan then, for this was before Ardhan existed as a kingdom, but the enchantment was strong enough to last through the Doom of the Wizards when the ancient world was ripped asunder, making the War Horns one of the great treasures of the resettlement. When raised in answer to a summons from the crown, the call of the Horns would sound in every corner of the kingdom.

As soon as Crystal was certain all the War Horns had been safely delivered, the queen walked out to the center of the "meadow-that-had-been-the-palace" and handed the kneeling Duke of Belkar his Horn. The entire town's population, massed about the edges of the meadow, held its breath as he lifted the ancient Horn to his lips and blew.

The note rose piercingly clear and hung in the air. It got into the blood and bones of the people and hung there. "To war!" it called, and the men and women who moved toward the gathering places moved a little faster.

Cei, then Lorn, then Hale, then Aliston; from the corners of the kingdom all the lords answered the call save Riven.

"He travels very slowly," Mikhail reminded Tayer as they made their way in procession back to Belkar's townhouse, "and is not likely to answer until he's at Riven Seat and has returned his family to the arms of the Mother."

What young Riven thought, as he moved slowly across the land with his preserved dead and his grief, he let no one know. But after the five Horns sounded, he drew even deeper into himself.

The man with the red-gold hair and the brittle blue eyes stood listening within his tower and when it became clear that the sixth note would not be heard, he laughed. Calling a gray-robed Scholar to him, he began to make plans.

"It's probably still not too late to go to Kraydak and surrender," Lapus said quietly as he and Crystal walked with the rest of the court through the streets. His tone was so matter-of-fact he might have been discussing the raisin buns they'd had for breakfast.

Crystal stopped dead and a minor court official stepped on the train of her gown. She didn't hear his muttered and fervent apologies, for Lapus had kept walking and she had to hurry to catch up. The minor official, thankful he wasn't to be turned into something unpleasant, left the procession at the earliest opportunity.

"I could what?" she demanded of the Scholar when she stood beside him again.

"Kraydak would then rule Ardhan, of course, but it would avert the war and save many lives."

"It wouldn't avert anything. They'd fight without me."

"I merely suggested an alternative."

"Alternative!" Crystal snorted. The day was hot, the ceremonial robes were heavy and she wanted a cold drink. "Lapus, you say some really stupid things sometimes."


On a hot summer day the court—the queen, her consort, their attendants, the Duke of Belkar, his attendants, the Elite, the Palace Guard, supply wagons, one Scholar, and the wizard—and seven hundred and forty-one soldiers in the newly formed Ardhan army gathered together to set out for Hale.

"Mother, save us," Crystal whistled softly as she cantered up to the head of the march with Lapus. "They're bringing everything but the scullery sink."

"Look again, milady. There, on that large wagon . . ."

Crystal looked where Lapus pointed and her eyes widened in astonishment. Touching her heels lightly to the sides of her horse, she rode the length of the column to where the queen stood, going over a lengthy list with someone Crystal assumed was the Quartermaster of the March.

"Mother," she called. "Is all this really necessary? We go to war, not off on the grand tour."

Tayer was tired and irritable. Most of the bureaucracy had died in the palace and although the new staff did their best, they had no experience in handling a move of this size. Besides Tayer and Mikhail, only six of the eight surviving upper servants had even seen a grand tour. No one since the time of the Lady had moved the court to war. Work the queen would normally delegate to someone else, she had to do herself.

"Yes," she snapped, "it is all really necessary. You may be able to conjure food and shelter out of thin air and the Elite may be ready to travel for days on journey bread and water, the rest of us mere mortals cannot."

Crystal jerked back in the saddle. She hadn't thought her gentle mother capable of that tone of voice.

"But we'll travel so slowly . . ."

"Kraydak has waited for you for hundreds of years, I doubt he'll care about a few more weeks." Then she turned back to the lists, clearly dismissing her daughter.

Sighing, Crystal turned her horse, about to head back to her place in line, when she noticed Mikhail standing and staring up into the branches of a large oak. Curious, for her stepfather wore the plain gray uniform of the Elite and his troops were some distance away from where he stood, she moved toward him.

"What do you make of those," he asked as she reined in. He pointed up at three huge crows perched in the tree watching the departure preparations with beady eyes.

"Kraydak's creatures," Crystal told him without hesitation. The carrion stench from them was so strong she wondered it didn't trouble the tree. She took the reins in one hand and covered her nose with the other. "He's probably using their eyes."

"We'll see about that," Mikhail rumbled. He waved three archers out of the ranks and they trotted over to his side.

"Do you see those birds?" he asked them.

They did.

"Do you think you can hit them."

The eldest of the three stared at Mikhail in disbelief. "Meaning no disrespect, milord, but we could hardly miss if we threw the arrows by hand."

Mikhail grinned and stepped out of their way. "Be my guest."

The three strung their bows; each put an arrow to the string, and let fly. The arrows traveled about three feet and then burst into flames so intense that they fell to the ground as a light shower of ash.

"Again," Mikhail commanded.

The same thing happened.

The archers stood shuffling their feet nervously. They didn't like fighting wizardry, especially when it was so obvious that they couldn't fight it. As one, their lips moved in a brief prayer to the Mother and they turned to stare at Crystal. Easily readable on their faces was the memory of the words she'd spoken to the assembled army the night before: "Remember, you won't be fighting the wizard, I will."

Crystal moved her horse forward until she sat almost directly under the tree, never taking her eyes off the crows. They stared back, three triangular heads turned to one side so they could each watch her with a bilious yellow eye.

"One chance, Kraydak" she called, squaring her shoulders and lifting her chin defiantly. She was acutely conscious of being observed by Mikhail and the three archers. "Recall your servants or lose them."

"Caw," replied a crow derisively.

"If that's the way you want it," Crystal said and her eyes began to glow, "then burn."

For a very little while nothing happened—the wizard stared at the birds, the birds stared at the wizard—then suddenly all three crows ignited and disappeared within sheets of flame.

One of the archers cheered as Kraydak's spies were reduced to greasy smears on the tree branch.

"Now that's more like it," Mikhail laughed, slapping Crystal's leg affectionately. "Well done." He coughed and waved his hand about to clear the noxious smoke, heavy with the smell of burned feathers and cooked crow. "We'd better get out of this stuff though, if we want to be in any shape to travel."

Crystal rode back to the head of the column in a much better frame of mind. She'd easily broken through the protective spells that Kraydak had wrapped around the crows. This was what she was meant to do, what she had been trained for. She would have been even happier had she thought Kraydak cared.

The archers returned to their place and told their mates of how the princess had let that murdering wizard know who ruled in Ardhan. The story spread and grew, becoming less accurate but more morale-boosting with every telling.

When the army finally got underway, it traveled as slowly as Crystal had feared. The queen, Mikhail, and the Duke of Belkar, accompanied by their standard-bearers, rode in front. Crystal and Lapus followed, the former letting her mind wander, the latter watching her expressions from the concealment of his cowl. And then came the remnants of the Palace Guard and the surviving Elite, both already recruiting from the body of the army. And then the army of Ardhan, cavalry leading infantry—an order the infantry heartily wished reversed, horses being horses. And then the wagons. And then, behind them all, a crow. Who looked as bored as Crystal felt.

The company kept to the King's Road between Belkar and Hale. It was not the most direct route, but it was the easiest.

"After all," as Crystal said with quiet sarcasm to Lapus, "there are the wagons to consider."

The first night, when they camped, the Quartermaster of the March escorted Crystal to her tent. He ignored her protests when she saw its size, and held open the flap for her to enter.

A curtain divided the tent into two parts. The outer section had been set up as a sitting room and furnished with several ornate pieces of furniture. Crystal recognized the large divan with the clawed feet as coming from the Duke of Belkar's townhouse. With a sigh she lifted the curtain and froze. In one corner of the second room was her bed from the townhouse with a fresh change of clothes laid out on the counterpane. In the other was a steaming bath smelling faintly of lilies of the valley, and waiting beside the bath was her maid.

The girl dropped a brief curtsy and managed not to giggle at Crystal's expression.

"Mother!" Crystal protested, barging into the queen's tent after a very unprincesslike dash across the camp. "No one takes their maid to war!"

"Queens and princesses do," Tayer told her calmly. And that was the end of that.

"As long as we're dragging the tub along with us, I suppose I might as well bathe in it. And actually," Crystal admitted to Lapus as they traveled, "I'm even getting used to the maid."

Lapus almost smiled. "They may make a princess of you yet."

"No." Crystal's mouth set in a hard line and a green tight flared in the depths of her eyes. "I am a wizard. I have to be."

"Then you had best learn to be both because, as you well know, you are also the only heir to the throne."

And Lapus told her the story—which she'd heard many times from the tutors she and Bryon had shared as children—of how the seven dukes and their people had come out of the North after the War between the Wizards and the Dragons destroyed their lands. They had settled in the land that would become Ardhan. Quarrels had erupted, and holding went to war against holding, duke against duke. When much of the land had been made waste and many people had been killed, the dukes came to their senses and were horrified at what they'd done. They cast lots and one among them was set up as king over them all, to be a judge, an impartial arbitrator they could bring their quarrels to instead of solving them by the sword. Then the land was divided into six relatively equal provinces which were given the names of the six remaining dukes: Belkar, Cei, Lorn, Aliston, Hale, and Riven. The king gave his name to the land but he would claim no province as his own, all and none of the land was his. The dukes planned a town where each would have a house, a capital city with a palace from which the king could govern. Again they drew lots, this time to choose the province in which the King's Town would be located, and Belkar lost the draw. From that first king came all the Kings and Queens of Ardhan in an unbroken line. The Ducal Houses might branch, but the Royal House stayed true.

The Royal House was the glue that held Ardhan together. It was the country's focus, its stability, and Crystal was the last of the line.

"If I lose," she sighed, "it won't be a problem."

"But the prophecy says you may win," Lapus reminded her. "What then?"

What then, indeed? Would she be willing to give up her power and be a princess for her people's sake? Would she even be able to or would the ways of wizard and princess be fighting within her forever? The weapon the centaurs had forged had nothing of the princess about it; could she hope to win with her powers thus flawed? She had a lot to think about as the army plodded toward Hale.


As the heat of the water worked its magic on muscles stiff from another day in the saddle, Crystal let her head fall back against the edge of the tub and her eyes drift closed.

*Oh, you have quite definitely won this point. Mother,* she thought, languidly moving her hands through the scented liquid.

"Shall I wash your hair, Highness?"

Crystal managed a nod and then sighed with pleasure as strong hands lifted the sodden mass of silver hair, added soap, and began to massage her scalp. *For this,* she decided, *I would almost agree to be princess.* She gave herself totally over to the skilled ministrations of her maid and let her mind wander where it would.

Contented and relaxed, nearly asleep, she felt the fingers change their motion and the pressure against her head became almost a caress.

"Time to rinse."

With no more warning than that, her head was shoved below the surface of the water.

"What . . ." As bathwater sucked into her nose and mouth with her involuntary gasp of surprise, Crystal fought to remain calm. She didn't struggle; she continued the motion of her attacker, sinking down to the bottom of the tub and out from under those hands. Then she twisted and rose, eyes blazing, to face her enemy.

"Very good," said a voice not her maid's, yet issuing from her maid's mouth. The girl's brown eyes had turned a brilliant blue. "And very nice."

Crystal clamped down on her power, releasing it now would only hurt the girl. Realizing the direction of the second comment, she snatched up her robe and put it on, ignoring the fabric floating about her legs.

"Get out!" she commanded, dragging a sleeve across the water streaming from her nose.

"As you wish, milady." The girl bowed mockingly and turned to leave the tent.

"That's not what I meant and you know it. Get out of Anna!"

"Anna?" Kraydak walked the maid's body back to its position by the bath. "What a pretty name." He picked up the mirror that lay on the bed and studied the face he wore. "So is she. Pretty." Features blurred and she wasn't any longer. He turned to Crystal and a lift of now scraggly brows said clearly, *your move.*

Carefully, biting her lip in concentration, for she had neither the older wizard's training nor his years of experience, Crystal rebuilt what Kraydak had torn down. She knew she did exactly as he wished, that, for reasons of his own, he tested her, but she couldn't refuse the challenge and let Anna suffer. Better her pride take the blow than an innocent girl.

Kraydak merely watched in the mirror, his eyes amused. "Very good," he said again when she finished, and caused Anna's head to nod approvingly.

Crystal flushed with pleasure at the tone of warm praise and then was immediately appalled as she realized it. "What . . . what are you doing here?" she managed at last in a voice neither as forceful nor as self-assured as she would have wished.

"Oh, I just came to see how you were getting along." He smiled a dazzling smile with Anna's mouth. "To let you know I need not rely on messengers but can be at your side in an instant, turning friend to foe." He looked her over, eyes lingering on breast and hip, the curves pressing damply through the thin cotton of her robe. "Now that I've got a good look at you, however, a few other ways of passing the time come to mind. But alas . . ." Anna's hands fluttered along her body. ". . . I find myself woefully ill-equipped."

"Well, if things are so woeful where you are, maybe you'd better go back where you came from."

"Throw me out," he told her, spreading his arms in a gesture of surrender. "You can do it. I can feel the power you command."

Deceiver, the centaurs had named him. Lies, they said, fell from his lips in numbers too large to be counted. But this time, did he speak truth? Was he so far extended, his power spread so thin she could, if not defeat him, at least cast him forth? The temptation to find out was very great.

"No. If I throw you out, I'll destroy Anna, burn out her mind."

"So? You don't particularly like her. What difference would it make?"

"It would make me no better than you." Her chin went up and her eyes narrowed. "I won't stoop to your tactics to win."

"You won't win, child." His voice was stern. "You haven't got what it takes. Winning means sacrifice. You aren't even willing to sacrifice this . . . this . . . nonentity to get me out of your tent. You amuse me,

Crystal." Again his eyes stared through her robe. "You fascinate me. But you are no danger to me." He smiled one last time and the brilliant blue of his eyes began to darken. "Until the battlefield." Suddenly the eyes turned brown again and Anna collapsed to the carpet.

Some hours later, Anna woke with no memory of her subjugation. Although mortified by the thought, she was willing to believe she'd fainted. Thankful that the girl had not been hurt, Crystal was still more relieved that she wouldn't be spreading panicked tales of the enemy's assault throughout the army.

Crystal herself told no one of Kraydak's visit. When nothing could be done—and nothing could—why add to the weight of worry? She had a fair idea of the power it took to so manipulate another's body and while it frightened her—for it offered further proof of just how great a power was his to command—it reassured her as well. He was too canny to deplete his reserves again as the battle drew closer. A wizard did not survive as long as Kraydak had by taking foolish risks.

But even as she comforted herself with this, even as she breakfasted, mounted, and moved one day closer to Hale, she scanned the eyes of everyone she met, knowing they just might be a certain uniquely chilling shade of brilliant blue.


No cheering crowd lined the road, for only fools and madmen cheer a war, but stragglers joined them daily and those who stayed behind looked up from their work to watch them pass.

Crystal felt the young woman's eyes on her from the moment the girl became visible by the side of the road. The intensity of the stare drew a throbbing line of power between them. Slowly, as they rode closer, features began to develop; average height, slightly plump, with honey colored hair worn short and curly. The original bright colors of her clothes were faded with many washings and she was barefoot. She stood with her feet apart, holding her elbows in large capable hands. She ignored the rest of the march, never moving her gaze away from Crystal.

When Crystal was close enough, she threw herself into the heart of the green fires. And surprisingly, because she had an anchor those fires couldn't touch, she pulled herself out again.

Crystal received a kaleidoscopic vision of the young woman's life. Chickens figured prominently. Chickens and a man, with a square jaw, a broken nose, and black brows that drew a line straight across his forehead. He was holding a chick, still damp and helpless from the shell, holding it, protecting it. Then it was a child who had his father's brows but his mother's eyes. Then it was a spear.

The exchange took only a few seconds. Crystal wanted nothing to do with it, she was responsible for the whole faceless mass of them, wasn't that enough? But asked, she saw no way to refuse. She nodded once. The girl nodded as well, then spun on her bare heel and headed home across the fields.

"A princess does not stare at her subjects," Lapus informed her.

The mood shattered. Crystal tucked the black-browed man safely away in her memory and turned to the Scholar.

"You've been promoting the princess a lot lately," she said wearily. "Have you been talking to my mother?"

"The queen is anxious for you to do your duty."

"Don't tell me about my duty, Scholar," the wizard growled. "I spent six years learning it from better teachers than you'll ever be." She gripped the sides of her horse so tightly that it turned its head and snapped at her knee, knowing full well she was not asking it to change its pace.

"The princess is your duty as well."

"I'm tired of duty!" The cry was from neither the wizard nor the princess but from Crystal, who was seventeen and so full of duty that there was little room left for her to be just herself. She looked at Lapus in horror, not believing what she had said.

For a second the reflection of the wizard flickered in Lapus' eyes and pity took its place. But only for a second.

"For some of us," he said flatly, retreating into the depths of his cowl, "there is no choice."

"For some of us," Crystal repeated just as flatly.

Except for the sounds of hooves and leather and a thousand marching men, the next few miles passed in silence.

She did indeed have a lot to think about as the army wound through field and forest on its way to Hale, but not all of it was distressing. Bryon invaded her thoughts more often than she was willing to admit. And each time he did, she felt the path of her future widening. The centaurs would not have approved. A couple of times, and this puzzled her greatly, Bryon's cheerful grin was replaced by the scowling face of the young Duke of Riven.

"Riven doesn't even like me," she muttered to her horse's ears.

Her horse, very wisely, refused to become involved.

As the deformed little man in the blue and gold livery entered Kraydak's sanctuary, the screams stopped abruptly. He stood just inside the gold lined door and waited. Once the screaming ended, his master would not be long. He waited patiently, ignoring the soft, moist sounds coming from the inner room.

When Kraydak emerged, his blue silk tunic and wide flaring breeches were spotless, his red-gold curls tumbled softly about his face, and his generous mouth curved in a satiated smile. His left hand was red to the wrist but that was undoubtedly due to the bloody bundle of skin he carried. Behind him, on a low bench in the center of the inner room, lay what appeared to be a fresh side of beef with long golden hair.

The wizard tossed the bundle to his servant—who caught it awkwardly (the only way his twisted body allowed him to do anything)—and the blood disappeared from his hand.

"She lasted longer than most," he said approvingly as the heavy wooden door swung shut behind him.

The servant—whose name had been among the first things taken from him—clutched the bundle tightly, spattering the costly carpet with thickening globs of red, and arranged his features into what stood for an ingratiating smile.

"There is good news, milord."

Kraydak settled himself behind his desk and raised an eyebrow. The servant shuffled forward.

"Kirka has fallen, milord. The plague has done its work."

"Did you doubt that it would?" And the servant's twisted body convulsed in pain.

"No, milord!" The pain stopped and the servant straightened as much as he could, dampness spreading down the front of his breeches. "The young and the strong survived, just as you said. Their tongues have been removed and they are being marched to the mines of Halda."

"A long march from Kirka."

"Yes, milord."

"Unlikely more than a few will survive the march."

"Yes, milord."

"A pity. Still, there are always more slaves."

"Yes, milord."

"And you will join them if that skin hardens enough to crack before you get it tanned."

The servant glanced down at the bundle in his hand, which was indeed beginning to stiffen, and began to shuffle backward to the door. He was reaching for the handle when the wizard stopped him.

"You forgot to thank me," said Kraydak softly, "for the pain."

"Forgive me, milord!" Had he been able to rise from them, he would have fallen to his knees. "It was exquisite pain, milord. Thank you. Forgive me."

"This time." Kraydak smiled. "But always remember, I made you what you are today."

The servant had only dim memories of a time when he had been a strong and brave warrior, the captain of an army that had dared to oppose Kraydak's might, but he knew what his master told him was true—for his master always spoke Truth.

"Thank you, milord. I remember." And he scurried away.

Kraydak steepled his fingers together and sighed. Kirka had fallen like all the other cities and countries before it. So much for Kirka's vaunted healers. He bent over the table and made a brief notation, a small bet with himself on how many survivors of the plague would actually make it to Halda. Not that he really cared; all his hopes now rested on the wizard-child and the battle that approached in Ardhan.

"And what I shall do when that's over," he said to the air, "I have no idea." He had survived the Doom. He was the greatest wizard ever. Nothing could touch him. He was indestructible. He would live forever. He was very bored.

His thoughts strayed back to the inner room and the low stone bench. He smiled and his blue eyes blazed as he went back to play with what lay upon it.

The servant had been very wrong when he assumed that life stopped as the screaming did. His own experiences should have taught him otherwise. There were ways to prolong the torment indefinitely and for what Kraydak had in mind, skin would have only gotten in the way.

# TWELVE

The army camped outside the walls of Hale's Seat. The Royal Party alone, consisting as it did of over twenty people, was considered to be enough of a strain on the town's resources in a time of war.

The Duke of Hale, a small, neat man in his late thirties, rode out to meet them. He paid homage to his queen, greeted Mikhail as an old comrade—the two men were of an age and had fought together in the Border Raids years before—informed the Duke of Belkar that his son had ridden in three days before with two hundred men and was even now waiting for him in town, and stared in astonishment at Crystal.

A trick of the evening sun turned her skin to burnished gold and at the same time ignited her hair into silver flames that danced gracefully on the breezes chasing about her. Her eyes blazed and all the greens that the Mother had given to the world in the beginning spilled forth with the fight and clothed her in glory. She towered over the rest of the company and the very air around her sang with Power.

For a moment there was nothing human about her at all, her beauty was so much like the Mother's first children and so very little like Man. The Duke of Hale, who was reckoned to be a brave man, began to tremble.

And then, incredibly, one long-lashed lid dropped over a glowing eye in what was unmistakably a wink.

Hale started and found the silver-haired girl regarding him levelly, her eyes containing nothing more than the reflected glow of the sun.

When they fell in behind Tayer and Hale for the ride through town,

Mikhail raised a questioning eyebrow at his stepdaughter. It took no power to know what he asked.

"He had to be sure of me."

"All right." Mikhail could see the necessity of that. "But the other?"

Crystal shrugged. "I didn't want him to stay frightened."

"Well, he may not be frightened," laughter hovered at the edge of Mikhail's voice, "but you've certainly confused the poor man."

That night, Hale gave a great banquet in honor of the queen. Whether because he felt she should not do completely without the pomp of the grand tour she'd missed or because he felt his own people could use the entertainment so close to war, no one knew. And no one would have been so ungracious as to ask.

Not up to arguing with her maid, Crystal allowed herself to be primped, painted, and laced into an elaborate gown.

"You look like a princess tonight, milady," enthused the girl as she pinned an emerald spray into the scented and piled mass of Crystal's hair.

"Yes," Crystal sighed, studying herself in the glass, "I suppose I do." She was the symbol of the continuation of the Royal House in Ardhan. She felt like a symbol, like an icon, and not a bit like herself. The wizard was hidden by yards of ribbons and lace and the beauty which had made the Duke of Hale tremble could barely be seen beneath the glory of the presentation. Only her eyes were unchanged, but no one looked a princess in the eyes.

"I'm not enjoying this," she whispered to Mikhail as they walked in procession into Hale's Great Hall. "I feel like I'm wearing a mask."

"You look lovely," Mikhail told her proudly. "And you've made your mother very happy."

"But it isn't me." Everyone seemed to have the idea that being a wizard was like being a farmer, a collection of skills that you picked up or put aside as needed. It was actually more like the difference between a cow and a horse, Crystal decided. There were certain physical similarities but that was as far as it went. *I'm a horse dressed up as a cow,* she realized suddenly. *I can never be a princess, and even less can I be queen.* She winced at the thought of making that clear to her mother.

"Cheer up," chided Mikhail, assuming the wince came from discomfort at her finery. "And look at the bright side. Hale always lays a fine table and tonight he's feasting us royally."

Crystal smiled weakly at her stepfather's joke and settled down to have a miserable evening. Her plans were ruined when the food arrived and she discovered more than one type of wizardry was loose in the world. Her mouth watered. She was seated between Hale's wife Alaina and the Duke of Belkar and as neither of them seemed inclined to talk, she applied herself to the meal. Glancing up some time later—from her second pastry stuffed with raspberries and cream—she found Lady Hale staring at her.

"I beg your pardon," murmured the older woman in response to the question on Crystal's face. "It's just . . . you're not what I expected."

"Oh?"

Alaina blushed. "I always thought wizards would be grimmer, more awe inspiring, not so . . . so . . ."

"Princesslike?" Crystal asked from behind her ribbons and lace and jewels.

"Hungry."

Crystal looked down at the remains of her pastry, considered the enormous meal she'd just eaten, and burst out laughing. The laugh had nothing to do with either the wizard or the princess, and she felt better than she had since Bryon had left the palace.

Bryon, who'd refused a seat at the head table and was eating with his captains, picked the laugh out of the sounds of a hundred people eating and arguing and making merry, and grinned. If she could laugh again . . .

Lady Hale smiled shyly. "I hope you're not offended. I'd always pictured wizards as being more ascetic and less concerned with fleshly matters."

"It takes a lot of energy to be a wizard," Crystal admitted, deciding she liked this woman who had accepted her so easily, "but if this wizard doesn't develop more asceticism she's going to be very concerned with fleshly matters." With a sigh she laid her hand upon her stomach, the dress showed a new animosity in places where it had merely pinched before dinner. She examined the soft curve of Alaina's pregnancy with frank curiosity.

"Is that very uncomfortable?"

As Alaina began to blush again, Crystal realized she'd probably said something she shouldn't have. "I'm sorry," she exclaimed before Alaina could say anything. "It's just that I've never seen a pregnant woman before. At least not that I can remember," she added thoughtfully. "Children don't pay much attention to that sort of thing and centaurs are all male."

Alaina, who'd been very nervous upon learning of the seating arrangements for supper, was no longer afraid of the great and powerful wizard. The look on the wizard's face reminded her too much of her five-year-old son who forever asked about things he shouldn't. She answered the wizard as truthfully as she would have answered her son.

"Sometimes it's uncomfortable." One hand rested gently on the curve of her stomach. "In the end, though, it's worth it."

"May I?"

A slender hand hovered over Alaina's own. When she nodded, it drifted down and ever so tightly touched.

For a few seconds Crystal sat silent, sorting the sensations that flowed up through her fingertips. And then she smiled. It was a smile few were privileged to see, for it was neither human nor terrifying. It was the smile the Mother wore when She looked about her and marveled at the beauty She had created.

"So tiny and so perfect," Crystal whispered, and her voice was the wind of summer caressing the earth. Her eyes glowed so deeply green her pupils washed away in the radiance.

Alaina, caught up in the light, felt herself falling into the whirlpools of Crystal's power. But instead of pulling her down, they lifted her up and wrapped her in wonder. A smaller light added its bit to the glory and she realized, with a wave of joy, that she saw the life of her unborn child. When the light retreated and she was herself again, she wasn't surprised to find her cheeks wet with tears.

The slender hand lifted slowly away, the green fires died, and the mark of the other world faded from Crystal's face. Her smile became very human and a little sad.

"Thank you," she said.

"When you have children of your own," Alaina began, but Crystal stopped her.

"Wizards have no children," she said flatly. "It's the price of our power. Only the Mother's Youngest create life." They sat silently for a moment and the sound of Tayer's laughter floated down from the center of the table. Crystal visibly brightened. "But you may have just solved a problem."

Before Alaina could ask how, or even what problem, the Duke of Belkar leaped to his feet shaking his fist. It took her a heartstopping moment to realize he wasn't shaking it at her but across her at Mikhail. Apparently the two men were approaching the climax of a disagreement.

"If we're to win this war," roared the red-faced duke, "we must take it across the border to the enemy's land!" His voice filled the hall, causing the musicians to falter and fall silent, and most of the diners to turn and stare at him in astonishment.

"No!" Mikhail slammed a mighty hand down on the table, causing the cutlery, and more than a few people, to jump. "Make him come to us! Make him fight on our terms!"

"The only way he'll fight on our terms is if we take those terms and shove them down his throat! We've got to goad him forth from his hole!"

"Let him wear himself out on the mountains and not on the bodies of our men!" Mikhail was on his feet now as well.

"Excuse me . . ."

"If we let him in, he'll be twice as hard to kick out! We can't let him set one foot on our land!"

"Let him run supplies across the mountains, not us!"

"Excuse me!"

"We'll be in and out so fast that supply lines won't matter!"

"What?! Are you crazy, our yeoman soldiers against his trained killers?"

"I said EXCUSE ME!" The air crackled with the force of Crystal's voice. Mikhail and Belkar stopped bellowing at each other and turned to stare at her.

"There's no need for this," she began reasonably, holding on to politeness for her mother's sake.

"Stay out of this, princess," growled Belkar. "You said yourself we were to fight the best way we know how." He glared at Mikhail. "And my way is best!"

"This isn't your concern, Crystal," Mikhail told her. "We have a decision to make just as soon as Belkar sees reason."

A booming roar rocked the room, the candles and lamps flared with green fire, and a sudden wind threw the combatants back into their seats.

"There is nothing to decide." Crystal rose to her feet, her eyes blazing no less furiously than the candles and lamps. It was just as she'd feared, whenever they made her be the princess they forgot about the wizard, and, worse yet, she began to forget as well. "Have you forgotten the palace? Squashed flat! And he wasn't even in the same country. He could easily do it again. Here. Tonight."

Faces blanched.

"You will meet his armies on the Tage Plateau because that's how he has it set up. I will meet him when and where he chooses. You're nothing but game pieces to him, you and his army both, added to make our conflict more interesting." The room darkened until it was lit only by the fire in her eyes and the glow of her skin and hair. "And you'd better petition the Mother that he makes a mistake because that may be our only chance."

Then, turning to Lady Hale, she apologized for the disturbance and stalked out of the room.


"Crystal, I'd like to speak to you."

"I thought you might." Crystal slid over on the garden bench, giving her mother room to sit beside her. Gone were the ribbons and lace, the wizard was back.

"There was no need for that vulgar display at dinner."

"Yes, there was."

"Oh?" One beautifully arched chestnut eyebrow rose.

"People are forgetting this is a war of wizards."

"You were being ignored and you didn't like it."

"Well, yes:" Innate honesty forced Crystal to admit there was truth in that statement. "But they ignored the situation, too."

Tayer sighed. "Of course they did. We're all caught up in something we don't understand and have no control over. If Belkar and Mikhail argue, they think they're doing something."

"But they aren't!"

"Does it hurt to let them think so?" Tayer's voice was very quiet. "A little hope can make the difference sometimes."

"This time?"

"Who knows. And if the army, can take care of itself, that leaves you free to deal with Kraydak." Tayer gathered the stiff and unresponsive body of her daughter into her arms. Slowly, very slowly, Crystal relaxed. A breeze wandered in and tentatively ruffled her hair.

Crystal inhaled the scent of her mother's perfume and was transported, just for an instant, back to the days before the centaurs had come. Things had been so much simpler then. "I can't be what you want me to be, Mother," she said at last.

"I know," Tayer murmured. She'd known it for some time; the raw power blazing from Crystal's eyes that night had forced her to admit it. "I guess I'll have to start wanting what you are. But I don't want to lose my daughter."

Not even the darkness could hide Crystal's smile. "Never that." She returned the pressure of her mother's arms and for an instant it seemed as if their hearts beat in the same time and they were not two women but one. Then Tayer pulled gently away.

"I've got to get back. The queen can't vanish into the gardens for too long." She kissed Crystal on the forehead, and stood. "Oh. One more thing."

"Yes?"

"You keep the maid."

The wizard considered hot baths and clean clothes. "Yes, Mother."

Tayer had barely disappeared into the darkness when Bryon appeared out of it. He threw himself down on the bench and hooked his thumbs in his belt.

"Quite the trick you pulled this evening."

"Not you, too."

"I especially liked the way the lights went out. Must come in very handy when you need to impress the masses."

"And you're not impressed."

"You've always impressed me." He grinned in a way calculated to set maidenly hearts aflutter.

Crystal didn't appear to notice and certainly didn't flutter.

They sat for a while in silence, Crystal staring thoughtfully at nothing, Bryon—whose night sight was very good—staring appreciatively at Crystal.

"Lapus was right," she said at last.

"Oh?" A wealth of meaning lurked behind the word, for Bryon suddenly found himself very annoyed that Crystal had spent the last few weeks, no doubt pretty exclusively, in Lapus' company. That this bothered him, annoyed him even more.

Crystal continued, oblivious to the inner turmoil of her companion. "Do you know the worst thing Kraydak has done? He's taken away our choices."

"What choices?"

"All of them. Mother had to become queen. Ardhan had to go to war. I have to fight him. I have no choice in what I do and very little in how to do it. That's the whole problem."

"No," Bryon corrected, transferring some of the annoyance he felt at himself to her, "that's only part of the problem. You've got this strange idea that you have to do everything yourself."

She whirled around to glare at him.

"I do."

"You think that because you're the last of the wizards, Kraydak is your sole responsibility."

"He is."

"You can't and he isn't. One day you'll realize it and you'll have to ask for help."

"Ask who?" Crystal demanded. "You, perhaps?" Eyes beginning to smolder, she sprang to her feet. He had no right to lecture her like she was a child.

"Why not?" Ridiculously, he felt better now that Crystal was upset. He was back in control.

"There's nothing you could do. You couldn't fight him."

Bryon had to admit that she was right, he couldn't fight Kraydak and frankly had no intention of doing so.

"I was thinking of myself more in the line of moral support." He stood up with lazy ease. "I've got to get back to my men, but maybe you should consider it." He blew her a kiss and was gone.

Gone? She felt vaguely cheated. He hadn't once touched her.

"Consider it?" she shrieked toward the receding sounds of his footsteps. "I've forgotten it already!" Sparks leaped off the ends of hair flung about in frustration. She was one of the two most powerful beings alive, why was she constantly being thrown off balance by that smug, self-centered, overbearing, incredibly good-looking young man?

She danced aside as a blue bolt charred the marble bench and with a furious gesture flung a green one back along its path.

"Stop showing off," she snarled. "I know you can reach this far, but I've enough on my mind right now without you!" And then she stomped back into Hale's Seat because neither the wizard nor the princess could think of a way to follow Bryon without looking like a fool.


Kraydak considered the green bolt with some surprise. He hadn't been surprised in centuries and he savored the return of the sensation. He congratulated himself on not attempting to circumvent the prophecy. This was fun.

The bolt had exploded harmlessly against his tower, not even ruffling his defenses, but he was rather astonished that it had gotten that far. The wizard-child showed more strength in her thoughtless response to his prodding than she had at any other time.

For a moment, he contemplated paying her another visit, this time in the mind of her young admirer. His eyes glowed slightly as he dwelt on the likely result of that encounter. But no, he'd made his point and repeating it would be a useless waste of power especially as she was, after all, coming to him. His time would be better spent arranging a suitable welcome for her when she got close enough.

"Perhaps," he mused, rubbing the scorched mark on the stone, "this young man brings out the best in her." The corners of his mouth twisted up. "Or the beast." He wiped his fingers and reentered the tower. "Something to remember."

# Thirteen

The Duke of Riven stood on the battlements of his manor and looked north. His brow was drawn down in a scowl and his fingers worried a loose patch of mortar into dust. Somewhere to the north, there was a battle going on and he had chosen not to be in it.

It had been over a week since he had returned his family to the arms of the Mother. For over a week he had sat each night in his father's chair with the War Horn of Riven on his knees, not listening to the old men—his father's counselors—nor the young men—his friends—as they urged him to sound the Horn and ride to war. Even his steward—a solid gray-haired woman whom he thought had more sense—advised him to fight. They were all very anxious to ride into the arms of Lord Death, but he had no intention of allowing it. No intention of allowing more to die for a wizard whose face he couldn't seem to banish from his mind. He wondered how she'd felt when the Horn of Riven hadn't sounded. Betrayed? He hoped so.

He shivered. Riven Seat was high in the mountains and even in summer, the east wind whistling through Riven Pass was cold.

"Milord, dinner is ready if you would come in."

People were hesitant around him, as if afraid to touch his grief. They didn't know that he'd laid his grief in the pit with the bodies of his family which the wizard—the word was a curse in his thoughts—had preserved. All that he had left was a dull pain wrapped tightly around his soul.

Meals were somber times now. Looking out over the company from under heavy lids, Riven could almost see the gray pall that hung over the room. Hesitant glances were exchanged, conversations were held in a whisper or not at all. Mostly not at all. This, too, was the wizard's fault. In his father's day the hall had been filled with light and laughter, but she had killed his family and darkness had followed.

After dinner he sat in his father's chair, with the War Horn of Riven across his knees, and stared at the green eyes that gazed up at him from the fire.

"Milord? There's a Scholar here who wishes to see you."

"I don't want to see him."

"He says it's very important."

"I don't care."

"He says he brings a message from the wizard."

"What!" Riven leaped to his feet, the Horn falling to the flagstones unheeded. "She dares send someone here?" His cheeks were flushed and his eyes were unnaturally bright. "Oh, I'll listen to a messenger from the wizard, and when he's done I'll have a message or two he can take back with him. Send him in."

The Scholar was a small, thin man with sunken cheeks and eyes so deep-set they looked like they were hiding under the arching dome of his forehead. His hands fluttered constantly, birds, trapped in the ends of his sleeves.

"Milord," the Scholar began, then stopped, his eyes darting around the Great Hall, from person to person. "Milord, I have been instructed that this message is for your ears alone."

Riven waved his hand. "Out!" he commanded.

The men and women in the Hall looked at each other in astonishment and several murmured protests to their companions. Garments rustled as positions shifted, but no one left.

"You should not be alone with him," protested the steward, stepping forward.

"Why not?"

"Well, because . . ." She couldn't think of a convincing argument. And she really had no reason, just a feeling. "Because . . ."

"I've got my sword, haven't I?" He put his hand to the hilt. "If he tries anything, I'll kill him."

The Scholar wet his lips nervously. His grayish tongue looked like nothing so much as a large maggot.

"Now get out!"

With a helpless shrug, the steward surrendered and herded the others from the room. One or two tried to argue, but she silenced them with a glare and a gesture and, grumbling, they went. She paused at the door and looked back. Riven stood glaring at the Scholar, his lips drawn back in what was almost a snarl and yet, despite the appearance of frailty, she somehow knew that the Scholar was the more dangerous man. She sighed and closed the door. She could do nothing except keep a guard ready and breathe a quiet prayer to the Mother.

"Well?" demanded Riven when he heard the door close. "What does she have to say?"

"She, milord?"

"The wizard. I was told you have a message from the wizard."

"I do, milord." He wet his lips again. "But from the other wizard."

"The other wizard?" Riven repeated. "What the . . ." And then he understood.

"Wait, milord. Before you call your guards, you should listen to what he has to say."

Riven had never liked being told what he should do and he had come to like it even less during the short time he had been duke, for there were so many things a duke should do, but some note of power in the Scholar's thin voice stopped the call to his guards.

"I will not listen to treason," he protested weakly.

"Milord, the Great Kraydak does not counsel treason. He asks only that you continue to do what you have been doing."

"I haven't done anything."

"Milord understands exactly. The Great Kraydak asks only that you continue to do nothing. He agrees wholeheartedly with your decision."

It was nice to be agreed with for a change.

"After all, who is this woman that your people should die for her?"

Riven had often wondered that himself.

"She is responsible for the death of your family."

"Kraydak crushed the palace," Riven was forced to admit.

"But only to get to her," the Scholar said soothingly. "Does that not make her responsible?"

As Riven had said as much himself, he had to agree with the man.

"And so, why should you defend the woman who killed your family?" the Scholar continued reasonably. "This is a battle of wizards. Let the wizards fight."

Let the wizards fight. Riven had said that all along. "My people may force me to sound the Horn and ride to battle."

"Would they have forced your late father?"

No, they wouldn't have. Riven couldn't imagine the old duke being forced to do anything he didn't want to. "No," he said and his fingers curled into fists.

"Are you not the man your father was?"

"Of course I am!" Riven stepped forward, two bright spots of color on his cheeks. "What are you getting at?"

"Only that I had not thought you a worse duke than your father, milord."

"I'm not a worse duke!"

"Then prove it." The high-pitched voice of the Scholar had suddenly turned very cold. Caught up in his own heat, Riven didn't notice.

"How?"

"Enforce your will. You do not want to fight, so keep Riven Province from riding to war. Can you do that?" The voice was colder still and a strange light surfaced in the murky depths of the Scholar's eyes.

"Of course I can. I'm every bit as much the duke as my father was."

"Of course you are. And can you convince your people to resume trade with Melac?"

"As you say, they're my people. If I tell them to resume trade with Melac, they, will."

"And merchants will not be killed as they cross through Riven Pass?"

"You have my word."

"Very good." He was once again an ugly little Scholar with no sign he had been anything else. "You had better get some rest, milord, you look tired."

"Yes." Riven passed a trembling hand over his eyes. All of a sudden, a dull throbbing had begun behind each temple. "I'd better get some rest."

Some hours later, after falling immediately into a deep sleep the moment his head hit the pillow, the young duke was shaken roughly awake.

"Stop it," he muttered sleepily. "Go away."

The shaking continued, so, with a sigh, he rolled over. It was very dark in his room, but as his eyes grew accustomed to the lack of light he could make out two figures standing beside his bed.

"Well?" he asked petulantly, after a few moments of mutual staring.

The taller figure leaned over, a menacing shadow in full battle armor. "I'd like to have some words with you, my son."

"Father?" Riven clutched the blankets so tightly his fingers went white. "But you're with Lord Death!"

"And just who do you think this is?" asked the old duke, indicating the pleasant and disturbingly familiar looking young man standing beside him.

"Lord Death?" Riven's voice cracked on the second word.

The pleasant looking young man smiled—his teeth were very even and very white—and then turned to the old duke. "You have two minutes only," he said, and politely moved away.

"It's all the time I'll need," snarled the old duke glaring down at his son, "to deal with this traitor."

"But, Father, I . . ."

"Traitor to your country! Traitor to your name!"

"But I haven't done anything!" Clutching the blankets, he moved back against the headboard. He had seen this man buried his own height down in the body of the Mother. His heart slammed against his ribs and the blood pounded in his ears . . . he tried to swallow but the muscles refused to obey.

"And why not? The War Horn has been sent and all you can say is, 'I haven't done anything.' That much is obvious."

"She killed you!"

"No one killed me. I died. But Kraydak killed your mother and don't you ever forget that."

"This is a wizards' war!" Even she had said that. What could mere mortals do in a wizards' war? Better to keep his people here, safe, so no more would die.

"You want to be Kraydak's bond boy and watch your people go to feed his demons? Is that it?"

"No, I . . ." Riven's brow creased and he tried to remember just what the little Scholar had said.

"Well, that's what you've just agreed to." The old duke sighed. "If I'd known you were going to make such a mess of things, maybe I'd have tried harder to stay alive."

"It wouldn't have done any good," murmured a soft voice from the shadows. Both Rivens ignored it.

"You left me alone." The young man's voice was almost a wail. Fear faded beside the pain. Once again, he saw the healer gently closing his father's eyes. *"He chose, milord,"* she said. *"I could not save him."*

"So that's it. Maybe I thought you were old enough to take care of yourself. I guess I was wrong."

"You loved Mother and Maia more than you loved me! You died and left me alone!"

The dead man sighed again and spread his hands, as close to a helpless gesture as his son had ever seen him make. "Your mother was a part of me, I'd have been only half alive without her."

They stared at each other for a moment, the new duke and the old, both knowing that was as close to an apology as was likely to be spoken.

"And you aren't exactly alone, are you?" The steel was back in the old duke's voice. "You're responsible for an entire province. People depend on you."

"It's not the same." Riven's chin came up in a belligerent way that made him look very much like his sire.

"No, it isn't. Tough. You've a job to do; it was mine and now it's yours. I suggest you do it and stop crying over things that can't be changed."

"Time." Lord Death stepped forward.

"Just one more thing, milord." With a frown that held more weariness than anger, the old duke drew back his arm and struck his son hard across the face.

The force of the blow flung Riven almost out of bed and stars exploded behind his eyes. It took him a minute to realize that the continuing light was not inside his head. He opened his eyes and sat up.

The sun shone through and around the green brocade that covered the windows; morning. The room could not have been dark only seconds before. His father and Lord Death had not come to him in the night. It had been a dream, vivid and disturbing, but only a dream.

He lay back against his pillow as his valet came into the room and flung open the curtains. Golden light poured through the tiny panes of leaded glass, banishing shadows and gilding fear.

"A beautiful day today, milord. There's a fog on the heights, but it should burn off in a couple of hours." The valet turned to face the bed. "And what . . . milord!"

"What is it?" Riven inspected his immediate surroundings. Everything seemed to be in place. He could see no reason for the other man's shocked exclamation.

The valet silently handed him a mirror.

Across his cheek, in the exact shape of his father's hand, was a massive purple and green bruise.


"The pass has been filled?"

"We've just finished it, sir, but I still don't understand why we don't let the Melacians into the pass where we could ambush them."

"I gave my word they wouldn't be killed in the pass." Riven smiled.

"I gave no word that the pass would still be there when they came to use it." His horse fidgeted under him and he let it dance about before bringing it under control. "You're sure the Scholar sent no messages before he was killed?"

"None that we were aware of. If he used magical means . . ."

"No matter," Riven shrugged. "Kraydak will know of our plans soon enough."

"Then why not sound the Horn?"

"Why make it easy for him? You'd better get back to your men, we'll be leaving soon."

"Yes, sir."

Riven watched his captain ride away and decided to stay a moment longer on the hill overlooking Riven's Seat. A warm breeze blew slowly along the side of the mountain and it carried with it all the smells he wanted to remember when he was in the midst of battle.

"He loved you very much."

Riven glanced down at the pleasant looking young man—who was still disturbingly familiar. No need to ask who Lord Death referred to. "He has a funny way of showing it." The bruise had faded a little, but the teeth on that side still ached when he chewed.

"You needed to have some sense knocked into you." Lord Death waved a white hand at the army forming in the valley below. "It seems to have worked."

"Why did you let him come back?"

"Why not? You couldn't possibly understand my motives, Mortal, so you needn't try."

"For whatever reason then, thank you."

Lord Death smiled. And wasn't there.

Not until much later did Riven realize that Lord Death bore a startling resemblance to his mother.

# FOURTEEN

The crescent moon was barely visible over the tops of the trees, campfires had died to embers and, with the exception of the sentries patrolling the perimeters of the camp and the surgical pavilion, regrettably never quiet, the army of Ardhan slept. No one saw the manshaped shadow slipping from shelter to shelter. Even the Duke of Belkar's guard failed to see it as it passed almost close enough to touch. What was one more shadow amongst the shadows of the night. Unnoticed, the intruder moved around to the back of Belkar's tent.

After checking that he remained unobserved, the shadow slipped a knife from his sleeve, the blade carefully blackened to prevent a stray bit of light from giving him away. Slowly, quietly, he slit the canvas wall and then slid through the hole. Only a thin black line showed he had been there at all.

It was dark, but the shadow deftly threaded his way around the furniture and the scattered pieces of armor. He made his way without incident to the center of the tent where, by the dividing wall, there was a bed.

The occupant of the bed stirred, rolled over on his back, and began to snore. Loudly.

The shadow moved silently forward. He bent over, but it was too dark to see the features of the sleeper. Not that it mattered, the snoring with its particular cadence and its volume said, "Here lies the Duke of Belkar" as clearly as if it were full daylight.

Stepping back a pace, the shadow raised his knife and struck. A moist thud cut the snores off abruptly.

The shadow turned, arms spread wide as if to embrace someone or something. Then, struck by a brilliant beam of silver light, Lapus fell to his knees.

"No, not Kraydak," Crystal told him sadly. "Nor will it be. He lied when he said there would be a way out."

Lapus could barely see the young wizard through eyes squinted shut against the glare, but he sensed she wasn't alone. Behind her, where the light was not so bright stood . . . the Duke of Belkar? He twisted around until he could see the bed. Empty; except for his knife which had cut right through the thin mattress.

"Illusion," he said bitterly. "Lies."

"Not the first. All Kraydak offered you was more of the same; illusions and lies."

"No!" Lapus got to his feet. Two guards stepped forward, but Crystal waved them back. "He showed me. It was real!"

"What he offered may have been real, but he would never have given it to you. I suspect that even had you succeeded tonight he would've ignored you just as he's doing now."

"No," Lapus repeated, burying his head in his hands and collapsing back on the bed. "It couldn't have been a lie." Then his head lifted and his eyes opened wide, pupils dilated against the light. "He showed me Truth!" Suddenly, he clutched at his knife and dove across the tent.

He was on them so fast that Crystal had no time to react. Already upset by the confirmation of Lapus as Kraydak's tool, the attack shocked her into immobility. Had she been the Scholar's target, Kraydak would have won in that instant, but Lapus pushed her aside and headed straight for the duke. Where he was met by a guard. And a sword.

He peered down at the steel that stuck out of his chest and gave a soft sigh as it slid free. The knife dropped from nerveless fingers and with the other hand he touched the blood flowing from the wound—gently, as if afraid to disturb the flow.

"I wish," he said tenderly, staring up at Crystal with a hopeless desperation, "we could have . . ." And then he died.

Crystal knelt beside him, closed his eyes, and kissed him tightly on the forehead. Then she stood aside so the guards could remove the body.

"Why did he do it?" asked Belkar shaking his head as they carried Lapus from the tent. He had liked the Scholar, enjoyed arguing with him, respected his mind. He had hoped that Crystal's suspicions were unfounded. "What could Kraydak have shown him?"

"Just what Lapus said he did, I expect. Truth. Lapus told me once that Truth was the only master." Her hands stroked up and down her arms as if afraid to be still. "Kraydak took Lapus to the top of the tallest mountain and offered him all the knowledge of the world."

"Eh?" The duke was puzzled. "What mountain? Where?"

The tent flap had barely closed behind the guards and their burden when it opened to admit Mikhail. He jerked a thumb over his shoulder—he must have passed the body on its way out—raised an eyebrow and asked, "Lapus?"

Crystal nodded.

"What about the others?" Belkar demanded.

"Thanks to Crystal, we got them all. The dukes are safe."

"And the Scholars?" Crystal asked, although she knew the answer.

"Child," said Mikhail gently, enclosing her shoulder in a massive hand, "they were out to do murder for a man who wants to put the entire country to the sword." He moved his finger under her chin and lifted her head so she was forced to look at him. Her face was very pale and her eyes were dim. "You said yourself that once Kraydak held a mind the only sure release was death. They had to die. We had no choice."

Crystal scuffed her foot by the damp, red stain on Belkar's carpet. This was another choice that Kraydak had taken from them. She felt as though iron bands had been riveted about her chest. "He was my friend."

"And mine," said Belkar.

"We've all lost friends," Mikhail reminded her and then realized that, until this moment, Crystal had not. Lapus and young Bryon were the only two friends she had. Her power, her rank, and her beauty had kept other friendships from developing. He opened his arms and offered a father's comfort if the wizard cared to take it.

The wizard cared to, very much. With a strangled sob, Crystal hid in his embrace, and cried for Lapus, for all the others, and, just a little, for herself.

"What of our lads?" asked Belkar.

"Only one of them was hit, but he's pretty bad. The knife went up under his ribs. I doubt he'll make it."

Crystal pushed herself away from Mikhail's chest, wiping her cheeks dry with the flat of her hand. This was how she could erase the memory of Lapus lying dead at her feet. "I can save him," she said, giving one final sniff, and starting for the door.

"No." Mikhail swung around and blocked her way. "Kraydak must know his plan failed and may try something else tonight. You have to be ready. Remember what happened last time."

She rubbed her nose across her sleeve, looking absurdly young as she did so, and remembered.

After the first meeting between the Melac and the Ardhan armies—in which Kraydak had sent out an innocuous probe and Crystal had smashed it back at him with a strength that surprised them both— Crystal had gone to the surgical pavilion to help. The area was already protected from infections by a long and complicated weaving of power, but she wanted to do more. The surgeons directed her to a young man with a deep sword slash across the belly. His cut and torn guts were bulging from the wound, masking the rest of the internal damages. The surgeons wondered why he was still alive and they doubted he could hold on much longer.

Feeling slightly sick at the sight and the smell, Crystal placed her hands lightly on the soldier's body and began to hum. A green flame grew in her eyes, spilled over and ran down her arms into the boy on the stretcher. Before the astonished eyes of the surgeons and those patients near enough to see, the edges of the wound began to glow and close. The bulging mass of intestine, now miraculously clean and whole, tucked itself back where it belonged. Muscle fibers reached across the gap left by the sword and quickly wove the muscle back into one piece. The edges of the skin flowed smoothly together, leaving no scar or any other sign there had ever been a wound.

But the young man, now seemingly whole and hale, still lay near death.

Crystal's song changed slightly, becoming less somber, less instructive. Those listening felt a surge of energy, minor aches and pains disappeared and several small wounds closed. Color flooded back into the young man's face as the life force he had lost was replaced. His eyes flickered, then opened. He looked around, wondered peevishly why everyone was staring at him, and demanded a beer.

Crystal smiled, then the light pouring from her went out, and she collapsed to the floor. Although healing the wound had drained her, it had not caused her to faint. She had replaced the lost life force with her own.

The soldier was no worse for his experience—except for a vague but disturbing memory of hunting horns and baying dogs—but Crystal lay unconscious for three days. During that time Kraydak did what he pleased, but it was observed that, although he created plenty of impressive loud noises and bright lights, his attacks caused confusion and fear rather than destruction. He was obviously biding his time until Crystal recovered.

Crystal woke to a demoralized army and a mother frantic with worry. The army was much easier to reassure. When Crystal explained what had happened, Tayer ordered her to leave healing to the surgeons. Realizing that in this both queen and mother were in full accord, Crystal reluctantly agreed and then blamed herself for every death which followed. If she didn't send her people to Lord Death, neither did she try to stay his hand.

\*     \*     \*

Crystal knew Mikhail was right to stop her. Her responsibilities made it as impossible to save the guard as it had been to save any of the others who had fallen. In addition, she was tired from the day's fighting and the small but constant drain of keeping the protection over the surgical tent. The power she'd used to trap the Scholars had tapped out almost all of her reserves. None of this made the almost certain death of the guard any easier to bear. Finally she nodded and Mikhail stepped out of her way. The wizard was back and wizards don't mourn what they can't change.

"Can I walk you to your tent?" asked Mikhail, who was not as convinced as Crystal seemed to be that the wizard and his daughter were two separate people. She nodded again and he turned to Belkar.

"Go on then," said the duke. "There's nothing you can do here. I'll just have someone change the carpet. And the mattress," he added thoughtfully. "Can't say as I fancy sleeping on that knife hole."

The camp was certainly busier than it had been one short hour before when Kraydak's Scholars had slipped through the shadows to do murder. Bodies had to be disposed of, troops reassured, and a life saved if possible. Mikhail and Crystal walked alone through the darkness. Mikhail insisted that Tayer always be accompanied by soldiers from the newly reconstituted Palace Guards but refused them for himself, putting his trust instead in his great black sword. Crystal, the princess, was assigned Guards as well but Crystal, the wizard, threatened to turn them into newts so they went elsewhere.

"I'd like to know how you knew," Mikhail said as they threaded their way through all the activity. Crystal had refused to explain her suspicions in case she'd been wrong. Considering Lapus' involvement, Mikhail now understood whom she'd been protecting.

"I could see myself in his eyes."

"In Lapus' eyes?"

"Yes."

"Is that unusual? I suppose I'd have seen myself reflected in his eyes had I cared to look."

"When I look in someone's eyes," Crystal explained, remembering

how shocked she'd been to first catch sight of herself in the Scholar's
gaze so many weeks before in Belkar's library, "I look into their hearts.
There could be only two reasons for me to see myself; his love for me
was so strong I was the only thing in his heart, or he had been blocked
by a wizard. There is only *one* other wizard." Her smile didn't quite
hide the pain of Lapus' betrayal. "I tried to convince myself that Lapus
had indeed lost his heart and almost succeeded until I met Hale's
Scholar. Maybe one man could fall in love with me at first sight, two I
couldn't believe, even though the centaurs had warned me how men
would be. Then I met Cei's Scholar, and Aliston's, and Lorn's, and I
stared out of the eyes of all of them. Once I knew Kraydak was involved, the plot became easy to discover."

Too easy, it seemed to Mikhail and it worried him. Kraydak, no
doubt, had his own reasons for doing sloppy work. Using planted
Scholars to attack the dukes seemed too much of a diversionary tactic;
helpful if it succeeded but no great loss if it failed so long as it masked
the more important maneuver. He only wished he knew what it masked
and feared it would be an attack, not at the army, but at his daughter,
who had been hit once already tonight. And although he would never
tell her, for the news would only add to her burden of pain, Mikhail
had reason to believe that Lapus did indeed care greatly for the princess. Mikhail was very familiar with the many faces of devotion; he
had worn them himself for years.

They arrived at Crystal's tent and the soldier guarding the door, the
young man she'd lifted from the grip of Lord Death, snapped to attention.
When told what she'd done, he'd pledged his life to the protection of his
savior. His lord, the Duke of Cei, had a strong streak of romance running
beneath his shrewd and pragmatic exterior and had happily released the
man from his service. And so Crystal acquired a personal guard she had
no wish for but couldn't get rid of. The relationship developing between
her guard and her maid was the only thing that made the situation bearable. She hoped she might soon lose them both to one another.

Mikhail leaned forward and planted a kiss between the silver
brows. "You did what you had to," he said softly.

*I wish we could have . . .* You did what you had to. She nodded, not trusting her voice, and slipped into the tent.

Although she crawled into bed exhausted, Crystal couldn't fall asleep. Every time she closed her eyes she saw Lapus charging across the room, knife raised, his face twisted with hatred. She hadn't always liked what he'd said, how he'd stressed the conflict between wizard and princess, but she'd come to care for him and had thought he cared for her. That his friendship was an act, engineered by Kraydak, made her feel slightly sick and very lonely. This, the centaurs had not warned her of.

Eventually, the exertions of the day overcame her grief and she drifted into an uneasy sleep.

Gradually, Crystal became aware of green. A soft springtime green, very peaceful, very nice, very soothing. She could move around and there seemed to be a solid surface beneath her feet but the green never changed. She knew she was asleep and somewhere deep within her own subconscious. The centaurs had promised to teach her ways of manipulating the dreamworld but there hadn't, in the end, been time.

"Not a very interesting place for a dream," she sighed, spinning about so that the white gown she wore flared about her ankles. She liked the way the silky fabric clung, the way it whispered across her skin, although she wondered why she'd dreamed so little material above the waist. And then she saw the man approaching and knew she wasn't dreaming; not quite. She tried to raise a wall of power between them and found she had no power to spare.

His hair shone red-gold, like sunlight on fire, and clustered about his face in loose curls. His eyes were the clear, merciless blue of a hot summer day. Above tight sapphire breeches and high black boots, he wore no shirt and the muscles of his chest and arms rolled smoothly beneath golden skin as he closed the distance between them.

Grace and power, Crystal realized. And something more.

His hand, when it took hers, was cool and dry. His lips, touched to the skin of her wrist, soft and warm. "At last," he murmured. "Face to face."

Crystal snatched free her hand, more frightened than she'd ever been in her life. That he could reach this far into her mind without even waking her . . . "Get out of my mind!" She kept her voice below a scream but only barely.

Kraydak smiled. "I had hoped that we might be friends."

Gathering up her courage, and holding dignity before her like a shield, she managed a tight smile in return and retreated a step. "I hardly think so."

"No? You wound me." He lay long fingers against his bare chest. "We have so much in common."

"We have nothing in common! You're a . . . a . . ." She searched for a word that would sum up the disgust and loathing she felt as anger rose to take the place of fear. ". . . an abomination. You destroy anything you touch." She turned her back on him and found he still stood in front of her. And still smiled.

One red-gold eyebrow arched. "Abomination? Child, you are hardly one to point an accusatory finger."

"I am not like you."

"No," Kraydak agreed smoothly, his smile twisting strangely, "you aren't."

"You use people."

"Yes," he agreed again, "I do. I assume you specifically refer to the late, lamented Lapus? A useful tool; your grief at his betrayal gave me access to your mind. I needed a surety to enter through, you see, so I built my own."

She remembered the red spreading into the pattern of the rug and felt sick. "You set him up, you set all of them up, just to get at me?"

He reached out and pinched her chin. "And she's clever, too. Yes, child, I did it all for you." A couch, the couch from Crystal's tent, appeared behind him and he sat, gracefully crossing one booted leg over the other. He shook his head in mock sympathy. "Oh, my poor child, if you insist on caring for creatures so far beneath you, you can only expect to be hurt. Humankind should be your plaything, not your partner." His voice became caressing and held a possessive note that ran like soft fingers down Crystal's back. "We are the last two of our kind.

The last two. No mere mortal could ever hope to understand us." The blue of his eyes deepened. "Come to me, Crystal."

To Crystal's horror she took a step toward him, under no compulsion save that of his voice and his presence. Red with shame, she stopped, determined at least to move no closer, no matter what he said.

He said nothing. He laughed low in his throat and held out his hand, his gaze fierce and compelling.

Well aware of the dangers of a wizard's eyes, Crystal dropped her own to avoid being trapped by his gaze. Red-gold hair curled in an inverted triangle on his chest, the lowest point trailing down the ridges of his stomach until it dipped beneath the blue of his breeches.

Her shins hit the edge of the couch.

"You needn't even try," Kraydak told her gently as she struggled to move away. "This may be your mind, but you'll find I'm in total control. Oh, and one more thing." He reached out and took her hand, pulling her down beside him. "These bodies are illusions, but they react like flesh."

He drew a finger down her cheek and her eyes widened at the responses such a simple touch caused. He manipulated reactions she didn't know she possessed and, not knowing, she had no way to defend herself. She dug her hands into the cushions of the couch, fighting the urge to touch him in return. Independent movement was possible it seemed, as long as it was not away from him. Cautiously she began to slide her essence, the core of her that was Crystal, deeper within this representation of her physical body.

Kraydak, one arm clasped lightly around her waist, pushed her back against the cushions. He felt her essence retreat and he let it go. She could not escape him, after all, and if she thought this warm bundle of flesh he held would resist his assault for long . . .

When he kissed her, she leaned into it and she heard herself cry out in disappointment when he stopped. Her thoughts and her feelings almost seemed as if they belonged to two separate people. And the sensations of her body, under Kraydak's skilled caresses, were rapidly overwhelming her mind.

"Patience," the older wizard chided, slipping the gown off her shoulders, "we have plenty of time."

He ran his fingers lightly over her breasts and she barely managed to hold her essence in place as her body arched under his touch. She became very much afraid that she would soon give in to the sensations now setting her body alight, and then she would be lost, his creature entirely.

"Someone has certainly prepared the way," he murmured into the soft skin of her throat. "I hope I get the chance to thank him."

Bryon. Crystal grabbed that thought and held on tightly. She closed her eyes and built his image on the inside of the lids. She remembered every time he'd ever touched her, the feel and the scent of him, and built of it a barricade between her skin and Kraydak's hands.

It wasn't quite enough.

Kraydak's hands dropped lower and began to tug at the silky cloth that draped her hips, twisting her about so that he straddled her. His mouth moved to her breasts.

When she remembered to breathe at all, it was in great shuddering gasps over which she seemed to have no control. With the small part of her mind still her own she knew she couldn't hold out much longer. The fires that Kraydak had lit would consume all she was.

*Bryon,* she cried, feeling the heat licking at her refuge, *help me!* And from the time before the centaurs, rose one more memory. A very young Bryon rolled in the dirt of the training yard, hands clasped between his legs; a very young Crystal stared in puzzlement at the quarterstaff in her hands while their fathers almost split themselves laughing. Child, this wizard called her; she would use a child's blow. She bit down on her tongue, hard. As the pain jolted her free from the pleasure, she gathered the remnants of her strength and slammed her knee up between Kraydak's legs.

The illusion did indeed react like flesh and Crystal possessed the strength of the tree. It was fortunate for Kraydak that he had already depleted most of it.

Kraydak's eyes widened, he made an incoherent noise, and sank slowly to the ground. The surrounding green turned yellow, then orange, then red, then black and Crystal woke up in her own bed, her heart beating so fast she was afraid it would escape.

She lay staring at the ceiling, hands clenched at her sides, and forced herself to consider what had almost happened. His touch still lingered on her body and she flushed with embarrassment when she realized that the fires he'd lit still burned. Not with the same intensity as they had in the dream world, but a definite heat radiated out from the places he had . . . She shuddered. Kraydak had defeated himself when he reminded her of Bryon; she wouldn't be that lucky another time. And Kraydak's power frightened her less than her own lack of resistance.

"The trouble is," she mused, chewing on her lower lip in a most unwizardlike way, "I can't fight what I don't understand."

What if he came again? There was one rather obvious solution and the enemy himself had given it to her. She unclenched her fingers, wiped her sweaty palms on the sheets, and noticed with some surprise that she was still breathing heavily. . . .

Bryon woke up to the peculiar sensation of being in a different bed than the one he'd gone to sleep in. It was softer, slightly larger, and it smelled good. He was still in a tent and, from the sounds filtering through the canvas, still in the center of the Ardhan army, but where . . . and then he became aware of a warm body in the bed beside him, and he recognized the scent. . . .

"Bryon," said Crystal earnestly, "I need your help."

"Is this a dream?" Bryon asked of no one in particular.

"Don't be ridiculous." Crystal poked at him and wondered if he was going to be difficult. "You can't be dreaming, you're awake."

"I am?"

"Yes, and I want you to make love to me."

"I'm dreaming," he said with conviction. "I've had this dream before."

"Bryon!" Her voice was sharp, this wasn't how she'd imagined things at all. She should have been in his arms by now. He should have been swept away by passion the moment he found himself in bed with her. Wasn't that the way it worked? "Kraydak attacked me tonight and you're the only one who can stop it from happening again."

"What!" He sat up in the bed, reaching for the sword that wasn't there. "Kraydak came here?"

"Not exactly, he was in my mind and he . . . uh . . ." To her astonishment, Crystal felt herself blushing. "He, uh, stimulated me."

Bryon sat back against the pillows, the corners of his mouth twitching. He appeared to have his passion well under control. "He *stimulated* you? Perhaps you'd better tell me just what happened and what you think I can do about it."

Slowly, and with long pauses while she struggled to put the experience into words, Crystal told Bryon of Kraydak's attack. She left out nothing, not the fear, not the . . . other. She finished with her plan to build a defense with Bryon's help.

"After all, as Mikhail says, the best defense is a strong offense."

Bryon considered what Mikhail's reaction would be if he knew his beloved daughter was sitting naked in bed with a man he'd been heard to refer to as "having more gonads than sense," but all he said was: "I don't think this was the kind of situation he had in mind."

"Never mind him," Crystal dismissed her stepfather with a wave of her hand. "Will you help me or not?"

Bryon took a long, appreciative look and said, "No."

"No?" It had never occurred to her he would refuse. Wasn't this what he'd been leading up to all along?

It came as a bit of a shock to Bryon as well and with an altruism he hadn't known he possessed, he tried to explain.

"If this was truly your idea, I'd be honored to make love to you. But it isn't. Kraydak took advantage of your innocence to try to gain control over you and I won't finish the job."

"But it isn't like that!"

"Isn't it?" Bryon's voice was gentle but his eyes were hard. "As much as you care for me, would I be here if Kraydak hadn't attacked you?"

"No, but . . ."

"No buts. When we make love," he picked up her hand and planted a kiss in her palm, "and we will, it won't be as an act of war."

Crystal wrapped her fingers protectively around the kiss and looked at him with glowing eyes, eyes that had nothing to do with being a wizard. "Bryon," she began.

"No, not tonight." His voice was beginning to sound strained. "Now you'd better send me back to my own tent."

She studied him for a moment and then smiled. She was still smiling seconds later as she watched the indentation of his body smooth out of the mattress. "Were you concerned because it wasn't my idea," she asked it, "or because it wasn't yours?"

"Well, one thing's for sure," she said to the darkness as she blew out the lamp and settled down for sleep, "he won't get a chance like that again." But whether she referred to Kraydak or Bryon was not entirely clear.

Hanna stood on the battlements and looked out over the valley kingdom of Halda. She shivered and pulled the heavy traveling cloak tighter around her although it wasn't the night wind that caused the chill. She'd lived in Halda for seventeen years now, ruled over it as queen for ten; its fall, its death, tore open a wound she would always carry.

"Majesty?"

She turned and the young guard, dark circles visible beneath his eyes even in the uncertain torchlight, bowed.

"They are ready?"

"Yes, Majesty."

He stepped aside to let her pass, every movement a fight against exhaustion. It had been three days since anyone in Halda had really rested. It had been three days since the defenders at the pass had fallen and the army of the Melacian Empire had swarmed into the valley. Three days of slaughter. Men, women, and children put to the sword; and worse, if the hysterical accounts of the few fleeing survivors could be believed.

Hanna moved sure-footedly through the castle's dark halls, the guard following silently behind. Next to the great Palace of Ardhan, the dwelling of Halda's royal family was a paltry thing, but it had been a home to her, which was infinitely more than the other ever had. She stopped on the threshold of the throne room to let her eyes adjust to the sudden light.

Against the long wall opposite her, wooden platforms were rising, stages to lift the archers to the arrow slits high in the granite walls, hammers and saws providing a background to every other noise in the hall. Some of the wood, Hanna saw, had been cannibalized from the castle furnishings. Stretching away to either side of her, weary men and women sat holding their weapons, waiting. Behind them, rich tapestries still hid the stone. Through the heavy oak doors at the room's end, a steady stream of people, servants and nobles alike, carried food and water and weapons. In the center of the room, healers moved among the wounded and blood pooled on the gold inlay mosaic of the floor. The air was heavy with the smell of smoke and sawdust and steel and fear.

At her back, the young guard cleared his throat, as much of a prod as he could give his queen. She took another moment to banish hopelessness from her expression, then, lifting her chin, she stepped out into the room, heading for the small knot of people by the great gilded thrones. She walked as quickly as she could but took the time to acknowledge those she recognized with a smile or a softly spoken word.

Behind her, although she couldn't see it, shoulders squared and furrowed lines of tension eased.

"Mama!" As she reached the dais that held the thrones, a tow-headed boy of eight threw himself at her legs. "Mama, Papa says he's not coming with us!"

She reached down and stroked his hair. "He can't, Jeffrey."

"Why not?" Jeffrey's voice rose. He was too tired and too frightened to be reasonable.

"Because he's the king. And the king has to stay with his people."

"But I want him to stay with us!"

Hanna's heart twisted and for an instant she closed her eyes in pain. *Oh, so do I, my darling. So do I.* When she opened them again, her husband was there.

Gregor, King of Halda, was not a physically imposing man. He stood a head shorter than his wife, and the square, solid body of his youth had become inclined to fat. His sandy-brown hair was graying and laugh lines bracketed his eyes. He shifted the girl-child in his arms and smiled.

He had the sweetest smile Hanna had ever seen and, as she had since that first day when he'd smiled up at her, she couldn't help but return it. They'd said their good-byes that evening, when he'd finally convinced her that the children stood a better chance if she went with them. His scent clung to her still. She couldn't decide if it would be a comfort or a torture in the hours to come.

Jeffrey twisted against her leg and glared up at his father. "I want you to stay with us," he repeated, lower lip beginning to tremble.

"I can't."

Something in that quiet voice got through and Jeffrey sighed. "Can I stay with you, then?" he asked.

"Who will take care of your mama and your sister if you stay with me?"

Jeffrey sighed again. "I'll take care of mama." His small hand slipped into her larger one. "But do I hafta take care of Ellen, too?"

Safe from reprisals in her father's arms, three-year-old Ellen removed her thumb from her mouth long enough to stick out her tongue.

"Ellen, too," Gregor told him. "I'm counting on you."

"She's a slug," Jeffrey muttered. "But okay."

Gregor turned the beauty of his smile on his son. "Thank you."

"Majesties." The Captain of the Royal Guard stepped forward, at his side a young woman clad in homespun and leathers. Although he was dark and her hair flamed a brilliant red, the whipcord leanness of their builds and the sharp wildness of their gazes bespoke a relationship. "Trin says you must go now if you hope to reach the caves by dawn."

Now.

Hanna looked at the captain's companion, who nodded.

Now.

"I will carry the child." Trin held out her arms.

Gregor bent his head and placed his lips for a long moment against his daughter's brow. Ellen squirmed as his hold tightened and she made a muffled protest around her thumb. His eyes were very bright as he handed the child over to Trin.

"Jeffrey." He went on one knee before the boy and took the small shoulders in his hands. "You are King in Halda after me. While you live, Halda lives."

Jeffrey, impressed by the tone in his father's voice, nodded solemnly. Hanna knew he didn't understand, not really, but he'd remember. Father and son embraced and Gregor's cheeks were wet when he stood.

A thick finger traced the line of Hanna's jaw. "So beautiful," the king murmured and then she was in his arms.

And then she was walking away, down the long length of the throne room. She paused at the great oak doors, taking one last look back.

*I never thought I'd love him.* She remembered the long ride from Ardhan so many years before. Her surprise—their mutual surprise—at how well they got along, at how many important things they agreed on. How friendship had grown to something more precious. Pain and the tiny lifeless body of their first child who had never taken a breath in this world. The joy of Jeffrey and Ellen. *I wanted to never leave him.*

Over an impossible distance, their eyes met.

Then she walked from the room, saving the only thing in Halda that could be saved. The future.

# FIFTEEN

On mornings when the fighting had not yet begun, the leaders of the Ardhan army met at dawn in the queen's pavilion. Although Bryon had the standing invitation issued to all the ducal heirs, he seldom attended, preferring to eat with his men. On the morning after his visit to Crystal's tent, he surprised everyone by not only appearing, but by having managed to wash, shave, and find a clean set of clothes.

He made an elegant bow to the queen, saluted first Mikhail, then his father and the other dukes, grabbed a plate and a mug, and found a seat beside Crystal. If he wanted to speak to her about the night before, however, he was to be disappointed. After greeting him with a somewhat absent smile, her mind, to all outward appearances, was wholly on the war.

"I'm afraid it's true, Majesty," the Duke of Lorn said sorrowfully as conversation resumed. "My daughter arrived last night with confirmation. Halda has fallen."

Tayer's eyes filled with tears and, almost involuntarily, she shook her head slowly from side to side. Mikhail appeared to be carved from stone.

"What of the Royal Family?" he demanded gruffly. Hanna, Mikhail's only sister was Halda's queen.

Lorn's daughter, Kly, a small, muscular brunette, spoke up. "The news I have is three days old, dating from when the pass was taken by the Empire. Then, the Royal Family was safe in their principal seat, but by now the castle must have been overrun. So long dependent on their mountain barriers, Halda has . . . had almost no defenses."

A sound, half moan, half sob, welled up from Tayer's throat.

"Do not despair, Majesty." Kly's matter-of-fact tone was more calming than sympathy would have been. "I believe the Royal Family escaped and are hiding in the mountains."

"Why?" Mikhail did not yet let himself hope. Better Hanna be dead than a captive of Kraydak or his men.

"I was in Halda often during my three years as a Messenger and I saw the escape plans. Halda's Guard Captain long feared this day would come. And, although it is not common knowledge, Halda's Guard Captain is a wer."

"Wer!" More than one member of the council spat out the word as though it left a bad taste in the mouth. The members of the race the wizards had developed were few in number, seldom seen, and almost invariably hated.

"Wizard spawn," growled the Duke of Cei, his fat face twisted with distaste. "More likely to side with Kraydak than against him!"

"No." Kly's voice was quiet and assured. "The wer hate the wizards with an intensity hard to imagine. The names of the wizards are curses to them and Kraydak's is the most cursed of all." She turned to Crystal and, with no change of expression, added. "They've still not decided about you."

Crystal inclined her head. What the wizards had done to create the wers was terrible beyond belief. The wers had a right to eternal hatred of their creators and, although it had happened thousands of years before her birth, she was a wizard.

"If it's not common knowledge," said Lorn, "how did you happen to find out that this man was a wer?"

Kly favored her father with a level gaze.

He blushed slightly and mumbled, "Never mind."

"Milord." Kly addressed Mikhail directly. "There isn't a person alive that knows the mountains better than Rayue. There are caves and passages that go on for miles and have served as emergency shelter for the wer for generations. I believe that, for now, the Royal Family of Halda is safe."

Mikhail held her eyes for a moment longer, then, finding hope in her certainty, nodded.

"Now, if you'll excuse me, I'd like to go check on my horse before the fighting begins." As she left, she exchanged grins with Bryon. She had been Messenger to Belkar as well.

The council broke up soon after her departure. It was getting light and the battle lines were forming on the Tage Plateau.

Crystal stood, as she had stood since the first day the armies had engaged, alone on a rocky outcropping with an unobstructed view of the battlefield. Her hair whipped about in the wind and she felt, with growing uneasiness, the power building in the east. The air hung heavy with it and the sky was growing a greenish black. She waited nervously, gathering her own power to counter what had to be a major blow. As always, she faced the day wondering why she had not already been destroyed.

Although she had no way of knowing it, Kraydak wondered the exact same thing. On each day of the battle he had sent a little more power against her and each day she had met it and managed to survive. Once or twice, as she turned his attack in a totally unexpected way, he'd felt that, maybe, there was more to this wizard-child than he suspected and, perhaps, it would be amusing to discover what. And then he'd remember the prophecy—out of Ardhan would come the last of the wizards, the last creature capable of defeating him—and he'd try again to destroy her.

On a hillock, not far from where his daughter waited, Mikhail and his staff sat surveying the scene. Messengers had become couriers and already the traffic was heavy between the commanders and Mikhail. He hated not being able to fight himself, but his skills as a tactician were needed much more than his skill with his great black sword. His eyes went to where the Elite were grouped to take the brunt of the day's charge and he wished with all his heart that he was among them.

The armies joined and Crystal braced herself for the release of

Kraydak's power. When it came, it was typical of his attacks but much more complicated than most. It began to rain. No ordinary rain, this was cold, and vicious, and selective. It rained only on the Ardhan army. Only the Ardhan troops got wet and cold, only their footing became slippery and treacherous. Even when soldiers grappled in close hand to hand combat, Kraydak's army stayed dry and sure-footed.

Crystal couldn't tell if Kraydak had wrapped each of his men in a force shield and then caused it to rain or if he was directing the rain itself. She faced a master weaving of many types of power with only a slight idea of how to begin unraveling it.

As the day progressed, and the battle raged, so too did the battle between the wizards. Crystal began to understand what Kraydak had done and was having some success at undoing it. The rain came in scattered bursts now, whole sections of the Plateau would be dry, while in others rain fell on Ardhan and Melacian alike. In places where she could not stop the rain, Crystal tried to turn Kraydak's power against him and so an Ardhan soldier, cold, wet, and miserable, found himself up against a Melacian who was wrapped in blistering heat and dehydrating rapidly. The odds began to even out and by midafternoon, although the conditions were both uncomfortable and unusual, neither side could say they had an advantage through magical means. The wizards now held each other in a precarious balance.

"Oh, well done." Kraydak could not have been more pleased had he trained the child himself. For her deft handling of the day's problems, he forgave her even the attack of the night before. And although it would not happen again, he treasured the experience; he didn't remember the last time he had actually been hurt. Of course, he couldn't let her think she was free to cause him distress and just get away with it. He checked the interweavings of their power and smiled. "Let's see how you deal with this then, little one."

\*       \*       \*

The Melacian army began to fall back and a cheer went up from the Ardhan side, a cheer that turned to cries of horror as the dead shambled up from the rear of the Melacian ranks. The fallen, gathered each night from the battlefield, had been patched together and reanimated in a grisly parody of life. Their feet dragged through the mud, their lips were pulled back from their teeth in a rictus grin, and they still bore the wounds that had sent them to Lord Death. Here lurched a man with a great hole in his chest through which could be seen a gray and rotting heart. There staggered one whose head lolled drunkenly to the side, for the muscles needed to support it had been ripped away. Others walked on legs or swung arms not their own and rude stitches showed where limbs in better shape than the originals had been attached. Some carried swords, some spears, but they all carried terror as an added weapon.

The dead were not skilled fighters, but they didn't need to be. The same ghastly power that gave them a semblance of life and sent them out to kill, also gave them a strength few living could match. They were tireless and almost impossible to stop. Killing blows had no effect, for they were already dead, and the weary men of the Ardhan army found it necessary to chop these new opponents into pieces to stop them. Even then, very often, the pieces fought on.

Had it been possible to turn and run—to flee screaming from corpses that fought wrapped in the gagging stench of rot; to hide where a clammy hand could not close round your throat and continue to squeeze even after it was no longer attached to an arm—there would have been few Ardhan soldiers left on the field. But there was nowhere to go, so they choked back their fear and fought on.

Kraydak's living soldiers took strength from the victories of their unliving comrades, and threw themselves back into the fray.

When Crystal saw the dead advance, she bit back a scream. These shambling horrors were the stuff of her nightmares and she had to deal with her own terror before she could deal with them. Each decomposing feature, each hideous parody of humanity, struck a blow at the barrier of her power.

"Can't you do anything?" she called to a young man weaving his way through the battle, pausing here and there beside those who had fallen.

"What they do with the bodies is none of my concern," Lord Death replied, his features changing constantly as he spoke, and then he continued on his way unseen.

Crystal clutched her courage tightly and reached out to smash one of the dead to the ground. The freezing rain began again. The delicate balance of power slipped and disaster threatened. Her heart in her throat, Crystal grabbed back control and realized that Kraydak had effectively tied her hands. If she destroyed the living dead, she lost control of the elements. If the Ardhan soldiers were forced to fight the crippling cold and wet as well as their physical enemies, the Melacians would easily win. But if she let the walking evil be . . . as she watched, one of Belkar's captains went down with a spear slammed through his chest by a crawling monstrosity that dragged its guts on the ground behind it.

From his vantage point at the Plateau's edge, Mikhail ground his teeth in rage. He couldn't think of a thing that would do any good. Maneuvering was next to impossible, almost the entire army fought one on one and far too many men fought those they had defeated once already.

"Milord," gasped a courier, riding up on a lathered and blood-flecked horse, "they're breaking through to the south. Aliston is falling back. The duke asks you send him reinforcements."

Mikhail scanned the Plateau. An arm of the Melacian army had curved around, forcing the Ardhans to fight on two fronts, the east and the south. Up against the living dead, the southern front was falling back. Much farther and the Melacians would be behind the Ardhan lines.

"Get through to the Duke of Hale," Mikhail barked. "Tell him to regroup his cavalry and get over there as fast as he can."

"Yes, sir!" And with a weary salute, the courier was gone.

Mikhail doubted even Hale's cavalry would be fast enough to reach Aliston before the line was breached, but meanwhile there was something he could do. The need for a tactician was over. He drew his great black sword, whirled it once around his head to hear it sing, and set his heels to his horse's sides. The beast leaped forward, as glad to be moving as its master was. They pounded down the hill and flung themselves into the battle.

Aliston's weary men rallied as Mikhail hit the Melacian line like ten men not one. The dwarf-made sword moved so swiftly it looked like a black flame and flesh and blood and bone went flying from everywhere it struck. The dead began to die again.

It was almost enough.

Then Mikhail's horse was cut out from under him, disemboweled by the dying blow of one of Melac's captains. He jumped clear and continued to carve his way forward, his height and strength giving him an advantage over the foe that even the loss of the horse couldn't totally remove. But numbers began to tell and for every man he cut down it seemed another two rose up to fill the place. Soon he was stopped and, back to back with Aliston, surrounded by corpses and twice corpses, the two warriors fought to hold what he had regained.

Although he was covered in blood and dripping with gore, Crystal knew her stepfather had less need of help than anyone else still fighting. As much as she wanted to blast an area of safety around him, she forced herself to look away and do what she could for those who needed it more. She had discovered that, although most of her attention was needed to hold back Kraydak in the heavens, she could still manipulate small areas on the ground.

The angle of a sword blow, that would surely have separated head from shoulders had it connected, changed slightly in the air and slid off the edge of a shield instead.

A Melacian stepped on a rock which rolled slightly and sent him flying.

An archer with a direct line of sight to the Duke of Hale drew back her bow and put an arrow into the eye of a comrade.

The barbs of a Melacian spear hooked on an Elite's heavy armor and while trying to free it, the spearman himself was speared.

A craggy-faced young man with brows that drew a black line across his forehead slipped on another's blood and fell jarringly hard to the ground. As he lay gasping for breath, one of the undead loomed suddenly over him, spear raised to strike. Whispering a good-bye to his wife and child, for he knew he was on his way to Lord Death, he watched in amazement as the stitches holding the creature's spear arm to his body came unraveled and arm and spear fell harmlessly to the ground. Even the undead managed to look slightly surprised.

"I kept my promise," Crystal told a breeze, and then sent it to tell a young woman with honey-colored curls.

Kraydak's power threw itself at her barrier in waves. With each strike, she could feel her defenses wearing away, crumbling under the subtleties of Kraydak's attacks and her own terror of the walking dead which she still fought to control. She feared this would be her last battle, hers and Ardhan's. The army couldn't beat the undead without the help she was unable to give. Her fists were clenched at her sides, sweat plastered her tunic to her breasts, and her hair flapped lifelessly in the wind. Her ears began to ring.

She began to hear horns.

Surely that couldn't be in her head.

It wasn't.

"To war!" called out the War Horn of Riven. "To war!" And out of the forest to the south streamed the men of Riven, the duke leading the charge with the Horn to his lips. He blew again.

All through the Ardhan army, hearts lifted at the sound and men and women found the strength to fight a moment longer.

"TO WAR!" Then the duke put aside the Horn, drew his sword, and the Riven warriors threw themselves at the backs of the Melacians who had almost broken through to the south.

The call of the Horn went through Crystal like a ray of light. She drank it in, gathered it up, and threw it as hard as she could at Kraydak's might. Which wavered but held. She added her joy in Riven's arrival, the hope that rose in every breast, and the love of the farmer's young wife. Kraydak's attack crumbled and the setting sun burned red and gold through the fleeing clouds.

At the touch of the sunlight, the undead paused and then, like puppets with cut strings, they collapsed to the ground. Riven's men soon drove the remaining Melacian soldiers into a full retreat while the Ardhan army leaned on their weapons and cheered.

Fewer people than usual gathered outside the queen's pavilion that evening. Lorn had died with an arrow in his throat. Cei was in surgery with a spear wound in his belly; his fat had saved his life. Hale would not leave his men, for few of their horses had survived and in Hale a horse was regarded with as much tenderness as a child.

At Mikhail's approach, Tayer forgot queenly dignity and threw herself on him regardless of the blood which stained her hands and gown a lurid red. An embarrassed Riven was welcomed with much backslapping, his lateness forgotten in the perfect timing of his arrival.

Crystal collapsed on a camp stool and begun stuffing herself with meat tarts in an attempt to fill the emptiness that clawed at her from within. She had come very close to using every last bit of power. Belkar came and stood beside her, his face gray beneath the dirt and blood.

"Have you seen Bryon lately," he asked, "have you seen my son?"

Crystal's face blanched and the remaining color drained from her eyes. "No," she said, realization dawning. "Not for hours."

They looked at each other and then both turned toward the battlefield. Was he out there? Did he lie staring up at the stars too wounded to move, bleeding, dying? Had he already gone to Lord Death?

"I'd know if he were dead," Crystal whispered, listening to the pain rising from the wounded and trying find Bryon's within it. "I'd know."

"Better dead than out there," rumbled the duke. "Mother knows how long until they find them all."

The thunder of approaching hoofbeats distracted them and they glanced up from their fears.

"Why the long faces? Didn't we win?"

"Bryon!"

Bryon smiled wearily. The joy in Crystal's voice and the welcome in her eyes made the whole wretched days almost worthwhile.

Crystal bounded to her feet, the meat tarts flying unheeded to the ground. Relief and something more flooded the places where power had been expended. "We feared you'd been killed."

"Not hardly. Not a scratch on me." He slapped at his armor with disgust. It looked a great deal like he'd spent the afternoon swimming in an abattoir. "All this blood belongs to somebody else. Several dozen somebodies, as a matter of fact." He kicked a foot free of its stirrup, but before he could lift his leg clear of the saddle, a blue bolt arced down from the sky and smashed him to the ground. Screaming in terror, his horse bolted.

"NO!"

The world stopped while Crystal threw herself down at Bryon's side, but he was already beyond any help she could give. He tried to grin, and as he died she saw herself reflected in his eyes.

# Sixteen

The roaring in her ears drowned out the normal sounds of the Ardhan camp as Crystal knelt at Bryon's side, cradling his head in her lap, her eyes closed and dry. She knew the Duke of Belkar stood behind her, tears cutting channels through the grime on his face, and she felt his grief more clearly than her own. She wasn't sure it was grief she felt.

A single beam of moonlight cut through the gathering darkness, rested briefly on Bryon's still body and then was trapped in the silver net of Crystal's hair. When she finally stood, it rose with her. She brushed by Belkar, not seeing him, and strode down the path to the battlefield.

"Crystal," Tayer called, but Mikhail put his arm around her and shook his head.

"I don't think she can hear you, my love."

"But she shouldn't be alone." Tayer wiped her eyes with a square of lace and linen pulled from her sleeve.

*I'm afraid she'll always be alone,* Mikhail thought, but all he said was, "No, she shouldn't."

They followed their daughter down the path, each resting a hand gently on Belkar's shoulder as they passed the old man who stood silently mourning for his son. When they reached the battlefield, Crystal already stood on her outcropping of rock, arms raised to the moon.

As they watched, her hair lifted and wove patterns in the air, gathering in the light and absorbing it. Her eyes were pools so deep that the green appeared black. She stood unmoving, a sculpture of white marble rather than living flesh and her beauty had never been more terrible. She looked so little like their daughter that Tayer and Mikhail suddenly found themselves more afraid of her than for her.

If Kraydak had thought to paralyze her with grief, he had made a grave mistake.

She knew what she was feeling now. She was furious. No matter that her own power had been depleted; there were other sources and her anger would act as focus for them.

Without warning, she ignited in a glorious blaze of silver fire. Every leaf, every twig, every blade of grass in the surrounding area stood out in sharp relief against their own tiny and impenetrable black shadows. Tayer and Mikhail staggered back, nearly blinded by the intensity. Behind them, they heard the rest of the army cautiously approaching, drawn like moths to the flame. The men and women carrying the wounded from the battlefield favored the wizard with a startled glance, then, giving thanks for the light which made their job easier, hurried to finish before it went out.

When the light of the wizard outshone the light of the moon, Crystal called. The mountains answered. The sound was so wild and inhuman that many of those who heard it fell to their knees in terror, fingers stuffed in their ears in a hopeless attempt to block it out. They sang together for a moment, the wizard and the earth, and then Crystal clenched her fingers into fists.

The song of the mountain ceased, replaced by a rumbling roar—rock, torn from its rest and hurtling earthward. The Melacian army was camped in the shelter of the mountains. Their screams could be heard all the way across the Plateau.

A blue bolt arced down from the heavens, but Crystal almost contemptuously swatted it aside. It was closely followed by a second and a third. The fourth she grabbed and held and threw it back the way it had come. There was no fifth bolt.

She clenched her fists again.

With a tortured scream, an entire cliff face sheared away and plummeted down on the Melacian camp.

Mikhail staggered up to his daughter, tears running from his burning eyes. Thus must the wizards of old have looked at the height of their powers, proud and distant and not the least bit human.

"Crystal!" He clutched at her arm and was surprised to find it icy cold. "Enough! You've done enough!"

She shrugged free of his grasp with such ease that Mikhail wasn't sure she even knew he'd been there. Her seemingly gentle motion flung him back and off his feet. Through slitted eyes, he saw a small form moving past him and up to face the wizard. "Tayer, no," he began and then realized that it wasn't his wife.

Her eyes squinted nearly closed against the glare, Kly pulled back her arm and punched the wizard as hard as she could in the stomach. She had intended a slap in the face but had discovered to her chagrin that she wasn't tall enough.

Crystal's gaze snapped back from the distance and she dropped it to the young woman's face. When their eyes met, Kly found the light no longer blinded her and she stared back fearlessly, not even trying to escape as she fell into the darkness. As she felt herself and all she was, probed, examined, and absorbed, the darkness lightened and grew green. When she returned to herself, the wizard looked down at her with eyes that glowed the deeper green of summer leaves.

"It wasn't because I loved him," Crystal explained, as much to herself as to Kly, her voice deathly calm. "It was because I never got the chance to find out."

Kly nodded. "I know," she said.

And because Kly understood, Crystal sighed and the light went out.


Kraydak's servants were used to the blue bolts that blazed out from the top of the tower. They knew that with each bolt went death and destruction for their master's enemies. They had never before seen one come back.

"Master?" He edged his twisted body around the door and peered fearfully into the room. He had not been called and the punishment for entering unbidden was severe, but the returning bolt had shaken the tower and he was sure he had heard his master cry out in pain.

"Master?"

There, against the far wall.

The servant scrambled farther into the wizard's sanctuary. The door swung silently shut behind him and he whimpered low in his throat. It was too late to turn back. He forced abused limbs into motion and shuffled painfully across the carpet toward the blue and gold bundle on the floor.

A thin trickle of blood ran from Kraydak's nose, streaking the sculptured beauty of his face. His eyes were closed and his head twisted back at an awkward angle, but the golden chest still rose and fell: he lived.

With a gnarled finger, the servant gently touched his master's blood. He stared at the scarlet stain for a moment then brought the finger to his lips. It tasted no different from his own.

Deep in the prison of his mind, the man he had once been woke and screamed, "Kill him! If he can be hurt, he can be killed! Kill him! You will never have this chance again!"

The servant awkwardly wiped the blood from Kraydak's face. He had learned long ago that it hurt much less to ignore the voices in his head. He would wait and his master would wake and he would be told what to do. Even now the wizard's eyes were opening.

Blue fires. Searing. Burning. Consuming. Killing.

The inner voice died first, then the servant's body spasmed and collapsed at his master's feet.

Kraydak kicked the broken thing aside and staggered to the inner room where he threw himself down on the marble bench.

"That wizard-child is lucky beyond belief," he snarled, checking the lump on the back of his head. "She dares to throw my power back at me! At me, Kraydak!" He winced as he probed the sore spot, his eyes glowed briefly, and the pain was gone.

"You have hidden depths, wizardling," he continued in a softer voice—a voice the servant would have recognized with terror had he been alive to hear it. "You destroyed my armies and you caused me pain." Twice now she'd hurt him, and that was beyond even his ability to forgive. "Of course, the army will be replaced, and while that game continues, we will play a new game, you and I. I will call you to my side and you will learn about pain." He reached down and stroked the skinning knife that lay on the bench beside him.

"Bryon was right." Crystal struggled to keep her voice steady and matter of fact. It held an edge, she knew, but none of the hysteria she had feared would appear the moment she opened her mouth. She'd spent the night, trembling in exhaustion and reaction, alone in her tent, not even her mother daring to force an entry. The earth sang quiet songs to her, filling the darkness with comfort, and by morning she had calmed herself. When she entered the queen's pavilion, and met the eyes of the council members, she knew no one would ever call her princess again.

"Bryon was right about what, dear?" Tayer asked kindly.

Crystal knew they humored her, but she didn't care. She saw the fear in the glances of the soldiers and didn't care about that either. Kraydak had also been right. Care about someone and you only get hurt. She wasn't going to care anymore.

"He said I couldn't fight Kraydak alone. That someday I'd have to ask for help."

"We'll do what we can," Mikhail told her, but wondered what sort of help mere mortals could give to a seventeen-year-old girl who could call to the earth and have it answer.

The wizard shook her head. "What can you do?" she asked bluntly. "What can any of us do? Last night my anger gave me strength, but I can't be angry all the time." She walked to the tent flap and looked out at the sunshine. The wind brought her the sound of metal on rock, the pitiful remnants of the Melacian army digging out their camp. For an instant, she reached out and touched the power she'd called the night before. It stirred and she backed quickly away from a seduction more dangerous than any Kraydak could attempt. Without her rage as focus she knew she lacked the skill to control the forces her power, small in comparison, could release.

The council exchanged worried glances and Belkar rubbed a hand over red and puffy eyes. They had buried his son with the dawn.

"Then what's left?" he sighed.

Crystal turned to him and her expression was more human than it had been at any time since Bryon had died. Even in her anger, she had realized his loss had been the greater one; he was an old man, he would have no more sons. "The Doom of the Ancient Wizards," she said almost gently. "The dragons."

"The dragons?" the council repeated in one voice, an incident that would have been funny any other time.

"The dragons," snorted the new Duke of Lorn, a wiry, brown man who resembled his sister Kly a great deal, "returned to the earth thousands of years ago. When the wizards died."

"But one of those wizards lives," Crystal reminded him. "If the legends are true, then so too must one dragon."

The wizards had created the dragons in a contest to determine, once and for all, who was mightiest. They had drawn up the very bones of the earth and changed them, reshaping them into giant flying reptiles, breathers of fire and frost. Each wizard poured his or her mightiest spells into a dragon, and when the great beasts were finished each wizard gave up a piece of his or her own life force so that the dragons might live. Each dragon was a part of the wizard who'd created it.

But the dragons were also made from the body of the Mother and, to their horror, the wizards could not control the creatures they had made. In great battles that lasted years and forever changed the face of the land, the dragons slew their makers. There was never any doubt of the outcome. In their conceit, the wizards had created too well. As long as the wizard who created it lived, so too would the dragon. And the dragons were stronger.

When the wizards were defeated, the dragons returned to the earth from which they were made. But if one wizard still lived . . .

"Then Kraydak's dragon must live!" Hope rang out in Tayer's voice. They had a chance after all.

But Cei was shaking his head, jowls jiggling with the motion. "Impossible. Firstly, if it lived, it would be fighting Kraydak, which it isn't. Secondly, Kraydak is many things, but I've never seen anything to make me think he's a fool and he must believe that the dragon is dead. You said yourself, he emerged from hiding when he realized he'd escaped his Doom."

"It's been thousands of years," Crystal replied. "Kraydak has to believe he destroyed the dragon during their last battle. How else could he still live?"

"How, indeed," muttered Lorn.

"But you don't believe the dragon is dead?" persisted Tayer.

"If Kraydak lives, the dragon lives. He may have stopped it, but he couldn't kill it without killing himself."

"And why hasn't Kraydak come to this conclusion?" Lorn demanded. "As Cei pointed out, he's no fool."

"Because he'd rather believe he escaped his Doom than believe it still lurks around some dark corner." Crystal shrugged. "He was the most powerful of the wizards, maybe he has convinced himself that he can't be defeated."

The council considered that. Kraydak's ego could indeed blind him, convince him that he must have killed the dragon and, alone of all the wizards, escaped the consequences.

"Maybe," said Lorn suddenly, "Kraydak's right. Maybe he did accomplish what he thinks."

"Impossible. The dragons were created as extensions of the wizard's life force, not as separate beings. If a wizard lives, a dragon must. The Mother doesn't break her own rules."

*But She's willing to bend them,* Tayer thought, watching her daughter and knowing that Crystal was something more than just the last wizard. *Moonrise came early last night.*

"Why," asked Belkar softly, "did you not think of this until now?"

Crystal turned slowly to face him. Why did you not think of this earlier, asked his heart, before my son had to die. "Until last night, I thought as Kraydak does; he is the most powerful of the wizards, he destroyed his Doom. But last night I touched the body of the Mother and it is stronger that he could ever be. The dragons were made of that body, he could no more destroy them than he could destroy it. Somewhere Kraydak's Doom still lives, and I swear to you I will find it and use it to destroy Kraydak."

It will not bring back my son, said Belkar's heart, but the old duke only nodded and gently touched Crystal's face, wiping away the tears she hadn't been aware she'd shed.

"All right," Cei said at last, "where do we find this creature?"

"I don't know. I'll have to ask someone who was there."

"That was a thousand years . . ." Cei began, but Tayer broke in. "The Grove!"

Crystal nodded. "Yes, Mother, the Grove. It's time to wake the trees."

Tayer sighed. She felt the peace of the circle of trees tugging at her heart. The one thing that had made all this death and destruction bearable had been the thought of the Grove, forever unchanging, waiting silently and patiently for her return. If Crystal had to wake the trees, there could be no hope that that peace would remain unbroken.

"But the Grove is weeks away," Hale protested. "Even riding the fastest horses with frequent changes."

"The wind can get there in a few hours," Crystal told him, "I'll ride the wind."

After what she had done to the mountain, no one doubted she could ride the wind; ride it, dance with it, and tie it in knots if she wanted to.

"But what of Kraydak?"

Silence fell as they all considered what would happen if Kraydak attacked while Crystal was gone. Very faintly, in the distance, could be heard the wails of the Melacian survivors.

Crystal almost smiled. "He set the rules for this game and they say we must both have an army. He'll be busy for a while."

"When are you going?" These were the first words Riven had said to Crystal since he had left King's Town so many weeks before. They weren't what he had intended his first words to be.

"Now." She brushed past him, uncomfortable with the way his eyes followed her—Bryon was dead—and left the pavilion, a breeze dancing ecstatically in her hair.

Tayer held tightly to Mikhail's hand as Crystal spread her arms and the wind began to rise. Harder and harder it blew, until tent ropes snapped and men had to scramble to keep the tents from flying away. Dirt and ashes spun through the air, blinding those who still had their eyes open. Then, just as suddenly as it had started, the wind stopped. When people could see again through watering eyes, the wizard was gone.

Crystal didn't so much ride the wind as become a part of it. Spread thinly on the air, she let it blow away her doubts, her fears, her anger. It was very tempting just to let go, to let it blow away her self as well, to give up form and failure completely and be one with the wind. Very tempting.

Fortunately for the Ardhan army, the centaurs had spent six long years implanting in Crystal the one thing that the original wizards had never acknowledged: with great power comes great responsibility.

The Grove stood silent and beautiful, untouched by the world outside. The peace within it was a warm and loving presence. A presence that fled with Crystal's arrival. The trees pulled back from her and their leaves trembled in a way that had nothing to do with the wind.

The centaurs had taught her more than one way to wake the Ladies of the Grove. She chose the fastest. She wasn't very polite about it either. Looking deep into the heart, of each tree, she wrapped lines of force about the life that slumbered there, and pulled.

Yawning and grumbling, the hamadryads were drawn forth. Twelve beautiful women, with silver hair, ivory skin, and leaf green eyes, stood ringed around a thirteenth. But the resemblance was purely physical between Crystal and these distant aunts, no emotion stronger than self-interest marred the expressions of the twelve, no breeze dared disturb the beauty of their hair.

"Well, Youngest," said one finally, "are you going to tell us why we were so rudely awakened or are you going to stand and stare at us all day?"

Crystal started. She hadn't realized she was staring; knowing you bore the face and form of an Elder race was one thing, seeing it something else. "I need your help."

"She needs our help," echoed another. "Did Milthra ask for our help when she started this mess?"

"No," continued a third. "And did They ask for our help when They planted that," all heads turned to look at the youngest of the trees from which no hamadryad had come, "in our grove?"

"No," finished a fourth. "But now the last of the wizards needs our help."

"You know me?" The last of the wizards knew she asked a ridiculous question. It annoyed her that she found the massed presence of the Mother's eldest children so intimidating.

"Know you? We watched you being conceived."

"And an ugly . . . mortal display it was, too." added the nymph who had spoken first. "My name is Rayalva. I am Eldest now Milthra is gone. You may address your plea to me."

Crystal was not in the mood to be patronized. She gritted her teeth and her eyes began to glow.

Rayalva smiled with total insincerity. "You have no power over us, wizard. Now, what do you want?"

Swallowing her ire, and reminding herself how badly she needed the information these infuriating creatures possessed, Crystal forced politeness into her voice. "I need to know where Kraydak's dragon is."

"If you want a dragon," yawned a nymph who had not yet spoken, "make one yourself. That's what all the other wizards did."

Crystal ignored her and her sisters and spoke only to Rayalva. "The dragons were tied to the life force of the ancient wizards. If Kraydak still lives, then the dragon he created must live also."

The Eldest stared at her in disbelief. "You woke us up to tell us that? Of course, the dragon still lives. He's sound asleep, mind you, but he lives. Didn't the centaurs teach you anything?"

"Yes, but . . ."

"For several centuries great forces have been stirring and making things decidedly uncomfortable for the sole purpose of creating you so that you could wake the dragon."

Crystal sat down rather suddenly on the grass. Her mouth opened and closed a few times. "They never told me that," she managed at last.

"It's something the centaurs would expect you to figure out for yourself," Rayalva said unsympathetically. "Men, idiots! You, no doubt, have been fighting Kraydak yourself."

"Yes." A blue bolt smashed Bryon from the saddle. Crystal cringed, her throat closed, and she seemed to have forgotten how to breathe. Because she had fought Kraydak, Bryon had died. The hamadryad's next words came from very far away.

"A waste of time, you can't defeat him. Well, maybe in a couple of thousand years you could," Rayalva was forced to admit, "when your powers mature. You can do many things, you know, not dreamed of by the wizards of old. All your mothers saw to that."

"All my mothers," Crystal repeated weakly, her gaze going to her father's tree.

Rayalva sighed. "You still haven't figured it out, have you?"

She forced herself past Bryon's death. At least she could learn how to avenge him. "Figured what out?"

"Who were the parents of the ancient wizards?"

"The male gods and mortal women."

"And what was the first thing the wizards did when they came into their powers?"

"Killed their fathers so there would be no more wizards."

"And their father were?"

"The male gods!" Crystal snapped, becoming impatient with the catechism.

"Leaving who to create more wizards?"

"If the male gods were dead . . ." She thought for a moment. "The female gods? But my father . . ."

Rayalva sighed again. "When the remaining gods saw that a wizard had survived, they pooled their essence and presented it to a daughter of the Royal House of Ardhan in such a way that she would be forced to create a child from it. Only Milthra's heritage kept her alive through that creation; a fully mortal woman would have been consumed." Rayalva began to slide back into her tree, the other hamadryads following her lead. "You have no father, child," she said almost kindly, "but you have a multitude of mothers."

"I knew we shouldn't have let the centaurs educate her," muttered a disappearing nymph.

"Wait!" protested Crystal, leaping to her feet and staring around the now empty grove. "You haven't told me where the dragon is!"

"With the dwarves," came the answer, and then even the leaves were silent.

Crystal was almost back to the camp when she felt Kraydak searching for her. He used only a tendril of his power, the merest fraction of what she knew he could call up, but it was enough. Dwelling on Bryon's death, she had forgotten to set barriers, leaving herself open to attack. Bit by bit, Kraydak pried her free from the wind and when he had re-formed her flesh, he dropped her.

Over a lake.

He still played games.

Crystal hit the water with enough force to knock the breath from her, plunging straight down to the bottom. Bound by the weight of her clothes, she began to panic. She thrashed toward what she thought was the surface, her violent movements erasing any chance of floating. Her clothes felt like lead sheets wrapped around her arms and legs. Her lungs burned. She had to breathe. She had to breathe. She had to breathe. She . . .

Suddenly, something grabbed her hair and hauled her head up out of the water. She forced herself to relax, to gulp great mouthfuls of air, and allow herself to be dragged to safety by the strong arm under her chin. In the shallows, the arm released her, but before she could try to stand, she was picked up and carried to shore.

"Are you all right?" asked Riven anxiously as he gently eased her down.

"I'm fine," she said, checking and discovering it was true. She looked up at Riven's worried face but couldn't quite manage to smile. He'd saved her life. Lord Death had been very close. What a stupid way for a wizard to die. She'd never been so embarrassed in her life. "Thank you."

Riven shrugged self-consciously and pushed his wet hair out of his eyes. His hand was fine-boned, an old scrape nearly healed across the knuckles. His eyes were deep-set under heavy brows and so light a hazel they were almost green. He was slender but obviously strong and . . .

Crystal couldn't believe she was lying there considering the appearance of the Duke of Riven. Bryon was dead. She struggled to her feet, pretending not to see Riven's offer of a helping hand.

"Where are we?"

"About two miles from camp. I was checking the patrols when I saw you fall." He watched her with an almost puzzled expression on his face. For just a moment the wizard hadn't looked like a wizard at all. Nor like a princess.

She nodded, and staggering only slightly, set out in the direction he'd indicated. Riven fell into step beside her and an uncomfortable silence prevailed.

"Did you find out about the dragon?" he asked at last.

"With the dwarves," she said shortly, not wanting to acknowledge his presence because then she'd have to acknowledge some disturbing thoughts, mostly having to do with the feel of his arms around her as he carried her from the water.

"The dwarves?" He stopped, then had to hurry to catch up as Crystal marched resolutely on. "But the dwarves refuse to have anything to do with humankind. No one has any idea of where to find them."

Crystal remembered Mikhail's great black sword and finally achieved a smile.

# SEVENTEEN

"The dwarves . . ." Mikhail stroked the hilt of his great black sword and stared thoughtfully off into the distance. He'd been only sixteen when he'd fought for and won the dwarf-made blade; twenty-two years and the golden caverns and carved halls of the master craftsmen still shone as bright in his memory as they had the day he'd left. The home of the dwarves was a sight to remember for as long as life lasted. Unfortunately for most of those privileged to see the caverns, life didn't last very long.

"The dwarves," Mikhail repeated. "Yes, I know where to find them." He smiled at a memory. "In fact, after you get to a certain point they usually find you."

"What point? Where?" Crystal asked, trying not to sound impatient and failing. Kraydak was busy bringing in fresh troops and supplies to continue the game, but that couldn't take him long. She had to wake the dragon before he turned his full attention back to her.

"North of the badlands of Aliston," Mikhail told her, snapping out of his reverie and moving to stand by the map. "Where the northern mountains end, there's a red sandstone pillar. Whether it was carved by the winds or the dwarves, I have no idea, but it marks the boundary of the territory they've claimed for themselves. Here," he pulled out a dagger and stabbed at the map, "as near as I can mark it, is where it stands."

The Duke of Aliston came over and peered closely at the point of Mikhail's dagger. "Rough area that." He clicked his tongue. "You'll

need one of my lads as a guide or you'll never get through the badlands."

"I have to go alone." *Always alone,* she thought, remembering her
reflection fading from Bryon's eyes as Lord Death claimed him. And it
was her fault he was dead. She was never meant to stand against Kraydak. She should have known it from the start.

"Crystal, no. Not alone." Tayer got to her feet and held out a hand
to her daughter. "If you can't use your powers for fear Kraydak will
notice what you're doing, you'll have to take soldiers; guards to protect
you."

Crystal pushed both her dead friend and her guilt to the back of her
mind and gave Tayer's hand a comforting squeeze. "Don't worry,
Mother, I'll be fine. Besides, there's nothing a guard could do to protect me from Kraydak."

Tayer wasn't very reassured.

"No magic, eh?" Belkar growled. "Then how do you expect to
wake the dragon?"

"I don't know," Crystal admitted.

"And how do you expect to get there?" Cei demanded, the thought
having just occurred to him. "Kraydak's on to your wind trick and we
haven't the time for you to ride. Aliston's badlands have got to be at
least a month away."

"Month and a half," put in Aliston, turning his nearsighted gaze on
the young wizard.

"I don't know," Crystal admitted again. "But I'll think of something."

"Without magic," Aliston pointed out, "you'll never make it
through the badlands without a guide."

"That has all been taken care of."

The entire council started, but it said a great deal for the timbre of
the voice that, although everyone in the pavilion was armed and nerves
were balanced on a knife's edge, not one weapon was drawn. When
they saw who had spoken, jaws dropped and the company stood and
stared.

The two centaurs were so large that their heads brushed the top of the tent. Their horse halves could easily carry a man as massive as Mikhail in full armor and their torsos were heavily muscled and equally as huge. The beards flowing in magnificent curls over their naked chests—only practical Cei noticed that they had no nipples—exactly matched the shade of their glossy hides. Their whiteless eyes seemed to hold all the wisdom of the ages.

A strangled cry caused heads to turn back to Crystal. The color had drained from her face and her eyes stood out like burning jewels. Her breath hissed through slightly parted lips and her hands, clenched into fists, began to rise.

The council edged back until the centaurs and the wizard faced each other in a circle of humanity pressed tight against the canvas. They had seen her, in her rage, call down mountains and all of them knew that power once taken up will be used again and again.

"Crystal!" Tayer stepped forward, away from the retreating council, and her voice threw up a wall between her daughter and the creatures she faced. "You will not do violence. These . . . persons . . . are guests in my tent!"

In the silence that followed, the wheeze of Cei's breath could be clearly heard and a breeze against the canvas roof was a booming roar.

The wizard locked eyes with the queen, who ignored their emerald depths and stood glaring at her furious child. "You will not do violence to a guest!" she repeated.

Slowly, Crystal lowered her hands and uncurled her fingers. "But, Mother . . ."

"Hush, child, I know." Tayer gently touched Crystal's shoulder and together they turned to face the centaurs.

"My thanks, Majesty." The black centaur inclined his head. "Although we are not sure she is capable of causing us harm, the release of such power would have definitely been detrimental to those around us. I am C'Tal." He indicated the palomino. "This is C'Fas."

"What are you doing here, C'Tal?" Crystal snapped before Tayer had a chance to speak. "Haven't you interfered enough?"

"We have been informed," C'Tal told her in ponderous tones, "that we were remiss in your education."

"You were given all the information," C'Fas continued in a voice equally as solemn. "We did not feel it necessary to tell you what to do with it."

"Others, however, suggested you were ill-prepared for the conflict you found yourself in." C'Tal shook his head sadly. "We feel you were as well-prepared as possible, considering the short time we had you in our charge. Given a century or two and perhaps . . ." he shrugged, sending fascinating ripples down the length of his body. "What we could have done is not the point but rather what we did."

"Or what they imply we did not do," broke in C'Fas with an edge to his voice.

"Precisely," agreed C'Tal, nodding at his companion. "Or what they imply we did not do."

"Who implied?" demanded Crystal, used to the considerable time centaurs took in getting to the point but no longer willing to put up with it. Not now. Not after Bryon.

"The hamadryads," said C'Tal, glowering down at her. "While we are firm in our contention that we did all we could in the time we had available, there is something in what they say. You should never have faced Kraydak yourself. We should have been more careful that this was made clear to you."

"I'm surprised the hamadryads cared." Crystal felt her anger lose its edge as guilt returned to the foreground. She had been told but hadn't understood.

"They do not. But they were most annoyed at being awakened, feeling, and perhaps rightly, that had you been told of the dragon as you should have been, there would have been no need for you to go to them."

"But why," asked Tayer, "are you here?"

"We have come to help."

"Where were you two days ago," Lorn snorted, remembering the arrow through his father's throat and the ranks of the undead, "we could've used help then."

Both centaurs turned to look at the duke, who was paring his nails with a slender knife and was not at all intimidated by their gaze. He gave them back glare for glare.

"Then you needed more heavy cavalry," said C'Tal.

"Now you need centaurs," finished C'Fas.

Lorn looked interested but not convinced. He wisely chose not to mention that the centaurs would make impressive heavy cavalry themselves.

"I will carry the wizard to the edge of the badlands." C'Tal stepped forward and laid a heavy hand on Crystal's shoulder. "While my brother will remain here."

"Well, we'll be happy to have him," Tayer began, nervously considering the creature's bulk and wondering how to entertain someone who was half horse, "but there really won't be much for him to do."

"He is not here to be amused, Majesty," C'Tal boomed. "We hope his presence will convince the enemy that the wizard is still here. If he does not probe too deeply, he will not be able to tell the difference between their life forces."

Tayer looked from the huge golden-haired centaur to her daughter. "Oh," she said.

Crystal tried to explain. "Centaurs are magical beings, Mother. They don't use the power so much as they are the power. If Kraydak has no reason to suspect I'm gone, and doesn't force his way below the surface patterns, he'll think C'Fas is me."

"Oh," Tayer said again, only this time she felt much better about it.

Mikhail stepped forward and stared belligerently up at C'Tal. He had to crane his neck to meet the centaur's eyes and that annoyed him. He'd never had to look up at anybody before.

"Can you protect her from the dwarves and the dragon?" he asked.

"That is not my concern," C'Tal informed him. "We will do no more than what I have already said." He turned to Crystal. "Now come, we must go."

Crystal stopped Mikhail from saying what he so obviously thought; he had never been good at hiding his anger.

"As much as it hurts me to admit it," she said softly, "he's right. That," a hint of steel came into her voice, "is not his concern. I can take care of the dragon."

"That dragon has only one purpose," Mikhail reminded her as he gave her a boost onto C'Tal's broad back, "to kill wizards."

"To kill Kraydak," Crystal corrected.

"Waking up in the presence of a wizard after sleeping for a thousand years may cause him to attack first and ask questions later," Mikhail said grimly.

"I'm not like any of the other wizards," Crystal reminded him in turn. "My heritage from the Lady of the Grove will protect me."

"What of your humanity?" asked Tayer gently, coming up to stand in the circle of her husband's arm.

Crystal's face grew bleak and she saw again her reflection fading from Bryon's eyes. "That died with Bryon," she said shortly. But catching sight of Riven's concerned face over C'Tal's shoulder, she wasn't as sure of that as she had been.

And then, as impossibly fast and silent as the centaurs had come, Crystal and C'Tal were gone.

"Stop that!" snapped C'Fas as Hale, horse sense overcoming common sense, ran a hand over a glossy haunch.


To ride a centaur is like nothing else in the world. Perhaps being strapped to a shooting star would give the same wondrous feelings of grace, power, and speed but Crystal doubted it, for a star would not have a convenient shoulder on which to rest your head. Her hard knot of anger at the centaurs began to dissolve; surely it was unreasonable for her to expect them to go against their natures. Used to dealing in centuries, they had done the best they could when forced to work with days and months and years. Gradually, the old feelings for her teachers began to resurface and for the first time since Kraydak had destroyed the palace, Crystal felt protected and safe. She paid no attention to the countryside they passed over; instead she locked her arms about C'Tal's waist, buried her face in the familiar smell of his back, and gloried in the ride.

It ended too soon. The Aliston badlands passed by in a rocky blur and they stopped before a red sandstone pillar. Suddenly stiff from so many hours in one position, Crystal slid awkwardly to the ground.

"The dwarves are past the pillar?" she asked C'Tal as she massaged the pins and needles out of her legs.

"We do not keep watch over the dwarves," C'Tal informed her imperiously. "Your foster father says they are on the other side of the pillar. We see no reason for you to distrust him."

Crystal straightened up and stared dubiously past the marker. The land consisted of a series of low rock ridges, split and blasted into strange and forbidding shapes. Everything was a dusty gray with no living green to break the monotony. The dwarves lived in that?

"Oh, well," she sighed, "if they're in there, I guess I can find them."

"If they are in there, they are more likely to find you," corrected C'Tal sternly. "Remember, you must not use your power. If Kraydak discovers what you are attempting to do, it will mean not only your death but the deaths of thousands of innocent people as well. I will be here when you emerge." He paused and looked down at Crystal with something very close to concern in his expression. "If we are truly responsible for what you have done, we are sorry."

"Sorry won't raise the dead," said Crystal softly.

"Nothing will raise the dead," replied the centaur. "It is therefore unproductive to hold fast to one who has died." He spun gracefully on one massive hoof and disappeared.

"I'm not holding Bryon," Crystal shouted after C'Tal. "I'm remembering him!" There was, as she expected, no response. Taking a deep breath, she stepped beyond the column. The landscape appeared no different, the red tower of rock was a marker, nothing more. She'd hoped it might be some sort of magical barrier, that once passed the home of the dwarves would stand revealed. A small gray lizard, so perfectly camouflaged she almost stepped on it, scuttled out of her way—the only life in sight.

Because it seemed like the only thing to do, she headed deeper into the badlands. Five miles and a blister later, she was very dusty and very thirsty and no dwarves had appeared. A fear lurked in the back of her mind, whispering that they might have moved on since Mikhail had won his sword, moved on and taken the dragon with them. And if they had? She tried not to think about it.

The centaur had dropped her off in the early morning and it was now midafternoon. "I could have flown this far in less than a minute," she muttered to a disinterested lizard.

She perched on the edge of a rock and mopped her forehead with the edge of her tunic. The dust covering both became a muddy smear. The sun beat down mercilessly and she looked longingly at the cool black shadow of a small cave.

A cave.

Dwarves lived in caves. Granted they were carved and built into caverns of great beauty, but they were still caves.

Crystal dropped to her knees and peered into the darkness. After the bright sunlight, it took her eyes a moment to adjust, but she was certain that the cave extended back quite far and eventually opened up. Carefully, she slid forward onto her stomach and began to inch her way into the darkness, pulling herself along by her elbows and toes. Her body quickly blocked any light coming from the entrance and the darkness became so thick it could almost be touched. A sharp rock dug into her elbow, drawing blood and a string of curses that would have horrified Tayer could she have heard them.

Inch by torturous inch, Crystal squirmed down the tunnel, wondering why she had been so sure it would open up ahead. If anything, it became more confining and began to slope quite distinctly down. Then, just as her eyes were beginning to adjust and she was able to distinguish between the denser black of the rock and the grayish black of the air, her elbows found no purchase and, scrambling for something to grab, she tumbled over the edge of a precipice.

A small one, fortunately. She lay on her back, breathing heavily, more frightened by her instinctive urge to break her fall with power

than by the fall itself. She had just realized that, unable to use her powers, she could die in a great many ridiculous ways . . . and this time
there would be no Riven to pull her out.

The sudden flaring of a lantern almost blinded her, but her hamadryad
eyes welcomed the light, absorbed it, and soon she could see again.

She had never seen an uglier man. He was short, bandy-legged,
barrel-chested, and had the arms and shoulders of a man twice his
height. The grizzled red beard did nothing to improve the scarred and
scowling face. Red fires burned in the depths of his eyes. Around his
waist, over a patched brown tunic, he wore a belt made of gold leaves
that was so beautifully crafted and so detailed Crystal was sure she
heard a breeze move through the leaves. He had to be a dwarf.

"Name's Doan," he growled at last. "I expect you've come for the
dragon."

Crystal opened and closed her mouth a few times, but words just
wouldn't come.

"Well, you look like her," Doan said, holding out a hand to help her
up. To Crystal's surprise, he appeared to be smiling. "But you sure haven't got her way with words. Coming?"

"Where?" Crystal managed at last.

Doan held the lantern up and she saw they were in a small, circular
cave. Tucked up against the ceiling was the tunnel she had fallen from
and opposite it, at floor level, was an arched doorway. Doan headed for
the door and she followed.

She had to duck to get under the arch, but the rest of the corridor—
such a work of art could not be thought of as a mere tunnel—was high
enough for her to walk erect. The dwarf moved quickly for all his
squatness and she hurried to keep up. There was no time to study the
carvings on the walls, although she was sure they told a story as so
many images kept repeating, there was barely time to notice the inlay
work and the beauty it brought to the stone.

"Doan," she said, before the silence became oppressive and reminded her that they were walking under almost a mile of solid rock,
"who is it you think I look like?"

Doan snorted. "You're the image of the Lady. And you know it. Even her sisters remarked on the resemblance."

"But we all look alike."

Doan snorted again, a rude noise he seemed fond of. "The Lady had more life in her than all those sticks of wood combined. So do you."

"Did you know her?"

"I'd hardly know you looked like her if I didn't, now would I." His harsh voice softened slightly and though he looked no less ugly, he was, for a moment, less frightening. "Aye, I knew her. She'd done me a favor, thousands of years ago by mortal time, so I watched them for her—her man and her boy—and I watched her die." He looked up at Crystal; the red fire blazed in his eyes and his voice was stone.

"Kraydak and Death could have the whole mortal lot of them if it was up to me." Then he sighed and the fires died. He waved her on ahead. "But it isn't, so there you are . . ."

Crystal stepped out into a cavern where the rock had been worked on and improved by hundreds of dwarves for thousands of years. And the cavern had been beautiful to start with. Gold and silver danced across the walls and diamonds refracted the light into countless tiny rainbows.

But the room was only a frame for the dragon.

More lovely than anything Crystal had ever seen, he lay sleeping, wrapped around a stone column that had been carved to resemble a giant tree. His scales were gold and shone with an almost iridescent light. He was grace and power and a terrible beauty. The mighty head lay pillowed on a curve of foreleg, and his golden lacelike wings were folded across his back. From his nostrils came two thin streams of pure white smoke and from his mouth . . .

Crystal turned to Doan in disbelief.

"He snores?"

Doan nodded. "And he stinks when he gets too hot. He's a bit whiff now."

A slightly unpleasant, musky odor was noticeable and it grew stronger as Crystal moved closer. She winced as her footsteps echoed, sounding unnaturally loud.

"Don't worry about the noise," Doan said, stomping along beside her. "We carved this cavern out around him, and if that noise didn't wake him up there's no sound loud enough to disturb him."

Crystal stood and stared up at the dragon. Had its jaw been flat on the ground, she would have just barely been able to look it in the eye. Tentatively, she reached out and touched it on the nose. Beneath her hand, the skin was warm and surprisingly soft. There was no indication that the creature was aware of her at all. She prodded it gently with the toe of her boot. Nothing.

"It's funny," said Doan, kicking the dragon and not gently, "that out of all the spells Kraydak threw at this creature to stop it, it was the simplest one that worked. Sleep, he said, and sleep it has." The dwarf shrugged. "Even the earth sleeps, so I guess those made of it must as well."

"But how do I wake it if I can't use my powers?"

Doan gazed at Crystal in astonishment, both brows raised nearly to his hairline. "Didn't the centaurs teach you anything?" he demanded.

"They taught me plenty," Crystal snapped. She'd settled with that and didn't need it brought up again. "They never mentioned this, is all."

"*This* is what you were born for, and they never mentioned it?" Doan snarled in disgust. "You can't count on those blowhards for anything. Kiss him!"

"I beg your pardon."

Doan sighed, "An enchanted sleep can be broken only by the kiss of a maiden both fair and pure." Critically, he looked her up and down. "The Lady was the most beautiful woman ever to walk the earth and you're her image, I guess that should be fair enough. How's your love life?"

Crystal remembered Bryon lying blasted on the ground and started to laugh. Kraydak had outsmarted himself that time. Had Bryon been allowed to live she, no doubt, would have been unqualified to wake anyone from an enchanted sleep by now. Kraydak would have the world to himself and . . . to her surprise she found herself cradled in Doan's powerful arms and weeping bitterly.

"Hush, child," he whispered as she clung to him, sobs racking her slender body. "Tears won't bring him back." He remembered another silver-haired maiden who'd wept in his arms, then dried her eyes, and walked away from her tree to her death. He cursed mortal men, individually and collectively, for the pain they caused.

Gradually Crystal calmed and pulled away. She felt surprisingly better. Was that all it took, then, to forget, to ease the pain, just a few tears? She checked her heart and found Bryon there as he always had been, but the cold fire surrounding the memory had been put out. Doan reached up and took the last tear off her cheek with the tip of his finger. It sparkled there for a moment then shimmered and changed; where the drop of water had been was a perfect blue opal.

"That's never happened before," Crystal sniffed, wiping her nose on the tattered edge of her tunic.

"You've never cried on a dwarf before," Doan told her, offering her the gem with an oddly gentle smile on his ugly face.

She managed a weak smile in return and tucked the stone in her belt. Then, with new resolve, she turned back to the dragon.

"Why me?" she asked. "Why a wizard? Wouldn't any beautiful virgin do?"

Doan snorted. "What would any beautiful virgin do with the dragon once she woke it? Hopefully, it'll listen to a wizard."

One silver eyebrow went up. "Hopefully?"

"That's the theory." Doan shrugged. "We won't know until you try."

"On the lips?"

"I don't think it has lips."

"Oh." Crystal squared her shoulders, leaned forward, and kissed the dragon on the exact center of his golden nose. Then she stepped back beside the dwarf and they waited.

The snoring, which had been a rumbling background noise from the moment they had entered the cavern, stopped. The dragon twitched, rubbed at his nose with the curve of a talon, and opened his eyes. They were the brilliant blue of a summer's sky and faceted into a thousand gleaming parts. Six feet of forked tongue snaked out and gently touched Crystal's face.

"Wizzzard." Its teeth were very large.

"Not your wizard," Crystal protested, as the tongue touched her again.

"Young," said the dragon. "Different. Tassste like treesss. Ssstill, wizzzard." In a blur of gold and blue, he reared back, opened his mouth, and shot forth one large but not very hot puff of smoke.

Doan almost collapsed, he was laughing so hard at the puzzled expression on the dragon's face.

Crystal, who had dived out of the path of what she expected to be a killing blast of flame, was not as amused.

"Well, what else did you expect?" she said, limping back to meet the dragon face to face. "You've been asleep for thousands of years."

"Thousssandsss?" For the first time he looked around and realized where he was. "Kraydak!" The softly sibilant voice grew to a roar that shook the roof. Crystal and Doan scrambled for cover as he surged to his hind feet and, talons extended, ripped and shredded the air. He fell back to the floor with a crash and began maneuvering his bulk around so he could get out the only tunnel large enough for him.

"Hold it!" Crystal grabbed a dragging wingtip and dug in her heels. She couldn't let this lizard and Kraydak destroy everything people had worked for over the last thousand years; the scars of their last conflict were barely healed. "Where do you think you're going?"

"Releassse, wizzzard," snarled the dragon, appearing very willing to take care of her first. "There isss job left undone."

"And it'll stay undone unless you listen to me. Kraydak beat you once, he can do it again."

"Accident."

"Maybe, maybe not; and he's been getting more powerful while you've been napping. This time he could kill you instead of just putting you to sleep."

The dragon glared at her suspiciously but he stopped trying to leave the cavern. "Lissstening."

Crystal let go of the wingtip. She was aware that the dragon considered her at best an annoyance to be eliminated and at worst, regardless of her differences, one of the race he was sworn to destroy. She wiped her sweaty palms on her thighs and met the glaring blue of his gaze. This, the hamadryads hadn't told her. She'd been created to wake the dragon, yes, but that couldn't be the end of it.

"Kraydak will have to be distracted if you're to have any chance of getting close to him."

"Ssso," he hissed contemptuously. "What dissstractsss wizzzard?"

She spread her hands and said simply, "Another wizard."

The dragon smiled. It was the most terrifying thing he had done so far.

"Yesss."


With Doan as a guide, the walk back to the sandstone pillar was pleasant and much faster than her earlier journey across the badlands. Although Crystal wanted to hurry, for she knew that C'Fas could mask her absence for only a limited time and she'd spent longer than she'd intended with the dragon, the wonders of her surroundings invited her to linger. The caverns of the dwarves were, indeed, as beautiful as legend described them. Thick pillars, carved to resemble fantastic animals, carried the weight of the roof—and the mountain of stone above it—on their massive shoulders.

"Not bad for just a few thousand years," the dwarf agreed as Crystal admired the jewel-encrusted mosaics covering the walls.

"A few thousand years? But the dwarves have been since the beginning."

"Been, yes, but not here. We came here to guard the dragon."

"Against what?" Crystal couldn't think of anything that would dare to harm such a magnificent and powerful creature.

"Against mortals," Doan snorted. "A plague on the earth they are.

Can't imagine what the Mother was thinking of when She created them. Consider the mess we'd all be in had a human stumbled on the dragon. When Kraydak emerged, they'd have led him right to it and we'd have the battles of the Doom all over again." He chuckled and suddenly sounded much more approving of mortalkind. "Of course, they'd have probably tried to make him pay for the privilege of destroying them. This is the way out."

Crystal took one last look around, then began to follow Doan up the narrow, winding staircase. "What I really mind," she said suddenly, "is having Kraydak be right."

"About what?"

"Well, he said I couldn't defeat him, and he was right."

Doan stopped climbing and turned to look at her. "Who told you that?"

"Everyone."

"Everyone?" The dwarf made it sound like an expletive. "Did I?"

"No . . . But I thought I was created to wake the dragon?"

"You were."

"And I wasn't supposed to fight Kraydak at all?"

"You weren't. But that has no bearing on whether or not you could beat him." He sighed at the expression on her face and motioned for her to sit down, seating himself on a higher step as she did so. "I've been keeping an eye on your battles . . ." A wave of his hand cut off her question. "Never mind how, let's just say I have. And I've been keeping my eye on you for a lot longer. You've got closer ties to the Mother than any of the old wizards ever did and every time you forget to be a wizard with a capital W . . ." He reached down and lifted her chin with the tip of one hoary finger. "Every time you're just Crystal and you hit him with what you're feeling, you whop his ass."

"I do?"

Doan grinned fiercely. "You do."

"Then I didn't need the dragon?"

"Maybe. Maybe not. You're young, comparatively untrained, and not even at seventeen can you exist on emotions all the time. The dragon is a tool for you to use, why not use it?" His finger under her chin increased its pressure and then withdrew. "But if it means so much to you, in my opinion, Kraydak is wrong. You can defeat him." He got to his feet and started climbing again. "Besides," he threw back over his shoulder, "that arrogant s.o.b. hasn't been right about anything for thousands of years, so why should he start now?"

As Crystal climbed after the dwarf, the last of the guilt wrapped about Bryon's death dissolved. While she'd thought it inevitable that Kraydak would win, Bryon had died because of her stupidity in accepting the older wizard's challenge. Now that she knew the truth, Bryon was still equally dead, but it wasn't her fault. Now, he could be mourned.

At the top of the stairs, they went through a red sandstone door and out to the badlands of Aliston. Even knowing it existed, Crystal could see no sign of the door on the pillar that marked the edge of the dwarves' territory.

"That's amazing," she breathed.

"On the contrary," lectured C'Tal from behind her, "as the dwarves are master of stone, it is not amazing at all. It would be amazing only for a hamadryad, or a mer, or a human to have built that door."

"It would be impossible," Doan grunted, turning and looking up, way up, at the centaur. "How're you doing, you old horse's ass?" He grinned as C'Tal pretended not to have heard. "Hear you've begun to believe your own legends."

C'Tal speared the dwarf with a condescending glare, his arms folded across his mighty chest. "What legends?"

"The legends that say centaurs are the holders of all knowledge."

One gigantic hoof gouged a hole in the dirt. "We do not feel there was anything amiss in our teaching. She possessed both the information and the ability to fashion it into an understandable whole. And," he emphasized the word with a mighty stamp, "all the free peoples of the earth should be grateful that with this wizard there will be no danger of her indulging in random and irresponsible behavior. If nothing else, we have instilled in her the belief that she must employ her powers for good."

"If nothing else," Doan agreed amicably, leaning against the pillar, both hands shoved behind his belt. "But it's not polite to talk of the child as though she wasn't here."

"She is not here."

"Wha . . ."

Crystal, spotting a flash of gold amidst the gray sameness of the badlands, had scrambled to the top of a rocky hillock to get a better look. Slowly at first, for his wings were stiff and unsure, the great golden dragon rose into the sunlight and appeared to burst suddenly into gilded flame. Crystal caught her breath at his splendor and one hand reached out as though to touch the glory. Her heart seemed to be beating too violently to stay within her chest. There were tears in her eyes as she wondered how such a creature would look in silver and green. . . .

"Do you think she'll survive?" Doan asked, after he had explained the plan that Crystal had given the dragon.

"Although her powers are great and still growing, she is, despite our teachings, relatively untrained and it is unlikely that she will prevail against one who is infinitely more experienced in both the means and the method of wizardry."

"Which means?"

"I do not think she will survive. The hope of the world can only be that she continues to amuse the Enemy long enough for the Doom to approach."

"Got a better plan?"

"No."

# EIGHTEEN

When Crystal arrived back at the Ardhan camp, it was late evening. She had been gone for four days. Kraydak had apparently not missed her.

The centaurs disappeared practically the instant Crystal's foot hit the ground. One moment they were there and the next they were gone. The queen and her council breathed a collective sigh of relief. Not only was their wizard—daughter, princess—safely back, but it hadn't been easy sharing close quarters with C'Fas for four days. A centaur is an awe-inspiring creature and trapped in a tent—for he had to stay out of sight of Kraydak's spies—he is overwhelming in the extreme.

The dwarves had replaced Crystal's tattered clothes from some hidden store, and had set her opal tear in silver. She wore it on a chain around her neck and it glowed softly in the folds of her tunic.

"Well?" asked Mikhail at last, for Crystal still stood where she'd dismounted, eyes unfocused.

With a barely perceptible jerk, the wizard returned to her body. "He is almost ready to attack again," she said. "We will be only just in time."

"We?" repeated Lorn skeptically, "Does this mean . . ." He broke off as Crystal turned to face him. He suddenly couldn't remember what he was going to say.

She swept the tent with her gaze and the questions that had not yet been voiced disappeared. Not until Doan pointed it out, had she realized her stupidity in mentioning the dragon to so many people. It was not beyond Kraydak's ability to lift the knowledge from their minds and thus gain the time to prepare himself for the attack. Crystal hated to alter the memories of her parents and their council, but it was by far the lesser of two evils. She could only hope she wasn't already too late, hope that they hadn't told everyone in the camp what they knew.

Tayer recovered first from the tampering. She blinked twice, looked momentarily puzzled, and then stared questioningly at her daughter. "You look exhausted," she said at last. "You need a hot bath, a light supper, and a good night's sleep."

"A heavy supper please, Mother," Crystal said as they walked arm in arm from the tent, leaving Mikhail and the council shaking their heads and wondering what they'd missed. "I'm starved." She'd need all her strength for tomorrow.

In the quiet hour between moonset and dawn, a great white owl lifted from Crystal's tent, circled once around the queen's pavilion, and headed east with strong, unhurried beats of its wings. The sentries that saw it go watched until it vanished in the clouds, then turned to each other and said in voices of wonder, "The wizard," as if that was enough to explain it. For them, it was.

Tayer and Mikhail slept on, wrapped in each other's arms, unaware that their daughter was changing the rules of Kraydak's game. They would have tried to stop her had they known, so she hadn't told them she was going.

Kraydak, safe in his tower, smiled as Crystal entered his territory. Given her previous displays of power, he had expected more resistance to his call. If the form she wore was intended to deceive him, it was an abject failure, for he had spotted her the moment she crossed the mountains. Mindshielded or not, there just weren't that many owls with a fifteen-foot wingspan.

Crystal flew on, thinking owl thoughts on the surface but behind the shield concentrating only on distracting Kraydak and bringing things to an end one way or another. She realized her end would probably come before his. Not even the centaurs who had trained her expected her to live. And if by some miracle she did . . . well, she doubted the dragon would allow the last of the wizards to continue to exist. She was calm now, accepting, but in the dark hours of the night she'd considered running, running and letting Kraydak and his Doom fight it out without her. The world would be ripped apart once more, but she would live a while longer. *It isn't fair,* she sniffed. *I'm only seventeen.* But still she flew on.

The foothills of the Melacian side of the mountains were passing far below her when the storm struck. Gusts of wind tossed her about, trying to slam her out of the air, and the rain beat through her feathers, hitting hard enough to bruise. The water was so dense she could hardly see, the wind ripped feathers free, and the thick down that should have kept her warm and dry was soaked through. She'd expected him to find her but not so soon. She had to survive, her death now would be too short a distraction.

"Distract me from what?" wondered Kraydak, who'd pried free a tiny piece of the thought.

Screaming a challenge, she dove for the first clear area she spotted and her talons sank deep into the soft mud beside a mountain stream. She threw back her head, the green eyes blazed, and a weeping birch, the silver's more flexible cousin, danced in the wind and lifted its leaves to the rain. The wind blew harder, but the tree bent gracefully out of its way, bent so far that its uppermost branches trailed in the swiftly moving water of the stream.

A huge silver salmon with green-gold eyes leaped away and sped downstream as the blue bolt came out of the sky and crashed into the earth where the tree had stood.

\*        \*        \*

Kraydak smiled, calmed the wind and stopped the rain, for they were no longer needed. She was very resourceful, this wizard-child, and he looked forward to making her trip an interesting one before welcoming her to his tower and finding out just what exactly she thought she was doing. If she fought the calling he'd laid upon her, she did it in a very peculiar way. He considered boiling away the stream and the rivers it ran into but decided against it; that would hardly be sporting and he did want her to arrive in one piece. He hadn't been so diverted in centuries. Where had she learned to think so much like a fish?

Crystal sped down the stream as fast as her powerful new body could take her. She was tiring but didn't dare take the time to rest. A moving target was, after all, more difficult to hit. She felt the amusement in Kraydak's questing thoughts and used her anger at it to reinforce her shield.

The ancient wizard laughed aloud. So she would hide her fishy thoughts, would she? He followed instead the pattern of the shield.

The current slowed and the texture of the water changed; the stream was about to join a major river. Once sharing its depths with a multitude of life forms, she'd be harder for Kraydak to spot and, if she remembered the maps correctly, the river ran through Melac's capital city and right past Kraydak's tower. With his attention on the river, he wouldn't be scanning the rest of the countryside.

"Why," Kraydak asked the skull, "would I want to scan the countryside?" He got only fragments of thought through the shield and this fragment made no sense. If she was trying to sneak assassins through Melac, they'd die before they reached the tower and he'd never have to become involved. Assassins were a stupid idea. He smiled. They must be getting very desperate.

"I wonder . . ." He tapped the yellowed ivory of the skull's teeth. "Should I scan the countryside?"

The skull grinned up at him.

He nodded. "Yes, you're quite right. She's played my game, so it's only fair I play hers . . . for a while. Besides, the countryside can hold nothing more interesting than the river. She shows such initiative, I almost wished I'd called her sooner."

A massive golden paw tipped with deadly claws split the water inches from Crystal's nose. Her panicked flip backward took her up and out of the water and dangerously close to the snapping jaws of a huge golden bear. She hit the water with a painful smack and raced back upstream. From the security of the bottom of a deep pool, she considered what she should do.

Crystal knew she really only had one choice. What happened to her was unimportant. She had to hold Kraydak's attention. The dragon had to get through.

She sent out a questing thought. The bear waited at the end of the stream. He blocked the water route completely, which left only one way to go. She rose to the surface of the pool, found the strongest flow of current, and started back downstream. Her fins and tail beat against the water and she swam rapidly toward the river. The current lent her speed and she moved faster and faster until she flashed through the water like silver lightning. When she felt the bear gather himself to lunge, she twisted her tail and jumped.

No fish jumps better than a salmon and no salmon ever leaped higher than Crystal. Up, up she arced, flashing silver in the sunlight. The bear, who had dived forward to scoop her from the water, was taken by surprise and although he reared and raked the air with his claws, he was far too late. With liquid grace, Crystal twisted and dove into the relative safety of the river.

As she swam away, she felt the bear's mind follow her. He seemed to be laughing. At least she'd managed to keep him amused.

Kraydak considered sending an otter into the river but decided against it. He had no need to exert himself for, after all, the wizard-child was coming to him. He would watch to see she didn't slip away and take care of her when she reached the tower. He appreciated her courage, secure in the knowledge that she could do him little harm.

The sun was a red-gold ball balanced on the western mountains when Crystal reached the tower. She swam slowly, trying to conserve her dwindling energies. Between holding the transformation and the constant fear that Kraydak would make a move she couldn't counter, she was nearing the point of exhaustion. And if she faced Kraydak, if she actually reached him and the dragon hadn't yet come, what then? Could her shield hold without distance to lend it strength? She was so busy worrying, she didn't notice the net until it was too late.

"Right then, we've got her! Heave to and let's get her beached!"

The four men put their backs to it, laboriously drawing the net and its thrashing cargo to shore. But what they pulled from the water was no fish.

"Holy shit," breathed a ruffian who was missing an ear and most of his nose. "I never thought I'd see one of those." He dropped the net and grabbed for his sword as the unicorn kicked itself free of the ropes.

It was over very quickly.

Sides heaving, its horn and hoofs dripping gore, the unicorn staggered-toward the tower. It shimmered and Crystal collapsed across the steps. Her skin and shift were covered in blood, not all of it belonging to others. There was a sword cut on her upper arm and her nose still bled freely. She shivered in the shadow of the tower and couldn't seem to catch her breath.

The great iron-bound door swung open. She was expected.

*At least he's still interested,* she thought, crawling forward. She pulled herself up until she sat on the bottom step, looked up at the apparently infinite length of stone staircase wrapped about the inside of the building, and giggled. She couldn't help it.

"You've got to be kidding," she called up the stairs.

The door slammed shut and latched with an ominous thunk. Kraydak thought he had her safe; now she had nowhere to go but up.

Crystal remembered the blue bolt smashing Bryon to the ground and added the memory to her shield. The dragon should be very close. If it was coming. If Kraydak hadn't already taken care of it. She set her teeth, pulled herself to her feet, and slowly began to climb.

High above the clouds, the dragon soared, his scales glowing reddish gold in the light of the setting sun. He banked and dipped and gloried in the strength of his wings.

"Perhapsss wait," he thought as he raced the wind and won. "Kraydak killsss wizzzard. Kraydak isss mine. No more wizzzards. Ever."

The sun dropped below the horizon and, for a moment, the dragon lit the evening on his own.

"Perhapsss wait."

On the hundredth step, Crystal knew she had to rest. Her blood sang in her ears and she couldn't, just couldn't lift her leg again. She sagged against the outer wall.

DEATH!

The scream in her mind shocked her so she slid down half a dozen steps before she could catch herself. Eyes wide, she reached out a trembling hand and touched the wall again.

DEATH!

Even prepared for it, the force of the cry caused her to jerk and snatch her hand away as if she'd been burned. She sat down, carefully staying away from the wall, and clasped her hands between her knees to stop them from shaking.

"Destroy him," said Lord Death from the step below her, "and free my people, too."

And then he was gone and she was alone again save for the screaming souls trapped in the walls. It was a long time before she could continue to climb.

The door to the inner sanctum was made of solid gold. The carved face of a demon leered out at Crystal as she mounted the last few steps and just before the door swung open, it bared its teeth. She stepped over the threshold and looked about. The slamming of the door behind her was so predictable that she didn't even flinch.

The walls of the room were covered in sheets of beaten gold, a cheerful fire burned in a small hearth, a huge desk took up over half the space, and strange and wonderful things were piled haphazardly about. A door seemed to lead to another room, although this first room took up the full diameter of the tower. There were no windows.

Kraydak looked very much as he had in her mind. Maybe better. He wore a robe of blue velvet which had fallen open to expose the golden muscles of his chest and he smiled kindly.

"Now what, little one?" he asked. "How are you to defeat me in single combat when you barely made it up the stairs?"

Clenching her teeth, Crystal pulled herself erect and reached into her belt. With what was almost the last of her strength, she sent the small silver knife flying straight for Kraydak's heart.

He plucked it easily from the air, turned it into a dove, and crushed the life from the bird with one immaculately manicured hand. He never stopped smiling.

Crystal hadn't expected it to work, but she had to try. Unfortunately, that used up just about all she had left. Where was the dragon?

"You're dripping on the carpet," Kraydak chided her. He waved his hand and she was warm and dry in a gown of green silk that dipped and clung to her body. Her hair floated around her like a silver-white cloud. His smile changed slightly and he licked his lips. His expression reminded Crystal of the demon on the door.

Crystal could only watch as her feet carried her within his reach.

He wrapped a hand possessively around her throat and she shuddered.

"It's been lonely for me these last thousand years. You don't know what it's like to be the only one of your kind, always alone." His smile saddened. "Of course, if you'd managed to kill me, you would've found out. But you can't kill me and, fortunately for us both, I have no need to kill you. Yet. When I do . . ." He shrugged. "Well, I am used to being lonely."

The hand around her throat was the hand he'd used to crush the bird. It was sticky with blood.

"You have lovely skin," he murmured against her cheek.

His hand began to stroke her throat and it caught on the silver chain. He drew it tight, so that the links began to cut into the back of her neck.

"Very pretty," he said, lifting the opal to admire it. "Dwarf work, isn't it? I never had much to do with the Elder Races. Perhaps I should remedy that when the novelty of your company wears thin."

*Where was the . . .*

"What?" Kraydak raised an eyebrow in inquiry. "Why don't you tell me what you're waiting for? Not dwarves, surely? Don't tell me you've recruited the Elder to your cause."

The Elder . . . Crystal concentrated what little strength she had left on forming the image of C'Tal in her mind, the great black body, the flowing hair and beard, each pompous and pedantic utterance she'd been forced to endure for six long years.

Kraydak easily brushed it aside. "A good likeness, little one, but you can't hope to block me with something I know far better than you. The centaurs taught all the wizards. It's what they do, and I stayed with them a very long time. An opportunity I could not allow you to take."

*Every time you're just Crystal . . .* said Doan's voice in her memory.

Bryon then. The laughter in his eyes, the touch of his hand, the feel of his breath on her mouth, his body lying crumpled and broken on the ground.

"Not bad . . ." The ancient wizard nodded thoughtfully. "But you let me in at the end. You forgot, you see, who put him on the ground."

Crystal held tight to her anger. It would not be a shield now, but a doorway for him to slide through and into her mind. Something that must not happen. Carefully, for this was her last chance, she built up layer by layer a silver tree. Not the ancient birches of the hamadryads, but the thirteenth tree in the circle, a young tree, barely marked by time. It was the tree that made her different, negated the superficial kinship between herself and Kraydak, defined from the very beginning the type of person Crystal would become.

Beneath the pressure of Kraydak's mind the tree bent and swayed, but it held. He drew the chain he still held tighter, golden brows drawn down with annoyance. "They say dwarf-made links never break. I could behead you with this. It wouldn't be pleasant."

Crystal thought of the tree.

"You will tell me what you're trying so hard to hide." He forced her chin up. "You've been quite a diversion, wizard-child, and I'm sure you'll find ways to amuse me for a long time to come but, for now, all I ask is that you look at me."

Crystal had no strength left to refuse. The tree withered and died and she met his eyes.

Blue. Very blue. Wrapped in blue . . . sinking in blue . . . wanting it to consume her.

*So that's what it feels like,* was her last conscious thought.

She didn't see the look of raw terror on Kraydak's face when at last he found what she had hidden and, seconds later, she didn't see the golden tail which sheared the roof cleanly from the walls, nor the expression of triumph on the dragon's face when the mighty jaws closed and the Wizard's Doom found Kraydak at last.

It was probably fortunate she didn't see the mess the dragon made as he fed.

Finished with Kraydak, the dragon looked down at the wizardling lying crumpled on the floor, opened his mouth to destroy her as well and suddenly changed his mind. She didn't look like a wizard, nor smell like one, and he was certain she wouldn't taste like one.

"Harmlesss," he decided and spread his wings to leave.

"If you leave her here, she'll die."

The dragon turned his head and fixed Lord Death in one sapphire eye. "Ssso?"

"You must return her to her people."

"Mussst?" The dragon snorted a brief burst of flame, as close to laughter as he could come. His wings beat at the air. "Mussst?"

Lord Death nodded. "You owe her. She woke you. She made it possible for you to destroy your creator. If you allow her to die, you're no better than he was."

"Better than wizzzard!" His tail, whipping from side to side in agitation, destroyed a large section of wall.

"Prove it. Take her home."

The dragon reared, but Lord Death stood quietly, staring up at him. Finally the great beast sighed and scooped Crystal up in massive talons. "Yesss." Then, wings spread for flight, he paused.

"Ssson of Mother . . ."

"Yes?"

"Why sssave?"

Lord Death reached up and untangled several lengths of silvery white hair. "I don't know," he admitted. "I really don't know."

"Crystal? Crystal? Mikhail! I think she's awake!"

"Crystal?"

She felt Mikhail's hand clutching hers, knew it was Tayer placing the wet cloth on her forehead, and struggled to open her eyes. Why was everything so blue? Gradually the blues began to fade, replaced by browns and golds and reds and blacks, colors which finally shifted to become her mother's worried face. She looked for her voice, found it, and croaked, in nothing resembling her usual tones, "I'm hungry."

To her surprise, Tayer began to cry and it was the Duke of Belkar who held the cup of soup to her mouth while Mikhail held his wife.

"What . . ."

"Drink up," Belkar commanded, not letting her finish, his own eyes bright with tears. "You're nothing but skin and bones. You look like you've been out a month instead of just a week."

Crystal obeyed, partly because she had no energy to protest and partly because satisfying the enormous hunger that clawed at her was more important at the moment than getting answers. When the cup was empty, she sighed and tried to sit up. It wasn't a great success and she sank back against the pillows, breathing heavily.

"What happened?" she managed to gasp.

"You tell us," Mikhail said, taking the cup from Belkar and refilling it. He propped Crystal up and she drank greedily while he talked.

"Eight days ago, we woke and were told you'd vanished. Late that night, something huge flew over, terrified the horses, and dropped you in the middle of the camp. You've been lying here, unconscious, ever since."

Finished with the second mug, Crystal tried a smile. Her lips felt stiff. "The dragon," she said. "Then Kraydak is dead."

Mikhail frowned. "Are you sure? He escaped before."

Crystal shook her head and wished she hadn't when the room danced with blue spots.

"Not this time." Her voice, rough as it was, held such conviction that they had to believe her. "The dragon brought me back after it killed Kraydak."

"How can you know?"

She spread her hands. "I'm here." It was the only answer that fit. She'd never know why the dragon had let her live; she didn't really care. Being alive was enough.

Belkar beamed down at her. "You said he'd have to make a mistake for you to win. He didn't, though, and you still beat him."

"No. He made a mistake."

"What?" scoffed the duke. "You were stronger. You beat him at his own game."

"That was his mistake." She peered up at Belkar from under suddenly heavy lids. "He never realized that I wasn't playing." A massive yawn threatened to split her face. "The war?" she managed as sleep pushed her back into the pillows.

"Over," said Mikhail, pulling the covers up under her chin. "The Melacians sued for peace the morning after you reappeared."

"Good," she murmured and slid into blackness.

With the resilience of youth, the heritage of the Lady, and what seemed like gallons of chicken soup, she regained her strength quickly, eating and sleeping and listening for only a week before she left her bed. Already plans were being made to go into Melac, find the true king, and put him back on the throne. Belkar was certain that the conquered countries would slip back into their previous boundaries, but Cei wasn't so sure. He felt there would be more bloodshed before the disintegrating Empire straightened itself out. Crystal agreed with Cei.

She soon discovered that most of the army had gone home; only the dukes and their people remained. And a young couple who refused to leave without seeing her.

"We couldn't leave until we got your blessing on our joining."

Crystal smiled at the young woman who had been her maid and the soldier she had taken from the hand of Lord Death. "For what it's worth, you have it. And my deep wishes for your happiness as well."

The two blushed and grinned and headed for the door where the ex-maid paused and shook her head. She turned back to the bed as if determined that a distasteful task must be done. "Promise me, milady," she pleaded, "that you won't wear red again. It simply isn't your color."

Crystal looked down at the robe borrowed from her mother, threw back her head and laughed. "I promise," she managed at last and felt better than she had in months.

The camp looked tattered and deserted as she walked across it her first day up. The leavings of the army blew about her as she moved slowly to the scar in the earth where the bodies of the fallen had been buried.

She stood at the edge of the mass grave and stared down at the scuffed and pitted dirt. A blush of green appeared which grew and spread until a thick carpet of grass covered the whole area. Buttercups unfolded velvet petals and nodded at the sunlight.

"Very nice."

Crystal transferred her gaze from the ground to Lord Death.

"Don't you ever," she hissed, "show yourself to me in that face again."

Lord Death backed up a step and Bryon's features were replaced with auburn curls, amber eyes, and a slightly nervous expression.

"I thought you might want to say good-bye," he explained.

"Oh." She smiled sheepishly. "Sorry, but I've already said good-bye." She waved a hand at the ground. "This is only tidying up. The dead are your concern, I should look now to the living."

"I was going to say that!"

"I don't think," Crystal told him kindly, "that I'm quite ready for the comfort of Death."

Auburn eyebrows rose, Lord Death snickered, and Crystal was alone.

A moment later, she saw her mother leave the large pavilion and she went to meet her.

Although thinner, Tayer practically glowed in the sunlight. The golden strands in her hair wove a shining pattern through the chestnut and the flecks in her eyes shone. A soft, secret sort of smile, curved her mouth. She greeted Crystal with a kiss and they sat together on a log worn smooth by its many weeks of service as a bench.

Tayer felt suddenly shy with her silver-haired daughter. With the last of the wizards.

"You were never much of a princess," she said at last.

Crystal smiled and cupped her hands so they could fill with sunlight. "The wizard was always stronger, Mother."

"I know. But you were the only heir and you had a duty to the people."

"I *was* the only heir?"

Tayer turned and met the now familiar green glow of her daughter's eyes. Her own eyes widened as Crystal's smile grew. "You probably knew before I did," she accused and laughed when Crystal shook her head, a picture of wronged innocence. "Well, I'm sure you had something to do with it anyway, O Mighty Wizard." Tayer was right, but Crystal had no intention of ever telling her that the moment they had shared in the Duke of Hale's garden—using the knowledge Crystal had found in Lady Hale's pregnancy—had righted the wrong done to Tayer's body at her daughter's birth.

The two women sat in a companionable silence, both considering the new life and the world it would enter. Both concluding it wasn't that bad a place, all things considered.

Finally, Tayer sighed. "You won't be returning with us, will you?"

"No. There's no place for me there."

"There's always a place for you," Tayer said sharply. "You're our daughter and we love you, whatever else you are."

"I know you do, Mother." She leaned over and kissed Tayer's cheek. "I meant there's no place for the wizard and I can't be just your daughter for very long."

"But you'll visit."

"Of course, I will! I'm about to become a sister, I've no intention of missing that." If Kraydak had been very lonely for the last thousand years, he had done it to himself, a mistake Crystal had no intention of repeating.

Tayer seemed reassured. "What will you do?"

Crystal spread her hands, scattering the sunlight. "Things are a bit of a mess right now; there'll be plenty for the last wizard to do straightening out what the second to last wizard did." She had a sudden vision of the way Riven's hair always fell over his face and her fingers itched to push it back. The green glow of her eyes deepened and she grinned, managing to look both more and less like a wizard.

"I think I'll start by helping to open Riven Pass."

# END

"Do you think she knows what she did?" Doan stretched out a hand and gently touched the trunk of the thirteenth birch. Although it was high summer, its leaves were brown and dry, its branches withered and dead.

C'Tal shook his head. "She thought she built an image, as she did with the others. She could not know that this would come of it."

"It saved her life."

"Yes."

"I wonder, what will become of her now?"

"That is not our concern. We have done all we were meant to do, your people and mine. The Enemy is defeated and the Doom has returned to the stone of which it was made. We may put the last of the wizards from our mind."

Doan looked up and met the Centaur's eyes. The great black orbs were solemn behind their heavy lids. "You really believe that, don't you?"

"Do you not? We have done," C'Tal repeated, "all we were meant to."

"Perhaps we have," Doan admitted. "But I think you're forgetting something."

"Forgetting?" C'Tal roared the words so loudly that the dead leaves dropped from the tree before them in a rustling shower. "Forgetting," he said again in a quieter and much more dangerous voice. "What is it you suggest I have forgotten, dwarf?"

"You've forgotten her mothers. She's unique, but they're a part of her and someday, I'll wager, they'll make their presence felt."

C'Tal snorted, as always his expressions at their most horselike when he was annoyed. "I remember her mothers." His voice dropped into a lecturing drone. "Seven were the Goddesses remaining when the Gods had been destroyed. Seven they were and . . ."

Doan raised a hand and cut him off. "Maybe you'd best remember that one or two of them . . ." He paused, snapped a tiny branch from the thirteenth tree and slipped it behind his belt, for memory's sake. ". . . were neither wise nor kind." Then he raised the hand again in salute and left the Grove.

C'Tal looked down at the withered birch. "Seven they were . . ." he said slowly.

# THE LAST
# WIZARD

For Fe, who freed the emotions
and refuses to let me lock them away again.

# ACKNOWLEDGMENTS

I'd like to take this opportunity to thank Doris Bercarich for technical assistance above and beyond the call of friendship. *I* wouldn't have lent me a disk drive.

# PROGENITOR

S even were the goddesses remaining when the gods were destroyed. Seven they were and these were their degrees:

*Nashawryn was the eldest; ebony haired and silver eyed, ruler of night and darkness, concealment and safety held in one cupped hand, a dagger of fear clenched tight in the other fist.*

*Zarsheiy, who closely followed night in age, ruled fire, and, claimed her dark sister, was ruled by it. Flame her hair and flame her eyes and flame, they said, her heart. Passionate and unpredictable, one moment giving, the next destroying, Zarsheiy's temper was legend amongst both Mortals and the deities they had created.*

*Most loved of all the seven was Geta, Freedom, who watched her twin brother Getan, god of Justice, destroyed by his wizard son and so hid her grieving face from Mortals all the long years the wizards ruled.*

*Gentle Sholah held hearth and harvest in the bowl of her two hands. Her dance turned the seasons, and she was the first who dared deny Nashawryn and have Zarsheiy heed her call.*

*Tayja was Sholah's daughter, carved for her of mahogany from the heart of a single tree by Pejore, the god of art. It was Tayja who dared go into Chaos and bring out the skill to harness Zarsheiy and she who fought always to strike the dagger from Nashawryn's hand. Craft and learning were her dominion and although she demanded much of those who worshiped her, of all the goddesses, save perhaps Geta, she gave the most in return.*

*Youngest of the seven was Eegri, and on her realm of chance even Tayja's reason blunted. She went where she would; into night; into flame; now revering freedom, now denying it; tripping through field and forge with equal abandon. She had no temples and no priesthood, but her symbol was etched over every door and among mortal kind there were many who lived by her favor.*

*The last of the seven claimed to have been present when the Mother-creator lay with Chaos and bore him Lord Death, her one true son. She claimed to be more passionate than fire, to be more necessary than freedom, to be the moving force of hearth and harvest, to be more fickle a power than even chance herself. Of craft and learning she claimed to be the strength, lending to poor mortals the incentive to succeed. Her name was Avreen, and she wore both the face of love and of her darker aspect, lust.*

As the dark age of wizards ended, these seven were all of the pantheon that survived; no longer worshiped, seldom remembered. But a goddess once created does not disappear merely because her creator has moved beyond and closer to the truth. As they watched the wizards rule, so they watched the wizards die. And they saw that one did not. The most powerful of the wizards, his father the most powerful of the gods long destroyed, still lived. Throughout the many thousand years during which he hid, the seven watched. When he emerged to rule the earth again, they were ready.

The gods had stood alone, each against his child; and lost. They would stand together.

The Mother-creator's eldest child, immortal first created, died for love of a mortal man. The seven used that love—for was not Love one of them—and formed a vessel into which they poured all that they were. They caused that vessel to present their essence back to the Mother's youngest, to a mortal woman, to the only aspect of all the Mother's creation that was in turn able to create, and she formed that essence into a child.

And the child, unique in creation, won where the gods had failed.

# ONE

"You waitin' for someone?"

"No."

"Mind if I set?"

"Yes."

The beefy faced man opened and closed his mouth a few times and a wave of red washed out the freckles sprinkled liberally across his nose and cheeks. "Think you're too good ta set with me?" His hard miner's hands clenched the edge of the small table.

"No." But the tone said yes.

It said other things as well, spoke a coldness that caused the miner's balls to draw up, even under his thick sheepskin trousers.

She lifted her head just a little and let a ray of lantern light fall within the confines of her hood.

The man's eyes widened. For a moment his jaw went slack, and then his sandy brows drew down in a puzzled frown. He knew something was happening; he didn't know what. An instant later, he lost even that and turned away, knowing only that his advances had been rejected.

She lowered her head and her face was once again masked by darkness.

"Not very polite," said her companion as the miner returned to his own table amidst the jeers and catcalls of his friends. "I never thought to see you use your power on such a trivial thing."

Crystal shrugged but kept her voice low as she answered. Although she had no objection to being thought overly proud or even peculiar, it wouldn't do to have the whole tavern think her insane; sitting and talking to a companion only she could see. She said as much to Lord Death, adding: "I wish to be left alone. That is not, to my mind, a trivial thing."

Lord Death drew his finger through a puddle of spilled ale, making no mark. "And your wish is to be that poor mortal's command?" His hair flickered to a bright red-gold, and for a heartbeat his eyes glowed a brilliant sapphire blue.

The hiss of breath through Crystal's teeth caused several patrons to turn and peer toward the dim corner. She quickly dropped her gaze to her mug of ale until, curiosity unsatisfied, they returned to their own concerns.

"You dare?" she growled when the attention had shifted away. "You dare show that face to me? To criticize *my* actions with it? To dare suggest I walk his road? Kraydak's road?" Kraydak of the red-gold hair and sapphire eyes and silken voice and blood-red hands. Kraydak, the most powerful of the ancient wizards, dead now these dozen years. Her hand had set his death in motion, but his arrogance had killed him in the end. His arrogance. His concern had been solely for himself, all others existing only to serve.

Lord Death sat quietly, chin on hands, watching the last of the wizards work her way through his accusation to the truth. In spite of a parentage that tied together all the threads of the Mother's creation, and more power than had ever been contained in a mortal shell, she was as capable of lying to herself as any other. But she seldom did and he doubted she would now. He'd spent a lot of time with her over the last few years, drawn by something he was not yet willing to name, and he'd come to respect her ability to see things as they were, not as she wanted them to be.

"I'm sorry." The whisper from the depths of the hood was truly contrite and both slender hands tightened about her mug. The pewter began to bend and she hurriedly stroked it straight. Forgetting how it must appear to anyone watching—and there had been inquisitive eyes on her since she entered the inn—she turned to face Lord Death. The shadows of the hood could not hide the brimming tears from one who walked in shadow. "I . . . I seem to be losing control of things lately."

The one true son of the Mother reached out to brush a tear away, but the drop of water slid through his finger and spun down to the scarred tabletop. He sighed and his mouth twisted as he withdrew his hand. "May I give you some advice?" he asked as they both stared down at the fallen tear.

She sniffed and managed a smile. "I don't guarantee I'll take it."

He smiled back but kept his voice carefully neutral, not letting the worry show. "Find something to do. Kraydak committed his worst excesses because he was bored." He waved his hand. "Go back to the Empire, there's enough to fix there to keep any number of wizards busy."

Crystal shook her head and pushed a spill of silver hair back beneath her hood. "I can't. The people of the Empire are too aware of the evil a wizard can do and I am too obviously—" she sighed, "—too obviously what I am. When they see me, they see Kraydak."

"You destroyed him. They'll come to see you in time."

"If you expect one act of good to wipe out ten centuries of evil, you expect too much of your people, milord. Even if I tried to make amends for every horror he ever committed—and I did try, in the beginning— they would still see only that I was a wizard, like him."

"Not like him," Lord Death reminded her.

"No," she agreed. "But in his Empire, wizard means terror and they see me as potential threat not savior." Her voice trailed off as she remembered how her help had been received; how she'd come to use her powers in secret if at all, hiding who and what she was rather than trying to fight the inheritance of fear Kraydak had left her, afraid herself that she would one day lash back and so become what they accused her of being.

Even here in Halda, even though King Jeffrey was a cousin of sorts, she kept her identity hidden. Kraydak's legions had cut through the valley country and a wizard would not be looked on kindly. Amid the

small crowd of men and women who'd braved the weather for companionship's sake, she could see a hook where a hand should be, a patch
covering an empty socket—the eye seared out by fire if the puckered
ridges surrounding it were any sign—and scars beyond counting. High
in the northern mountains, this mining village had been hit less hard
than others she'd seen, but once having felt a wizard's power they
would not likely welcome it again. Fortunately, the bitter cold—
noticeable in the tavern even though fires roared at both ends of the
long room—wrapped everyone in the anonymity of heavy clothing and
she was not the only one huddled deep within a hood.

A problem to involve her mind and her power would go a long way
toward settling the turmoil she'd live in lately; thoughts and feelings
boiling beneath the surface, occasionally bubbling up as they had with
that poor miner. It seemed, sometimes, as if each individual facet of
her personality fought for a life of its own, only rarely, coming together
to work as one harmonious whole. There were days when she dreaded
opening her mouth for fear of what would come out.

"Perhaps," Lord Death broke into her thoughts, "you should go home."

She briefly considered it. Her twelve-year-old brother and the seven-
year-old twins were enough to keep an army of wizards busy. "No,"
she said aloud, "it's too soon. Mother would be sure something was
wrong and she'd fuss."

"Maybe she could help."

"Help with what? There's nothing wrong." Crystal wondered if he
could see the heat rising in her cheeks. He sat silently, smiling slightly.
*He knows me too well,* she thought, but for some strange reason that
pleased her. "There's nothing wrong my mother can help with," she
amended and was rewarded by a fuller smile. "And besides, the adula-
tion of the Ardhan people is as hard to take in its own way as fear and
suspicion."

Fear and suspicion.

Which brought it full circle back to the Empire. Without her help, it
would be many, many years before the effects of Kraydak's tyranny
were erased from the land and the people—but she suspected that this

slow healing was for the best. Only time would convince those who'd survived the crushing weight of Kraydak's yoke that they were their own masters again.

"The trouble is," she said at last, "no one needs me."

Lord Death had no response to that so he merely sat and watched the last of the wizards drink her ale. He enjoyed watching her, not only because she was stunningly beautiful and inhumanly graceful, not only because she was intelligent, witty, and powerful, but because . . . He broke off the thought, as he always did at that point, and glanced around the room. An ancient man, sitting as close to the fire as he could without igniting his old bones, lifted his mug in salute. Lord Death smiled and returned the salutation. He appreciated a graceful exit. A number of the relic's friends peered about, wondering whom he greeted. By the coarse jokes and ribald poking at the old man's supposed gallantry, it was obvious they saw only Crystal. After living their lives in a land where winters were often eight months long, they were well practiced at judging a person's gender despite the heavy clothing.

If Crystal noticed any of this, she chose to ignore it as she ignored the other noises of the crowd, letting sounds wash over her in an undifferentiated rumble. Her table, back in a corner and away from the fires, was isolated, cold, and a little dark. Save for the one miner who'd approached at the drunken urging of his friends, she'd been left alone from the moment she'd slipped quietly back there and sat down. Even the young man who served her ale came back as seldom as he thought he could and shivered the entire time he was forced to linger so far from the fires. He'd asked her once if she wouldn't like to move closer, more for his sake, she suspected, than hers. She'd told him no, and he hadn't brought it up again. If she thought about the cold at all, she welcomed the drafts that skirted her ankles and tugged at the edges of her cloak; they kept the odors of humanity, steaming woolens, and stale beer down to a bearable level. An enhanced sense of smell, part of her heritage from the Mother's Eldest, could be a distinct disadvantage at times.

She wasn't sure why she'd even entered the inn. She had no need of food or warmth; she had no wish for companionship; but when the last light from the setting sun had picked out the gilding on the tavern's hanging sign and it had flared like a beacon in the fog she'd taken it as an omen.

What kind of omen an inn called The Wrong Nugget would be, Crystal had no idea.

She sighed and let her gaze drift over to the stairs that led to the second floor. Each step dipped from the wearing of countless footsteps and the wood was polished almost white. Any place that kept the stairs so clean, she decided, could be trusted to keep the bugs in the beds to a minimum. Perhaps she would stay the night.

But tomorrow?

Maybe she could return to the centaurs. It had been seven years since they'd taught her the delicate manipulations of the dreamworld. Perhaps enough time had passed that she could handle their pompous and pedantic utterances again. She thought of C'Tal. "Are *you entirely certain that your spiritual growth has proceeded sufficiently for you to be instructed in . . .*" No, seven years wasn't long enough. There had to be something else.

She sighed.

"No one needs me," she said again, and finished her ale.

"*Self-pity makes me sick!*" The voice blazed between her ears, disgust and anger about equally mixed.

Crystal flicked a glance behind her. Only her shadow grayed the rough log wall. Only Lord Death was close enough to have made the remark.

"I beg your pardon?"

Lord Death looked startled at the frosty tone. "I didn't say anything," he protested.

"You didn't?"

"No."

She had to believe him. He had never, to her knowledge, lied. She wasn't sure he could. "Then who . . ." She rubbed her forehead with a pale hand. Wonderful, now she was hearing things. Just what the world needed: a useless, *crazy* wizard.

With a scream of frozen hinges and a roar of winter wind, the outer door burst open and slammed back the wall. After an instant of stunned silence, the sudden blast of freezing air brought a number of the patrons to their feet and a bellow of: "Close the Chaos damned door!" ripped out of a dozen throats.

The man who staggered into the light wore furs so rimed with ice it was only common sense that said he wore furs at all. He half dragged, half carried a man-sized bundle, equally white. Just over the threshold, he stopped and swayed and stared, eddies of snow swirling about his feet through the open door.     ·

The men and women in the tavern stared back, caught by his desperation but not knowing how to respond, as the room grew colder and the lamps guttered. Finally, the young server pushed through the crowd and wrestled shut the door, alternately kicking and cursing at the lumps of ice that had followed the stranger inside. When warmth no longer leeched out of the tavern, he placed a tentative hand on the stranger's arm. The man didn't appear to notice. Even blurred by layers of clothing, every line of his body screamed exhaustion. His sway grew more pronounced and he toppled to the floor, curled protectively around his burden.

"Get the poor bugger a brandy," someone suggested, breaking the silence.

"If yer buyin', I could use one meself."

"Brandy'll kill'im. Have Inga here give'im a kiss."

"That'll kill'im fer sure."

Amid appreciative laughter at this string of wit, the server knelt down beside the body, advice and drunken speculation continuing until one voice above the babble, sharp and clear:

"What is going on out here?"

The tavern fell as close to silent as taverns ever fall, and every head still capable of the motion turned to the kitchen door. Physically, the woman who waited there for an answer was not the type to inspire such quiet. She was short, thin, with close cropped red curls, and a wide mouth—currently pressed into a disapproving line. The apron she wore over winter woolens was stained, for, proprietor or not, she did much of the cooking herself. A smudge of ash marked her nose. "Who," she demanded, dusting flour off her hands, "left the damned door open? We can feel the cold all the way into the kitchen. I've told you lot before that I've no intention of heating all of Halda."

"It's a stranger, Dorses," the barman called out and the rest of the explanation was lost as everyone tried to shout out their version of events.

She sighed, signaled the barman to stay put—his skill with beer or brandy was undeniable, but the man was useless in an emergency—and made her way across to the door. Experience told her it would be faster to see for herself than to try to sort out over twenty voices. When she reached the stranger, she touched his shoulder with the toe of her shoe.

"Is he dead, Ivan?" she asked the server.

"No." Pale brows drew down toward a snub nose. "But he's not good."

Dorses shook her head and turned a withering gaze on her clientele. "And I suppose it occurred to none of you to get him over by the fire and out of those wet furs?"

As several of the more sober blushed and muttered excuses, she looked back to her server. "What are you trying to do?" she demanded as Ivan continued to tug on the stranger's arms.

"I can't get him to let go of his bundle," he grunted, lower lip caught up between his teeth.

"Then let him be." She scanned the faces present. "Nad?"

"He's in the pot."

"Nay, I'm back."

The man who pushed his way forward was of average height and anything but average width. His shoulders were so broad he seemed a foot or so shorter than he actually stood. Pleasant features were arranged about a mashed caricature of a nose in an expression of eager curiosity.

Dorses twitched Ivan out of Nad's way and said: "See what you can do."

Nad flexed his massive shoulders, bent over the stranger, and taking each fur covered arm in a callused hand, lifted. A foot, then two, the stranger rose and although he maintained his grip the bundle's own weight pulled it free. Nad grunted in satisfaction, moved a bit to the left, and gently lowered the man back to the floor.

"Chaos," breathed Ivan, his eyes widening. "That's a brindle pelt he was carryin'. Looks fresh killed, too."

The stranger lay forgotten in a puddle of melting snow while they all examined what he'd been clutching so tightly. Dorses bent and stroked the long, brown and black fur.

"It's brindle all right," she said, lifting a corner and looking beneath. Her tone remained unchanged as she added, "It's also a body." After eight years of running this tavern, she'd pretty much lost her ability to be surprised by anything.

"My brother," the stranger's voice was a reedy gasp. He rose shakily to one elbow and removed the half-frozen wool scarf from in front of his mouth. "Wounded in the mountains." Beneath a drooping mustache his lips were pinched and white. "Needs . . ." Then he collapsed back to the floor.

"Help," Dorses finished, her hand slipping beneath the fur and resting on the throat of the wounded man. His pulse barely shivered against her fingers. "Ivan, take care of . . ." Without a name, she waved a hand in the general direction of the stranger. "I want his brother here up on that table. Don't unwrap him, Nad!" she snapped as huge hands reached down and started to roll the brindle free. "Lift him as he is."

"But Dorses!" Nad protested, scarred fingers sinking into the plush fur. "Just think on it! A week at my forge wouldn't bring in what this pelt will. You don't use brindle as a stretcher! You can't!" His tone was horrified.

"Why not? It's almost a shroud. Now move!"

With a miner on each side of the torso and another lifting the legs, the body and the pelt were hoisted onto a hastily cleared table. Nad bit back a cry as the preferred fur of kings settled gently on top of biscuit crumbs and spilled beer. At a curt nod from Dorses, he almost reverently folded back the outer edge, and then the inner, pulling slowly but steadily for the pelt was frozen stiff and stuck to something beneath.

"Mother who made us all," he breathed, and his hands dropped to his sides.

Even Dorses paled.

The stranger's brother looked about thirty and was a slightly built man, thin but muscular. A week's beard glinted gold in the lamplight, some shades darker than the wire-bound braids. His skin was pale and he had a delicate beauty seldom achieved by men; just barely saved from being effeminate by the stern line of his mouth, uncompromising even so close to death. Above the waist, his clothes bore russet brown stains. Below, they were shredded and the flesh beneath was no better. Not even the stiff and reddened strips of hide that bound them could disguise the extent of the injuries. Only by courtesy could these hunks of meat still be called legs.

The tavern fell silent. One of the men, up on a neighboring table for a better view, scrambled down off his perch and vomited into a bucket. Everyone ignored him, their eyes on the dead man. Oh, he still clung to life, although the Mother only knew how, but there wasn't a person watching who would grant him a place amongst the living.

"Jago?" Pulling free of Ivan's help and leaving the young man holding his sodden furs, the stranger fell onto the bench by the table and took his brother's face in cracked and bleeding hands. His hair was nearer brown than blond and pulled back into a greasy tail. Although pain and exhaustion made it difficult to tell for certain, he appeared five to seven years older than the wounded man. "Jago?"

"Give me your knife," Dorses said quietly to Nad. "Those bindings have to come off."

"Those bindings are all that's holdin' the flesh on his bones," observed a woman in the crowd.

"Aye," Nad agreed from his vantage point. "You'll have a right mess if you cut him free. And the whole lot's froze so you'll have ta pry the bindings up and likely take a bit of leg with it. Wouldn't be surprised if what's left is frostbit, too." He handed Dorses his knife and added,

" 'Course, far as he's concerned it won't make much difference either way."

"While he lives, we do what we can." And her tone left no room for argument.

The knife was sharp but the bindings were tight, wet, and becoming slimy as they thawed. Only the shallow and infrequent rise and fall of his chest said Jago still breathed. Although her eyes never left the delicate maneuvering of the blade, Dorses checked between each repositioning of the point; just in case. She'd fight to save the living, but she'd not waste her time on one already gone to Lord Death.

"Are you a healer?" The stranger looked up from his brother's face, his eyes and the circles beneath them nearly the same shade of purplish gray. His accent gave the words an almost musical inflection but did nothing to hide the desperation.

"No." Dorses' mouth pressed into a thin white line and the tendons of her neck bulged as she forced the knife through the hide.

"We've no healer here," Nad explained, putting one foot up on the bench and leaning a forearm on his thigh. "And few anywhere in Halda. When the Wizard's Horde went through twelve year ago, they were all killed, from apprentice ta master. When the wizard fell, and the horde with him, there was no one left ta teach the youngsters until Ardhan sent aid. E'en then there was so much healin' needed doin' they'd no time ta teach at first. Dorses was joined ta a healer though and he . . ."

"He couldn't have done anything here." As the flesh beneath the bindings began to warm, her nose told her what she'd find. She had hoped it was the untanned brindle hide she smelled, and in part it was, but with even a small fraction of leg exposed the putrid stench rising from the black bits of flesh could only mean gangrene. The one question remaining was how the man still lived with legs clawed to shreds and rotting off his body.

"Have you a name?" She asked the stranger.

The stranger nodded. "Raulin. This," he added, "is my brother Jago. We were traveling north across the mountains when we were attacked by the brindle. Jago screamed and screamed, but I got my dagger in its eye . . ."

"In its eye?" More than one eye in the tavern measured the length of the pelt. A full grown brindle stood more than seven feet high at the shoulder and its eyes were two feet higher than that. Of course, if it was feeding . . .

"I climbed on its back," Raulin continued, as jaws dropped throughout his audience, "and put my dagger into its eye. It's a long dagger. It died. Jago stopped screaming." Tears dripped from his face onto his brother's. "Five days ago. Maybe four. He hasn't screamed since. I did what I could. I promised to get him to a healer." He began to struggle to his feet. "You said no healers. We have to go on."

Dorses' hand on his shoulder pushed him back down and a steady pressure kept him there. She was stronger than she looked.

"You're in no condition to go anywhere," she said, her voice as gentle as anyone had ever heard it. "And your brother is well on his way to Lord Death."

In the quiet corner, as far removed from the drama near the door as was possible while still remaining in the room, Crystal raised her head and met Lord Death's eyes. He nodded.

"He's mine, or yours," he said.

She peered through the nearly solid wall of wool and leather covered backs and then at the Mother's one true son. Already his hair was beginning to lighten and a faint line of beard coarsened his jaw as the features of the young man on the table moved onto Death. She couldn't save every handsome young man destined to die. But she could save this one.

She made up her mind.

"He's mine."

The scrape of her chair, moving away from the table as she stood, sounded unnaturally loud. A miner turned, nudged his neighbor, and in seconds the crowd had spun on its collective heel to look at Crystal.

There was no longer any point in avoiding attention.

She threw back her hood and let the cloak slip from her shoulders.

Hair, the silver-white of moonlight, flowed almost to her waist and danced languidly about in the still air as though glad to be free. She stood taller than the tallest man in the room. As she stepped forward, her eyes began to glow; green as strong summer sunlight through leaves. There could be no mistaking who she was.

The ancient wizards had been bred of gods and mortal women and they'd ruled the earth for millennia until their arrogance destroyed them. All but one. All but Kraydak. And in less than a thousand years on his own, Kraydak had engendered as much carnage as all of the others had accomplished together over five times as long.

But from Ardhan came a prophecy, that from Ardhan would come Kraydak's Doom.

Crystal. A weapon forged by the goddesses in a mortal womb, shaped by the strength of the Eldest.

Crystal. The last wizard. Only seventeen when she'd faced Kraydak and defeated him. Only seventeen when she'd saved the world. Twelve years later, she looked barely older.

The crowd parted, moved by surprise and other emotions, less well defined, with a guttural, multitoned murmur. Her gaze shifting neither left nor right—the tavern might have been empty from the way she moved—she approached the table, a song of power building in the back of her throat. It wasn't a sound yet, but the hair on every neck in the room stood up. She looked down at the wounded man and then at his brother.

For the first time in five days, Raulin's eyes held hope.

"Save him," he said.

She nodded, laid long pale fingers on the torn and rotting legs, and sang.

# TWO

The soft crackle and hiss of flame, the pervasive scent of smoke mixed with wool and wood, the warm weight of blankets shielding her body against the chill that touched her uncovered face, the musty taste of time's passage in her mouth . . . Crystal opened her eyes.

Above her, parallel lines of logs, bark still clinging, slanted down to the right. She turned her head and followed their length until they ended in a wall, also of rough log, and liberally chinked with mud and moss. Barely below the eaves, two small windows made of glass so thick it appeared green let in weak and watery winter sunlight. She shifted and heard the rustle of straw as the mattress moved below her.

Inside. And in bed. What else?

Rolling her head back to the left, she saw another wall, with a door, and close beside the bed a small table that held a half-burned candle, a heavy ceramic pitcher and a matching mug. Her nose wrinkled. There was water in the pitcher.

Moving carefully, for muscles shrieked protest at the gentlest activity, Crystal managed to free an arm from the constricting bedclothes. She reached out, a long pale finger touched the edge of the jug, and she paused.

As much as she needed to drink—and her mouth felt as though a family of mice had moved in for the winter—she knew the water, or more specifically the swallowing and the weight in her stomach, would only intensify the craving for food she could feel beginning. Until she could satisfy *that* she'd best not make it any worse. Whoever put her here—in this bed, in this room—would soon return, for the fire sounded as if it had almost burned down.

She let her hand fall and concentrated instead on remembering what had happened. There'd been a man. No, two men. And a healing. Frowning in disgust over her lack of recall, she grabbed at the memory and yanked it forward. Jago. She'd healed Jago's legs. Or more accurately, rebuilt them, and then rebuilt Jago. She remembered his life-force fluttering beneath her power like a wounded bird trying to beat its way free. But she'd held and healed it, pouring her own life-force into it until it could manage alone. The last thing she remembered was hitting the floor, the fall closely followed by a confused babble of voices. She grimaced. No, two confused babbles of voices; one of them reverberating inside her head.

"So. You're awake." Dorses said, and paused in the room's doorway to study the wizard.

Long silver hair spilled across the pillow, not moving now but not exactly lifeless either. Green eyes were partially hooded by pale lids, and the one hand that lay outside the covers seemed almost translucent. It was easy to believe that this ethereal beauty was a child of the Mother's Eldest, less easy to believe that she held the power of life and death in those ivory hands.

"Please . . ." Crystal's voice had an unused rasp. "Please, I need food."

Dorses watched for an instant longer, keeping her expression carefully neutral. Did feeding this wizard indicate approval beyond what she had already? And if it did, did it matter? No, she realized, it did not. A moral judgment had been made when she'd had the helpless woman carried upstairs. That would have been the time to deny her, not now. She twisted her head and called over her shoulder, "Ivan, fill a tray and bring it up."

The half-lidded eyes opened a bit wider and a definite twinkle sparkled in the emerald depths. "Rather a lot of food."

"Ivan!" The yell was a practiced, long-distance command. "Fill the large tray."

Crystal's lips flickered into a smile, but the expression took too much effort to maintain. She sighed and tried to move the taste of mold out of her mouth.

"Can you use a drink?" Dorses assumed nothing, but the wizard certainly looked like she *needed* a drink. Hardly surprising, all things considered.

"Will Ivan be long?"

"No."

"Then I would love a drink."

The intense longing in Crystal's voice made Dorses thirsty as well. She moved to the bed licking her lips, filled the mug, and held it to the wizard's mouth.

The water had sat in the pitcher for some hours and was beginning to go stale and flat, but it couldn't have tasted better to Crystal had it just been drawn fresh from a mountain spring. She drained the mug and with the strength it gave her pulled herself shakily up to recline against the headboard of the bed. The fire, she could now see, burned in a small black stove, squatting against the opposite wall.

"If I may . . ." Dorses offered. Slipping an arm between back and headboard—and the wizard was not as light, as she looked—she rearranged both wizard and pillows in a more comfortable position.

"Thank you."

"More water?"

"Please."

Using both hands, Crystal managed to hold the mug and drink. She tried to ignore the spasms of hunger, concentrating instead on the very real pleasure in her mouth and throat. When the cup was empty again, she carefully put it on the table, and turned to the innkeeper.

"How long?" she asked.

As she'd already asked about the food, Dorses assumed the wizard wanted to know how long since the healing. "Two and a half days." She moved to tend the fire, going over all she wanted to know, ordering the questions, wondering how best to begin. When a wizard, the last of all the wizards, collapses in your common room, a number of questions need answering. She opened the stove's door and began to rebuild the fire. Two and a half days ago she'd seen a dead man come back to life, blackened and rotting legs made whole and pink, but the why of *that* was wizard's work and no business of hers. "Why," she finally asked without turning, "did you fall?"

For the shelter and the food, Crystal felt the innkeeper was entitled to an answer. Her fists clenched against the hunger, she tried to explain. "He was too close to Death. Healing the legs wasn't enough. I had to give some of my life to keep him alive." She forced the fingers of her right hand to relax so she could indicate the room with a wave. "Why did you . . ." Why did you have me carried upstairs? Why did you see that I was comfortable and protected? Why did you shield me from those who would take advantage of my helplessness? And there would be those, there always were. All that conveyed in only three words.

Closing the stove door, wiping the wood dust from her hands, Dorses considered the question. This was not the first time she'd been asked it in the last two and a half days. Perhaps it was time she found an answer. After a moment, she stood and met the wizard's eyes. The motion of her hand was a reflection of Crystal's. "You gave some of your life to keep him alive," she said.

There were more questions in the silence but Ivan, arriving with the laden tray, pushed them into another time.

"I brought some of everything that was ready," he panted, maneuvering his bulky load through the door with the ease of long practice, "'cause you never said what you wanted on . . ." He stopped as he felt Crystal's eyes on him and all the color drained from his face. *It's one thing to know you serve a wizard; it's another thing entirely when that wizard sits up in bed and stares at you.* He took a step backward and his mouth worked soundlessly.

"Put it by the bed," Dorses ordered sharply, afraid he was going to turn and run.

Ivan's gaze snapped to Dorses, and finding nothing there, at least, he didn't understand, he moved tentatively forward and eased the tray down on the small table.

No longer able to control herself, Crystal grabbed for the steaming bowl of soup.

Moving backward much faster than he'd advanced, Ivan retreated out of arm's reach, then paused to watch. His pale face grew paler as the hot soup disappeared, but he stood his ground, fascinated.

"Ivan!"

He jumped. He'd forgotten that Dorses still stood by the stove. "Yes, Dorses?"

"Haven't you anything to do?"

"Uh, aye."

She waited, arms folded across her chest.

"Uh . . . right I'll get ta it now." After a last astounded look at Crystal, who had finished the soup and was reaching for the tray, he ran from the room.

"Your apprentice?" Crystal asked as she broke open a fresh biscuit and spread it thickly with butter.

"Aye." Dorses hooked the room's one chair out of the corner with a toe and sat. "He's a good worker when he remembers there's work to be done." A nod at the tray. "Enough?"

Besides the soup and biscuits, the tray held a meat pie, a bowl of rabbit stew thick with potatoes and carrots, a small baked squash, and two apple tarts.

"It should be, thank you."

Dorses peered a little nearsightedly at the woman on the bed. "I'm curious; did you know this would happen? The collapse? The hunger?"

"The hunger, yes. The energy I use has to be replaced." Crystal flushed. "But the other, I'd forgotten. It's been a long time since I've healed someone so close to Death. I forgot what it would cost to bring him back." She paused and licked a bit of gravy from her lip. Suddenly it occurred to her that Lord Death had suggested the healing. Somehow, she doubted he'd forgotten and she wondered why he'd put her in such a position. "By the time I remembered," she continued, resolving to question the Mother's son when next he appeared, "it was too late to stop."

"Could you?"

"Have stopped? Yes."

"Why didn't you when you realized that this," Dorses waved a hand at the bed, "would come of it?"

Finished with the stew, Crystal started on the meat pie while she searched for a way to make her position clear. "Once I'd started, it wouldn't have been right to stop. I'd made him my responsibility by beginning and I couldn't just let him die. Giving him the life-force he needed, even knowing it would leave me helpless while it kept him alive, seemed the lesser of two evils." She sighed, blowing pastry crumbs over the bed. "Although I'd have rather not had to do it."

"Ah." Dorses thought about that for a moment. This was the first wizard she'd ever heard of who considered the *lesser* of two evils. For that matter, she could think of very few people who would save a stranger at their own expense. "And what would you have done," she asked at last, "had you just been hungry?"

The wizard grinned. "I'd have staggered outside to the nearest grove and become a tree until spring when the body of the Mother would feed me."

"If you weren't chopped up for firewood," Dorses reminded her dryly. "Winters are long here."

Crystal acknowledged the truth of that with a smile. What a way for a wizard to die. She licked bits of squash from her fingers. "When I fell, what happened?"

Dorses shrugged thin shoulders. "Nothing much. No one wanted to touch you, which wasn't surprising considering who and what you are. So, after we got our other invalids up into bedrooms, I had Nad carry you up here before liquor overcame common sense."

"Nad wasn't afraid to touch me."

"Nad does what I ask."

Crystal had a pretty good idea that most of the village did what this strong-minded woman asked. "Thank you."

"You're welcome." She spread her hands. "Now what?"

Crystal flushed again and put down the second tart. "I can pay you for all of this."

Dorses cut at the air with a dismissive gesture. "It isn't a problem. There could be blizzards every night and the place'd still be packed. You're good for business. You could eat that way for another five or six days and still not eat up all the profits you've made me in the last two nights. What I meant was, now you're here, do you plan to stay?"

Crystal thought about the aimless wandering she'd been doing lately, about the fear that greeted her wherever she went save home and the mindless adoration that greeted her there. So far, there'd been none of that here. She had spoken more to Dorses than she had to anyone outside her immediate family in years. Except, of course, Lord Death. It felt good.

"If you don't mind," she decided suddenly, "I'd like to stay for a bit."

"Mind? Weren't you listening? You're good for business." The innkeeper rose, glad to have it settled, and pleased the wizard was staying; not solely for the increase in custom. "Ivan!" she called down the stairs. "Come up for the tray."

He must've been waiting at the bottom of the stairs for the summons, he reached the room so quickly.

"Chaos," he breathed, spotting the empty dishes. He lifted the tray gingerly, it had been used by a wizard, after all. "I only ever saw Nad eat that much before." It was this, not the miraculous healing, that marked her as truly powerful in his mind. Food, he understood. He tried a tentative smile. To his shock and joy it was returned.

"Thank you, Ivan." Her voice was a summer breeze.

"You're welcome, L-Lady," Ivan stammered and floated from the room, so totally oblivious to his surroundings Dorses had to move out of his way.

Puzzled by the young man's behavior, Dorses glanced questioningly toward the woman on the bed and suddenly saw what Ivan had; a soft, exotic beauty with a hint of need and a promise of passion. A beauty more a matter of expression than eyes or lips or cheek. She pursed her own lips in admiration; this was a power *she* understood.

"At least he no longer fears me," Crystal explained softly, letting the expression fall, becoming no less beautiful but certainly less accessible.

"If you think Ivan in love will be easier to manage," the other woman said dryly, "I wish you joy of him. Do you thus lay the fear in all men?"

"No." Her laugh was a little embarrassed. "Two years older or two years younger and that wouldn't have worked." She remembered other men who'd howled curses at her, or pleas, or just howled. Ivan's uncomplicated sweetness was like a balm across the memories.

"Well, if you're well enough," Dorses spoke over her thought, "there's one man I wish you'd see. That Raulin's been driving me crazy trying to get into your room."

"Raulin? The brother?" She wondered what he wanted. Over the last twelve years she'd learned they always wanted something. "I guess I'd better see him."

"Good, I'll tell him . . ." Dorses paused in the doorway, nodded once, and added, ". . . Crystal." Then she was gone.

*A long time,* the wizard thought sadly, *since someone said my name in friendship. Except,* she added upon reflection, *for Lord Death.*

It was too soon for the food to do any good, even in a wizard's system, but Crystal imagined that she could feel her power grow. It frightened her being helpless; there were too many who would love to make a wizard pay for a wizard's crimes. She studied the ceiling and reached out just a little.

The logs were pine. The branch now growing into the room at her urging, fully needled, and tipped with a pair of pinecones, proved it.

"More power back than I thought," Crystal muttered. She'd only intended a light touch. "This could be embarrassing to explain."

Out in the hall she heard Dorses trying to make an impression on someone who didn't appear to be listening.

". . . and you will not stay long. She'll be here for a few days, you'll likely see her again before you leave."

"I only want to thank her. That's all."

Crystal wasn't sure, but she thought she recognized the voice, although when she'd heard it last, it had quavered with pain and exhaustion. Raulin. He spoke in a kind of lazy drawl she found pleasing. The voice of a man who smiles a lot she decided; smiles and means every one.

"Lady?"

Rested and fed, Raulin was much more attractive than he'd been that night in the tavern. It wasn't so much the features—the nose a bit large, the gray eyes a bit deep, the brows a bit too definite, the mustache more than a bit . . . Crystal paused, uncertain of how to describe the mustache but it was more than a bit, that was for sure—but rather how he wore them: with laugh lines, and a twinkle, and a willingness to be delighted by life.

"Lady?" he repeated and stepped into the room. "Mind if I come in?"

"You're in," she pointed out.

He smiled. "And you don't seem to mind."

No, she didn't. She returned the smile and said, "You wanted to see me?"

"I've been trying for the last two days," he admitted. "In fact," his smile grew broader, "Dorses would say I've been very trying."

Crystal gave a gurgle of laughter, the sort of uncomplicated response she thought only her younger brother could evoke. "I really doubt Dorses would," she told him.

"Maybe not." He reached the edge of the bed and dropped to his knees. His face grew serious and his eyes stared fearlessly into hers. "You saved my brother's life," he said. "I can never thank you for that, there aren't the words, but I wish you could know how I feel."

Maybe later she would warn him about the dangers of looking into a wizard's eyes.

An emerald spark appeared and Crystal took the gift Raulin so innocently offered, moving across their gaze into his heart. It held little darkness, she found, and much light. At the center of the light was Jago. The younger brother, much loved and protected. The companion, the right arm, the other half. A man to guard his back, a friend to guard his dreams. Could he lose this much of his life and still have a life remaining?

Crystal didn't know she was crying until a gentle finger wiped away a tear.

"Lady?"

She caught his reaching hand and held it for a moment. "I do know how you feel," she said, so softly he had to lean forward to catch the words. "And I am well thanked for your brother's life."

To her astonishment, he brought the hand that held his to his lips and kissed its back, his mustache drawing fine lines of sensation across the skin.

"Lady," he told her, allowing her to reclaim her arm, "I will continue thanking you all the days I live." His smile returned. "And never has gratitude been expressed so willingly."

Was he flirting with her? Crystal tilted her head and gazed at the man in puzzlement.

"And if my thanks could be expressed in some more tangible way . . ."

She recognized that tone. He *was* flirting with her.

"You have only to command me, Lady. I long to fulfill your every wish." The florid words were accompanied by a mighty flourish of an imaginary hat.

"Uh, no wishes at the moment."

"Well, then . . ." He stood and dusted off his knees. "I'd best get back to Jago." The smile became a grin. "He's not as pretty, but I don't want him to spill soup in the bed. We can't afford a second one." He bowed, winked—she was quite sure he winked—and left.

Crystal shook her head. What an unusual man. His gratitude seemed truly to come with no strings. And Dorses appeared to want her around only because, for some unsaid reason, she liked her. Did everyone she'd met today play a very deep game or were they actually aware of her as a separate being, not necessarily evil because she was a wizard and not some thing to take advantage of because she had power? Had she stumbled on a small pocket of crazy people? Or perhaps, her expression grew slightly wistful, had she found the last of the sane?

Lord Death stood in a corner of the room and watched Crystal's face, wishing he could read her mind to see what prompted such a soft and dreamy look. She wasn't aware he could be with her unseen and he had no intention of telling her. If there were dead or dying present, she always saw him, but at other times he often chose to just spend time invisibly watching.

He was pleased to see he'd been right about Dorses. This woman could accept what Crystal was. He'd thought as much when he'd urged Crystal to heal that young man, knowing what it would take out of her, knowing it would throw her on the mercy of the innkeeper. The wizard needed to spend more time with people and less time brooding about her future. Brooding would lead her nowhere good.

He wished she'd confide in him about what had been bothering her lately. He wanted to help but didn't know how. Perhaps she'd say something to mortal ears. Once it was in the open he'd be able to do something.

The pleasure faded as he considered Raulin. It was so easy to forget Crystal had a mortal heritage as well and he greatly feared she now found herself in the company of one who would appeal to that side.

He didn't want to understand the pain he'd felt when the mortal touched her.

He was Lord Death and pain was not a part of that.

He looked up and the pine branch died.


The next morning, Crystal left her room, wandered down to the kitchens, and astounded the innkeeper by not only suggesting a new way of doing turnips, a staple in the local diet, but by then preparing the dish herself.

Dorses, knowing Crystal's background as both princess and wizard, for who in that part of the world did not, assumed it was something she'd learned in the dozen years since the defeat of Kraydak, made a note of the recipe, and asked no questions.

Crystal, thanking the vegetarian centaurs for teaching her at least one skill that served some purpose in the mortal world, offered no explanations. She had no wish to underline differences, not when she felt so content.

While they worked, the two women talked, and firmed their tentative feelings of friendship.

When Ivan came in from morning chores, he brought a dried and delicate wild rose, found perfectly preserved, mixed in with the summer's hay. Wordlessly he presented it to Crystal, accepted her thanks with glowing eyes—few wizards' had ever been so bright—and pink with pleasure, watched her wind it in her hair where it slowly softened and lived again.

The afternoon, Crystal spent with Raulin. He made her laugh with his wild flattery, and she felt herself beginning to respond to his obvious interest. In his own way he was as single-minded as those who saw only the wizard, but it was a single-mindedness she couldn't help but appreciate. It was a nice change.

Although he never mentioned it, his accent told her he came from the Empire. She wondered how he'd managed to survive the long years of Kraydak's rule with his good nature intact.

That evening, she lay on her bed, listening to the sounds rising up from the common room, one hand gently stroking the velvet petals of Ivan's rose. Dorses had asked her to come down, but she hadn't the courage to face the locals and risk their almost certain fear and rejection.


"There," Nad sat back on his heels and beamed down at his handiwork. He'd just set new andirons into one of the common room's giant hearths and he was pleased with the way the design looked. "You see," he said, "they've got ta be large enough ta carry the load but not so large young Ivan here can't move them out ta clean the ashes like. And as this is a public place," he looked up at his audience and smiled, "then best make 'em easy on the eyes."

Crystal grinned back and tucked one foot up under her on the bench. With both hearths unlit, the room was far from warm. "They're certainly very pretty," she agreed. "I've never seen irons shaped like stag horns before."

"Stag horns!" Dorses snorted from behind the bar where she was counting stock. "All I asked was that they be thick enough not to melt out of shape and he brings me stag horns!"

"Actually, they don't look very thick," Crystal said softly to Nad, not wanting to get him in trouble with the innkeeper and her quest for durability. "Are they likely to melt?"

"Nay." The blacksmith's brow puckered and he scratched at the bald patch on top of his head. "But they may sag a tad the next time we have a cold snap and some stonehead overloads the fire."

"That would be a definite shame." She slid off the bench and onto her knees beside him. "May I?"

"Be my guest." Nad waved a hand, puzzled but gracious.

Crystal leaned forward and lightly touched both antlers. The iron flared a sudden brilliant green. "No fire built in this hearth can affect them now," she explained as the glow faded. "They'll always be as lovely as they are today."

"Well, I'm much obliged," Nad's broad features were rosy. Praise always made him blush, for he could see the flaws he'd left even if no one else could, and this was high praise indeed. "That's a right handy trick." He gave her a sly grin. "Can you straighten nails?"

She laughed and held out her hand.

The nail Nad dropped on her palm had certainly seen better days. It was bent not once but twice, and touched with rust as well.

She held it gently by the head and stroked the index finger of her other hand down its length. No green glow answered. The nail turned cherry red and melted into slag.

"Good thing we were on the hearth." Nad observed philosophically.

Crystal stared down at the tiny puddle of molten metal. She didn't understand; the power had begun to answer, then it had twisted off as if responding to another call. She wiped suddenly sweaty hands on her thighs. "That's . . . that's never happened before."

"*Idiot,*" sneered a voice in her head.

"You shouldn't get upset about it." Nad grasped her shoulder lightly with a warm and comforting hand, misinterpreting Crystal's bleak expression. He liked the girl. Let others argue the mortality of wizards— and they had been for the three days this one had been at the Nugget—she was kind and she was beautiful and that was enough for him. He loved beauty and tried to put a little into everything he made; from pickaxes, to plows, to andirons. "I couldn't have used that nail agin anyway, not bent as it was," he continued, smiling sympathetically. "I guess you were still fired up." His blunt chin pointed at the stag horns. "From doin' t'other."

"I guess." She managed a small smile in return because the blacksmith looked so upset at her distress. She wanted to accept his explanation. She hadn't been paying much attention to the nail, it was such a small thing, and she could easily believe she'd used too much power. Foolish, for attention should be paid to the smallest of power uses, but not frightening. Except for the voice.

"Well now, look who's comin' down ta join us," Nad got to his feet and extended a massive hand to Crystal.

She took it and stood, fortunately enough taller so that Nad's huge shoulders weren't blocking her view.

Slowly descending the stairs, placing each foot firmly but with care, was Jago. He'd been shaved, his hair washed and rebraided, and no trace of his injuries was apparent, but knuckles showed white in the hand that gripped the banister and his gaze never rose from his path. Raulin followed closely behind, his expression as proud as if he'd taught Jago to walk.

"Well, you certainly look a sight better than you did," Nad boomed, striding forward to meet the brothers at the foot of the stairs. "Just tryin' out the new pins are you."

"Yes," Jago said shortly. He was out of banister and it was a good five feet to the nearest bench.

Nad looked at Jago, looked at the open space he must cross, and understood the hesitation. "You've nothin' ta worry about, them legs of yours are as good as new."

"I know that," Jago's tone was polite, but only just barely.

"I've been telling him the same thing," Raulin put in. "Not that they ever were much . . ."

"Raulin . . ."

"And it'd not be polite to let the lady wizard think you didn't trust her healin'," Nad added.

Jago's lips narrowed. "It's not that, I . . ." He trailed off, unsure how to explain.

"It's just you saw your legs," Crystal said gently, stepping into his line of sight. "Before you lost consciousness you saw and you knew what you had to look forward to if you woke. And no healing can erase a memory like that, not if the Mother-creator Herself had been the healer. You know your legs are whole, but you can't believe; not quite, not yet."

"Yes." He nodded, both with respect and relief that someone understood. "That's it exactly." He took a deep breath, avoided Raulin's reaching hand, and walked to the bench. Then he sat, visibly unclenched his jaw, and smiled up at his brother. "What do you mean they never were much?" he demanded.

Below his mustache, Raulin's smile was identical. It was the one feature they held in common. "I meant in comparison, of course."

"I think," Nad turned a beaming face on Dorses, who watched from behind the bar, "this calls for a drink."

"Not surprising," the innkeeper said dryly, "you think everything calls for a drink." But she filled five tankards with ale and joined the others at a table.

Crystal studied Jago's face while he drank, and when he lowered his tankard he caught her at it. He met her eyes as forthrightly as his brother had, his own holding neither fear nor suspicion, only a cautious reserve. Raulin had laid himself open for her taking; Jago only acknowledged that she could. His eyes were a very dark violet and he was among the handsomest men Crystal had ever met. She looked away first, found Raulin studying her, flushed, and ended up staring into her ale. This showed all the signs of becoming very complicated.

". . . certainly the most excitin' night we've ever had at the Nugget," Nad was saying. "As if you three weren't enough, we found at closin' time old Timon had already left with Lord Death."

"What"?

"Oh, nothing ta worry about," the blacksmith hastened to explain, "he had ta be ninety if he was a day. Just his time." He took another drink of his ale. "Still, the Nugget's not likely to see another night like that in a hurry."

"Nor want to," Dorses said emphatically.

"Now I don't know about that," Raulin drawled, winking in Crystal's direction. "Everything turned out for the best."

Jago raised his tankard to his brother. "Next time *you* distract the brindle."

"Brindle tried to eat me, I'd choke him."

"You've always been hard to swallow." Jago's tone was light, but his face had tensed. It didn't take a wizard to see memories crowding up against the banter.

"Dorses?" Ivan stuck his head in from the kitchen. "It's near sunset and the biscuits aren't . . ."

"Near sunset? As late as that?" Dorses leaped to her feet and scooped the tankards from the table. "Put the dry ingredients together, I'll be there in a minute."

Ivan's head disappeared.

"You lot can stay or go as you please," Dorses told them, dumping the tankards behind the bar and heading for the kitchen. "But sunset's when I unbolt the doors. Crystal, if you don't mind, the fires, we've not much time . . ." And she was gone.

*Crystal, if you don't mind, the fires . . .* She turned the words over in her mind, oblivious to the others in the room. *Crystal, if you don't mind, the fires . . .* Of all her many acquaintances, over all the years, only the old Duke of Belkar had treated her power as though it was a useful tool.

"Lady?" Jago's worried voice brought her back to the Nugget's common room. "Are you all right?"

"Yes," she turned the brilliance of her joy on him. "I've seldom been better." *Crystal, if you don't mind, the fires . . .*

She waved a hand at the new andirons and they disappeared beneath a load of wood. She turned to the other hearth, found the wood already laid, pointed a finger at each and said, "Burn."

A flare of green and both hearths filled with flame.

"She's good with fires," Nad confided to the brothers as the room began to warm.

"*Ah,*" sighed the voice in her head.

It sounded pleased, but Crystal was too pleased herself to notice.

"Will you stay a while and enjoy the fruits of your labors?" Raulin asked, more than one invitation apparent in his voice. "Seems like a pity to waste such heat."

Pleasure faded and Crystal headed for the stairs. "No," she said without turning, "I can't."

"Crystal . . ."

A murmur from Jago cut off Raulin's next words, and she escaped to her room.


"I have had it with this!"

Crystal glanced up from the potato she was dicing. "Had it with what?" she asked.

"This!" Dorses glared at the disassembled pieces of the water pump. "Nothing but trouble and Nad's off at the mine today." She rubbed at her forehead, leaving a smudge of rust behind. "I don't suppose you could fix it."

"Sorry." Crystal shrugged. "But pump repairs were never something they taught me."

Dorses sighed. "I didn't think so."

After the incident with the nail, the strange and sudden twist, Crystal was hesitant to use her power on the pump, but neither did she want to let Dorses down. "Perhaps I could look at it anyway."

"Couldn't hurt," the innkeeper admitted standing aside. "I'm out of ideas."

With her index finger, Crystal pushed a metal ring along the counter. It clinked against a stubby cylinder. The wizard took a deep breath. There had to be almost twenty bits and pieces of metal spread out in front of her and she had no idea of what to do with any of them. She wanted desperately to repay some small part of Dorses' kindness.

Her left hand lifted a tiny bolt and fitted it into the plate in her right hand. Crystal bit back a scream. Her hand had moved; she hadn't moved it.

"Crystal? Are you all right?"

"Fine," she managed, watching her fingers screw two totally incomprehensible things together. Dorses must not find out what was happening. Her right hand attached something to the pipe at the top of the pump. She couldn't bear it if this pushed Dorses away, as it must. Her left hand placed a second piece on the first. Her mind still seemed her own, but her hands moved at another's command. Strangest of all, behind her surface terror stood a wall of competence and calm.

*"Relax,"* suggested a voice.

*"React,"* sneered another.

The first voice was new, but the second she'd heard before.

With a sharp snick of metal against metal, her hands fixed the rebuilt cap onto the pump, tightened the collar, then fell limply to her sides. For a very long moment, they burned and itched with the not exactly unpleasant sensation of returning blood, then that faded and they were hers again. She raised them to her face, studied the palms, turned them over and studied the backs. Fortunately, the feeling of calm remained, distancing her still from what had just happened.

"You didn't cut yourself?" Dorses was a little worried; Crystal stood there so quietly, staring at her hands.

"Uh . . . no."

"Let's see what . . ." The innkeeper moved around the wizard's motionless body. "Mother-creator, you've rebuilt it!" She grabbed the handle and began to pump vigorously. "Let's hope it wasn't in pieces long enough for the pipes to freeze."

"Do they?" Crystal asked, only because she felt she must say something.

"Chaos, yes. Once the cold weather sets in, Ivan's up every couple hours in the night keeping the water moving." A cough and a sputter and a splash of cold liquid shot out the mouth of the pump. Dorses smiled in satisfaction. "I hate having to melt snow," she confided to Crystal. "I thank you from the bottom of my heart."

Crystal opened her mouth, unsure of what she was going to say but uneasy over taking credit for something she hadn't done. To her horror, words spilled out without her willing them. "Consider it a gift from the goddess." And the calm disappeared.

"Think highly of yourself, don't you," Dorses laughed, still facing the pump, not seeing the fear that robbed all power from the wizard's features. "I've a barrel of beer that could use a blessing then; it's going skunky."

"Maybe later . . ." Crystal choked out, and fled. For one of the few times in her life, she thanked the centaurs for their insistence on emotional control—although for them control meant denial—drummed over and over into the child she had been until it became almost second nature to hide what she felt. Those lessons served her now, keeping all the terrified bits of her together and moving.

"Crystal?" Dorses turned, but the kitchen was empty. She wondered if she should follow. Had she said something wrong? But the soup boiled over on the stove, and once that was taken care of the pies needed finishing, and the moment for following passed.

Up in her room, Crystal lay in the center of the bed, knees drawn up to her chest, eyes squeezed shut, arms wrapped tightly around her head, and her hair a silver veil over all. Only her lips moved. Over and over they formed a denial, of the voices that whispered and roared and of the knowledge of what those voices meant. "No, no, no, no. . . ."

Unseen beside her, Lord Death reached out a hand. It hovered a moment close above a shoulder he couldn't touch and when he withdrew it, the fingers closed to form a fist. *The comfort of Death,* he thought, *is a cruel joke.*

\*       \*       \*

"Crystal?"

The banging on her door was persistent and loud.

"Crystal, open the door!"

Slowly she unfolded and still more slowly stood. She waved a hand and the door swung open.

Raulin, his hand raised to bang again, took a quick step into the room. "Are you all right?" he demanded anxiously. "Dorses says you've been up here since morning. She figured if you could keep the door closed you must be fine, but me, I wanted proof." He moved forward and brushed her hair back off her face, leaving his hand resting gently against her cheek. He had to tilt his head slightly to meet her eyes. "What's wrong?"

Crystal wet her lips, She'd fought all day, banishing the voices, building and reinforcing shields in her mind. Her nerves hung balanced on the dagger's edge and she could not allow herself the luxury of hysterics, not inside, not where others could be hurt. "I think," she said softly, "I don't want to be alone." Then, as Raulin continued to meet her eyes, she blushed deeply.

His answering smile banished much of the day's terror.

"No," she corrected hurriedly, not that. She moved her face against the warmth of his hand. "Not yet."

"Then come down to the common room," he suggested, marveling at the satin feel of her skin, daring to trace one finger down the curve of her throat. Not yet meant later. He could wait. "Jago's down there now, he's enough of a wonder to hold them. They won't even notice you."

She cocked her head to listen and noticed for the first time the noise sifting through the floor. "Is it as late as that . . ."

As she obviously didn't require an answer, Raulin concentrated instead on coaxing her to the door. When she balked on the threshold, he slipped an arm around her waist. "You did say you didn't want to be alone," he reminded her. He withdrew his arm as an emerald glow reminded him who he held. Cautioned but undaunted, he tucked her arm in his and, when that provoked no objection, kept her moving toward the stairs.

The common room was packed and, as Raulin had said, Jago stood in the center of an admiring court, the more vocal of whom were trying to get him out of his pants.

"Come on, laddie," called an old woman with a voice like crushed stone, "let's see them legs!"

"Let's have some skin," cried out a much younger one.

Most of the crowd had obviously been drinking heavily. Jago did not appear to be having a particularly good time.

"He hates being the center of attention," Raulin confided to Crystal as he steered her to a table in the back, the same table she'd sat at the night it all began.

"And you'd have your pants off?"

"In a minute." He grinned. "There's little I hate more than false modesty."

Over the multitude of heads, Jago—boosted up on a table by Nad, partially to give everyone a good view, partially to keep him safe—met Crystal's eyes. She knew he saw her, it wasn't a mistake she could make, but in no way did he acknowledge her presence. It showed a sensitivity to her feelings she hadn't expected and she found herself warming to the younger man. With nothing to draw their attention, the crowd indeed didn't notice her and she sat unseen until Nad innocently gave it away, only wanting Crystal to share in the glory. "And there's the Lady," he called, with a happy smile and a pointing finger. "The one who did the healin'."

The crowd fell silent as they turned and the weight of their gaze pushed Crystal to her feet. She felt her power build in answer to theirs. A crowd could become a mob very quickly, she knew, and quicker still when drink had blurred the boundaries.

"Wizard?"

The sound rose in a questioning wave and could still break either way when a man with an eye patched pushed to the front of the pack and said, "Where's my son, wizard. Where's my boy?"

Crystal kept silent. No answer she could give would satisfy. It never had before. She felt the familiar tightness in her stomach.

A woman, with a steel hook where her right hand should be, stepped forward to stand by the one-eyed man and the mob took them as their center and formed about them. Some murmured names. Others rubbed scars. They all remembered the day, twelve years before, when the Wizard's Horde had come.

"Wizard."

A growl now, an unpleasant rumble.

The funny thing was, if she actually was what they accused her of, they wouldn't dare accuse.

She saw Jago tense, his place on the table giving him an advantage in the fight that was sure to begin. Nad, his honest face puzzled, looked from one friend to another, unsure of what was happening. Beside her, she heard Raulin stand, and felt him ready for battle. She was very glad Ivan stayed safely in the kitchen.

"Wizard!"

Their common voice rising to a howl the crowd surged forward, arms reaching to clutch, but they slammed against a barrier and continued to slam against it as the wizard walked through them and up the stairs.

In the upper hall she paused. The crowd had not yet turned its attention on those who'd stood beside her. Before it could she reached out, wrapped Raulin and Jago in her power, and twitched them to safety; one heartbeat there, the next gone. Even if Raulin hadn't enough sense to stay in their room, Jago, she strongly suspected, would keep him locked inside. She heard Dorses' voice, falling like cold water on the din, slapping down and relocking the passion.

Not until she reached the safety of her own room did she allow the barrier to fall. They were all the same, the ones who hated, they never realized they couldn't hurt her.

Physically.

The voices kept her company all through the long night that followed. Not until morning did she regain enough power to push them back in their place.

# THREE

"Chaos, Jago, you owe her! The least we can do is tell her and let her choose." Raulin stuffed a heavy wool shirt into his pack, and reached for a pair of thick gray socks. His brother's hand clamped down just above his wrist.

"Those," Jago pointed out, grabbing the socks and tossing them in his own pack, "are mine." He released Raulin's arm and returned to methodically folding his own spare clothes and neatly placing them inside the oilcloth bag.

"I don't believe you, that you'd begrudge your own brother a pair of socks," Raulin muttered. "Your own brother . . ."

"*I* remember what old Dector told us; up in the mountains a pair of warm, dry socks could save your life."

Raulin released his pack and threw both arms up into the air. "Which is exactly the point I'm trying to make. Do you *want* to depend on a pair of socks? She's a wizard, Jago! For the Mother's sake, think of what that means!"

"I have thought of it, which is obviously more than you've done."

"Look," Raulin managed to keep his voice reasonable as he began ticking points off on his fingers, "she saved your life. If that sort of thing happens again wouldn't you want to have her around?"

Jago's lips tightened. "Yes," he admitted.

"And then last night, you know as well as I do that she pulled our asses out of the fire with that trick. We'd have been sleeping with Lord Death if she'd left us there."

"That's *not* what you said last night."

When the brothers had found themselves suddenly up in their room instead of in the middle of a howling crowd, Raulin had been furious. First, at the crowd for daring to raise a hand against the woman who'd cured his brother. Second, at Crystal for removing him before he could lift his hands in return. Had Jago not kicked his feet out from under him and then sat on him until he settled down, Raulin would've stormed back down the stairs and thrown himself into the fray.

Causing exactly the sort of riot Jago suspected Crystal was trying to prevent.

Raulin, once calmed and convinced Crystal would not want to see him, went to bed and fell quickly asleep. Knowing *why,* he didn't care *how* she'd gotten them out of the tavern and into their room, nor did he worry about the implications of the act.

Jago, however, lay for hours, staring at the ceiling, his thoughts tumbling to the cadence of his brother's snoring. Such power expended on their behalf made him nervous. One hand dropped to rest on his thigh. They already owed this wizard more than they could repay and now the debt had grown. With Raulin so ready to take up arms in her defense, he'd have no choice but to stand by the wizard's side. Although, he was forced to admit, he'd have stood there for the debt's sake as well. And for hers . . .

For two and a half days he'd carried a piece of her life and that tied them in ways he had no wish to be tied. Not to a wizard. Not even this one, beautiful and desirable as she undeniably was.

Their city had been conquered by Kraydak's Horde in their great-grandfather's time—although Kraydak was not known as a wizard then—and by the time of Jago's birth the excesses of the conqueror were an accepted part of existence. People lived their lives and did what they could to avoid coming to his attention. During the Great War, when Kraydak had stood revealed as what he was, nothing had changed. People tried harder not to be noticed and prayed to whatever they still believed in that they wouldn't be called upon to serve.

"And now," Jago had muttered to himself, "twelve years after surviving *that* we're not only noticed but serving." He'd sighed, elbowed Raulin to stop the snoring, and finally fallen asleep.

"I said, last night was different!"

Jago started, snapped out of his reverie by Raulin's voice. "Sorry. I was thinking."

Raulin tied down the last thong on his pack. "You think too much."

"Yeah? Well, I'm thinking for two."

"And," Raulin continued, ignoring the dig, "you never, listen."

"I never . . ." Jago yanked at the cord around his neck and pulled a small leather pouch up from under his shirt. "Well, all right then." He whipped it over his head and threw it across the room. The pouch smacked in the center of Raulin's chest. "Go ahead. Give it to her. But don't be surprised if she thanks you very kindly, tells us we've no business meddling, and pops off with it. Remember your own words; she's a wizard."

"And so, in spite of everything she's done for us, we're not to trust her?"

"I didn't say that!"

"You think she'll betray us?"

"I didn't say that either."

"Then what are you saying?"

Jago opened his mouth to remind his brother of the creed they'd lived their lives by and then closed it again. They'd been noticed; there was no retreating from that. And he did trust her; he couldn't not. But still, she was a wizard and accepting her did not deny that wizards had always, without exception, made their own rules. "I don't know," he said finally.

Raulin reached out and gave one of Jago's braids an affectionate tug. "Don't worry, little brother. We'll just ask her, she'll say yes or no, and that'll be the end of it." He slipped the cord over his own head but left the pouch hanging loose. "We'll pack the sled later." He headed out the door. "Come on."

"*Who* never listens?" Jago sighed, grabbed up his vest, and followed.

*　　*　　*

"So you're really goin' then?"

Crystal nodded, gray circles beneath her eyes mute testimony to a sleepless night.

"I wish you wouldn't," Nad muttered, staring down into the deep mahogany of his morning tea. "I'm sure they'd come ta like you in time." Then his lips twisted and he shook his head. "Nay, they wouldn't either." He looked up and sighed. "It's too bad there's nothin' great for you ta do, nice a shaft collapsin' or the plague or somethin' that'd bring them ta need you."

"You're not suggesting she collapse a shaft, are you?" Dorses asked, wrapping Crystal's nearly unresponsive fingers about a mug of steaming tea. She kept her tone light, hoping to lift the pall of gloom that hung about the woman. A half smile rewarded the attempt while Nad sputtered and tried to explain.

"I understand," Crystal said finally as Nad's sentences became more and more confused, "but it doesn't matter, not really. If a shaft collapsed while I was here, no matter how many lives I saved the fault would end up mine. And any plague I cured I would also be accused of causing."

Nad's eyes glistened. "You can't win." He blinked back tears and cleared his throat. "You just can't win."

Crystal felt her own eyes fill and bit her lip to keep the tears from spilling. Nothing undid her control faster than sympathy and understanding. She took a hurried gulp of tea, scalding her mouth but glad of an action to hide behind.

"Yo, Crystal!" Raulin peered in from the empty common room. "Can we talk to you a moment?" His brows waggled and beneath his mustache was an enthusiastic grin.

The Nugget's kitchen was warm and safe and with the prospect of leaving the inn before her, Crystal wanted to stay both warm and safe for as long as she could. But Raulin had stood beside her and Jago had shared her life so she set down her mug and got slowly to her feet.

As she brushed by Raulin—he remained in the doorway holding open the door, leaving very little room for her—she wished for an instant he'd come to her last night and she could have lost the pain in his arms. Except she wouldn't have, and she knew it. Too late now . . .

"We . . ." He pushed the door shut and stepped away from it into the common room. "Jago and I have a proposition for you."

Crystal looked from one to the other, from Raulin's enthusiasm to Jago's wary stare. "What?" she asked finally.

"We have a map that will lead us to one of the ancient wizards' old towers." Raulin patted the pouch hanging on his chest. "We want you to go with us."

Emerald eyes blinked twice and Crystal shook her head. "What?" she repeated but with an entirely different emphasis.

Raulin put a foot up on a bench and propped his elbow on his thigh. "Look, I know it's hard to believe, but it's true. After you defeated Kraydak, things went a little crazy in the Empire, every two-copper power mogul trying to gain control. While things were, well, stirred up, we found this map."

"We stole it from the office of Kraydak's city governor."

"Jago!"

"If you're telling her at all, tell her the truth."

"He was dead. He didn't need it."

"Wait." Crystal held up her hand, cutting the incipient argument short. "Did you kill him?"

Jago showed teeth in an unpleasant smile. "Not exactly."

"While I warned His Excellency that a lynch mob waited out front," Raulin explained in a flat voice, "Jago led them to the rear exit."

"And when he tried to slip out the back they ripped him to shreds?" Crystal asked, although she didn't really need to.

Once again Raulin's smile matched his brother's. "Eventually."

The city governor had been Kraydak's hand, a hand holding Kraydak's whip; Crystal spared him little sympathy. After twelve years of being the only wizard in a mortal world, Crystal had come to feel there was almost an excuse for what Kraydak had become; there wasn't so much as a rationalization for the mortals who had turned on their own kind. What the brothers had done had been as necessary as stepping on a roach.

"You *found* a map?" she prodded.

"Oh, yeah." Raulin pulled himself free of memories. "I only noticed it because the Right Honorable Scum-sucker dropped it scurrying out the door. I grabbed it . . ." He paused, decided the rest of what he'd stripped from the room had no real relevance to the tale, and continued. "Mother wanted to be a Scholar, couldn't of course, it was an outlawed discipline, but she read constantly and even managed to get her hands on a number of the forbidden texts. She recognized the sigil on the map."

"A bleeding hand," Jago interjected, "on a circle of black. Aryalan. One of the ancient wizards." His tone, unlike Raulin's, held no enthusiasm, no excitement. Raulin told a story. He reported facts.

Crystal felt Jago's disapproval, it surrounded him like a fog, but she was uncertain whether he disapproved of the weight of history that accompanied the wizard's name, the situation he and his brother now found themselves in, or her hearing of it.

"How can you be sure," she asked, "that the map leads to her tower."

"We can't," Raulin admitted cheerfully. "No one can read the script. What's more, it must have been recopied so many times over the centuries it's got a virgin's chance in Chaos of retaining any of the original wording. But it does lead to something of the wizard's, something important and big. That much we're sure of. Think of it, Crystal," he leaned forward and his hands clutched at dreams, "a treasure house of the ancients, lost since the Age of Wizards ended. Ours for the taking. Yours too if you'll come. Chaos knows, your talents could come in handy." Then his voice softened. "And we'd like your company."

For an instant Crystal thought, *So, he would find use for me after all,* then realized she did Raulin a disservice. It took no wizard to see that he wanted her more than he wanted her power. The power was only a useful addition. She glanced at Jago and he answered her silent question with a terse nod; more conscious of the wizard than his brother and therefore more wary of the woman.

This was what she'd been looking for, a new venture to involve her power now that the purpose she'd been created for was done. Something to give her life direction; for she had no doubt that although this pair of mortals might be able to breach the wizard's tower, there'd be power within it only she could handle. If she went with them, she'd be necessary again.

And more than that.

Companionship on the trail, laughter to chase away the loneliness, warm arms instead of cold power wrapped around her at night.

Raulin's gaze was a caress and, behind the caution in Jago's eyes, warmth lurked.

She felt herself respond, an answering heat rising. To her horror, she felt something rise with it, stirring behind the heavy shields that blocked the voices, felt it through the barriers, its strength bringing all the other bits and pieces with it and threatening to fling them free.

Crystal clutched at her concept of self. "I can't," she gasped, turning and fleeing. Halfway up the stairs she paused and let go enough to face them again, saying softly, "Be careful."

Raulin only stared, but Jago answered in tones matching hers, "You also."

And then she was gone.

"Well," Raulin said after standing a moment in stunned silence, "you were a lot of help."

"Huh?"

"I'm not surprised she ran, with you glowering at her like that."

"I wasn't glowering."

"You certainly weren't being too encouraging."

"Yeah? At least I wasn't leering."

"And I was?"

"When aren't you? Every woman we meet, it's the same story."

"I don't leer."

They started up the stairs, both very aware of having given Crystal enough time to reach the safety of her room, both well aware that bickering covered concern there seemed to be no way to express. They'd seen fear enough to know it, even on a wizard's face.

\*      \*      \*

"Lady?" Ivan slid out from behind the tree and moved tentatively forward. "I, I just wanted ta say good-bye."

From somewhere, Crystal found a smile for him. She'd slipped through the village unnoticed—those not at the mines were blind behind the heavy felt pads that covered the windows, blocking the winter drafts—and wondered how he knew she'd take this path. Known in advance, she realized. He'd been waiting for her to arrive.

"'Twas easy," he told her when she asked. "You wouldn't want ta pass the mines, not after . . ." He colored and continued, leaving the sentence hanging. "And I heard you tell Nad that you were headin' north when you stopped. If you were still goin' north, well," he shrugged, the motion almost buried under his heavy furs, "unless you changed ta a bird, this is the way you had ta come."

They both turned and looked down the only negotiable way up the cliffs that shielded the village from the furies of the north wind.

"And if I had turned to a bird?"

Ivan smiled. "Then I'd have seen that," he said simply, "and have waved." His eyes dropped to snowy boot toes. "But I'm glad you didn't," he added.

"I am, too," Crystal told him, and meant it. In the small pouch that held the few things she treasured—a birch leaf, withered and brown, a strand of her mother's hair, a smooth gray stone from Riven Pass—was Ivan's wild rose still, and always, blooming. She suddenly wanted to give him something that would mean as much to him, regardless of what the power use might open within her.

The heavy clothes she wore were more for conformity than necessity and although every breath hung in a frosty cloud and the sky had the brittle clarity that only comes with bitter cold, her hands and head were bare. She pulled free two long, silver hairs and, brows drawn down in concentration, braided them into a ring.

"Give me your hand."

Ivan obediently removed his mitten and extended his arm.

Crystal slipped the ring on his smallest finger. It fit perfectly.

Speechless, Ivan stared at his hand like he'd never seen it before. Then he gasped as he took a closer look at the ring. From an arm's length, it appeared no more than a thin silver band such as anyone might wear, but up close the solid metal became again the intricate weaving of two of the wizard's long silver hairs.

"I . . . I don't know what ta say," he managed at last.

"Well," Crystal gently slipped the mitt back on his hand as he seemed incapable of doing it himself, "you came to say good-bye."

The youth nodded and bit his lip. "Good-bye, Lady." He took courage from the warm feel of the ring about his finger and met her eyes. "I hope you find what you're lookin' for."

When he came up out of the emerald glow that had enveloped him, he was alone on the cliff top and his were the only tracks that marked the snow. He slid his thumb inside the larger part of his mitten and touched the ring. It was a beautiful gift but not the greatest the wizard had given him, for before he'd lost himself in her power he'd seen tears glisten in her eyes and he still felt the soft pressure of her silent good-bye.

Suddenly, he grinned and threw himself down the steep trail back to the village, bounding and leaping like a crazed mountain goat, his whoops echoing back from the cliff face and filling the valley with sound.

The last piece of equipment lashed tight to the sled, Raulin straightened and stared to the north. They'd follow the path young Ivan said she'd taken only to the top of the cliff and then swing west. He sighed and his breath laid a patina of frost on his mustache.

Jago stepped out of the Nugget, pulling on his mittens, and followed the direction of his brother's gaze. He couldn't help but be glad they were going on alone. Breaching a wizard's tower with another wizard in tow struck him as one wizard too many. Probably *two* too many, but he hadn't been able to convince Raulin of that and going along had seemed the answer. Besides, if they did win through . . .

"Jago?"

"What?" He slapped his pockets until he found his snow goggles and slipped them on.

"I wasn't leering, was I?"

"Afraid you scared her away?"

Raulin turned to face the younger man, his expression hard to read. "Yes," he said simply.

Jago shook his head. "No," he put as much conviction in his voice as he could, "you weren't leering. You didn't scare her away." He shrugged. "If one of us scared her, it was me. She knew, in spite of everything, that I didn't completely trust her. But I think she had her own reasons for running."

"Yeah. Me, too. Did you pay the innkeeper?"

"Of course." Jago went to his place behind the sled and got a firm grip on the pushing bar while Raulin slipped the leather traces over his shoulders. "I gave her the brindle pelt."

"You what?" Forgetting he was now held to the sled, Raulin turned so quickly he almost threw himself to the ground.

"Why waste our coin?" Jago asked practically. "We had no time to have it tanned and it was beginning to go gamy."

"If I'd known you were going to throw that much payment at her," Raulin growled straightening himself out, "I'd have asked for another bed."

"I don't know what you're complaining about," Jago muttered, rocking the sled from side to side to break the runners free. "You're the one who snores."

"I don't snore!" Raulin threw his weight against the harness and the sled jerked forward, cutting the start of the path shown on the ancient map in the snow.

The great white owl drifted silently on a breeze, the tip of each wing barely sculling to keep it aloft. Its shadow kept pace, a sharp edged silhouette running along the moon silvered snow. Suddenly, with powerful beats of huge wings, it dove for the ground, talons extended.

Had the hare frozen it might have lived, for owls hunt by sound more than sight, but it panicked and fled, kicking up a plume of snow that clearly marked its position. The shadow reached it first. Frantically, it twisted and spun and died as the talons closed and the weight of the owl drove it into the ground and snapped its back with a single clear crack.

The owl shook itself free of snow and bent its head to feed.

Perhaps the bird's bad eyesight explained why it continued to eat, apparently unaware of the man who stood less than a wingspan away, observing it with distaste. Perhaps.

"How," Lord Death asked with a shudder, "can you eat raw rabbit in the middle of the night?"

The owl clicked its beak in Lord Death's direction but made no other answer, save to eat a bit more raw rabbit. Not until its meal had been reduced to a patch of blood on the snow did it turn, blink great green eyes, and change.

"It could be worse," Crystal told him, spinning herself new clothes made of snow and moonlight—the cloak she clasped round her shoulders was red. "Compared to some, owls have fairly civilized eating habits."

"You realize that with no time to digest you have a stomach full of . . ."

"I realize."

"And?"

"I try not to think about it." She smiled. "I'm glad to see you."

Lord Death smiled back; he couldn't help it. He hoped she never discovered how much a slave to her smile he was. Except for the times he hoped she would discover it, and therefore smile more often.

Occasionally—this moment—Crystal wished she could trust the expressions on Lord Death's face. Did it mean anything when he smiled at her in that way, his eyes soft and questioning? Or did it merely mean that one of mortalkind had died wearing that expression?

They walked in silence for a time and then both began to speak at once.

Crystal laughed and waved a regal hand. "You first, milord."

"I merely wondered why you continue to travel alone." He'd put some effort into choosing the phrasing and it had, he thought, just the right touch of curiosity mixed with polite interest. Enough to get an answer but not to give away how much the answer meant. He wished he knew why the answer meant so much.

"There was . . . I mean, I . . ." She sputtered into silence and came to a halt.

Momentum moved Lord Death a farther pace or two, then he stopped, turned, and studied the wizard's face. "What are you afraid of," he asked, recognizing her expression. His voice grew cold. "What did he do to you?"

Puzzlement replaced fear for an instant then realization replaced that. "He didn't do anything." Crystal wondered what Lord Death had thought to turn his cheeks so red.

"Then what?"

Should she tell him what she suspected was happening? That the threads of power that made her what she was were one by one coming untied. He couldn't help. But then no one could and didn't friends tell each other what troubled them? Still, they weren't the usual friends, not the last surviving wizard and the Mother's one true son. Or should she just make something up to satisfy him?

"I can't tell you," she said at last, gifting him at least with no lie.

His voice deepened to a growl. "Why not?"

Helplessly she spread her hands. Why didn't she want Lord Death to know she was, perhaps literally, going to pieces? Why did it matter so much that she not shatter the image she knew he held of the perfect Crystal?

"Could you tell him?"

"Him? Raulin?" Strange question. She considered it. She hadn't told him, but could she? Raulin held no image of her the news could break and their friendship hadn't had the chance to develop to where what he thought of her mattered. "Yes," she said thoughtfully, "I could tell Raulin . . ."

Lord Death's face nickered through several expressions and ended up wearing none at all. "Oh," he said. And vanished.

Crystal stared at the place Lord Death had stood, her hand half raised to pull him back. "He wanted me involved in mortal lives again," she told the wind. "How could I betray him when I answered the question he asked?" she demanded of the shadows. "I never knew he carried mortal feelings," she confessed to the moonlight and opened her mind to call him back.

Across the meadow a tree burst into flame as the presences in her mind surged out of the place where the shields had penned Stem and grabbed for her power. Crystal screamed and dropped to her knees as burning hands beat at the inside of her skull. Below her, the snow hissed and melted. Voices howled and voices shrieked and voices screamed at other voices, but outside Crystal's head the night continued quiet and serene save for the one tree consumed in a tower of orange and gold.

Crystal felt her body rise, the movements small and sharp, directed by an unskilled puppeteer, or by one whose efforts were hindered by another fouling the strings. She staggered, almost fell and felt her feet jerked back beneath her. One voice, its cadences the hiss and crackle of the dying tree, snouted defiance.

"*I will have her!*"

"*No!*" purred another equally heated but infinitely more controlled. "*Mine, for I was the key.*"

Arms flailing, Crystal lurched first one way then the other, every two or three steps leaving a steaming hole in the snow. Her clothes, power created, dissolved, leaving her wearing only the pouch of memories on a leather belt around her waist and a blue-green opal, hanging from a silver chain about her neck. She felt the cold and then she didn't and then the pain was too intense for her to tell.

Then a third voice moved from the tumult to the forefront of her mind and the burning within became almost bearable. Her legs steadied and lengthened into a runner's stride.

With her fists clenched so tightly the nails cut half moons into her palms, Crystal clutched at the shards of her power and tried to force her shields back into place. Nothing remained to force; the shields had been obliterated and the voices fought over the ruins. When she tried instead to regain control of her body, something slammed her against a tree with enough violence to have her cry out in purely physical pain. Muscles and joints protested as the voices battled among themselves, twisting her from side to side. When the running began again, she let it.

Through the forest, across a small meadow, up a rocky cliff face and down an impossible trail, all done at close to full speed, the third voice fighting off the others while directing Crystal's feet. In shattered bits and pieces, Crystal felt the calm that had cushioned her while her hands repaired the Nugget's kitchen pump.

A small building appeared at the edge of her vision, her body changed direction slightly and ran toward it.

"No!" howled a voice.

The leg just lifted off the ground spasmed and when it came forward again, refused to bear her weight. Crystal pitched forward, rolling at the last second to avoid slamming her face into a granite outcropping. Her body racked with convulsions, she fed what little power she held to the third voice. She had to get to that building—she didn't know why, but its call nearly drowned out the chaos—and the third voice seemed also to be trying to get her there.

The convulsions eased and the puppeteer pulled heir to her knees, then her feet, then she was running again. The second time she fell, she tasted blood as her teeth went through her tongue.

The building stood barely two body lengths away, maybe less.

The convulsions returned and locked her muscles. She couldn't rise, not even to her knees, so she rolled through snow and rock and blood and vomit, rolled to the threshold and slammed up against the door. With the last of her strength, with the third voice falling before the other two, she lifted her arm and fumbled at the latch.

Her fingers refused to obey so she slapped at the piece of metal, drove her hand up against it, used the pain as a focus to keep control of her arm.

The door swung open and she flopped inside. . . .

Silence.

No sound save the soft murmur of the wind in the trees and the beating of Crystal's own heart.

She dragged herself forward, and with a swollen and bleeding foot pushed closed the door.

The wood beneath her cheek was cedar and from the spicy smell masking the stink that she knew had entered with her, the rest of the building was as well. A silver square of moonlight marked the floor a hand-span from her nose. She lay quietly, gathering together her splintered power, motionless until she held enough to feel whole again, then slowly, very slowly, she pulled her legs beneath her and pushed herself up until she sat.

The building was small and square, a door in one wall, small windows in two others flanked by cupboards filled with the supplies a traveler might need. Opposite the door was a fireplace, and wood stacked floor to ceiling. At a comfortable distance from the hearth, sat the cabin's only piece of furniture: a chair, arms and back intricately carved with leaves and vines, the whole thing lovingly polished to a satin finish.

The Mother's chair.

The Mother's house.

Small cabins maintained by those who lived in the Mother's service. Blessed with the Mother's presence. A place of peace, not only for the mind and spirit but for the body as well for no weapon could pass the door and no hand could be lifted in anger within the walls.

Crystal had had no idea such a sanctuary existed here on Halda's frozen border.

Carefully, she reached within. The bedlam had been calmed by the Mother's presence although the pieces that had created it still remained apart. She searched among them gently until she touched the presence that spoke with the third voice. "Thank you," she said to it.

"*You're welcome, child,*" replied the voice. "*They called me Tayja when I had a life of my own. Know me as your friend.*" And then the presence withdrew, leaving Crystal to herself, but the calm that came with it lingered.

Moving gingerly, for she hadn't the power to repair the damage done, Crystal crawled toward the chair, wincing as a torn bit of flesh caught on a rough piece of flooring. She knew she needed to eat and sleep, but she needed to think even more. When she reached the chair she sighed, and rested her head where the Mother's lap would be.

Tayja. Goddess of craft and learning.

It was just as she feared.

When the Age of Wizards ended, there were few powers left in the world. Out of all the pantheon that mortals had created to help them understand the Mother's creation and their place within it, only the seven goddesses remained. In time they caused one last wizard to be formed, a power to fight an ancient evil, and into that vessel they poured all that they were.

"And now that the evil is defeated," Crystal realized, her aching head pillowed on abraded arms, "some at least have no further use for the vessel."

Fire. Zarsheiy. Now she could name the hissing and howling voice, the first she'd heard, the part of her that fought the hardest to be free.

"And *that* is the problem . . ." Her eyes began to close and she sighed again. "They are a part of me and without them I am not. I wish," she murmured sleepily, "that just once there'd be an easy answer."

As she drifted to sleep, still leaning against the Mother's chair, she thought she felt the soft touch of a sympathetic hand against her cheek.

# FOUR

For two days Crystal did little but eat and sleep, slowly healing her damaged body as her returning power enabled her to do so. On the third day, she allowed the fire to die down to embers and, sitting with her back to the Mother's chair, slipped into trance and then deep within her own mind.

Green, a deep rich summer shade lightening to springtime as she went deeper still. A tendril of thought rose up to meet her and she paused, knowing that in the Mother's house only benevolent forces could stir.

"Why have you come?" Tayja asked, her tone sharp though not unkind.

"We need to talk." The wizard concentrated and the green light fractured into a forest grove, the two women standing within a circle of silver birch.

The goddess smiled, the white of her teeth startlingly bright against the darkness of her skin. "Ah . . ." She sank to the velvet grass and stroked a hand along the blades. "So long . . ." Then her face grew serious and when she looked up at Crystal it bore the stamp of the mahogany of which she had been made. "You are safe enough with me, but do not attempt this with the others. It will only intensify their struggle to be separate once again."

Crystal nodded and sat, folding her legs beneath her. The Grove was an image so much a part of her that it took little power to maintain. "What is happening to me?" she asked.

"I thought you had discovered it."

"Well, yes, but . . ."

"But you wish me to clarify? Very well." Tayja sat straighter and cupped her hands before her. "Consider yourself to be the crystal you are named." As she spoke a crystal appeared on her palms, rough cut, multifaceted, and a little smaller than a clenched fist. "You should be neither surprised nor fearful," she chided, for the living Crystal had stiffened at the other's manipulation of her mind. "I am, after all, a part of you." A green light shone through the stone. "As you can see, the joinings between the many facets are obvious and this one more so than the others." She traced a finger down the line and the portion of the crystal it delineated began to glow red.

"Zarsheiy?" Crystal guessed.

"Yes. A necessary but unenthusiastic part of your creation. She has always been unstable and had all our power not been necessary . . ." The goddess shrugged, a most ungoddesslike gesture, and continued. "While you were focused there was no problem." The crystal flared; green light submerging the red section back into the whole. "But as you lost purpose . . ." The green faded and the red glowed strongly once again. "Zarsheiy began to make her presence felt until . . ." A sharp crack and the red fragment of crystal broke free. "This weakened the structure and gave Avreen, who was always closest to Zarsheiy, ideas of her own." Tayja looked suddenly amused. "Actually, child, you gave her some ideas yourself."

Crystal felt her cheeks grow warm as she considered the aspects Avreen wore. "Raulin?" she asked.

"Raulin," Tayja agreed. "Not in itself a bad thing, but it strengthened Avreen and when next you used your power she twisted it, hoping to break free." Another facet flared along the edge of the larger stone, this one a deep flesh pink. "She didn't quite manage it, but her attempt and Zarsheiy's continuing fight to wrest control made the matrix increasingly unstable." The definition of the remaining contact lines intensified and each facet began to take on a color of its own, making the original crystal seem more a puzzle than a single piece. One, a deep brown, well marbled with green, became for a moment the dominant color.

Crystal touched the brown portion gently. "You?"

"Me," Tayja confirmed, her expression twisting slightly in embarrassment. "I found I could work on my own, and you wanted so badly to fix the pump. I am sorry, though, I had no right." She sighed and shook her head. "Three nights ago, however, it became fortunate that I had strengthened my will or, if you wish, the part of your will which is mine.

"When you opened yourself to call Lord Death, you lowered all barriers and both Zarsheiy and Avreen took advantage of the opportunity." The red fragment grew suddenly radiant, the crystal writhed in Tayja's hands, and the pink fragment lay free as well. "They began to fight for control of your power. Because I have always been integrated more fully into your personality, I can call to my use a greater part of your power than either of them but in order to do it, I had to take their path."

Crystal noticed that even when the brown broke free of the larger mass, much of it remained green.

"With your help, I brought you to this house, where both of my ambitious sisters lie dormant and no others can break free to challenge you. Use this quiet time to rebuild your shields so that when you leave, as you must, they will be contained."

Crystal stared into the goddess' hands. The red and the pink had become colorless. The brown remained unchanged. Deep within the multihued stone—for four goddesses had not yet taken up their aspects—she saw a core of green. She realized that little bit of green would be all that remained if all the goddesses broke free and Crystal knew it wasn't enough to sustain a life.

"What must I do?" she asked, searching Tayja's face for the answer. "How do I become whole again?"

Tayja spread her hands, the stones vanished, and she shook her head. "I do not know, child," she admitted, "but two things I can give you. First, as much as we seem separate, we are all a part of you. We gave up our lives at your creation and now have none of our own. Second, the whole is always greater than the sum of its parts." She frowned. "Not a great deal of help, is it?" The goddess clasped Crystal's hands for a moment. "Now you know me, you better know one part of you and there is always strength in that."

The Mother's house was cold when Crystal returned to it, the embers she had left, mostly ash. Carefully, she rebuilt the fire using only mortal skills. Not until it roared red and gold, and heat began to rise again, did she consider her meeting with the goddess.

"I suppose," she said to the Mother's chair, thoughtfully nibbling on a handful of raisins, "that if Tayja truly is a part of me and *I* don't know what to do then *she* can't. I do know I can't go on like this." Not only for her own sake but for the sake of the world as well. The ancient wizards had refused to control their appetites; her lack was less a matter of choice, but the results were likely to be the same if any one of the goddesses gained control—death and destruction. She twisted a strand of hair about her fingers and frowned. As much as she disliked the idea, the centaurs seemed to be the only solution. Maybe they knew something that could help.

*Our knowledge,* C'Tal had often said, *begins with the Mother's creation of this world and we have constantly added to it ever since. This aside, we do, however, prefer you to work out your difficulties yourself. That is why we taught you to think.*

Crystal sighed. "Oh, be quiet," she murmured at the memory, and it obediently stilled.

She spent the rest of the day tidying the small cabin and restocking the woodpile. The night she spent in meditation, rebuilding her shields around the goddesses, using the knowledge Tayja had given her to anchor them securely. In the morning, in clothing made of cedar and woodsmoke, she closed the door of the Mother's house firmly behind her and headed west.

As she walked, her power-shod feet barely dimpling the snow, her thoughts turned back past her recent breakdown to Lord Death and his sudden departure. Going over their conversation once again, she was forced to conclude his actions most closely resembled those of a jealous man.

"Which," she pointed out to a curious chickadee watching from a juniper bush, "is ridiculous. Lord Death is . . . well, Lord Death. He *isn't* a man."

As she continued walking, she didn't see the small bird's panicked flight nor the evergreen wither and die.

Crystal had not been celibate in the twelve years since she'd defeated Kraydak, but men who could deal with all she was were few and far between. She remembered Raulin's solution and smiled; in his desire to deal with the woman he merely acknowledged the wizard and for him that was enough. She suspected Jago would not have settled for anything so simple.

Deep below the shields, Avreen stirred.

Startled, Crystal shifted her thoughts away from the brothers, a little embarrassed they affected her so strongly that even such gentle memories could cause the goddess of lust to rise. She almost conceded that, if Lord Death was indeed capable of jealousy, perhaps he had cause. She shied away from the thought for that would mean he had reason and somehow that frightened her more than all seven goddesses.

Puzzling over her reaction to the Mother's son—and his to her and hers to that—Crystal walked around a granite outcropping and nearly died. A high-pitched and undulating howl echoed off the mountains and shattered the silence into a thousand sharp edged pieces. Blind panic threw her back as a massive brown and black body slammed through the space where she had been. Her heart in her throat, she rolled and looked up, dashing the snow from her face.

Brindle. A young male, barely five feet high at the shoulder. Small black eyes, well shaded beneath their protruding brow-ridge, glared down at her. His angry snorts made great gouts of steam in the frigid air. Muscles tensed and, silently this time, he charged.

Crystal just barely managed to avoid the strike. The soft whisper of fur against her cheek as she twisted to safety gave her an indication of the animal's speed. Had he been older and more practiced at judging distance, even the agility that came of Crystal's mythic heritage might not have been enough.

As his prey disappeared again, the brindle checked his lunge almost in midair, flipped his heavy body about with a fluid grace, and, growling in irritation, attacked once more.

Crystal caught hold of her power and slapped a portion at the brindle's nose.

He stopped dead, his eyes narrowed, and his upper lip drew back to show a mouth full of needle sharp teeth.

Trying to calm her breathing, Crystal began to back cautiously away. The brindle snarled a warning and she decided it was safest to stay right where she was. Slowly, so as not to provoke a response from the watching animal, she sat on a bit of windswept rock and wondered what to do.

She remembered hearing that brindles never abandoned their chosen prey; tracking it for days across hundreds of miles, worrying at its heels, waiting until a chance presented itself and then moving in for the kill.

Had it been night she could've turned into the owl and flown—not even brindles could track a trail through the air—but she daren't risk the bird's sensitive eyes to the glare of winter sunlight.

Raulin had killed the brindle that attacked Jago with only a dagger. Crystal studied this brindle, much as it studied her, made note of the claws, each a dagger's length and cruelly curved, and realized just what that meant. She measured its bulk against her memory of Raulin. This brindle could make four or five of the man and the beast that had attacked the brothers had been larger still. In her mind's eye she saw him, clinging to the thick fur at the animal's throat, driving the dagger into the eye again and again, desperation lending strength to the blows until finally one pierced the brain. She shuddered.

She couldn't use enough power to flip the brindle away, as she had Raulin and Jago at the inn, for that would weaken her shields and leave her helpless against Zarsheiy and Avreen. She doubted she could count on Tayja saving her again. If she had a choice, she preferred to face the brindle.

They were said to be intelligent, cunning, and ferocious; vulnerable only when feeding, for their gluttony made them careless. They did not peacefully coexist with any other living creatures and barely tolerated each other. Up to a dozen might live scattered throughout a clan range which was ruled absolutely by the oldest female, and if male brindles were thought to be bad tempered . . .

Crystal smiled.

The brindle howled at this display of fangs, puny though they were, then jerked what was to be his killing charge to a stop before it actually got moving. Where heartbeats before his prey had waited, an old scarred female, survivor of many matings, now reared and raked the sky with her claws.

Crystal opened her brindle mouth and roared.

The young male spared an instant to wonder what had gone wrong, then instinct took over and he ran.

The female brindle dwindled back to human form and the wizard grinned. A half grown male simply did not argue with a matriarch, no matter how unexpectedly she appeared. He would not stop running until he was miles away. From deep within, she felt the touch of seven smiles as the goddesses approved, for once in complete agreement, and just for an instant she knew how it would feel when she was whole once more.

?

Crystal's head snapped up and to the northwest. The touch came again.

?

Her power pulsed in response. The touch changed. Called.

!

Almost involuntarily, she stepped toward it. Something in the mountains, something with power, needed her help. She crossed the snow marked by the brindle's prints and walked into the fresh white beyond before she dug in her heels and asked the obvious question.

What called? Or who?

She knew the touch of all the Mother's Eldest, and this was none of them. She knew the sacred places where the Mother's power resided most strongly, and none were in these mountains. It had the feel of wizardry. But the ancient ones were long dead and even Kraydak, the one survivor from that earlier age, had joined them a dozen years ago.

*!*

Could she have triggered the relic Jago and Raulin searched for? She wished she'd asked for a look at their map.

*!!*

"All right." She picked up the thread of the call. "You needn't shout."

She checked her shields. They remained strong, for the illusion had taken little power. The centaurs would always be available for questioning, but this summons could end as abruptly as it began and Crystal *needed* to know where it came from. The goddesses would have to wait. She only hoped they would.

Throughout the day, as the mountain terrain grew bleaker, the call grew stronger. At sunset, she walked between towering peaks at the edge of the tree line. With moonrise, she flowed into her owl form and took to the air. It made no difference to the call, it stretched before her, a pathway of power, easy to follow.

*Too easy?* she wondered and took a moment to consider the idea that she might be moving into a trap. If the call did come from an ancient relic, this was a very real possibility. The wizards of old had thought as little of each other as they did of the world at large.

But if the call came from something else, if there was a power out there that could speak to hers, surely that was worth the risk? Not the promise perhaps, but the suggestion of companionship and perhaps help.

Yes, she decided, it was.

When her wings began to tire, she found shelter of a sort between two boulders, and, taking back her woman shape, wrapped herself in power and slept for the remainder of the night.

In the morning, with her stomach making imperious demands,

Crystal glared around at the rock and snow and cursed herself for not having taken the time to hunt the night before.

*!*

She could safely feed off her power for a little time; the peak was no more than half a day away, if she reached it and the call came from farther on she would go back and hunt before continuing.

At midmorning she found a cave. The call came from within.

Long and narrow and twice the height of the wizard who stood just inside its mouth, the cave sloped downward into the mountain. It seemed a natural fissure, rough walled and rubble strewn, but when Crystal laid long fingers against the wall, the power that had formed it in the distant past still echoed faintly in the stone. So the call came from the ancient ones after all. For a long moment she stayed half in, half out of the cave, disappointment warring with curiosity. Then she sighed and stepped forward as curiosity won.

When a sharply angled turn cut off the light spilling in through the cave mouth, patches of lichen dappling the rock began to faintly glow silver-gray, keeping the path from total darkness.

Suddenly, the cave narrowed to a vertical slash leading into the mountain's heart. To follow the call, Crystal would have to slide sideways, her movements confined on either side by the mountain itself. If there was a trap this would be the place to set it. She paused and pushed her hair away from her face. Was curiosity reason enough to attempt such a passage? The call continued to tug at her power and, moistening dry lips, she pushed into the crack.

"As long as I've come this far . . ."

The weight of the mountain flattened her voice, making it small and toneless.

Forty sidling footsteps later, she realized the lichen patches no longer provided the only light. A few steps farther and it had lightened quite definitely to gray. Another step, a struggle around a corner that seemed to clutch at her chest and hips, and the end of the passage was in sight; a pinkish-gray ribbon of light. Heartened, she moved as quickly as she could toward it.

Five steps away, four, and a body blocked her view of the cavern beyond. Lord Death stood where the passage widened, his hands outstretched toward her, his features flickering through a multitude of faces each wearing an identical expression of horror.

Was this a warning, Crystal wondered, biting back a startled shriek. Why did Lord Death block her path and why didn't he speak?

And then he did.

"Free my people," he pleaded and vanished from her way.

As puzzled by his cryptic utterance as by his appearance, Crystal hesitantly advanced.

The cavern felt enormous after the confinement of the passage, but the opposite wall was actually no more than fifteen feet away. Before she could scan the rest of area, her attention was snagged by the pattern in the stone of the far wall. Set into it were hundreds, maybe thousands, of bones.

"I see," piped up a shrill voice, "that you admire my map."

Crouched in the corner where the wall of bones touched one of mere rock, was a twisted and misshapen parody of a man. Its back was humped so high its head appeared to come from the middle of its chest, its arms were too long, its legs too short, and mottled gray skin fell about it in wrinkled folds. Its eyes were black from lid to lid, two vertical slashes served it for a nose, and the mouth that split its face from ear to ear was as empty of teeth as a frog's.

Crystal felt her jaw drop as once again the power that had led her here touched her own. There could be no mistaking the source, not so close. This was what had called her. She stumbled back a step.

"Who?" she managed. "What?"

"It is called a demon," said Lord Death, now standing at her side, lives still playing across his face, "and it is quite mad."

"I am sane enough when I choose," the demon protested, clambering to its feet. "Madness is my escape."

"You're trapped here?" Crystal asked, trying to make some sense of what was going on.

The demon threw wide its arms. "I am imprisoned here!" it

shrieked. It flung itself forward to land on its knees at Crystal's feet. "I beg of you, free me."

It smelted of cinnamon, sharp but not unpleasant.

"You have the power. You answered my call. Now you have seen me in my misery. You cannot leave me here."

Crystal glanced behind her. The narrow entrance to the tunnel was unbarred. She reached out with power. Red and black bands wrapped around and through the stone cocooning the cavern even to the small spring in one corner. Identical bands but black and red cocooned the demon. It was the oldest power she had ever felt.

"How long have you been here?"

"Eternity," sniffed the demon.

"Six thousand years," said Lord Death softly. "The wizard Aryalan bound it just to prove she could. Then she left it here."

"Left me," agreed the demon. "Bound me and forgot me." It turned from Crystal, crawled to the wall of bone, and began rubbing up against it.

The bones were not six thousand years old. Although many were yellowish gray with age, many more were still ivory.

The demon chuckled at Crystal's expression. "You like my map?" it asked. "He would not free me when I called to him, but he sent me things to do."

"Who did?"

"The sunny gold one. With eyes like bits of sky."

"Kraydak?"

Gray shoulders shrugged. "He never said his name. When there were two powers in the world he was one. Now there is only you." Its eyes narrowed. "And I do not want more man-things sent. I have finished my map."

It could have only been Kraydak, Crystal realized, called as she had been. He had refused to free the demon and later amused himself by sending mortals to it and to their deaths.

Raulin and Jago had gotten their map from Kraydak's city governor.

Desperately, Crystal searched the demon's prison for signs of a fresh kill. Even considering the three days she'd spent in the Mother's house, they could not have been that far ahead of her.

There were no bones except those in the wall. No blood, wet or dry. No bits of . . .

She jumped as the demon took her hand and pulled her forward. Its grasp was cool and dry.

"The bargain," it whispered to her, "was with the other. But if you free me, you may have the map instead."

"He said he would free you if you made him the map?"

"Yes, yes, he did."

"He lied." No guess but a surety. Kraydak always lied when he could.

The demon began to cry. "I know. Everyone lies to me. But it was all I had to offer him."

"What does the map show?"

"The way to her hole." It polished a bit of bone with a flap of skin. "To the Binding One's hidden place."

The way to Aryalan's tower. Kraydak had offered the demon freedom in exchange for the way to Aryalan's tower. He must have hoped to plunder it but had died before he got the chance.

Crystal reached out and lightly touched the wall.

*DEATH!*

She jerked her hand away and slowly turned to face the one the voices summoned.

"That which binds the demon in," Lord Death explained, "binds these mortal lives as well. I cannot take my children home. Free him, Crystal, and free them also."

She moved carefully away from the wall and looked down at the demon as sternly as she was able. "If I free you, what will you do?"

"Do?" Its mouth worked for a moment but no sound came out. "Do?" it repeated at last. "I shall go home. Go home. HOME!" The last word rose to a howl, a scream of anguish that ran up and down Crystal's spine with razor edges. The sound filled the cavern, thrummed within the rock, and was joined by the cries of the multitude in the wall.

The demon and those trapped with it shrieked out the agony of their long imprisonment.

Deep within Crystal's mind, darkness stirred and wakened. It surged outward, a roaring tide that slammed through shields and over defenses. Nashawryn answered the demon's call. Crystal added her scream to the others as the eldest goddess broke free within her.

# FIVE

*Blackness.*
    *Screaming terror.*
*Fire in the darkness that gave no light.*
*A hundred knives that cut and twisted.*
*A thousand years of pain.*

Driven deep within her own mind by the darkness and the fear, Crystal searched desperately for the core of self that Tayja had shown her. If it still existed, it lay beyond her reach. Nashawryn held sway over all.

Here, the nightmares that had dimmed her childhood.

There, the paralyzing dread of the young adult.

All about her the horror of the woman; madness, the shattering of her soul into a myriad of pieces that could never be joined again, each brittle shard dying cut off from the others.

A hundred voices wept and hers was more than one of them.

The noise pushed her this way and that, adding bits of her to the cacophony every time she tried to resist, moving her closer and closer to the precipice where fear and reality became one and Nashawryn would be all that remained.

And then . . . and then she cried alone.

The blackness trembled.

Crystal forced herself to be still.

Beyond the curtain, something called.

Her nose twitched as she smelled the soft leather of her father's

jerkin. Her fingers curved as they held the silken masses of her mother's hair. She rested for a moment in the memory of their arms.

Then she stepped forward. The blackness tore.

She gathered close the piece of self she had almost forgotten and
opened her eyes.

Raulin was just forcing himself around a tight corner in the passage
when the howling began. The sound echoed alarmingly within the corridor of rock. He winced, instinctively jerked his head away, and swore
as the back of his skull slammed against the rough stone. He felt Jago's
hand close on his shoulder, but any words were lost as a woman's
screams began to weave a high-pitched descant of terror throughout
the continuing howl.

Raulin ripped free of the mountain's grasp, leaving cloth and bits of
skin behind, and flung himself down the last few feet of passage and
into the cavern.

*Crystal.* He'd known it from the moment the screams began, though
he didn't know how. Her head was thrown back, the lovely white column of her throat was ridged with strain, her eyes were clenched shut,
her hands were fists that beat the air, and her mouth stretched wide to
let the sound escape.

He wasn't quite in time to catch her when she crumpled to the
ground but reached her side a second later, lifting her thrashing head
and shoulders up off the rock and onto his lap. With one arm cradled
protectively around her, for her constant movement threatened to
throw her free, he reached up with the other and fumbled with the
fastenings on his jacket. Her clothing had disappeared when she fell
and she needed protection from more than just the winter air. Abra-
sions, slowly oozing red, already marked the satin skin. He wished
he still wore his huge fur overcoat—removed before attempting the
narrow passage—for that was more the kind of protection she
needed.

The jacket was tight and hard to manage one-handed, harder yet when arms were full of a beautiful, naked woman who would not hold still, but Raulin managed to drag himself out of it and get the heavy fabric wrapped at least partially around Crystal's body.

On some level, his mind reacted to her desirability. He was only mortal man, after all. But those feelings were deeply buried and he held her as he would have held Jago in the same circumstances.

Her screams had died to whimpers. A trickle of blood, where teeth had scored her lip, trailed across her cheek. The jacket held her arms confined, for which Raulin gave thanks as his ears still rang from the force of one random blow. She kept trying to draw her knees up, to curl into a ball, to hide from whatever had done this.

Every time her knees came up, Raulin pushed them back. She was the stronger, he the more determined, finding what he needed to stop her in the memory of his father who had one day given up, curled into a ball, and while his wife and young sons watched, had died. He murmured soothing things to her, nonsense, bits of lullabies, anything to quiet her, to reach her.

And the howling that had started it all, went on and on.

He turned his head, saw the source, without really registering what he saw, and snapped "Shut up!" at the misshapen thing.

It did.

Now the only screams were Crystal's.

"Crystal?" He caught a flailing hand that had fought out of the jacket to freedom. "Crystal, it's Raulin. I have you. You're safe."

Suddenly she stilled; her breathing hoarse and labored, her body trembling with tension.

"That's it," he whispered and stroked her forehead with his cheek for both his hands were full. "Now come back. Come back, Crystal, I have you."

Her nose wrinkled and the tension went out of the free hand as the fingers curved around something he couldn't see.

"Crystal?"

She sighed, the warm weight of her settled onto his lap, and she opened her eyes.

*      *      *

The howl of loneliness hit Jago like a solid blow. He staggered and
would have fallen had the mountain not held him so securely. He
clutched at his brother's shoulder, seeking reassurance in that touch,
reassurance that the emotions ripping through his head weren't his.
When the thousand voices added their pain and the howl became a
choir, his hands went to his ears. He saw Raulin throw himself forward and disappear out of the passage. The sound held him pinned
and he could not follow. He was left alone with the lament.

Alone.

An eternity alone.

He ground his palms against his head. It made little difference.

Free us. Free us. Free us.

Fear.

The last was a single call, a silver thread running through the tumult. Jago inched himself forward. It was not the best of guides, but it
was all he had to follow.

He squeezed around the tight corner, repeating over and over, "I
will get to Raulin," using his brother's name as a talisman against the
loneliness. And the fear.

When the passage widened and the mountain no longer supported
him, he took only a single step before the howling beat him to his
knees.

It went on and on and on and Jago felt an answering scream rising
up within him to join it.

Then, just as suddenly as it began, it stopped, and only the silver
thread of fear remained.

Crystal. He'd carried a bit of her life and could not mistake it.

He stood, and with one hand against the rock for support—his
body still trembled in reaction—he made his way out of the passage
and into the cavern.

Raulin knelt in the middle of the floor, his jacket off and wrapped
about the wizard who twisted in his grasp. A vaguely manshaped thing

crouched at the junction of two walls, one the bare bones of the mountain the other inlaid with a fantastic pattern of . . . of bone.

"Crystal?"

The screams had died to whimpers and he could hear his brother clearly.

"Crystal, it's Raulin. I have you. You're safe."

And behind him Jago heard a moan; a soft sound, pain filled.

Slowly, he turned.

An auburn haired man stood staring down at Raulin and Crystal, shoulders slumped in despair. Feeling Jago's gaze, he lifted his head. Surprise replaced the pain in the amber eyes so quickly Jago could not be sure he'd even seen it. Then the despair was gone as well and the new stance denied that it had ever existed. The man smiled slightly.

"Do you not know me, Jago?" he asked. "We were very close once."

Jago felt his mouth move. It took him a few seconds to manage an audible sound and even then the roar of blood in his ears threatened to drown it out. "Lord Death."

Lord Death inclined his head. "Our previous encounter seems to have given you something few mortals enjoy, the pleasure of my company."

There was nothing Jago could reply, so he inclined his head in turn.

Lord Death waved an aristocratic hand toward the center of the cavern. "Your brother is very clever," he said and to Jago's ears the words came out with an edge. "He appeals to her humanity. Gives her something with which to fight the fear." The Mother's son grimaced and Jago shuddered, the expression was such a strange mix of sorrow and anger. "It is lucky you arrived when you did."

Lucky. Jago heard the contradiction between the voice and the words. If Raulin, however he did it, pulled Crystal up out of the fear, then it *was* lucky they'd arrived at the cavern when they did. Lord Death had admitted as much but not with pleasure. No, not with pleasure.

"Crystal?"

Raulin's voice had softened, the tone so different, that both Jago and Lord Death turned.

Lord Death stepped forward, then jerked himself back.

Crystal sighed and-opened her eyes.

*Why did father grow that ridiculous mustache?* Crystal wondered as focus returned. Then the face behind the mustache came out of shadow and she smiled and said weakly, "Raulin."

He returned the smile and stroked damp hair back from her face. "Welcome back."

"Jago?"

"Uh . . ." Raulin suddenly realized he had no idea if Jago had followed him, remained in the passage, or . . . He began to twist but stopped at the familiar feel of his brother at his back.

"I'm here." Jago kept his voice low, pitched to reassure, glancing back over his shoulder as he spoke. The features of the dead moved across Lord Death's face and he could get no idea of how the Mother's son felt. *Tread carefully, my brother,* he thought as Raulin shifted Crystal into a more comfortable position on his lap, *there is more here than even you will be able to deal with.*

"Are you better now?"

Crystal squeaked as Raulin's grip abruptly tightened. The concerned features of the demon poked into her line of sight.

"You were making a lot of noise," it accused. "Shrieking. Wailing."

"What in Chaos' balls is that?" Raulin demanded, trying to shield her body with his own.

"It's a demon." Crystal pushed against his arms until they relaxed enough to let her breathe. "It's trapped here."

"Is it dangerous?"

"Maybe," the demon said cheerfully.

"Jago!"

Jago, his dagger in his hand, took a step toward the demon, putting the point of his knife between it and the two on the floor. "Go on," he commanded, "get back."

The demon opened wide its lipless mouth and closed it on the metal.

Startled, Jago snatched the dagger back and stood staring down at the hilt. A thin wisp of smoke was all that remained of the blade.

"Cheap," muttered the demon and retreated to the corner to sulk.

The brothers exchanged incredulous glances, then looked in unison down at Crystal who had begun to giggle softly.

"I'm sorry," she sputtered, "only the look on your faces . . ."

The laughter built until her body shook with it and the sound began to take on a hysterical edge.

"Crystal?" Raulin shook her gently, but she continued to laugh although tears ran from her eyes and she trembled uncontrollably. "Crystal!"

Jago dropped to one knee beside them. "Hold her," he said.

"I *am* holding her." He fell silent as Jago took the wizard's jaw in one hand, turned her head to face him, and slapped her, hard. Then again.

With a shuddering sob, Crystal buried her face against Raulin's chest, and clung. "I'm sorry," she said again, her voice even weaker than it had been, but calm. "I don't . . ."

"Shh." He stroked her back, murmuring the words into her hair. "It's all right. Do you want to get up?"

She shook her head and clung tighter.

Raulin met his brother's eyes.

"Perhaps you'd better go get the packs," he said softly.

Jago's eyebrows went up.

Raulin glared. "Don't be stupid," he snarled, his hands continuing to soothe the woman in his arms.

Jago flushed, touched his brother's shoulder in a wordless apology, rose, and slipped silently from the cavern.

They'd left the packs back where the passage had narrowed so suddenly. Their sled, with the bulk of their gear and supplies, they'd had to leave a short distance down the mountain when the way became more rock than snow and the trail too steep to wrestle it farther.

Jago studied what had to be moved; the two packs and both massive fur overcoats plus a pile of assorted hats, scarves, and mittens. The packs would have to be moved one at a time, and perhaps emptied to get them around that tight bit. He rubbed his chin, absently scratching at the golden stubble, and decided that since the packs contained no clothes it might be best if he got the coats through first. He remembered how little Raulin's jacket covered, added how quickly comfort could warm, and recalled the expression on Lord Death's face. Not the despair, the anger that had followed.

"Definitely the coats." He heaved them up into his arms and turned to face the narrow passage with gritted teeth. At least he had something to take his mind off the fear that being underground always evoked.

Dragging some forty pounds of uncooperative fur through the mountain's heart was among the less enjoyable things he'd done lately, but when Jago reached the cavern and saw the way in which the positions of Raulin and Crystal had subtly shifted while he was gone, he knew he'd made the right decision. Although Raulin would not take advantage—he'd deserved Raulin's anger for implying he would—Jago didn't doubt his brother would be willing to cooperate and this was neither the time nor place.

"Here." The fur flopped like a live thing to the ground, one arm draping over Crystal's legs. "This'll do you a lot more good than that little jacket."

"She doesn't get cold," Lord Death pointed out from his place by the passage.

"Perhaps not," Jago replied without thinking, "but Raulin does, and he needs his jacket."

Crystal's head snapped up and she stared from Jago to Lord Death.

Raulin merely stared at his brother. The demon crouched out of Jago's line of sight and as far as Raulin was concerned that left Jago talking to empty air. "What are you babbling about?"

"You can hear him?" Crystal asked, her arms sliding down from around Raulin's neck.

"Hear who?" Raulin wanted to know.

"And see him?"

"See who?"

The wizard's silver brows dove into a deep vee. "I've never heard of a mortal being able . . ."

"Able to what?"

Jago sighed. "Why don't you tell him while you dress," he suggested to Crystal, nudging the fur with a booted foot. "I'll go get the rest of the gear."

The packs, as he suspected, had to be unpacked, for neither force nor ingenuity could get them around that last tight corner before the cavern. Rather than reload everything, and then unload it again six meters away in order to use it, Jago carried the bits and pieces into the cavern in armloads. The tableau remained unchanging from trip to trip.

Crystal, regal now and no less beautiful in the enveloping fur, explained in animated detail just what she suspected had happened when Jago had come so close to Death.

Raulin listened intently, his eyes never leaving Crystal's face. Jago wondered which motivated Raulin more, concern for his brother or an inability to look away from emerald eyes and ivory skin. The demon sat silently in its corner, its expression impossible to read. Lord Death stood just as silently by the rectangular cut that marked the passage and he kept the dead parading across his face to hide what might otherwise have been revealed. But his eyes, throughout all their many permutations, never moved from the two in the center of the cavern.

Each time he passed the Mother's son, Jago grew more certain he understood both the earlier pain and the anger that followed. Survival in the Empire had consisted for the most part of an intimate knowledge of the pecking order; a skill that translated in the survivors into a finely honed ability to judge their fellow men. To Jago's eyes, Lord Death was deeply, and hopelessly, in love.

Without really knowing why he did it—to protect his brother was no more than an admittedly valid rationalization—he stopped as he carried in the last armload of gear and said in a voice not intended to travel far from where he stood, "Why don't you tell her?"

Lord Death turned and the changing eyes and identical expressions of terror flowed into the features of the auburn-haired man whose amber eyes regarded him coldly. "Tell her what?" he asked in a voice equally quiet.

"Uh . . ."

"Do not presume, mortal. I am fully capable of running my own . . ." A wry smile twisted the full lips. "I am fully capable of running my own . . . life."

"Now let me get this straight." Raulin raised a steaming cup of tea to his mouth. "You talk to Death?"

The four of them, Raulin, Jago, the wizard, and the demon, sat around a small campstove, the red glow of the coals providing more of a focus point than actual warmth. The demon, its captivity explained, sat quietly and pouted. Crystal had refused to let it show off its handiwork, merely informing the brothers that the wall contained the remains of the demon's previous visitors, "and could we please leave it at that." Then she'd smacked its fingers away from the fire. It projected an air of injured innocence which no one paid any attention to.

Jago swallowed a mouthful of hot liquid and nodded.

"And he talks to you?"

Jago nodded again.

"And he's a regular guy? You can see him, touch . . ."

"No," Crystal interrupted, a little sadly, "you can't touch him. Nor can he touch you."

"Is he here right now?"

"No." Jago and Crystal spoke together, looked startled, then exchanged shy smiles. Neither knew when the Mother's son had left. One moment he'd been there, the next gone.

Raulin settled his back against the rock wall of the cavern. "How can you be sure?"

Crystal jerked a thumb over her shoulder at the wall of bones. "When the dead are present, I can always see him. Only when there are no dead, can he choose."

"Why?"

She shrugged and Raulin wished the motion had not been covered by the heavy fur. "I don't know. That's just the way it works."

"If he wants you to free the dead, why didn't he stay?" Jago asked. He remembered the thousand voices and their plea. He hadn't needed Crystal's explanation to know what they wanted.

"I think he leaves me to decide without the pressure of our friendship."

Her voice was troubled, as if she suspected a deeper meaning in Lord Death's sudden departure.

Jago considered, for a brief instant, telling her himself, saying, *He loves you, wizard,* but he didn't. Just because the last few weeks of his life had been a bonus, because he really should've died after the brindle attack, it did not mean he wanted to give the *rest* of his life away. So all he said was, "Freeing the dead frees the demon," as if he recognized that as the cause of her trouble.

Crystal sighed. "Yes."

"I am harmless!" protested the demon.

All eyes turned to the wall of bone.

"Well, mostly harmless," it whined. "Oh, please free me. Please . . ."

Jago's hand shot out and grabbed the demon's arm. "Do not howl," he snarled.

The demon looked piqued and easily shook itself free. "Wasn't going to."

Raulin listened to his brother and Crystal talk, sipped his tea, and studied the wall of bones. He couldn't find it in him to blame the demon for the men and women who had died to set that pattern, not even considering that he'd missed being a part of it by only a few hours. If they'd arrived at the cavern before Crystal . . .

He was disappointed that the treasure of the ancient wizard had amounted to nothing more than a strange creature with an appetite for iron. Then his mind slipped back to those moments spent holding Crystal in his arms and he decided the trip hadn't been a total loss. Still, he touched the leather pouch hanging about his neck, they'd had such hopes when they first found that map.

Map!

"Hey!" Jago threw himself out of the way as Raulin leaped up and dashed across the cavern. He twisted and glared at the older man who was running his fingers along the ridges of bone and muttering under his breath. "What do you think you're doing?"

"It's a map, Jago!"

"Yes! Yes!" The demon bounded over to its creation and began patting the wall. "A map! A map!"

"A map?"

"Yes. Look!" Raulin pointed out a triangular wedge of bone that ran diagonally up from the floor, cutting off the lower corner. "This is the mountain range we're in." He touched another pattern. "This is the canyon we followed to get here, before we started to climb." He slapped the wall where a bit of femur jutted from the mountains. "This is where we are!"

"Here! Here!" The demon agreed.

Jago slowly stood and stepped over to the map. "Then these," he said, "are the mountains they call the Giant's Spine."

"Aptly named," Raulin added, for they were delineated on the wall in vertebrae.

"And this," Jago continued, ignoring him, "must be the way . . ."

Both brothers looked up to the top left corner of the wall where a skull looked back. Barely visible on the yellow-gray bone was scratched the sigil of the bloody hand.

". . . to Aryalan's tower," Raulin finished.

"Yes! Yes!" The demon hopped up and down in excitement, looking even more froglike than it did at rest. "The Binding One's hidey hole!" Then it stopped jumping and added solemnly. "But you mustn't go there. It's dangerous."

"You should listen to it." Crystal still sat by the tiny stove, bare legs tucked up under the fur. "Aryalan trapped it, remember. It knows what it's talking about."

"Aryalan's long dead," Raulin scoffed.

But Jago said softly, "You knew, didn't you? That this was a map?"

Crystal nodded.

"And you weren't going to tell us."

She smiled and rubbed her cheek against the soft fur of the collar "No."

"Why not?" Raulin returned to her side and dropped to one knee to better study her face. "Think of what we could find there."

Her gaze flicked past him to the wall of bone. "Think of what you've found here."

Raulin dismissed the cavern, the bones, the demon with a quick wave. "We're not likely to find its type," he nodded at the demon, "inside the wizard's tower."

"There will be other dangerous surprises."

"And that's why you weren't going to tell us about the map? I'm not afraid of the unknown."

*I am,* she thought, shying away from the dark places Nashawryn had left when she retreated. *I am very afraid of the unknown. Now.* But she kept silent and only looked from Raulin's gray eyes, alight with a fierce joy, to Jago's violet ones. "Now you know the path," she said, "you'll go, won't you, no matter what I say?"

"Yes," Raulin told her.

When she looked to Jago for confirmation he nodded, although she realized he went not for the adventure, or even the possibility of wealth, but because his brother did.

Crystal's head went up and her expression firmed. "I could take it from your minds. I could make you forget the map existed."

Raulin's head went up as well, his jaw tensed and his eyes grew stormy. *Jago was right,* he thought. *Wizards can't be trusted. None of them.* His mouth opened, but Jago spoke first.

"You won't," he said.

"How do you know?" She turned the green of her eyes on him and released enough power so they began to glow. *Let Nashawryn get loose again; she'll burn it from their minds fast enough.*

Jago smiled, a little sadly. "Because I know you."

Crystal sat silent, aghast at what she'd thought. Nashawryn must never get loose again. How could she think . . . and then she felt the laughter and realized she hadn't. Zarsheiy. Stirring up what trouble she could. "I don't even know myself," she murmured.

"Then take my word for it."

Raulin was ashamed at his sudden anger and at the same time mildly amused that he and Jago seemed for an instant to have reversed opinions. He reached out and ran a strand of silver hair between his fingers. It felt cool and soft and finer than silk. "Come with us," he said.

"You asked me that before. At the inn. I said no."

"A lot has changed since then. But even if your answer remains no, we are still going on."

"Yes."

"Yes, you'll come with us, or yes, you know we'll go on anyway."

Crystal could spread herself on the wind and reach Aryalan's tower in hours. Deal with it and destroy it before the brothers even found the trail. But that way moved too close to oblivion even when all was in balance. Now she dared not risk it. She could, as the owl, still beat them to the tower by days. Deal with it and destroy it while they struggled over the mountains. But although the owl had nothing the goddesses could grasp and use, she would have to exist on power and all her power must be used to remain whole. Or what stood for whole these days. And besides, she was lonely.

Lonely. She held back a sigh as she turned the word over in her mind. From the moment the centaurs had taken her from her parents she'd been alone in one way or another. Why, she wondered, her hand creeping up to twist in the fur over her heart, did alone suddenly mean lonely? Perhaps because when she was alone she no longer knew the person she was with. Perhaps the demon had put the word in her mind. Perhaps because there seemed to be an alternative and friendship had become, for the first time since she was eleven, a very real possibility.

"Yes, I'll come with you."

Slowly, Raulin smiled, hearing at least part of her reason for agreeing in her voice.

Jago, who heard the part that Raulin didn't, stepped forward until he could see Crystal's face over his brother's shoulder. "What are you afraid of?" he asked softly.

His return unnoticed, Lord Death raised his head to listen.

Crystal looked down into the depths of the fur—looking into the depths of herself was out of the question—then she sighed, spread her hands, and said simply: "Me." If she traveled with them and their lives also were at risk, they deserved to know.

"There were seven goddesses remaining when the wizards ruled . . ."

She told them all of it, what Tayja had told her and the background they needed to understand, keeping her voice as emotionless as she could. It was safer that way.

The brothers sat enthralled, barely moving throughout the telling. The demon whimpered twice but otherwise sat still and quiet.

"So you see," she finished, "if I do go with you, you won't be getting a mighty wizard capable of blasting away all opposition. No more snatching you out of danger before the danger really begins. I'll be using most of my power just to stay intact." For the first time in the telling, she met their eyes. "Do you still want me?"

Without looking at Jago, Raulin answered for both of them.

"Yes," he said simply.

"Because you feel sorry for me?" The words slipped out before Crystal could stop them.

"Because we want your company," Raulin told her softly, hearing the fear behind her words. He leered in his best exaggerated manner. "Chaos knows why, but we like you." Then he grew serious. "And I can't deny we could use whatever help you can give."

He would've gone on but Jago, who sat where he could see the rest of the cavern, grabbed his arm and quieted him with a small shake of his head.

"Why didn't you tell me," asked the one true son of the Mother, "when this, began?"

Shaking back the silver curtain of her hair, Crystal met Lord Death's eyes. Answering one question, it seemed, led only to others. She shrugged, trying to lessen the importance of her answer for the wrong weight here would lead to questions she knew she couldn't deal with. "I was afraid you wouldn't like me if I wasn't perfect."

Lord Death blinked once or twice in surprise. Of all the possible reasons she might give for shutting him out, for refusing to confide in him, he hadn't expected that. His lips twitched as he thought about it, then he smiled. "You have *never* been perfect," he said.

She returned his smile, partly in response, partly in relief that their friendship seemed back on its old footing, with the awkwardness of the past two meetings buried by that quip. She couldn't know that she had given him hope.

An irrational hope, all things considered, Lord Death acknowledged with an inner sigh.

"Is she talking to *him?*" Raulin hissed.

Jago nodded.

"Is he talking back?"

Jago nodded again.

"I don't think I like this."

"Better get used to it, brother." Jago levered himself to his feet by grasping Raulin's shoulder. His legs had grown stiff from sitting so long in one place while Crystal told her story. "We can't spend the night in here, most of our gear is on the sled. And I don't know about the rest of you, but I'm getting hungry."

On cue, Crystal's stomach grumbled loudly. "Hungry," she agreed, "is definitely the word for it."

Raulin stood and in mirrored moves the brothers each held a hand out to the woman on the ground. Their gazes crossed as each made note of the other's gesture, then locked in near identical glares.

Crystal stared from one to the other in surprise, quickly suppressed the grin threatening to break free—the last time she'd seen those expressions they'd been on the faces of her youngest siblings and had rapidly degenerated to yells of "Can too!" and "Can not!"—and used both offered hands to pull herself up. She supposed it was equally childish of her to feel pleased at being the bone of contention. She didn't care. Perhaps, just perhaps, things were going to work out.

*The centaurs,* reminded a quiet voice in her mind.

*Shall I leave these two alone to be slaughtered?* she thought back at it and it stilled.

"Crystal," Lord Death called softly. "My people?"

The demon crept forward and tugged on the edge of the coat. "Free me," it pleaded.

She reached down and touched the demon's head with one pale finger, "Yes." For it had suddenly come to her how she could.

She moved to the center of the cavern and the coat slid down off her shoulders and to the stone floor. A breeze, an impossible breeze this deep beneath a mountain, fanned her hair into a nimbus of silver light. Green fires blazed up in her eyes and she reached out with her power and drove the green between the red and black that bound the demon.

Those who watched saw the muscles of her back roll and twist and her hands snap up to shoulder height and the knuckles whiten as they closed to fists.

The red and black were weakening and her power became a silver sword to cut the bindings loose.

Her arms went up, the fingers taut, and when she brought them down again, the wall of bone came down, too.

"FREE!" No longer gray but an iridescent blur, the demon spun once in place, its arms outstretched, and disappeared.

"FREE!" screamed the dead, and Lord Death vanished too, carrying his children home.

Crystal grabbed the shattered power of the ancient wizard and threw it up in the path of Zarsheiy, the first of the goddesses to attack the weakened shields. Howling with rage, the fire goddess hit the barrier, hit the jagged pieces of red and black and was stopped. It had been a binding power after all.

*Well done.* The velvet voice of darkness sounded amused and Crystal felt the presences retreat to their own corners once again.

Pleased with her solution, and even more pleased that it had worked, for she hadn't been sure it would, she took a deep breath and relaxed.

"Crystal?"

Jago stepped forward, once again offering her the coat. He kept his eyes carefully on her face but their outer edges crinkled as he said: "For Raulin's sake . . ."

# INTERLUDE ONE

Back in the bright beginning, when the Mother-creator had formed the world from her body and the air about it from her breath, when She had given life to the lesser creatures of the land and air and water, She paused to rest in a grove of silver birch. As She rested, She grew lonely and so called to life the spirit of the tree She sat beneath that She might have company.

And because She stayed for a time in that place, the glory of her spread out into the surrounding land. In the Grove itself, the Peace that was the Mother remained.

When the Age of Wizards ended, a band of mortals desperately seeking peace were drawn to that land. The Grove became a sacred place. A respectful distance from it, they began to rebuild their lives. They drew boundaries along mountains and rivers and called that which was bounded, Ardhan. These mortals, the Mother's Youngest, had no way of knowing that the echo of the Mother's presence called to others as well and that they shared their new land with creatures out of legend.

The Elder Races, those created of the Mother's blood, paid little attention to the newcomers. Their lives moved in different ways and only occasionally touched. The Elder Races were few in number and the land was large enough for all. Most of the time. As the years passed, Ardhan gained a reputation as a place where wonders happened.

It was in Ardhan that the Eldest and the Youngest briefly joined.

From Ardhan came the last of the wizards.

In Ardhan, the Council of the Elder Races met.

*       *       *

From his vantage point on the ridge, Doan could see the entire meeting place. Three centaurs. He grunted. Three too many as far as he was concerned. And one, no, two, giants. They sat so still his gaze tended to slide past them for all their size.

"Might as well get on with it," the dwarf muttered to the breezes. They chuckled as they sped away. "Oh, sure," he complained, heading down to level ground, "you can laugh. You don't have to stay."

He dropped the last eight feet, and, mildly disappointed that none of the centaurs shied, started right in. "What I want to know," his hands were on his hips, his chin jutted forward aggressively, and his breath was a plume on the winter air, "is why here? Why not the Grove?"

*when we move the water*

*to*

*the Grove*

*the sisters get angry*

The thoughts rose up out of the deep pool near which the land-bound Elders had gathered. Although ice clung around the edges, the center, despite the frigid temperature, was clear. Below the surface of the water, pale green and blue bodies wove in and out in a pattern as graceful as it was complicated. The exact number of mer who had answered the Call could not be determined for the waterfolk were never still, but it scarcely mattered for a thought held by one was shared by all.

"And," added the tallest of the centaurs, his coat gleaming like ebony in the early morning sun, "as the Ladies of the Grove cannot leave their trees, little of the outside world concerns them."

"Told you to take a hike did they, C'Tal? Can't say as I blame them."

C'Tal's eyes narrowed and he stared down his nose at the dwarf. "If you do not wish to be here, why did you choose to answer the call?"

"You think I volunteered? Ha!" Doan hacked and spit into the snow at C'Tal's feet. He disliked centaurs for a number of reasons. Their pomposity, their "Elder-than-thou" attitude, and their lack of anything remotely resembling a sense of humor headed the list, but mostly he disliked them because the Elder Races were supposed to get along and he enjoyed being contrary. "Chaos, no. I had everyone in the caverns begging me to answer so they wouldn't have to risk death by boredom. Now," he shoved his hands behind his broad leather belt, and rocked back on his heels, "what could possibly have got you so twitchy you were willing to associate with the bubble brains."

*better bubbles*

*than stone*

C'Tal's tail snapped back and forth in short jerky arcs. A centaur did not "dislike" anyone, but C'Tal certainly disapproved of Doan. Sarcasm and cynicism barred clear thinking. He expected the dwarf's opposition in what was to come. The mer, for all their frivolity, were logical creatures, and he had no doubt he could convince them. The giants, so motionless they appeared more a bit of the earth poking up through the snow than living beings, could decide either way, but C'Tal took comfort in the knowledge that they would at least listen without interrupting.

"We would not have Called had we not thought this to be the gravest of emergencies."

"Too cold for horseflies," Doan mused. "Weevils got into your nosebags?"

*quiet Doan*

*or*

*we'll be here*

*all day*

C'Tal looked smug.

*and you half-horse*

*speak*

*we*

*have places that need us*

Irritation visible in his flattened ears, C'Tal crossed his arms over his massive chest, drew his brows down into an impressive frown, and announced, "It is the wizard."

"I might have known," Doan sighed. "Every time one of you gets colic you blame it on her." He shook his head. "Why don't you leave the poor kid alone?"

One of C'Tal's companions stepped forward, tossing heavy chestnut hair back out of his eyes. "Surely even you felt the surge of power she called to her use and the breaking of ancient bonds. Are you not curious to discover what she has done?"

Doan smiled unpleasantly. "No, C'Din," he said. "I'm not. And you, you four-footed busy . . ."

*she has freed*

*Aryalan's demon*

Shocked, the three centaurs and Doan stared down into the water. Even the giants stirred, although they only looked at each other and smiled their slow smiles.

A pale blue body, small enough to fit easily into C'Tal's hand, arced out of the pool, turned once languidly in midair, then disappeared again into the ebb and flow of mer.

*the demon's prison had a spring*

*we*

*go where water is*

"All right," Doan said to the general area, "she freed the demon. So? About time the poor thing got to go home. And yeah, I felt the power surge; it was completely contained. Nothing to do with us."

"That," declared C'Tal ponderously, "is not the problem. It merely alerted us to that which we have called the Elder to discuss. She . . ."

"Hold it," the dwarf held up a callused hand. When C'Tal paused, his lips drawn into a thin line, Doan climbed nimbly up the tailings of the ridge he'd followed from the caverns, kicked the snow from a narrow ledge, crossed his legs, and sat down. "Talking to you on level ground," he explained sweetly, "gives me a pain in the neck."

"We are aware of herbal remedies," offered the third centaur, a glossy palomino, "that will relieve such pain."

"How about relieving a pain in the ass?"

"Yes," the golden head nodded thoughtfully, "we can ease that also."

"Later," C'Tal bit the word off, his teeth white slabs against the black of his beard, well aware the dwarf was being deliberately irritating. "We believe that when the wizard freed the demon she discovered the location of Aryalan's tower."

"So that's the burr under your blanket." Doan sighed and relaxed. It was just like the centaurs to get upset over something trivial. "I suggested years ago we let her deal with the remaining towers. I said it then and I'll say it now, the poor kid needs something to do. I'm glad she found one on her own."

"She is a danger, the towers are a danger," C'Din pointed out quietly.

"Hold that thought, hayburner," Doan interrupted. "You lot trained her, why not have some trust in your training?"

C'Din shook his head, his forelock falling back down over his eyes. "As you and others have pointed out, we trained the ancient wizards as well." He paused. When no one filled the silence with a reminder of what the ancient wizards had become, he continued. "We feel—now, as we did at your suggestion years ago—that the wizard at the tower is one danger too many. She is already the most powerful being now living. When she reaches the tower and adds the power within to what she already carries, will that not be an undesirable event?"

Doan kept a grip on his temper. C'Din was being very reasonable, for a centaur. And what was worse, he had a valid point. "Why," he growled, "will that be an 'undesirable event'?"

"All power corrupts," C'Tal intoned. "Absolute power corrupts absolutely."

The dwarf's eyes began to glow red and he pulled himself slowly to his feet. The cold of the outside world meant nothing to the Elder, but the chill radiating from Doan caused two of the centaurs to step away and, although he stood his ground, long shivers rippled the skin of C'Tal's back.

*stop*

*cliché becomes cliché*

*because of truth*

*power*

*does*

*corrupt*

The red dimmed but did not die. "I will listen to no more of this. You've got my opinion, not that you'll pay any attention to it. I've stayed at this farce long enough." Doan leaped to the ground, but a huge arm bared his way.

"Wait." The larger of the two giants looked down at him, her face expressionless.

Doan seethed, but until she moved her arm he wasn't going anywhere and he knew it. With ill grace he did the only thing he could. He waited.

"When you called us, C'Tal, what did you intend the Elder to do?" Her voice was strong and deep but softer than her size would lead many to expect. The giants had no need to shout.

C'Tal shrugged. "In some manner, we must prevent the wizard . . ."

"She has a name," Doan snarled.

"Very well." C'Tal's tone made it obvious that he merely humored the dwarf. "We must prevent Crystal from reaching Aryalan's tower."

"No," the giant said.

"No?" chorused all three centaurs.

Doan grinned, his good humor suddenly restored. "You heard her, she said no."

*why no*

"The remaining towers of the ancient ones *are* a danger and should be dealt with. The wizard is the only possible solution."

"That's not what you thought a dozen years ago when we discussed telling her about the towers," Doan groused.

Again the giants exchanged their slow smiles.

"We changed our minds," said the smaller one.

"So," Doan moved to stand before C'Tal, peering up at him through narrowed eyes. "That's two against sticking our noses in and two for."

*three against*

*one for*

*this wizard must be as free to take her own path*

\*as every other creature\*

\*we cannot say\*

\*this is right\*

\*this is\*

\*wrong\*

C'Tal dug at the ground, packing the snow into ice, his ears flat against his head, his companions equally upset. "So we are to stand by and let the Age of Wizards come again?"

"No."

Doan turned on the giants, hands on his hips. "What? Changed your minds again?" His lip curled and his voice dripped sarcasm but the giants appeared not to notice.

"Power can always be misused, we recognize that . . ."

The centaurs calmed a little.

". . . so we will watch to see that it is not."

"You?"

"Me," the smaller giant said softly. "I know the land the tower is in."

"Not exactly inconspicuous are you?"

"I will offer my help openly."

"And why should she take it?"

Once more the slow exchange of smiles.

"Will you two stop doing that," Doan snarled.

Both giants inclined their heads in a unified apology and Doan rolled his eyes.

"She'll take my help," the smaller continued, "because I have been in the tower."

The silence that followed was so complete that the sound of the mer moving through the water could be clearly heard.

For a change, Doan and the centaurs were in complete accord; his look of incredulity was reproduced in a larger scale on their faces as he demanded: "What in the Mother's name did you do that for?"

The smaller giant looked unperturbed. "I was curious," she explained.

"Aren't you a bit big to get curious?"

The two giants looked down at Doan. Quite a way down, for although the smaller was no more than twelve feet tall, the dwarf barely topped four.

"Aren't you a bit small to take such a tone?" the larger chastised him gently. "We get as curious as any race."

"Not so I've ever noticed."

Two sets of earth-brown eyes twinkled. "You live too fast, dwarf."

*what was in*

*the tower*

"A great deal of unpleasantness." The smaller giant sighed. "I did not go all the way in, but from what I saw, Aryalan trusted no one. The way is well trapped."

Doan's eyes narrowed. "And you're willing to go back?"

The larger giant took a deep breath and began to explain again. "The tower must be dealt with. The wizard is the only one who can do it, but the wizard should be watched."

"I am the logical choice to watch the wizard. I will therefore go back," the smaller concluded and spread her hands. "Where is the difficulty?"

C'Tal beamed and bestowed his highest accolade. "An explanation worthy of a centaur." He ignored Doan's snort. "Are we all agreed then?"

*we*

*agree*

"And I," said C'Din. The palomino nodded solemnly.

"Doan?"

The dwarf scratched his chin, stared off at the horizon, and finally threw up his hands. "Oh, all right." His brows came down and he glared up at C'Tal. "But not because I think the kid'll misuse anything. I want everyone to understand my position on that."

"You have, as usual," C'Tal said dryly, "made your point of view known."

"Good." He twitched his leather tunic straight. "Remember it." And stomped off.

*we*

*are leaving also*

*watch well large ones*

"We shall."

And then the pool was empty.

"You have," C'Tal intoned, "our thanks for discovering a solution to the problem. And you will," he continued, "I am sure, not only watch but take steps to ensure there is no abuse of power should such a situation occur."

"We shall."

"Then we also will be departing."

The three centaurs bowed in unison then, still in perfect synchronicity, whirled and galloped away.

The two giants sat quietly while the spray of snow from the centaurs' departure settled. Then they sat quietly for a few hours more while the pool iced over and the sun disappeared behind the silver-gray of a winter's sky.

"You didn't tell them why you went only a short way into the tower," said the larger at last.

"No."

"Nor did you tell them that you can't go farther than you did and that if the wizard does, she must go alone."

A curious jay landed on the broad ledge of the smaller giant's shoulder, making a bright patch of blue against the brown. She shrugged carefully so as not to disturb him. "Everyone is happy and I saved much time that would have been spent arguing. The tower must be dealt with. I'll know by then if the wizard must."

"And if she must?"

"I will deal with it. But I see no reason to worry now."

And again they exchanged slow smiles, then sat motionless until the jay grew bored and flew off.

# Six

E ven with two pulling and one behind, the sleigh seemed to gain in weight on every uphill climb.

*And these damn mountains,* Jago thought to himself, putting his shoulder against the rear crossbar and shoving, *are more uphill than down!* "Chaos!" The last he cried aloud as his feet lost their purchase and he slammed to his knees on the heavy crust. He reached out to grab for the sleigh then changed his mind as, unbraced, it slid back an inch or two. He heard Crystal gasp and Raulin swear as they took up the extra weight. Moving carefully, for the light cover of dry powder made the crust doubly treacherous and the footholds the two pulling had chopped were out of his reach to either side, he got one foot under him, shifted his balance, fell flat on his back, and slid twelve feet back down the mountain to slam up against a granite outcropping.

Kraydak's Empire had not been a pleasant place to grow up in, but some things are better learned in adversity. Jago took full advantage of his education as he cursed the sleigh, the snow, the rock, and then his brother.

"Should you be laughing" Crystal murmured to Raulin as they carefully backed the sleigh down the mountain. On this footing neither could hold the weight alone so the other could go for the brake and Crystal had promised the brothers that, for her own sake, she would use power only when the problem could not be solved in mortal ways.

"He's okay," Raulin grunted. Leaning back against the drag of the sleigh had twisted the harness so the straps cut into his armpits. Jago deserved whatever damage he'd done himself for that extra discomfort. "Fortunately, it sounds like he landed on his head."

Jago scrambled out of the way as the sleigh eased up against the rock. When it rested securely, he grabbed one of the handles and gingerly pulled himself to his feet.

As the pressure eased off the straps, Crystal freed herself and hurried around to his side. She wore Jago's spare pants, one of Raulin's shirts, and an old green sweater both of them laid claim to.

*"We know it isn't much," Jago had explained when they'd laid the clothes out for her, "but at least you'll be protected if you lose control again."*

*She reached out one hand and lightly touched their offering. Although not enough for warmth—no matter, a wizard, even an unstable one, was not at the mercy of the elements—it was enough to cushion flesh in a way that clothes woven of power could not when the power was no longer there. "I can't shift when I'm so confined," she said slowly. "If I wear these, I'll be bound to this form."*

*"Suits me." Raulin smiled and winked.*

*His words made the decision easier for her and she wondered if he'd known that when he spoke; wondered if the seemingly careless words actually held care. She dressed and then sculpted herself a pair of soft gray boots from woodsmoke.*

*"Function follows form," she explained, slipping them on. "Or at least that's what the centaurs always told me. I could as warmly go barefoot, but this will keep my mind from the task and yours from my feet."*

*And both brothers had shuddered at the vision of bare feet on snow.*

"Hey, I'm okay," Jago protested as Crystal reached for the strings that tied the heavy fur cap to his head. "I barely felt it." He knew better than to try to push her hands away. Early on, they'd discovered that her physical strength at the very least matched either of theirs. Occasionally, Jago wondered if she held back for fear of doing damage to their tender male egos.

Tossing the hat aside, Crystal probed the back of Jago's skull with gentle fingers. She shook her own head in irritation as he winced and tried to hide it when she found the tender spot.

"Don't worry," she reassured him, although exasperation touched her voice as well. "I use more power than this breathing." Her eyes flared briefly as she healed the bruising and blocked the incipient headache.

"Don't suppose you could do something about the significant lack of grace while you're in there?" Raulin called, sinking down on the front end of the sleigh and not bothering to unhook.

"This from a man who trips over shadows," Jago snorted, jamming his hat back on and securing it. He half-smiled his thanks at Crystal, too tired to get his entire face to cooperate, and pulled his heavy overcoat out from under the loose bindings that secured it. Now that they were no longer working, he was beginning to feel the cold. He yanked Raulin's coat free as well, and threw it at his brother's back. Without turning, or removing the harness, Raulin shrugged into it. It bunched up where the traces connected the harness to the sleigh, but it covered him enough to provide warmth.

All three of them looked up at the twelve feet they'd lost. It seemed like a hundred. The shadow of the mountain turned everything, path, sleigh, spirits, to a bleak and unyielding gray.

"Trouble is," Jago sighed, leaning against the sleigh and scrubbing at his face, "the man following has no traction." He waved at the axes Crystal and Raulin had been using to break through the ice. "He doesn't have his hands free to chip footholds, and that crust is too damn thick to stamp through."

"Trouble is," Raulin echoed, "the man following is a lout."

Jago's violet eyes narrowed. "Crust isn't the only thing that's too damn thick around here."

The underlying good humor, usually present in the brothers' bickering, was noticeably absent. Tempers were short, particularly the more volatile Raulin's. Crystal suspected that only the numbing exhaustion of the past few days had kept things from exploding all over the mountainside. They needed some kind of release from the drag of the sleigh and the constant cold, and, she was forced to admit, the tension her presence caused.

Physical attraction—not quite desire, not yet—stretched between her and Raulin like a bowstring. Explored, it would be easier to live with, but they hadn't had that chance. For the sake of warmth during the bitterly cold nights, the three shared a bed, her wizard's body generating enough heat for them all. If she used power to create privacy, she doubted she'd be able to contain Avreen once they began. If Jago would only take a walk for a couple of hours. . . . But they couldn't ask. Not in the winter. Not in these mountains. And Jago. Healing him was like healing herself, everything just seemed to fall back into place. The bond with him was a comfort—not a torment, not even an itch—and that was a relationship that needed defining as well.

Now this.

She glared back up the mountain.

Three hundred feet, maybe less, and they'd reach the pass and be on level ground for a while.

She kicked at the crust.

And then again.

"I think," she said slowly, "I may have an idea."

Both men turned to look at her, faces blank. Below her feet, the snow began to steam. With a crack, the crust broke and she sank up to her ankles in the softer snow beneath.

"No," they said simultaneously.

"Look," she explained, stepping out of the hole, "it's no more than I do at night when I raise my body temperature. You two pull and I'll push, melting myself a stairway as I go."

"It might work," Raulin said thoughtfully, pushing down his scarf and pulling bits of ice from his mustache.

"No," Jago repeated. "It's too dangerous for you to bleed off power. We can't risk the goddesses getting free." He met her eyes. They were the only green they'd seen for the last two days. "No. We'll think of another way."

Raulin twisted around and glared but remained silent.

Crystal bit back a sigh. Lately, it seemed she was the only thing they didn't actually fight over. She recognized the stubborn set to Jago's jaw and realized she was just too tired to muster the enthusiasm necessary to change his mind. Let the mountain change it for them, she decided, and pulled herself up on the rock to wait.

So they thought about other ways. Every now and then, one of the brothers would snarl something, the other would growl a negative reply, and silence would fall again. Crystal let them keep it up until she knew they could feel the cold creeping in under their furs and then she said softly, "There is no other way."

Raulin muttered an obscenity under his breath, then stood, tossing his coat back to Jago as he did. Jago ducked the heavy fur, letting it fall on the sleigh, slid out of his own, and secured them both. He walked up front and buckled himself into the other harness. Without speaking, in no way acknowledging each other's presence, they began to pull the sleigh away from the rock. When there was enough room, Crystal slipped in behind and began to push.

The first twelve feet went quickly, for only Crystal had to break the crust, and then they slowed as Raulin and Jago began to swing the axes once more. Still, with all three on firm footing, progress was neither as arduous nor as slow as it had been.

Safely in the pass, with the brake shoved deep into the snow, they collapsed.

"I say we make camp here," Raulin panted. "I'm beat."

"Still a couple of hours of day left," Jago argued, getting slowly to his feet. "I'd like to see what's on the other side of the pass."

Moving carefully, Raulin stood as well and began to unlash the gear. "Life is too short," he growled, yanking at a knot, "to waste it by dying of exhaustion."

"And we get little enough daylight to waste it because *you* can't make it get any farther." Jago stretched, leaned against the rock wall of the pass, and crossed his arms. "Getting old, Raulin?"

One step, two, Raulin moved toward his brother. His lips pulled back from his teeth and his hands clenched into fists. *Smart-assed little snot. Had as much of that smug, pompous smile as I can take . . .*

Jago straightened and dropped his weight forward onto the balls of his feet. *Time that arrogant asshole learned he doesn't run my life . . .*

*Should I stop them?* Crystal wondered. *Perhaps this is the release they need.*

Mortals, snorted Zarsheiy's voice in her head. With Crystal's power turned to heat, the fire goddess stayed close to the barriers that kept her penned. *You'll never understand them.*

Watching Raulin and Jago circling for an opening, Crystal admitted Zarsheiy was probably right.

The tension built until even the mountain seemed aware of it. A deep rumble, felt rather than heard, drew all gazes upward. Another rumble sent one or two tiny white balls dancing down the weight of snow poised above the pass.

"We can't stay here," Crystal said softly, voicing the obvious in case the brothers were too wrapped in anger to realize. "It isn't safe."

The tableau stayed frozen a moment longer, then Raulin spun about and grabbed up a harness.

"Try and keep up," he snarled as he jerked the sleigh into motion.

Jago snatched up the second harness and fell into step. They crossed the three miles of the pass in silence.

Late afternoon sunlight bathed the northwest side of the mountains, giving everything a rosy glow. A long, smooth expanse of pinkish-white snow spread down from the pass for a mile, maybe more, unbroken by rock or tree, and ended in a dark line of forest.

For a long moment the brothers just stood and stared, at the light, at the color, at the lack of gray. From her place behind the sleigh, Crystal saw some of the stiffness fall from their shoulders.

"Forest'd be a good place to spend the night," Raulin observed at last, squinting into the sun. "We'd have lots of wood and a good sized fire for a change."

" 'Course we'd have to get there before dark," Jago added, kicking at the snow. It was still crusted, though covered by about six inches of powder.

"Angle's a little steep. Stopping could be tricky."

Jago grinned at him. "Worry about that when we get there."

Raulin Shrugged and returned the grin, the last few days suddenly forgotten. "Why not."

With a whoop that echoed back from the peaks above them, the brothers yanked off their harnesses and tossed them on the sleigh. While Raulin checked to make sure everything was secure, Jago pulled their coats free. Crystal stood watching, openmouthed.

"What are you doing?" she asked.

"Trust us," Raulin told her, doing up his coat and wrapping his scarf more securely about his head. "You steer?" he asked Jago.

Jago nodded as they pulled the sleigh to the edge of the slope. "Suits me."

Careful not to start things moving too soon, Raulin scrambled up onto the load, settling himself as securely as possible. "Okay, Crystal, come on up."

Crystal began to get the idea. She looked down the mountain. A steep, straight run into a wall of trees. She looked at Raulin and Jago. They flashed her nearly identical, maniacal grins. *I'm as crazy as they are,* she thought as she climbed on and eased herself down between Raulin's legs. *Release is one thing but this* . . . She leaned back against his chest and felt one arm go around her.

"Hang on," he said into her ear.

All things considered, that seemed like good advice, so she did.

"Okay, Jago, let'er rip!"

The crust that had worked against them all the way up the mountain worked for them now. Jago threw his weight against the crossbar and the sleigh began to move. It picked up speed. Running full out, Jago tightened his grip and yanked himself forward, up onto the backs of the protruding runners.

Faster and faster. The runners roared against the snow.

Crystal squinted into the wind and the stinging load of snow it carried. Pushed back against Raulin's comforting bulk, she realized they were totally at the mercy of the slope. The thought terrified, but was at the same time strangely exhilarating. She stared ahead and tried to re-member to breathe.

The slope was not as smooth as it had appeared from the pass.

The sleigh bounced over a hillock. Jago threw his weight in the op-posite direction and the airborne runner slammed back onto the snow.

A sudden drop caused Crystal and the sleigh to part company for an instant. She bit back a shriek and hung on tighter. *I should've—ouch—walked!* She thought, as Raulin howled something wordless into the wind.

The sleigh moved off crust and onto granular snow. The roar of the runners softened, but they lost no speed. The forest began to approach very quickly.

Crystal clutched at Raulin's arm. "How do we stop?" she yelled.

A shrug and a wild laugh was the only answer she got.

The forest separated into individual trees.

The sleigh lunged into the air. When it landed, Jago yanked back hard on the brakes and they slowed. A little. Not enough.

This far north, at this time of the year, little or no underbrush filled in the spaces between the trees. The trees still grew too close together to allow the sleigh to pass.

Crystal gathered the power she'd need to stop them before the for-est did.

Jago reached forward over the crossbar and slapped Raulin on the left shoulder. Raulin nodded and leaned hard to the right, pulling Crystal over with him. The snow passed as a white blur, distressingly close. As the left runner ran up a ridge, Jago released the left brake and yanked down hard on the right.

"Mother-creator . . ." Crystal felt the sleigh twist beneath her . . .

. . . a strap broke . . .

. . . Raulin's hands on her waist . . .

. . . wind . . .

. . . air . . .

. . . cold . . .

. . . and the sudden shock of impact.

White. All she could see was white. Slowly, checking to make sure everything still worked, Crystal pulled her face out of the snowbank and turned. The sleigh lay on its side, half its contents fanned out over the snow. Raulin, she realized, had tossed her free. Raulin, who now roared with laughter and clapped his brother on the shoulder in congratulations. They'd dumped the sleigh on purpose! And they knew they would have to dump it right from the beginning! Her eyes narrowed as she dug snow out of her ears. Why those two . . .

The first snowball took Raulin just above the elbow. The second clipped Jago on the thigh. The third hit the edge of the runner now up in the air and sprayed wet white powder over both of them.

They turned, startled; and two lovely large handfuls caught both of them in the face.

"Oh, so that's the way it's going to be, is it?" Raulin yelled, scraping his face clean. He ducked another missile, scooped up a double fistful of snow and began returning fire.

Crystal twisted nimbly out of the way. "You'll have to do better than that," she taunted, tossing her hair back behind her shoulders. She bent to pick up more snow and Jago, who'd crept around the other end of the sleigh, scored a direct hit.

For the next little while the air was white as snowballs flew thick and fast. Sometimes two against one—and not always the same two—and sometimes all of them for themselves, but it soon became obvious that Crystal got hit far less often than the other two.

"I think," Jago shouted to his brother, currently an ally sharing the dubious shelter behind the sleigh, "she cheats."

"Does she now . . ." Raulin drawled. A snowball chose that moment to curve around their barrier and smack him in the side of the head. "Well, cheaters," he grinned, "never prosper." He jerked a thumb up and Jago nodded. Together they swarmed over the sleigh. Raulin hit her high. Jago hit her low.

Howling with laughter, in a tangle of arms and legs and great fur coats and flying silver hair, they rolled the last twenty feet to the forest and thudded up against the trunk of a young pine. The tree rocked, shook, and dumped its entire load of snow on their heads.

Lord Death stood quietly and watched the camp take shape just inside the shelter of the forest. Although he could not have been seen, he kept to shadow. It suited his mood.

"I am tired of watching," he said softly to the wind. It whirled about him, unable to offer comfort, and a clump of snow blew from a branch above. He held out his hand and the snow passed through it, in no way affected by his presence.

"I am tired of watching," he said again, his eyes on the silver-haired woman by the fire. "But I don't know what else I can do."

"What I want to know," Jago unwound the copper wire securing the end of one braid, "is how you got to be such a deadly aim with a snowball."

Crystal smiled and poked at the fire. Behind the shields Zarsheiy stirred and the blaze flared up, but as the fire goddess seemed content to merely vent her frustration, Crystal ignored her. "The centaurs," she explained. "They live on the great plains. No hills but lots of snow. They seemed to think it would improve my coordination."

"Seems like too much fun for a centaur to approve of."

"They'll approve of anything, as long as there's a lesson in it."

Jago snorted and shook his head. Free of the braids, his hair fell to his waist in a rippling golden mass. "Doesn't sound like much of a childhood," he said, beginning to comb it.

The wizard shrugged. "It wasn't so bad."

"I suppose. Still, it sounds . . . HEY!" He whirled and swung at his brother's legs, but Raulin had already backed out of reach. "He's jealous," Jago told Crystal, rubbing his head where Raulin had plucked out a hair. "Just because he's losing his . . ."

"Ha!" Raulin stepped over the log they were using as a bench and dropped down onto it. He reached for the blackened metal teapot and poured himself a cup. "Your vanity is going to get your ass in trouble someday. Should've had that whole mess chopped off years ago."

"Mess?" Jago turned, his hair glowing gold in the firelight, the wooden comb pointing at Raulin's face. "I'll cut my hair when you get rid of that growth on your upper lip."

"I'll see you in Chaos first."

"More than likely."

Their words held the cadence of a litany and Crystal relaxed, savoring the heat of the fire, the sweet strength of the tea, and the comfort of companionship. Just for an instant, she thought she saw something move in the darkness under the trees. She dropped her gaze into her mug, losing the image in its contents. The darkness was Nashawryn's realm and she had no intention of loosing that dread goddess again.

Out under the trees, Lord Death sighed. Once, she would have looked for him, but she didn't need him now. Still, she was happy. He'd never heard her laugh the way she had that afternoon. Wasn't that what he wanted? Wasn't it?

Raulin settled his forearms on his knees and watched his brother and the wizard. They looked, he thought, like the sun and the moon come down to share his fire. He had a sudden vision of the two of them entwined, great lengths of gold and silver hair wrapping about them and the rush of desire that accompanied it left him momentarily weak. As though aware of his thoughts, Jago turned to look at him and Raulin raised his mug in a slow and silent toast. Jago grinned, raised both brows, and returned to freeing a tangle. Coincidence, Raulin decided. Although the love between them was the strongest and best thing in both their lives, it had never expressed itself as mind-reading. Not even when they'd been children and could've used it. . . .

With his attention apparently on his hair, Jago managed to keep both Crystal and his brother within sight. He had a sudden urge to shout, "Would you two get it over with so I can figure out where I fit in!" but he held his peace. Would talking to Raulin do any good? He doubted it; his brother never welcomed interference in his love life—Jago smiled at memories—as much as he'd always needed it. . . .

Crystal stared into the fire, acutely conscious of the man to either side of her. They were so much the same in so many ways and yet she reacted completely differently to each. She wished she'd learned more about men in her twelve years of wandering. Twelve years. The fire danced with visions of the battle on the Tage Plateau, with the pyramids of bodies Kraydak had built across half the world. Kraydak and his armies. Kraydak's Horde. The men of the Empire.

"Raulin, how old are you?" she asked softly, because she daren't ask the other question, the question that naturally followed her line of thought.

Raulin sighed. "Thirty-seven. Jago is thirty-three."

"Then you were . . ."

"Part of Kraydak's armies?" He shifted, snagged the pot, and poured more tea. He'd wondered, off and on, how long it would take her to make that connection. "I was. Jago wasn't."

She turned over a number of responses in her mind, sure of how she felt but unsure of how to express it. Jago broke into the silence before she got the chance.

"Does it matter?" His voice was flat. "He didn't have a choice, Crystal. When they took you, you went. Or you died. They never came for me. That's the only difference. He didn't fight for anything he believed in. He only fought to stay alive. When you destroyed Kraydak, you freed Raulin as much as you freed countries under Kraydak's yoke. Does that make him the enemy now?" His face remained expressionless as he stared at her, but in his heart he prayed for her to say no, to not tear down the delicate friendship that had begun to grow among the three of them.

Crystal raised her head and Jago fell into the brilliant green of her eyes.

*You've always hurt for him, haven't you?*

He felt the question, knew it hadn't been spoken aloud. He felt her take his answer. Across the bond that stretched between them, across the bond woven of bits and pieces pulled from both their lives, he felt her say: *I hurt for all of them.*

He felt her pain and knew she meant every life that Kraydak had touched.

And he felt how it cut and tore when they wouldn't let her help but ran in fear and suspicion because she came of the same race Kraydak did. Felt her despair and burned with shame that he had considered even for an instant she would forget who the real enemy had been.

Then he again sat beside the fire, looking into a crystal tear that ran down the curve of an ivory cheek. His face grew hot and he tried to turn away, but she laid a hand along his cheek and stopped him.

"We carry the pain," she said softly, "because it is all that we can do."

The why, made up for both of guilt and doubt and caring, they didn't have to speak of.

A second tear joined the first. "I never realized before that I wasn't carrying it alone."

Jago turned his head, not taking his eyes from her, and softly kissed the palm that held him. She smiled, a little tremulously, and drew the hand away to wipe the tears dry with the place his lips had touched.

The bond between them strengthened, for only one thing was stronger than pain shared for love's sake and that was love shared for the same reason.

Raulin watched the only two people in the world who meant anything to him, and nodded. They'd worked it out. He wasn't sure how and he didn't care. He could leave it there, but though he knew what her answer would be, he needed her to tell him as well.

"Am I the enemy, Crystal?" he asked.

She turned to face him, pushing her hair back off her face as she moved, the warmth of her smile reaching across the distance. "You never were."

There had been only one enemy in that war and Crystal knew that better than anyone. But he still released a breath he didn't remember holding as her words dissolved a bitter doubt he hadn't known he had. He returned her smile with an equal warmth and then tried to calm his pulse when she flushed and looked away. He wondered how Jago would feel about looking for more firewood.

Off in the distance, a wolf howled, the lonely sound filling the night and giving all three a chance to regain a little composure. Raulin threw another log on the fire, Jago began rebraiding his hair, and Crystal began to sing.

It started as a formless kind of a hum, an outlet for the emotions that threatened to overflow. She stared off at nothing as the music began to form patterns and then the pattern evolved into a song. It was an old song, from before the Age of Wizards, a ballad of how the last of the air elementals fell in love with a mortal woman.

Jago's fingers began to move to the rhythm of the song. He remembered the last time he'd heard it; his mother sitting in their one comfortable chair with her old worn mandolin in her lap, Raulin sprawled on the hearth replacing the leather strapping around the handle of his dagger—replacing it with a strip torn from one of *his* vests if Jago remembered correctly. That had been about the last night they'd shared as a family. Soon after, Raulin had been taken and he'd been gone barely a month when their mother had died. The mandolin had been sold to pay for her pyre. He smiled as he wound off the braid, holding only the memory of that last night, letting the others go.

The centaurs had taught Crystal to sing as a means of focusing her power. She went one step beyond on her own.

Raulin's jaw dropped as, in the air over the camp, the song came to life. In a tiny patch of clear blue sky, Laur-anthonel swooped and dove and raced the wind. His hair was the color of sunshine, his eyes a storm-cloud gray. From the stunned expression on his brother's face, Raulin assumed Jago saw the same. An arm's reach away from the reality of woodsmoke and trampled snow, Laur-anthonel exalted in his freedom as the song named him more than mortal and less than god; he ruled the winds, no one ruled him. For once more aware of the wizard than the woman, Raulin relaxed and let the music take him.

Crystal sang on, oblivious to anything but the song. The goddesses, with no weakness to give them opening and no calling to their aspects, remained quiet.

Enthralled, Jago stared as the tiny image of the Lord of Air passed over the lands of men, heard singing and stopped to listen—little knowing that he heard his doom as well.

As the song changed, so did the vision; the blue sky of Laur-anthonel's domain replaced by a tower room in a stone keep where the King of Valen's youngest daughter sat at her loom and sang. The shuttle flicked in and out as, with Crystal's voice, Kara poured out her heart, weaving her hopes and dreams into the music. Ten thousand years later, in the air over the camp in the mountains, Laur-anthonel lost his heart again. He paused at her window, and she, feeling the breeze, turned and met his gaze. They exchanged a look so piercingly impassioned that Crystal fell silent, fearing the music might shatter it, and for an instant the image, and that look, hung in the air alone.

Kara found her tongue before the Lord of Air, and Crystal sang of her sudden love for this man who had come in answer to her dreams. She let her own undefined yearning seep into the music, lending Kara's words a sweet poignancy. In the pause between verses, as she drew a breath to continue, a strong rich baritone took up Laur-anthonel's response.

At first, Crystal thought the breezes sang with her, for they often did, and then she realized, shocked, that it was Raulin. She whirled to face him, the image in the air fading as her attention moved from it. Still singing Laur-anthonel's pledge of eternal devotion, Raulin raised an arm and indicated the barely visible lovers. They firmed as Crystal let the music take her up again.

Laur-anthonel, Jago was certain, had never behaved in such a way before for he could see the image of the Lord of Air take on his brother's mannerisms. And his brother's strengths. And, as the courtship progressed, his brother's feelings. He wondered if he should be watching such an outpouring of emotion, decided the music excused him, and knew that, right or wrong, he couldn't leave before the last note faded.

Free to sing Kara's part alone, Crystal found herself involved as she'd never been before. Her heart nearly broke with Kara's anguish at what she thought was love's betrayal and her spirit soared along with her voice as love proved true in the end. She forgot Jago listened, forgot everything outside the music, and sang to Raulin only; her yearning no longer undefined.

When Kara and her love were joined at last, the lines between the passion of the song and the passion of the singers blurred. Their joy rose into the night clear and strong, and then, as though they had rehearsed it, both voices fell to barely above a whisper as they spoke their vows to love.

*Never before,* Jago thought as the final vow gave way to silence, Raulin's voice wrapped around the core of silver that was Crystal. *And never again.* An intensity like that happened once in a lifetime and he thanked the Mother that he'd been allowed to hear it.

As the crackling of the fire and the movement of the trees surrounding the camp began to fill the quiet, Raulin, never taking his eyes from Crystal's face, held out his hand. Silently, for all that was necessary had been said, Crystal laid hers in it. He pulled her into his arms and bent his head to hers . . .

Jago shook himself free of the spell and for his own sake, for he knew they had forgotten his existence, went for a walk in the woods . . .

. . . where he discovered he had not been the music's only audience.

"What can I give her to stand with that?" Lord Death demanded. "How . . ." He buried his face in his hands and gave a long shuddering sigh. When he looked up his face showed red from the pressure of his fingers. "I can't even touch her, you know."

Jago nodded. "I know." Without thinking, he held out his hand.

Lord Death stared at it until he drew it back, and then, with only a small bit of the pain still in his face, he left Jago alone in the night.

Behind him, from the circle of firelight, Jago heard another song rise, the oldest song of all, and was glad Lord Death had at least been spared hearing it.

# SEVEN

A motionless silhouette against the winter's sky, the giant faced into the wind and read the news from it. The weather would hold, and that was all to the good. Giants seldom worried about weather, able by both sheer bulk and temperament to wait out the fiercest storm, but she wanted to remain on schedule. Both her pace and her path were carefully planned. She would meet up with the wizard and her companions close enough to the tower to be of obvious assistance.

A breeze ruffled her close-cropped brown curls and she smiled at the information it volunteered. It seemed that at the moment the young wizard had little interest in ruling the world and had found a more pleasant pastime.

*And I wish her joy of it,* she thought, picking a careful way down the steep and icy trail, *for the Mother knows she's had little enough joy in her life until now.*

According to the demon's map, Aryalan's tower lay north and west of the forest. As the sleigh could not be maneuvered through the trees, the way due north was closed. Therefore, they moved west for three days, skirting the edge of the woods until the forest dropped down into a valley which angled almost exactly in the direction they needed to go.

"This," Raulin declared upon seeing it, "was on old frog-face's wall."

As Raulin remembered their path in greater detail than either Jago or Crystal, and as the valley offered shelter and obvious signs of game, they descended into it, still following the forest.

Jago watched Raulin's and Crystal's backs and grinned. They weren't holding hands, but they might as well have been; he doubted he could slip a dagger blade, between their shoulders. Separated by the sleigh and the length of the traces, he couldn't hear what they said, but he had a pretty good idea they weren't whispering lovers' platitudes. For starters, he didn't think Raulin knew any.

As though aware of his thoughts, Crystal raised her voice, ". . . because it's a woman's song and when you change the lyrics so that a man can sing it you change the meaning!"

Raulin's reply was pitched too low to carry back to his brother but Crystal's response of "I am not being sexist!" filled in the words. They disagreed without the tentativeness of most new lovers and through that Jago recognized the depth of their feelings. It sounded remarkably similar to the way he and Raulin argued and they'd had over thirty years together.

To his surprise, he felt no jealousy at this closeness. Not of Crystal for coming between him and his brother. Not of Raulin for monopolizing the only woman they would likely meet for some time. Crystal hadn't come between them; while they hadn't exactly grown closer, the rising tension was gone. And Raulin, he knew, did not demand that Crystal remain exclusively with him. Their mother had raised them to believe in a woman's choice, and the brothers had shared bed-partners before. Somehow, though, Jago couldn't see himself with Crystal. It had nothing to do with his mistrust of wizards; he'd lost that back in the demon's cave and in a short time she'd become almost as important to him as Raulin. That was it. She felt like the sister he'd never had.

He watched her reach up to tug on Raulin's mustache and nodded sagely. Yes, like a sister. His sister and his brother and . . . He shook his head and left that line of thought dangling. Taking the analogy too far dropped him into murky waters indeed. Enough that they found pleasure in each other and that he in no way felt excluded from their company because of it.

Besides, the gear had never been in such good repair. Now he went over it for at least an hour each night before retiring to the shelter the three of them still shared.


Crystal found Raulin both an enthusiastic and a considerate lover, as straightforward and uncomplicated in bed as out of it. She thanked the Mother-creator that Jago approved of their relationship and treated the inevitable silliness with amused tolerance. Two things disturbed her. Avreen had made no attempts at freedom in spite of the amount of energy directed toward her aspect. For that matter, none of the goddesses made their presence felt during her nights with Raulin, almost as if something blocked them out . . .

*I've seen more fire in wet wood.*

. . . although Zarsheiy made a number of sarcastic comments during the day.

She wasn't complaining, lovemaking had never felt so, well, so complete, but Avreen's silence puzzled her. The second thing that disturbed her was the continuing absence of Lord Death. Not for years had he gone so long without appearing. In spite of the companionship of both men, she missed him. He was, after all, her oldest friend.


Raulin had decided early in life that women and men were not intended to understand each other. He therefore refused to analyze the experience during those few times when they seemed to. He stuck to that principle now. Lovemaking with Crystal lifted him to the heights every night. He cherished it, he enjoyed it, he didn't worry about it. Fortune beckoned, and he traveled to it with a beautiful woman by his side and his brother at his back. What more could any man ask for?

*        *        *

Their first morning in the valley, they crossed rabbit spore three times, and once a huge buck, his head held high under a majestic spread of antlers, regarded them somberly for an instant before spinning and bounding away.

"Snares tonight," Raulin declared, rubbing his hands in anticipation, "and meat tomorrow!"

Crystal laughed, suddenly looking wild and fey. "Meat tonight, I think."


Doan sprawled in the curve of a giant stone foreleg, his brow furrowed in thought. He often came to the Dragon's Cavern when he had a particularly knotty problem to work out and wanted to be uninterrupted. His brother dwarves had developed the habit of avoiding the cavern when the dragon had been alive—not from fear; a large dragon in a confined space in warm weather smelled impossibly unpleasant—and now, although the dragon curled about the center pillar had returned to stone, the habit remained.

"I could," he said, "let the giant handle it." He twisted into another position and drummed his fingers against his thigh. It bothered him that the giants considered Aryalan's tower enough of a danger to get involved. The notion that Crystal herself might *be* a danger rather than *in* danger, he discarded completely. He admitted, reluctantly, that the centaurs might have reason for paranoia, considering how the last wizards they trained had turned out. He also admitted, more reluctantly still, that this wizard was an image of the Eldest, of Milthra, the Lady of the Grove, and that might, perhaps, be influencing his thinking.

Snarling at nothing in particular, he swung down to the ground.

"Only one way to be sure," he informed the dragon, slapping it affectionately on its sandstone nose. He hitched up his pants and went to collect his weapons from the forge.

"Heading off again?" asked a brother, glancing up from his anvil where a vaguely axehead-shaped piece of iron glowed red hot.

Doan pulled his favorite sword off a wall where a large number of weapons hung. It annoyed him that so few of them ever got used. It annoyed him even more that no one paid attention to his complaints. "You got a problem with that, Drik?"

"Nope." The smith swung his hammer and the iron sprayed sparks. "Just curious. This trip got anything to do with the Call?"

"Might."

"I thought the Council decided to let the giants handle it."

"Yeah, well you know what they say," Doan buckled on the sword-belt and settled the familiar weight across his back, "if you want a thing done right, do it yourself."

"Figure you'll need your sword?"

"What do you think, slag brain?" Grumbling beneath his breath that anything in Aryalan's tower would be a welcome change, he picked up a dagger and stomped from the room.

"Pleasure talking to you too, Doan," Drik called after him, shook his head, and returned to work.

The huge white owl opened its talons, releasing the hare it carried into Raulin's arms. Raulin staggered a little under the weight of the dead animal, then shifted his grip and held it out by the ears.

"Fresh meat!" he exclaimed.

"So I see." Jago set a pot of snow on the fire to melt. "Are you going to clean it or do we spend all night looking at it?"

Raulin tossed him the carcass. "You do it. You need the practice."

"I'll do it," Jago agreed, pulling out his knife and laying the hare on a patch of clean snow, "because *you* are inept." He slit the belly and scooped out the entrails. "You want these, Crystal?"

She stepped into the firelight and bent to pick up her clothes. "Not now thanks, I just ate. Maybe later."

"You know I consider you my heart's delight," Raulin said, watching her dress with deep enjoyment, "but that's disgusting."

Crystal pulled the sweater over her head, her expression thoughtful. Lord Death had said much the same the night things between them had fallen apart so badly. Was he still angry with her? She hadn't seen him since . . . since the demon's cave, weeks ago. Uncertain whether anything could go wrong with the one true son of the Mother, she still began to grow uneasy at his absence.

"Crystal?" Raulin gently lifted her chin. "Please don't look worried. I didn't mean it."

She managed a smile, pushing her concern for Lord Death back out of sight. "It's okay." She snaked her arms under his open overcoat and around his waist. "When I'm not in feathers I find it pretty disgusting, too." Leaning forward, she kissed him hard and when her mouth was free again, added: "I try not to think about it." Which, she suddenly remembered, releasing Raulin to pull on her boots, was exactly what she'd said to Lord Death. All the concern came tumbling back.

*Best make up your mind,* Zarsheiy taunted. *The quick or the dead.*

*What?* Usually Crystal ignored her, but usually the goddess' jibes made sense.

*Poor child, don't you know your own mind?* False sympathy dripped from the thought.

*That's hardly surprising,* Crystal gave a mental snort, *since I've squatters in most of it.* Her hair, she realized as she straightened, curtained her face from Raulin's view so she carefully schooled her features before it fell back and he grew upset again. For reasons unknown, it didn't seem right discussing Lord Death with Raulin. Maybe if she had some time alone with Jago . . .

"That tickles," she said lightly, as he traced a finger along the edge of her left ear.

He grinned and winked. "You know, I've never kissed a bird before."

"A number of birdbrains," Jago put in, skewering the cleaned hare and setting it over the fire. He shielded himself with the teapot as Raulin took a quick step in his direction. "Hurt the cook and the cook burns dinner!"

"As you're just as likely to burn it without my help that's not much of a threat I'll . . ."

They never heard just what Raulin planned as an anthem of wolf howls drowned out his next words. The three froze as the chorus climbed up the scale, then faded.

"Great bloody Chaos," Jago breathed, trying to wet his lips with a tongue gone dry.

"Great bloody Chaos' balls," Raulin expanded, swallowing convulsively. "Both of them." He drew a long shuddering breath and added, "In a sling."

Crystal clutched at a wandering breeze. "They have us surrounded . . ." She twisted, seemed to reach for something neither brother could see, and threw up her hands in disgust. "There's more, but it won't tell me."

She seemed frustrated rather than afraid, so the brothers took their cue from her. They began to breathe almost normally again. Raulin continued to stare into the darkness, but Jago sank down to tend the fire.

"Think the meat attracted them?" Raulin asked, trying to forget that howl despite the chills still running up and down his back.

"Perhaps." Crystal tossed her head. She stepped toward the trees, then back, then twisted her hair with her hands. "But there's lots of game around here. They can't be hungry enough to approach the fire."

"Well, they haven't yet," Jago offered, pouring the snow, now transformed to boiling water, into the teapot, dumping it, tossing in a handful of herbs, and refilling the pot.

Suddenly, golden eyes glowed just outside the ring of light and then just as suddenly disappeared.

"And then again," he continued, his voice steady but the hand that set the pot back on the coals shaking visibly, "who wants first watch?"

"Wolves do not attack people." Crystal pronounced each word clearly and calmly, but whether she spoke to convince herself, the brothers, or the wolves, not even she was sure.

"Maybe they don't," Raulin admitted, his head jerking back and forth as he tried to watch all directions at once. He pulled off his mitts and wiped his now sweaty palms. "But they don't act like this either. Jago, you take first watch. Crystal second. I'll take last."

Not even Crystal's wizard-sight saw the wolves that night, but they continued to make themselves heard. No golden eyes broke the darkness, but howls shivered through the silence, time after time. Crystal wove a net of power about the shelter, blocking the noise so the two within could get some sleep.

Nashawryn stirred each time the wolves called.

Sitting alone on second watch, she fed wood to the fire and power to the barriers that held the dark goddess confined.

At dawn, the howling stopped. Daggers drawn, while Crystal stood by ready to help if necessary, Raulin and Jago slipped into the woods and separated, each circling half the camp. Just before they completed the circle, following tracks now deserted by their makers, Jago dropped to one knee and beckoned to Raulin. "Come take a look at this."

Raulin came, looked over Jago's shoulder, and whistled through his teeth. "Big bugger," he said, carefully noncommittal.

"Big bugger? That's it? Look at the depth of that print!" Jago put his fist against the snow and pushed. "This stuffs damp under the trees; it compacts. This wolfs gotta weigh more than it should."

"I hate to break it to you, junior, but that's not our biggest problem. There's a track as large on the other side of camp that wasn't made by any wolf."

Jago stood, brushing snow off his pants, his eyes beginning to look a little wild. "Then what?"

"Looks like a cat."

"That big?"

"Uh-huh."

"You know what I think?"

"Uh-huh. You think you should've stayed home and found honest work."

"How did you know?"

Raulin draped an arm around his brother's shoulders. "It's what you always think when our ass is in the fire."

"Do we tell Crystal?"

"Only if you intend on living to an honored old age."

"Good point."

They took one more look at the oversized print, at the whole line of oversized prints, and headed back to camp.

When told, Crystal looked thoughtful.

"What is it?" Raulin asked, buckling himself into the harness.

"I don't . . ." She shook her head and bent to pick up the other trace. "I've got the feeling I'm forgetting something very important. Something someone once told me."

"Oh, that's very definite." Raulin watcher her shrug the harness on, leered, and reached out a hand. "Let me help you settle that strap."

Crystal grinned, the thoughtful look vanished, and she slapped his hand away from her breast. "Is that all you ever think of?"

"Yes!" Jago called from his position behind the sleigh. "It's all he's thought of since he turned thirteen. Now, can we get going before our visitors return for breakfast?"

One silver brow rose. "Thirteen?"

Raulin threw his weight forward, straightening out his trace with an audible snap. "So what're we going to do, just hang around here all day? Let's go."

Except that the way was easier than any they'd traveled for some time, the morning passed no differently than others they'd shared. The quiet of a world muffled in snow soothed ragged emotions and, gradually, night terrors faded. They made good time, pausing only once to rest, and covered nearly ten miles.

"Hey!" Crystal yelled at the brother's backs. "Let's stop for lunch, I'm starved."

". . . and a huge conservatory . . ." Raulin spread his arms, deep in his favorite topic of conversation: spending the gold he knew they'd find at the tower.

"What do you want a conservatory for?"

"For plants . . ."

"I know that's what it's for, you uncultured boob, I just couldn't figure out why you'd want one."

"Guys! Food?" Crystal tried again as Raulin swung, Jago ducked, and neither heard her. She sighed, they'd never hear her now. A strong tug and the metal prongs of both brakes dug deep into the snow. The sleigh stopped cold and she used just enough power to ensure it couldn't move farther.

Raulin, being heavier, kept his balance. Jago's feet took a step his body couldn't complete, his arms wind-milled, and he sat down.

"Oaf," Raulin said fondly and extended a hand to help him up.

Back on his feet, Jago turned to face Crystal, who shrugged, and smiled.

"It got your attention," she pointed out. "Let's eat."

Jago's stomach chose that moment to loudly express its agreement. His mouth, open to deliver a blistering retort to Crystal, closed. He unbuckled his harness. "Well, I guess that's my vote. Raulin?"

The older man squinted into the sunlight then along the direction they had to go. "We're making such good time . . ."

"We won't get anywhere if we feint from hunger."

"True enough." He tossed his harness on top of his brother's. "I'll be back in a minute."

As he walked into a nearby copse of trees he heard Jago say, "You notice how he only has to go when there's work to do?" Distance cut Crystal's reply down to a musical murmur. Raulin grinned, the sound reminding him of murmurs into his chest, inarticulate expression of contentment. He swung behind a scruffy jackpine.

*Crack!*

The grin vanished and he froze, the image of giant tracks in his mind's eye. The hair on the back of his neck lifted and he felt himself watched. In the silence he could hear the tree's needles rub together, a faint *shirk shirk* that now seemed sinister. He managed to do what he had to—the sound was not repeated—then backed slowly out of the trees.

Branches, he knew, often cracked in the cold. He really wished it was cold enough for that to be a valid explanation.

Crystal looked up from the small blaze that heated the ever-present teapot, and frowned. "Raulin, are you all right?"

Jago snorted and tossed his brother a hunk of leftover rabbit. "Probably left it out too long and it froze."

"Something was in those trees with me." He kept his voice matter-of-fact; no sense in causing panic by frothing at the mouth.

Crystal stood to kick snow over the fire, but Raulin stopped her.

"We still have to eat. And the fire's a weapon if we need it."

*Acknowledgment at last!*

*Shut up, Zarsheiy!*

Conversation was strained and no one felt the urge to linger over tea.

They hadn't traveled more than a couple of miles when Jago held up his hand for a halt. "Raulin," he called without turning, "did you by chance *see* what joined you in the trees at lunch."

"No. Heard something. Why?"

"Because something is pacing us, something big and black. I've caught sight of it a couple of times now."

"Last night's visitor?"

"Could be."

Crystal's eyes flared as she tried to see through rock and trees and get a good look at their companion. Finally she gave up. "Wolves hunt at night."

"It isn't hunting, just following."

"Well, if it decides to move in . . ." Raulin unstrapped an oilskin bundle and laid it carefully on the snow. Squatting, he cut free the lengths of tarred rope that held it closed. As he opened it and lifted free what it contained, his expression was bleak. The crossbow was a soldier's weapon, easy to manufacture, easy to use. Raulin had been a soldier. He'd hoped he'd never have to be one again. Memories of men and women screaming and dying stirred. With an effort, he pushed them back.

"Are you sure . . ." Jago began, recognizing his brother's discomfort, knowing the source.

"Yes." He stood, slinging the deerskin quiver over one shoulder, and shoved the oilskin on the sleigh where the weight of his pack would hold it securely. Letting the head of the bow fall forward, he hooked the heavy bowstring with the cocking lever and shoved the toe of one boot into the iron bracing ring. A hard pull and the string snapped safely behind the trigger.

"Loading it too?"

"An unloaded bow is a fancy club." He heard the armsmaster's voice in that and his lips curled into a mixture of a snarl and a smile. He slipped a quarrel into position and laid the bow carefully on top of the load, the head pointed toward the trees at the left, the stock inches from where his hands rested on the crossbar of the sleigh.

He looked up and met Crystal's eyes; met not unearthly power, only concern and a question. So he smiled, a real smile this time, and answered it.

"I'm okay."

She nodded and reached out her hand. Although the length of the sleigh separated her palm and his face, he felt her stroke his cheek, leaving a residue of warmth and comfort behind.

"If you don't watch that," his smile quirked up into a grin and he waggled his brows suggestively, "I'll start howling myself."

The geography of the valley limited the sleigh to two directions; forward the way they'd been going, following a river course now buried under half a winter's accumulation of snow, or back the way they'd come. They went on. Crystal and Jago each kept one eye on their path and one eye on the trees and scrub that lined their path. Raulin followed blindly, trying to watch both sides of the trail at once.

As though aware it had been spotted, the creature pacing them took less care to remain unnoticed. They heard it on occasion, the crack and crash of a heavy body forcing its way through the brush, and once or twice saw sumac sway and shake off its load of snow as something unseen pushed past.

The sun sank lower in the sky, the trees began to thin as the forest they'd followed for so long began to end, and they reached a place where the slope to the valley's edge ran clear.

"Higher ground might not be a bad idea," Jago suggested as they paused to consider their next move.

"Maybe," Raulin agreed, "but that slope'll . . . Chaos!"

A huge black wolf stood in the clearing. Teeth bared, it growled.

It stepped forward and the growl grew louder.

Raulin's hand dropped down to the crossbow, rested a moment on the stock, and lifted back to the sleigh when the wolf moved no closer. Unless it attacked, he wouldn't fire. He wasn't sure he could. "Let's move it," he said quietly, throwing his weight against the crossbar and almost running the sleigh up the back of Jago's legs. "Just keep it smooth and quiet and I think we'll be all right."

As the wolf and the path from the valley fell behind, Raulin felt cold fingers brush against his spine. He knew those golden eyes continued to watch and he kept his own locked on the silver sway of Crystal's hair, fighting the urge to turn and walk backward, keeping the enemy in sight. *Enemy,* he snorted to himself. *Try to think of it as a big dog. You'll be happier.*

A flash of black among the trees to the left and they knew they were accompanied still.

"There!" Crystal called, and pointed.

A smaller gray wolf sped across a clearing on the right and disappeared into cover.

"Two," Raulin grunted.

From the left a howl, and from behind an answer. And then another. And then another. And then the valley filled with sound. As the last echo died away the sun slipped below the valley's edge and suddenly, although true night was still hours away, shadows ruled.

"Run!" Raulin barked, catching up the crossbow and ramming his shoulder against the sleigh. "We're too out in the open to fight."

So they ran. With wolves to either side and wolves behind. Jago floundered on a patch of soft snow and almost fell, but Crystal grabbed his arm and yanked him back onto his feet. Forced off the river's path, they scrambled up hills, heading due north into the rougher going of the mountains.

*Why don't they attack?* Crystal wondered. *What are they waiting for?* Sleek shapes, just on the edge of her vision, kept pace but came no closer. The power needed to protect Raulin and Jago would weaken the shields and free the goddesses. She could only hope that in leaving Zarsheiy would do more damage to her enemies than to her friends.

Ahead of them waited a jumble of rock and a cliff-face that rose eight to ten feet out of the mountain.

"The cliff," Raulin panted. "Get our backs against it!"

With the end in sight, they managed another burst of speed.

The front curve of the right runner caught under a rock and the sleigh slewed to a stop. The leather straps dug into Crystal's breasts as dead weight caught up to her and she plummeted to one knee, gasping, all the air forced out of her lungs. Jago's runner kept moving, spinning sleigh and Jago to the right, whipping both feet out from under him. Raulin's chin slammed into the crossbar and he bit his tongue. His eyes filled at the impact but he stumbled forward, half blind, grabbed Jago, and pulled him to his feet.

"Crystal!" He yelled. "The harnesses!"

A flash of green and the harnesses split.

Raulin pushed his brother on ahead and turned back to help Crystal. "The cliff, it's our only chance!"

Plunging forward, they almost crashed into Jago who had stopped and stood staring at their intended refuge. "I think not," he said quietly. Raulin and Crystal rocked to a halt beside him.

The black wolf stood on the cliff top. Its teeth gleamed white even in the dusk and its open mouth made it look almost as if it laughed. Then it leaped.

Raulin raised the crossbow and pulled the trigger.

The wolf's scream, when the quarrel drove into its haunch, sounded like nothing out of an animal's throat and when the body hit the ground almost at Raulin's feet, a young man snarled up at them—a young man with thick black hair that grew to a peak in the front and down to the center of his back like a mane, with fierce golden eyes, with very white teeth, and with a crossbow quarrel through one muscular thigh. As they watched, he warped and changed until the great black wolf crouched and worried at the arrow. A little blood matted the fur, but the shaft blocked most of the bleeding.

Jago's mouth worked, but no sound came out. Even Raulin seemed to have nothing to say. And Crystal finally remembered what had nagged at her all day.

*Morning council in the queen's pavilion the day after Halda had fallen to Kraydak's Horde; Kly, the Duke of Lorn's daughter, had tried to reassure Mikhail that his sister, Halda's queen, still lived. "The mountains have hundreds of caverns and passageways, milord," she had said. "The wer have used them for generations."*

"Wer," she repeated aloud. "He's wer."

"Good guess, wizard. Jason, come here."

Still snarling, the wolf rose and trotted past them on three legs, the uneven gait detracting not a bit from his strength. Their gazes never left him and they turned like puppets following his direction.

Four wolves, two mountain cats, and a man stood between them and the sleigh. Jason, apparently ignoring the arrow, went to stand at the man's side, his injured leg tucked up, paw resting inches above the snow.

The man was naked and shivered slightly in the cold. In his hands he carried a rod almost two feet long crafted of amethyst wrapped in bronze wire. His hair grew like Jason's, proclaiming him kin, and his smile was feral and most unpleasant.

"We don't like wizards on our land."

Kly's voice came out of the past again. *"The wer hate the wizards with an intensity hard to imagine. The names of the wizards are curses to them."*

The rod came up, its bronze tip pointed at Crystal.

Her thoughts ran out like water; the harder she tried to hold them the faster they moved. The void that remained wrapped her in warmth and comfort. Her vision fogged. She swayed, felt Raulin's arms go around her, felt herself slide to the ground. She heard Raulin's roar from a distance, heard an answering roar from one of the great cats, and saw a ginger colored blur go past. Her head refused to turn, so she watched the snow instead of the fight, deprived of the energy to care.

The fight finished before Jago had a chance to help. The great cat returned to its position on one flank of the group and Jago looked down to where Raulin sprawled on the ground. He appeared winded more than hurt. The cat's front paws had slammed into his chest but done no real damage.

"We give only one warning, mortal. Move toward us again and you die."

Jago forced his breathing to calm. Forced reason to win out over anger. "What do you want?" His voice sounded almost normal and only he knew what it took to keep it that way.

"The wizard." The wer spat the word into the air.

Raulin struggled to his feet and tried to surge forward but Jago grabbed his arm and held him back. "Stop it, Raulin," he commanded. "You can't help her if you get killed."

The man's upper lip lifted to reveal his teeth and his eyes narrowed.

"You can't help her. You are no match for Hela alone," the ginger cat looked smug, "and we bind the wizard's power."

*So that's what happened,* Crystal thought muzzily. She wondered vaguely if he bound the goddesses as well, but it really didn't matter much.

A gray-brown wolf, almost matching Jason in size, flowed into his manshape. "I will take her, Eli, as Jason is injured."

Eli nodded, handing over the rod. "Hela, Gel, watch the mortals." Then he returned to fur.

As the man and both great cats approached, Jago kept his hand on Raulin's arm, not for restraint, but for knowledge; Raulin was the fighter. When Raulin's arm tensed, he flung himself forward, hand grabbing for his dagger, seeing Raulin do the same only much less quietly.

Gel met aim in mid-leap. A forepaw hit Jago's head with the force of a club, driving him to the ground. His head rang. His vision exploded into orange and yellow lights. He couldn't see or hear, so he slashed out blindly at the musky smell. Claws ripped through his mitten and into his hand. He lost his grip on the dagger and barely felt the pain when another blow to his head plunged him into darkness.

Raulin rolled as he dove forward, coming up under the cat's attack, driving both feet into Hela's chest and throwing her to the ground.

Then he had his arms full of claws and teeth. His dagger went flying. Bringing her back legs up, Hela kicked, shredding his clothes. Raulin screamed as the claws tore into skin. He lost his grip on her jaw. Her teeth closed on his throat.

"Not good, not good." The giant shook her head at the news the breeze had brought. She would have to hurry.

# EIGHT

"You're lucky the inner pack wanted you alive, wizard."

*Alive.* Crystal caught hold of the word and used it to drag herself a little way out of the pain. She tried to open her eyes, but even so delicate an action was beyond her. Her arms dangled in air, her face bounced against bare skin, something hard dug into her stomach. She forced the information together. Carried over a shoulder.

The shoulder dipped and she dropped onto rock.

New pain and old pain reinforced almost washed her away once more, but she hung grimly onto awareness.

"Cap her," husked a distant voice.

Again she tried to open her eyes. The lids trembled but wouldn't rise.

Rough hands yanked her into a sitting position. Ribs ground together. She whimpered and power flowed sluggishly, responding to the hurt. A smooth band, cold but too heavy to be metal, settled down around her head. Another of the same stuff curved under her chin and snicked into the first band just in front of each ear. She jerked at the sound; very loud, very sharp, and somehow very final.

The hands released her and she collapsed, the band chiming musically as it slammed against the stone. Her throat spasmed as she fought for air, sucking it through her half open mouth. No air got through the ruin of her nose. She tasted blood.

Slowly, very slowly, power began to smooth the jagged edges. Her breathing eased and her body relaxed enough to allow healing. She lay on her side, knees up, arms pressed tight against her chest, and tried to remember.

*What had happened to Raulin and Jago?* The wer, she remembered, and the rod, and the binding, but there her memories ended. Once over the gap, her thoughts seemed clear enough. Had the binding worn off? To test it she would have to reach for her power . . .

No. Best let the power continue repairing the damage her body had taken. It would do that without her interference and she didn't know what would happen if she attempted control. She was a little afraid to try.

The wer, the rod, the binding . . . and what then?

Beginning softly, an eerie harmonic discord rose in volume to bone shaking intensity. Not the wolves, this was a scream not a song. Shoulders hunched against the sound, Crystal brought her hands up and rubbed at her eyes. She had to see. Something sealed her lids shut. The upper layer crumbled under her touch. Most of the lower, gummy and warm, scrubbed away. Her lashes matted and stuck, but she managed to force her eyes open.

Blood. Smeared across her palms. She touched one eye again and the fingers came away red. Her blood then. Better than the alternative.

The undulating cry went on. And on. And on.

*What had happened to Raulin and Jago?*

Gathering her returning strength, she placed both bloody palms against the rock and pushed. Ignoring the protest of her body, she managed to almost sit up.

She lay against the wall of a large, roughly circular cavern. Flickering torches, jammed into random niches in the stone, barely lit the space. In the center of the cavern, a number of the great cats surrounded a flat topped boulder. Muzzles lifted, the cats wailed. On the boulder were two black . . . things.

Crystal remembered.

The wer had hoisted her up and bent to sling her over one shoulder, moving her line of sight to include, for the first time since she'd fallen under the rod, Raulin and Jago. She saw the cats attack. She saw the brothers go down. She heard Raulin scream. That had penetrated the mists sifting through her mind. Still outwardly blank, still bound by the rod, deep within her head she'd raged and torn at the walls of her prison.

Something gave.

The cats had burned.

And not with an external flame that could be doused but from inside, with goddess fire. The cats had screamed and thrashed as they died, torment flicking them through change after change. The wolves had circled and snarled but found nothing to do until Jason had flowed into his manshape, hobbled forward to where Crystal lay limp and exulting and had beaten the wizard senseless.

In the cavern, the cats fell silent and began to move away. Two changed and lifted the bodies from the boulder. One followed his kin, the other approached Crystal, the charred remains held tenderly against his chest. A body-length away he stopped and stared down at her with topaz eyes.

"You killed my mate," he said.

Crystal refused to let his grief throw her into guilt. Straightening as much as she could, she stared back at him. "She was killing mine."

He hissed and spat, then turned his back on her and walked from the cavern.

Carefully, Crystal leaned back, easing her weight off her arms and letting the wall support her. She stretched out her legs, the movement hurting less than she'd anticipated. The worst of the pain seemed over, but the healing went on and would for some time. She saw that her feet were bare, and rubbed her cheek against the sweater's shoulder. The brothers lived, for their places within her were still filled, but they were also injured and she had no idea how badly.

*If they die because of you*, she vowed silently to the wer, *you shall see what wizardry is capable of.*


"Mortal, wake! You cannot die if I refuse to take you!"

Jago stirred and regretted it. He opened his eyes and shut them instantly. The moonlight seemed to burn holes in his brain.

"You try my patience, mortal!"

Squinting, although the action hurt his head, Jago managed to focus on an auburn-haired man, whose amber eyes flashed with anger.

"Lord . . ." He swallowed and tried again. "Lord Death?"

"Jago?" Raulin's face pushed into his line of vision. He didn't look right somehow. "Jago, wake up!"

"S'what he said."

"Who?"

"Lord Death."

"You're not dead!"

Jago pulled in a shuddering breath. "I know. Hurts too much." He figured out what bothered him about Raulin; the skin of his face seemed almost gray. "You don't look too good."

Raulin's mouth twisted. "You should see the other guy."

Jago rolled himself up on one elbow. The world spun, the insides of his head with it, and he spewed all over the snow. He felt Raulin's arm around his shoulders and when his guts stopped heaving, his brother lowered him gently back down.

"You think you can lie quietly for a few minutes?"

The stars began to whirl. "I don't think I've got a choice." He refused to close his eyes, and concentrated on making the stars behave. Somewhere over to the left, he heard Raulin banging things together loudly. Very loudly. Much too loudly. The sound bounced about the inside of his skull setting the stars, which had just begun to calm down, jigging once more. He wondered where Lord Death had gotten to and . . .

"Crystal!"

"Take it easy. Let's try sitting again, I brought a pack for you to lean on." As he spoke, Raulin eased his brother up, very slowly, until he reclined against the pack.

Jago clenched his teeth against the nausea and sucked in lungful after lungful of cold air. His head stopped spinning and settled into a steady, tormenting throb. Answered by a sharper throbbing . . . He raised his right hand and looked at a mangled ruin.

The throbbing turned to the brindle's roar, teeth dug into his legs and . . . No! He got control of himself, although his legs continued to ache in memory. He met Raulin's worried eyes, Raulin who no doubt suspected what he was thinking, and searched for something to say that would ease that look of strain.

"I guess," he said at last, "I won't be playing the harp anymore."

"You can't play the harp," Raulin said gruffly.

"Then I guess I won't be playing it any less."

Raulin's relieved smile was all Jago could've asked for and he managed a small one of his own.

"Here," Raulin wrapped the fingers of Jago's good hand around a warm mug, "drink this while I bandage."

Jago took a cautious sip, recognized the bitter brew as a painkiller from their emergency kit, and relaxed.

When Raulin saw Jago actually drinking the potion, he turned his attention to the mangled hand. The great cat's claws had ripped through skin, and flesh, and hooked down into the tendons. Several of the small bones had been displaced and one knuckle barely remained attached. Shreds of tissue were white with frostbite for the hand had lain half buried in snow. Miraculously, most major blood vessels seemed intact. Ignoring Jago's groans, Raulin rebuilt what he could and wrapped the whole tightly in clean linen. It was a better field dressing than any he'd had time to do during the war. He appreciated the irony that experience gained in such wholesale slaughter had twice now come to Jago's aid. Not that this in any way compared to the brindle.

"You know," he said, tying off the end, "when your head starts working again, this is going to hurt like Chaos."

"It already does."

"Good."

"Good?"

"If it can hurt, it can heal. Can you move your fingers?"

The fingers moved a little although Jago turned gray with pain during the attempt.

"What happened?" he asked, just managing to keep the scream from breaking through.

Raulin laid Jago's hand gently in his lap. "Well, it's my guess, they didn't have Crystal bound as tightly as they thought 'cause when we went down those cats started to burn. Think you can stand? Your clothes get wet from sitting in melting snow and you're going to be a lot worse off."

Jago remembered not to nod. "Yeah. I think so."

With an arm around Raulin's shoulder, Jago got slowly to his feet and stood swaying until the world steadied, then the two of them made their way over to the sleigh.

"Probably a good thing you'd already gone out," Raulin continued, "because the smell of those cats burning . . . Anyway, I flopped over and played dead." His voice grew grim and much colder than the winter night. "I could still hear what they did to Crystal."

"She lives."

Jago turned to face Lord Death who walked at his other side. "I know." The bond between Crystal and himself had not broken.

"They dragged her off. I saw where they entered the mountain." Raulin had either not heard his brother or had assumed the words were directed to him. "And we're going after her as soon as you're steady on your feet."

"The two of us against a mountain full of wer?" Jago asked as they reached the sleigh and Raulin released him.

"Yeah."

"Should be interesting."

The smiles they exchanged came from a lifetime of standing together. Some things got done regardless of the odds; this was one of them.

Raulin brushed the clinging snow off his brother's back and helped him into his huge fur overcoat. Jago, who'd just begun to notice a creeping chill, sighed thankfully and sank down on the front of the sleigh.

He watched Raulin strip their gear to bare essentials, his grip on the world not yet strong enough to help. "What about you?"

Raulin snorted and pulled his scarf down off his throat. Almost invisible in the beard stubble were four punctures, two on each side of his windpipe. "Teeth had hardly touched," he said, "when the cat started to burn and lost interest. I got off light."

"Only because he ignores the rest of the damage."

"He what!"

Lord Death nodded and Jago whirled on Raulin who stared at his brother, completely confused by the sudden outburst.

"Open your coat!"

"Why?"

"Just do it!"

Raulin sighed and slowly unhooked the fasteners. Under his coat, the clothing he'd been wearing hung in tatters. Under his clothing, eight angry, red lines marked where Hela's claws had torn through to skin.

"Only scratches, I swear." He tried to close the coat, but Jago glared it back open.

"Get me the emergency kit."

"Look . . ."

"Get it!"

He got it, then stood almost still as, one-handed, Jago pulled bits of cloth from the cuts, all at least a quarter inch deep and most already looking pink and inflamed. Two started bleeding sluggishly again as the scab holding the remains of Raulin's shirt inside the wound came free.

"Cat scratches," Lord Death said, as Jago reached for the roll of linen, "often become infected. You'd better disinfect those."

Jago nodded thoughtfully and reached instead for the bottle of raw alcohol.

"Now hold it, what're you going to do with that?"

"What do you think?" Jago asked, pouring some of the liquid on a cloth balanced on his knee. "That mess has to be cleaned.'"

"Not with that stuff, it doesn't." Raulin backed away, but Jago grabbed a corner of his coat.

"Knock me over," he warned, "and I'll have a relapse."

Raulin sullenly stopped moving.

Jago flipped the coat open again and wiped at the scoring with the alcohol laden cloth. "Stop squirming. Cat scratches often become infected."

"Says . . . CHAOS! . . . who?"

"Lord Death."

"When did he become a . . . DAMMIT JAGO! . . . healer?"

"I am the Great Healer," said Lord Death quietly. "Mortals come to me when all other healers have failed."

"What did he say?' " Raulin could tell by Jago's expression that the Mother's son had answered the question himself.

"He's expounding philosophy. If you'd stop dancing away, this'd go faster and we could start after Crystal."

Raulin growled an inarticulate curse but stood motionless while Jago finished.

Lord Death watched Jago's ministrations with a number of emotions warring in his breast. He needed Raulin reasonably healthy to rescue Crystal, but he resented the time spent on healing when every moment Crystal stayed with the wer put her in greater danger. He hated the thought that these mortals could attack the wer without his help and he could do little without theirs. And a very small part of him enjoyed Raulin's pain.

A linen bandage soon covered Raulin from armpits to waist. Although exposed flesh rippled with goose-bumps, he only shrugged his coat closed. Putting on freezing cold clothes underneath it would do more harm than good at this point. A fire would draw the wer. The small campstove threw heat only to the cooking surface; not enough to warm clothing.

"I'll be okay," he answered Jago's silent question, bending to complete the packs. "The coat's warm enough for fighting."

Jago nodded, there not being much else he could do, and in a little while Raulin helped him into his pack. He tried to ignore Lord Death, whose patience appeared to be growing short.

"He won't need that," Lord Death snapped as Raulin settled his own pack and loaded the crossbow.

"Why not?" Jago asked, waving Raulin quiet.

"Because I will lead you to Crystal on paths the wer do not walk."

"You?"

"What's he saying?" Raulin demanded.

"He says you don't need the crossbow. That he'll lead us to Crystal on paths the wer don't walk."

"He will?" Raulin turned over the idea. Lord Death could see the wer, but the wer couldn't see him. Jago could follow his direction and he, Raulin, could follow Jago. "It might work." He unloaded the bow and hung it from his pack by the quiver, out of the way but near to hand. His brow furrowed. "Ask him if . . ."

"He can hear *you*," Jago interrupted.

"Yeah, well . . ." Raulin straightened and spoke where Jago pointed. "If you can get in and out of there without being seen, why do you need us?"

"Tell your brother," Lord Death said to Jago, "that I cannot carry Crystal if it comes to that." He paused and fought to keep anything at all from showing on his face or in his voice as he added, "He can."

Crystal sat alone in the cavern for what seemed a very long time. She ran her fingers lightly over the band on her head and decided it was the same material as the rod. It fit snugly, almost as if it had been made for her head. It was a power binding of some kind, of that she was certain. Tentatively she reached in and directed the healing that still went on. Her power responded.

Cautiously, she manipulated and tested and discovered that everything appeared to be under her control. Her shields had remained up and not even Zarsheiy was missing. That surprised her, for there had been nothing containing the fire goddess when the cats had burned. Nor could she understand why Zarsheiy stayed so silent; this situation should've called forth scathing remarks.

*She's sulking.*

Crystal recognized Tayja's voice.

*The link between you and her and Avreen was so strong that she found herself back behind the barriers before she could even think of freedom.*

*Avreen worked with me?*

*Of course, child, you've given her ample reason to stay.*

Crystal felt herself flush. Raulin. She sighed and wondered if Raulin realized they had more of an audience each night than Jago, who patiently killed time by the fire. She touched the places the brothers held in her heart, knew they continued to live, and reached out with her power to call them.

Pain.

Screaming and writhing, she clutched at her head. Hot knives drove into her brain. A vise tightened and crushed. Then, as suddenly as it began, it stopped.

"So you have discovered what the cap can do."

Gasping, she scrambled back into a sitting position, her fingers tearing at the bands.

The old wer who stood over her smiled. "You cannot remove it," he said, "and if you try to use power against it, or to augment your strength, or in any way it finds your actions aggressive," he shrugged, "you now know what will happen. The wizards," his lips curled back in a snarl of pure hate, "built their devices of torment well." He flicked a hoary nail against the cap. "With this they could keep their fellows captive, healthy, whole, and helpless. You cannot use your powers to escape."

Hoarse from screaming, Crystal rasped, "They made this to use on each other?"

He spread his hands. "Who else has power to trap? As the wizards grew more powerful, their only adversaries were each other. Did you not destroy the only other one of your kind?"

"That was different!"

"He is still dead."

"I'm not like other wizards!"

"I see no difference."

Crystal worked her weight up the wall until she stood looking down at him. Small things hurt, but even her nose had begun to function again. She could smell the heavy animal scent of both the caverns and the wer who faced her. Basically, she was whole. For now. "Why," she asked with dignity, "am I alive?"

"Now? Specifically?" He slid his hands beneath the loose poncho he wore, a piece of clothing easy to slip out of in wolf form. His smile showed a broken tooth and dripped with malice. "We've waited many generations to catch a wizard. To visit on you some of the torment your kind laid on us. When we escaped during the Doom, we stole what toys we could. One brought you low. One you wear."

"But I had nothing to do with your creation . . ."

"It doesn't matter!" He spat the words. "You are wizard!"

For an instant a craggy gray wolf stood before her, its lean and hollow flanks jutting from the poncho. Pale eyes blazed with rage. Then the old man stood there again, breathing heavily through his nose, obviously fighting to keep his emotions under control.

"It's been thousands of years," Crystal said, shaken, "why do you still hate wizards so?"

"You see," he snarled, "but you do not understand." He turned and began to walk across the cavern. "Follow. I will make you understand. And then you will begin to pay."

The wolf on guard at the entrance to the wers' tunnels reclined, head on paws, half asleep. Young and complacent, sure the wer were the only predators in the valley, the attack took him by surprise. In the brief struggle, he flicked into his manshape and Jago slammed him behind the ear with his dagger hilt. As he fell, he became wolf again.

"We can't tie him," Jago pointed out, grabbing him by the forelegs and dragging him away. "If he changes, the rope will slice his hands off."

"Do you care?" Raulin asked, remembering the sounds of heavy feet and fists pounding against Crystal.

"He's just a kid . . ."

Raulin sighed. "Yeah, I guess."

They blocked the tunnel, hoping more to slow the guard than to stop him entirely.

"What if he doesn't try to follow and just goes for help."

"This is the only way into the valley from the mountain," Lord Death explained, eyeing the rock pile impatiently. "If he goes for help, it will take him some time and accomplish the same thing as far as we are concerned."

They advanced into the mountain, their eyes adapting in the darkness enough to pick out the darker shadows that marked companions. Moving as quietly as they could, Raulin followed Jago who followed Lord Death who made no noise at all.

Not a great deal of time had passed when Jago flattened against the rock. Raulin mirrored the move a second later. They'd come to a fork, one branch black and deserted, the other lit—although the torches burned so far apart they gave a twilight effect at best. No sounds came from the inhabited passage but given the freshness of the torches, wer could not be far.

Lord Death walked forward, passed the torch, and disappeared into the gloom.

The brothers waited. And waited.

Raulin wrinkled his nose against the overpowering odor of pine. He picked a crushed needle out of his mustache and fought the urge to sneeze. *Not many walking pine trees in these parts* he'd pointed out when Lord Death had suggested they hide their scent.

*And there are no mortals at all,* Lord Death had pointed out in turn. *The wer will react less to the smell of pine than the smell of meat.*

Meat. Raulin hadn't wanted to ask.

Jago started as Lord Death stepped out of air in front of him. The movement jarred his hand and he bit back a curse.

"I suggest you keep it quieter," Lord Death warned. "We are reaching the inhabited sections of the mountain and must go carefully. Come, this section is safe."

They passed the first torch and came to a small cave angling back into the rock. Faintly, over the smell of pine clotting their noses, came the musky scent of cat. The brothers froze.

Lord Death, no longer sensing them following, stopped, turned, and glared. "I said it was safe. They will not wake for some time, I have touched their dreams."

His mouth close to Raulin's ear, Jago repeated Lord Death's words.

As they moved on, Raulin shook his head. *Dreams touched by Death*, he thought. *Nice.*


The old wer led Crystal to a small cavern spilling soft lamplight into the tunnel; a higher level of technology than any she'd yet seen. Jason's wolfshape lay across the door, not on guard for his attention was turned within. When he caught their scent, he whirled, rising into manshape with the move. Gray paste covered his arrow wound.

"What are you doing here, wizard?" he growled.

"I brought her, Jason."

"Why?"

"To show her why we hate."

A whimper from the cavern and Jason's hands clenched into fists. His golden eyes filled with fury "Show herrrr." The last came out more growl than word as the great black wolf trembled with the effort not to attack.

Another whimper spun him back into the cavern.

"Go." The old wer pointed and Crystal stepped forward.

The cavern, the size of a large bedchamber, held a low table and a stool, rough shelves cut into the rock walls and filled with carvings of wer in all their shapes, and a large box bed, heaped high with furs. The lamp sat on the table, close by the bed. An ancient woman knelt by the box and crooned, soft and comforting, too low to be heard more than a few feet away. The young woman on the bed was obviously in labor.

"In the early months," the old wer said softly in Crystal's ear, "the mother's changing does no harm, but after the wolf is ready to be born she must stay in womanshape to carry the mortal half to term. If she changes, the child and usually the mother as well dies. This is the torment the wizards gave us; strong emotion sets off the change outside of our control. Surprise, anger . . ." He paused and the woman on the bed whimpered again as a contraction rippled her swollen belly. ". . . pain."

"Then why . . ."

"Our lives are long and in wolfshape the urge to mate is very strong. Although wer did not ask to be created, neither do wer wish to die. Do you wonder why we hate you?"

"The cats . . ."

"Are more indolent by nature so their time is a little less hard. They have three males for every female. We have five."

Even as Crystal recognized the singsong cadence of the crooning, she saw the trance it was meant to maintain fail.

"Jason?" The young woman's eyes tried to focus as the pain pulled her out of her hypnotic state.

He poked his nose into her hand and she clutched at it, then stroked the cheek of a worried young man.

To Crystal's wizard sight the fingers of the hand seemed shorter than they should and the russet hair grew too thickly across the back.

"No!" she cried aloud, heard an answering cry within, felt the shattering of a goddess bond, and began to move.

The Eldest of the Elder Races had a part in Crystal's making and with Milthra's strength she met Jason's charge and hurled him aside.

When she reached the bed she was already singing, throwing power into her voice regardless of what the cap would do. She rested one hand on the woman's head and the other on her stomach and sang her an easing of pain. The change, barely a heartbeat begun, stopped. The fingers grew longer, the hair less. Then Crystal went deeper, wizard and goddess acting as one, touched the core of the wer, found the flaw, and healed it.

The cry of a newborn blended for a moment with her song, then it continued alone.

When Crystal raised her head, wer jammed the door, drawn by the use of power.

"What . . ." The old wer spread his hands searching for the words.

Crystal swayed, the place where her power had been was an aching void. The fire, the repairing of herself, and now this; she had nothing more to give. "I healed her. She controls her changes now."

"How? The cap . . ."

"The cap works to prevent escape." Her head throbbed and the places beneath the cap felt bruised. It had reacted to the power, but it hadn't tried to stop her.

"Why?"

Crystal looked at the girl-child sucking lustily on her mother's breast, squirming as her father licked her clean. "I am not like other wizards," she told him, and tumbled into the void.


Lord Death stopped, head cocked as though he listened. "Lives. A number of them," he said suddenly, waving Jago toward one of the small caves. "Hide there until I return for you."

Jago pulled Raulin through the arched doorway, a small portion of his mind noting that it could never have been naturally carved. "Someone's coming," he hissed in explanation. "Hide."

They pressed up against the wall where the angle was too sharp for them to be seen from the passage, packs pushed hard into the rock. They heard the questioning cries of puzzled cats first, and then the soft thud of pads running on stone. The sounds grew louder, filled their ears, then faded.

Raulin relaxed his grip on his dagger, silently released the breath he'd been holding, and sagged against the wall. The wounds under his bandages ached. He stretched, trying to remain flexible but knowing he was stiffening up. He felt Jago still tensed beside him.

"What is it?" he leaned over to whisper.

A nervous smile glimmered briefly. "I started thinking about all the rock piled up above us."

Raulin bit back a laugh. "With all the things we have to worry about . . ." After the strange half-light of the tunnels his eyes adjusted quickly to the greater gloom of the cave. He saw the sweat sheen Jago's face and touched his brother's arm. "These mountains have stood for thousands of years, they'll last a few hours more."

Jago nodded. He plucked at the sling holding his injured hand immobile against his chest, and forced his thoughts away from the great weight of stone they moved under. *Crystal needs you. Think of Crystal.* From deep in his mind came a wisp of song. He sighed and the knots in his muscles eased.

"Hey." Raulin leaned over one of the shadowy bundles that almost filled the cave. "Tanned hides."

Intrigued, Jago moved beside him. The corner of hide felt butter soft between his fingers. "Trade goods?" he guessed.

Raulin shrugged. "Makes sense."

"The danger has passed. Come."

"He's back?" Raulin asked, reading Jago's reaction.

"Yeah." Jago tried to calm his pounding heart as he rose and turned. Lord Death stood in the entrance, the light from the passage igniting copper strands in his hair. He cast no shadow into the cave.

"Things have changed," said the Mother's son, his expression unreadable. "We must hurry."

"I can't decide; are you brave or stupid? I mean, considering that you expected the cap to fry your brains."

Crystal tried to focus. Browns and blues swam in front of her and finally arranged themselves into a young girl with wild chestnut curls and cornflower eyes. She didn't look much like one of the wer.

The girl grinned.

Pale greens swirled about in soothing patterns and Crystal realized where she was. "I'm not awake."

"Out cold," agreed the girl. "Your power is slowly rebuilding but for now, you're stuck here."

Crystal's stomach spasmed. "I'm starving."

"You surprised? You better hope they feed you soon or, even after you regain consciousness, you'll be mush for days." The girl spun about. "The others can't get this high in your head with no power to use, but I go where I want."

"Are you trying to get free?"

"Maybe. Maybe not."

"You're Eegri." she smiled, despite the hunger, as one long-lashed lid dropped in a saucy wink.

"Maybe. Maybe not."

"You weren't the one who . . ."

"Don't be ridiculous," Eegri snorted, "I don't do babies." Then she looked thoughtful. "Not after the initial gamble. No, you broke Sholah loose with that stunt, shattering the remaining matrix. Geta's still sulking, but the rest of us are rummaging about quite separately. So," she drew her legs up and sat cross-legged on nothing, "answer my question. Brave or stupid?"

Crystal considered it for a moment, weaving a strand of hair through her fingers. "I guess," she said at last, "you could say I took a chance."

Eegri stared at her, then burst into peals of laughter. "I like you, wizard!" Her smile fell on Crystal like a benediction and a delicious smell filled the air. "You got lucky. They're feeding you."

Her mouth flooding with saliva, Crystal felt herself pulled back to consciousness. "Did you do that?" she asked the fading goddess of chance.

Eegri's smile hung on an instant longer. "Maybe. Maybe not."


Crystal opened her eyes to see the ancient woman who had knelt by the birth bed. In age-twisted hands, she held a large clay bowl filled with heavy porridge. Her gray eyes, while not kind, were at least neutral.

"You saved my granddaughter and her child," she explained. "Eat."

She backed quickly away as Crystal grabbed up the bowl and began shoving handfuls of the warm food into her mouth. Then, recovering, the wer admonished sharply, "Eat slower. You'll choke." Male voices from the passage admonished her in turn, but she snarled them into silence as she left.

Crystal felt the rumble of moving rock, and ignored it, concentrating on the food. The porridge only just took the edge off her hunger, but its weight was a comfort in her stomach, and when the bowl had been licked clean she felt able to look around. She was in a small cave, about eight feet square, and a single torch was jammed into a crack by the door—by the blocked door. She got up, put her palms against the stone, and pushed.

As she expected, nothing happened. "I am going to get my strength back," she muttered, sitting back down, "and then I am leaving. Cap or no cap."

Lord Death sped down the passageway, Raulin and Jago keeping up with difficulty. "Soon we'll come to a short passage that leads to the central cavern. Cross the passage quickly and quietly. The wer meet to decide Crystal's fate."

"Meet where?" Raulin wanted to know when Jago had echoed the information.

"Where do you think," Lord Death said coldly without turning.

"In the central cavern," Jago translated.

"Wonderful," Raulin muttered and reached behind him for his crossbow.

The passage was indeed short. Crossing it, quickly and quietly as instructed, the brothers could clearly hear the debate going on in the cavern.

". . . healed Beth, we let her go."

"And who will heal my daughter when her time comes? No! We keep the wizard chained to do our bidding as her kind once kept us!"

"Wizards are the pain givers. Kill her!"

"She healed Beth!"

"But why?"

"Wizards can't be trusted, her reasons . . ."

The voices faded in the distance. They ran about a hundred meters along secondary passageways until Lord Death stopped before a roughly circular boulder pushed tight against the rock wall. "She's behind this."

Raulin shook his head, put his shoulder against the curve, and pushed. The boulder rocked. He bent and studied the floor. "Grooved," he said, standing. "Can't be moved from the inside, but the two of us should manage fine. Jago."

With a sound like half the mountain falling, the huge stone rolled out of the way.

Raulin straightened up and took a deep breath through gritted teeth. He waited until the pain smoothed out of his face, then ducked into the cave, his eyes half closed as though afraid of what he'd find.

Jago leaned a moment longer against the stone. *Lucky they're arguing too hard to hear that,* he thought, following his brother through the opening. *We won't get a chance like it again.*

Raulin had caught Crystal up in his arms, ignoring his injuries as he pressed her against his chest, and covered her face with kisses. "I knew you were alive. I knew it." But the shadows in his eyes said he'd had his doubts.

Crystal's fingers danced over every bit of Raulin she could reach.

He touched the cap and his expression hardened. "Is that what they hold you with?"

She drew his hand away, not allowing him to see how his tugging at the band sent slivers of pain into her head.

"We've got to get out of here," Jago said softly. She turned to face him then and he felt her joy, less demonstrative than her response to Raulin, but just as deep.

"You're both injured. I have no power . . ."

"It doesn't matter," Jago told her, wishing he could wipe the helplessness from her voice, "we have no time either. Come on."

The three of them stepped back out into the passageway and Crystal froze.

"You've come back."

Lord Death smiled hesitantly at her. "I couldn't leave you in the hands of your enemies."

"But . . ." She looked from Raulin to Jago.

"I brought them to you." When she stepped toward him, the smile vanished, and he turned away, feeling too exposed with Jago watching. "Now, I will take you out."

Crystal quickly hid the hurt but not before Jago saw it and vowed to have a word or two with the Mother's son.

They traveled as quickly as they could, tossing caution aside with all the wer accounted for in council. The air freshened, the light changed subtly, and at last they could see the silver of moonlight on snow.

"It's still the middle of the night," Crystal marveled, sagging against Raulin with a sigh. "It feels like it should be days later."

"Well, we've cut days off our time," Jago told them peering out into the night. "We've come out on the opposite side of the mountain."

Just then the faintest of howls drifted up along their trail.

"I think," said Raulin, propelling them out of the mountain, "you've been missed."

They fought their way down the icy slope, almost blinded by the sudden brightness. The howls grew louder. Four legs move much faster than two, especially with injuries and a long night beginning to take their toll.

"Leave me and save yourselves!" Crystal cried as a sharp edge cut into her bootless feet. She stumbled and fell to her knees.

"None of that," Raulin snapped, pulling her up. "We stay together, all of us."

As they ran, his arm tight about her waist, she left a bloody trail on the ice.

Jago tripped on a hidden branch and reached out to steady himself on an oddly shaped outcropping. His fingers clutched at cloth.

"Gaaa . . ."

"Gently, mortal, I will not hurt you." The giant picked up Raulin and Crystal who had careened into an outstretched arm, and drew all three of them against the shelter of her body. "You are safe. There is no longer any need to hurry."

And then the wer were upon them.

# NINE

Crystal buried her face against the giant's warm side and refused to think about the wer howling around them. Her power had dropped to such a level that her bare feet actually throbbed with cold. Raulin and Jago were both wounded and she could do nothing for them. Hunger tied knots in her stomach. Her head hurt. One more thing and she'd break down and cry. She'd deal with the wer later.

Raulin enfolded Crystal protectively in his arms. The giant still held them loosely and he felt as if they'd reached a safe harbor. Let the wer slaver and growl, he was certain that the giant could take care of them.

Jago sagged and whimpered as his weight fell forward on the ruin of his hand. A gentle grip lifted him and settled him comfortably against a massive thigh and a soft touch along his back eased the pain. He saw his brother and Crystal safe against the giant's other side, thanked the Mother-creator for their good fortune, and relaxed.

The wer circled, two dozen wolves and half that number again of cats. They moved constantly, a seething wall of eyes and fangs gleaming in the moonlight, with here and there a pale flash of skin quickly clothed again in fur.

The giant sat patiently, held their prey, and waited.

Finally Eli padded out of the pack and shifted to his manshape.

"You have something that belongs to us, Elder," he called.

"Yes," she said, her slow, pleasant voice neither acknowledging the wer as a threat nor threatening them in turn, "I believe I do. You may come in and remove it from the wizard's head and we shall be on our way."

Eli looked puzzled, then he caught sight of the cap lying deeply purple against the silver of Crystal's hair. "Not that toy," he snarled. "The wizard."

"But she can't *belong* to you. One person can't own another. If I remember correctly, that's what your people cried out to the wizards who tried to own you."

"She is a wizard!" Eli almost screamed it. "The wizards kept us in torment. Created us so we would always exist in torment!" His emotions overcame him. He flowed back into wolfshape and raised his muzzle to the moon. The pack joined in.

The giant waited silently until the echoes of the howl finished bouncing back off the mountains, then said, "What you say is true, but as this wizard had nothing to do with that and is in fact younger than a number of you I fail to see your point."

Another wolf rose to two legs and growled, "We could take her."

"You could try," corrected the giant gently. "I wouldn't advise it." A quiet certainty radiated with the words, lapping over the wer, calming them. When most had stilled, she raised her voice, just a little. "I am taking these children to my camp. You may spend the night outside in the dark and the cold watching if you wish, but we will still be there in the morning. If you have anything else to say, you may say it then."

"We can't just let the wizard go," wailed a manshape of one of the cats.

"I *said,* we will be *there* in the morning."

He opened his mouth, closed it, snapped back to fur, and began vigorously washing a hind leg.

"Can you mortals walk?"

It took the brothers a second to realize that she was speaking to them. Raulin's chest burned with lines of fire, but he nodded. "Yes, I can."

"Me too," Jago straightened, taking elaborate care not to jar his hand. He was beginning to have fond memories of the mauling he'd taken from the brindle, at least he'd been out through most of that.

"Then follow in my footsteps," she said, standing and scooping a semiconscious Crystal up in her arms. "I will always take the easiest path. Don't worry," she added comfortingly, ignoring the wer who scrambled out of her way, "it isn't far."

They looked at each other, they looked at the wer—who appeared more confused than aggressive—and they did as they were told. Her huge footsteps were easy enough to follow, even in the uncertain moonlight. Jago estimated her height at close to twelve feet and at most only four of that was leg. As tall as she was, she actually looked taller sitting down.

*It isn't far* can be a dubious statement when uttered by a giant, but she led them only a short way down the mountain to where she'd set up her camp within a small copse of trees. In the center of the clearing a fire burned, and on the embers at the edge of the fire, just beginning to steam, sat a teapot.

Jago started. It looked like their teapot; but theirs had been left with the sleigh on the other side of the mountain. Except—his eyes bulged a bit—wasn't that their sleigh drawn up on the far side of the fire? And that shelter . . .

"Uh, Raulin . . ."

"Yeah. I see, I see."

The giant laid Crystal gently down on the sleigh, turned, saw the brothers' bewilderment, and smiled. "The breezes told me where to find your equipment, so I brought it with me when I came. Now," she squatted by the teapot and filled three enamel mugs, "drink this and shortly you may sleep."

Raulin stuck his nose over the mug she'd handed him, and sniffed. The painkiller from the emergency kit and something else. He took a cautious sip. Raspberries?

"Doesn't taste like goat-piss anymore," Jago muttered.

"No reason why it should," pointed out the giant, leaving Crystal, who after a number of mouthfuls was managing on her own. "I can do nothing for your hand," she told Jago sadly. "It is beyond my skill. But in the morning . . ."

He nodded. "Crystal can take care of it." That thought had kept him from screaming hysterics or black despair all night.

"But you," she advanced on Raulin, "you, I can soothe." She flipped open his coat and had the old bandages unwrapped before he had time for more than a single yelp. Clicking her tongue at the flaming red lines, she fished a flat metal container from a pocket, and spread the ointment it contained over the wounds. Even before she finished they looked less angry. She cocooned him in fresh linen, and pulled one of his spare shirts, warm and soft, over his head. Lifting the empty mugs from two sets of lax fingers, she pushed the brothers toward the shelter.

"The wizard will join you when she's had something to eat," she admonished as they hesitated. "Sleep."

"Well, I'm not going to argue with her," Raulin muttered, dropping to his knees and crawling inside.

Jago half turned, gave a small bow in the giant's direction, and followed.

"Now," she loomed over Crystal, "first we will remove this ugly piece of work." Her large hands circled the cap and she added, "I'm sorry, child, but this may hurt." Then she pulled.

Crystal's back arched and she tried not to cry out as, with a crack that seemed to shatter her skull, the band broke. Panting, she collapsed back on the sleigh as the giant methodically snapped the polished amethyst into tiny pieces. "Please," she said, when she thought she could control her voice, "I need food."

"Yes, of course you do." The giant placed a large biscuit in Crystal's hand.

Crystal took a tentative bite, sighed, and crammed the rest into her mouth. When she finished swallowing, the giant handed her another.

"I haven't had these since the centaurs," she said through a mouthful of crumbs. The taste conjured up wild runs across the plains; the thunder of hooves pounding against the ground, the smells of centaur and upturned sod blending and becoming one, her hair blowing into a tangled cloud as she clung to a broad back and rode down the wind. She could feel strength seeping back. "I could never get enough of them."

"I think you've had enough at present," the giant chuckled. "Just one of those horse-cakes could keep your teachers fed for a whole day. They may, as the dwarves assert, be pompous and pedantic," she said, sliding her arms under the wizard and carrying her over to the shelter, "but they can cook."

Crystal yawned, suddenly more tired than she'd been since her battles with Kraydak. "Have you a name," she asked.

"I have a number of names. Today, I am Balaniki Sokoji."

"Sokoji," Crystal repeated, crawling inside. "Pretty. I like it." She snuggled down between the brothers and fell asleep with Raulin's arms about her and Jago's breath warm on the back of her neck.


"Good morning, Sokoji."

"Good morning, Crystal. How do you feel?"

"I have less power back than I expected to," she shrugged, "but I had more power to replace than I'm used to." She stretched and smiled. "I guess I feel fine."

"Good." Sokoji bent over the fire and stirred the porridge that bubbled and steamed. "Come and eat and you'll feel better still."

Crystal, her feet healed during the night, glided forward an inch above the snow. She reached out, caught a plume of woodsmoke rising lazily on the still morning air and from it formed herself new boots.

"It would be more practical," observed the giant, "to visit a cobbler."

"It would," Crystal agreed, accepting a huge portion of the oatmeal and nodding her thanks. "But by the time I realized that, there were no cobblers around." As she ate, she told the giant everything; the first time she'd heard the voices in her head, the healing of Jago, her fight with Lord Death when Zarsheiy nearly broke free, the demon, agreeing to accompany the brothers to Aryalan's tower, and the wer. She didn't know why, exactly, but she felt Sokoji should know.

Sokoji sat immobile while Crystal spoke. Much of the story, she knew. The goddesses, however, she would have to think on. *They* were an aspect even the centaurs had not considered.

"Crystal?"

She turned to see Raulin crawling out of the shelter, his bandages brilliant white in the morning sun.

When he spotted her and saw that she was all right, his worried expression vanished. "I woke up and you weren't there . . ." he said, spreading his hands. He reached back inside for more clothing, but Crystal stopped him before he could put it on.

"Wait." she said, wrapping warmth about him. "I want to look at your chest."

"It doesn't even hurt anymore." Raulin began, going to her side. He noticed the giant sitting motionless on the other side of the fire. "Is she okay?"

"She's fine," Crystal assured him, undoing the dressing. "Her name is Sokoji and she's thinking. Lift your arms."

He did. "She looks like she froze during the night."

"The centaurs once took me to visit a giant. She sat like that the entire two days we stayed. Apparently she'd been thinking for almost six years."

"What about?"

"No one knew."

The eight parallel lines on Raulin's chest no longer looked dangerous. Although the cuts themselves had not healed, the flesh around them appeared healthy and firm. Crystal set her fingertips just under the collarbone where they began and, humming softly, traced each line. The wounds glowed briefly green and vanished. Then her hands moved a little lower.

"Crystal! We're not alone!"

"Prude."

"Whoops! Excuse me if I'm interrupting."

Raulin flushed deep red and pulled the heavy undershirt, still clutched in one fist, over his head.

Jago tossed him a shirt and sweater, grinning broadly. "I noticed you hadn't got dressed this morning. Guess now I know why."

"You don't know anything, you little . . ." Raulin stopped in mid diatribe, his eyes widening. "Your hand!"

Both Jago's hands were whole.

"That's two I owe you," he said softly to Crystal, his eyes bright with emotion. "Thank you."

*I have less power, than I expected to.* And she had no memory of healing Jago. As it healed her when she needed it, whether she directed it or not, her power had also healed him, using the life-bond between them.

"Come and eat," she said, suddenly unsure of what this closeness would demand of her. "Power alone can only do so much."

As the brothers ate under Sokoji's unwinking stare—Jago having been reassured as Raulin had been—Crystal spotted movement in the trees and went thankfully to meet it.

Raulin rose in protest but Jago dragged him back, mouthing the words "Lord Death." He'd sensed Crystal's discomfort, knew it had something to do with him and Raulin, and wished, not for the first time, that Lord Death had a more corporeal form. As much as he had grown to love the wizard, Jago suspected that her kind could never be happy with mere mortals.

They stood silently for a moment, Crystal gazing down at the branch in her hands and stroking the needles, and Lord Death staring off at nothing, then they both began to speak at once.

"Please, go ahead."

She hesitated but realized he would not speak until she did. "I missed you," she said at last. "What kept you away?"

"Would you have me sit at night and keep company with them?" Even to his own ears, he sounded bitter.

"Why not? You've sat with me in mortal company before."

*But I meant more to you than the company then,* he thought to himself. *Ironic, isn't it, that someday those two will die and be mine and you I can never have.* All he said aloud was, "No."

"Have I upset you somehow, I . . ."

Her distress at his refusal showed in both face and voice and while he cursed himself for hurting her, he also marveled that he could. "Two mortals, a giant, and a wizard make a crowded campsite." That to lighten the *no*. And then he took a chance. "But if you want me, step away from the fire and call."

"And you'll come?"

"If you call me," he reiterated, meeting her eyes, wondering why he put himself in such a position, "I will always come." *What if she never called? What if she did?*

Crystal heard a deeper meaning beneath his words and knew she could probably force it out. But did she want to? Was it something that could survive being dragged out and totally revealed between them?

*Not yet*, murmured a voice.

*Idiot,* snapped another.

"You must do something about the wer," said Lord Death, not totally unaware of the turmoil he'd caused and pulling away from it for his own sake.

"What?" The sudden change of subject caught Crystal off balance.

"You cannot leave them as they are when you can heal them."

"The changes?"

"Yes. You can right a very great wrong." Young women and infants, faces feral and in great pain, flickered across his features.

She shook her head, hiding behind a curtain of silver hair until he wore his own face again.

"I am Death, Crystal, and often I seem cruel, but these have been robbed of even a chance at life. I am not as cruel as that. Too many come to me too young."

She thought of the power it would take to heal so many, how her shields would weaken. She thought of the goddesses breaking free. She opened her mouth to say she couldn't, looked at Lord Death and knew he expected her to say she would. Although he had seen the excesses of the ancient wizards, he had never, she realized suddenly, expected her to follow their path. *Free my people* were among the first words he'd ever said to her. She would not have *Heal the wer* be the last.

"I will heal them," she said and felt that his smile of approval well rewarded her for the risk.

\*       \*       \*

When Crystal returned to the campsite, Raulin and Jago sat nervously watching the giant who, as far as Crystal could see, hadn't moved.

"I have to speak to the wer," she said.

"Are you crazy?" asked Raulin, standing and striding over to her. He took hold of both her shoulders and gave her a little shake. "You barely escaped from them with your life. Go near them and they'll zap you with that rod again."

"They won't dare, not while Sokoji is with us."

"In case you hadn't noticed, Sokoji is not with us."

"I am only thinking, mortal, I am not dead."

Crystal suppressed a smile as Raulin paled. She gently patted his cheek and whispered. "Don't worry, they're used to it." Sliding out from under his hands, she crossed the camp until she stood at the giant's knee. "I need to speak with the pack. Will you come with me?"

Sokoji nodded. "I will."

Crystal raised her voice slightly, turning her head so she faced the trees beyond the giant. "Then I will speak with the pack, the entire pack, when the sun has moved a handspan in the sky. They will speak with me because they remember what I did for Beth. The Elder will see that we both, the pack and I, are no threat to each other."

A shadow separated itself from the shadows of the forest and moved off toward the mountain.

"I knew it," Raulin muttered, still a little rattled by the giant's sudden return to awareness. "I knew we were being watched."

One handspan of the sun later, Crystal stepped out of the trees and faced the wer, the giant on her right and the brothers on her left.

*"You can't leave us behind, Crystal," Jago had said quietly. And he was correct. She couldn't.*

The wolves had grouped in the center of the slope, the cats in their regular flanking position to each side. Of the sixty-two wer assembled, all but two walked on four legs. A young woman stood at the back of the pack, warmly dressed in leather and fur, holding a squirming bundle in her arms. It had to be Beth. A great black wolf wove about her legs, every now and then whining and sticking his nose in the bundle.

"You will not, of course, be using that," Sokoji called out.

Crystal followed her gaze and saw the amethyst rod between the forepaws of a wolf she thought she recognized as Eli.

"We will not use it if we are not attacked," Beth replied, settling the baby more securely in her arms, "but we must be able to defend ourselves, Elder."

Sokoji looked unconvinced. "I would prefer it with one less likely to use it."

Beth shrugged. "Eli is hunt-leader."

"It doesn't matter, Sokoji." Although she spoke to the giant, Crystal's voice carried up the mountain. "I'll give him no reason to think his people under attack."

"And if he uses it anyway, I'll rip his tail out and strangle him with it," Raulin muttered, not at all comfortable standing so exposed before the wer.

Crystal ignored him and continued. "I have only one thing to say. If you wish it, I will remove from the women the flaw of the ancient wizards and heal them all as I healed Beth, a gift they will pass on to their daughters."

The silence on the mountain was so complete the sun could almost be heard moving across the sky. For different reasons, Raulin and Jago were as shocked as the wer. Only Sokoji seemed unaffected.

Then one of the cats changed and a tawny-haired woman with eyes as green as Crystal's asked suspiciously, "Why only the women, wizard?"

"That is *my* flaw. I am sorry, but I have nothing in me to touch the men."

"No!" An old man crouched on the mountainside. "Each generation we grow more stable, some of the younger ones are able to walk with mortals and keep them unaware of what they are. We don't take anything from wizards!"

"Some? Two! Two! only!"

"Each generation we grow fewer!"

Bodies shifted out of wolf and cat all over the pack, ignoring the cold in the need for a voice.

"What good is it, if she cannot change the men?"

"It's women who die!" screamed a girl, barely in her teens. The male wolf beside her bared his teeth and growled. She slipped into wolfshape, rolled on her back and exposed her throat, but before he could close his teeth on the soft fur Jason threw himself between them and cuffed the male away.

"She's right," Jason snarled, taking on his manshape but looking no less furious, "it is the women who die. This is their choice. Not ours."

"But what of us," whined the male, shifting only long enough to form the words and not rising off his belly.

"It is too soon to tell, but I think," Jason looked back at Beth and his features softened as he met her smile, "when the women have control, it will help us remain calm."

"And what do you want for this great gift, wizard?" Eli stood, the rod dangling from his fingers.

Crystal's face hardened.

"I want you to ask me. Come to the camp when you've reached a decision."

Then she turned on her heel and headed back into the trees.

The brothers held their peace until they reached the camp but only just.

"Crystal, you are out of your mind! They almost killed you and you want to help them?" Raulin stomped about, one hand twisting at his mustache, the other waving in the air. "Put yourself at risk for *them?*"

"*They* are women and children, Raulin." She explained about the random changes and what that meant to childbirth. Her shoulders squared. "I can't allow such suffering to continue when I could banish it."

"And if the goddesses break free while your power is elsewhere?" Jago asked quietly.

"Sholah, I know, is with me in this."

*We cannot leave them as they are,* agreed the goddess, although only Crystal could hear her.

"And the rest'll shatter you into nothing!" added Raulin, still driven to stomp around the clearing by the force of his emotions.

"I'll take that chance."

"No." Lord Death's quiet tone carried a finality just bordering on the melodramatic.

"Listen, Crystal," Raulin began. Sokoji laid a massive hand on his shoulder.

"Gently, mortal, let the Mother's son have his say. He seems to agree with you."

"What? Is he here?" Raulin glared up at the giant. "And you can see him too? Oh, great." He threw himself down on the sleigh beside his brother. "Well, maybe he can talk her out of sacrificing herself."

"Maybe he can," Jago murmured, watching Crystal, watching Lord Death.

"I didn't realize what I asked of you," Lord Death told her, his eyes locked on her face.

"I'm ashamed you had to ask." Crystal flushed. "For all my talk, I am more like the ancient wizards than I suspected."

"You needn't do this to prove yourself to me."

She smiled. "I'm not. I'm proving myself to me."

He nodded slowly and she saw he understood. Something blazed for a moment in his eyes, something that caused her heart to pound and then both it and Lord Death were gone.

Raulin got to his feet and Jago, knowing his brother was neither as brash nor as insensitive as he pretended, wondered what he would say, even having heard only Crystal's side of that conversation.

But, concern the single emotion in his voice, Raulin only said, "Can't it wait? Just until you get the goddesses under control?"

"And if I never do? Should I let more innocents die because I'm afraid to take a risk?" She cupped her hands, letting them fill with sunlight, then wove a garland out of glowing golden strands. With a disdainful toss of her head, she let it dissolve. "Do I spend the rest of my life using only enough power to do pretty tricks? I am the only one who can help them. They need me."

"We need you, Crystal."

"No," she corrected gently, "you want me and as wondrous as that is, it isn't the same thing. If I turn my back on the wer, I am no better than the wizards who created them, denying the responsibility of my power."

He lifted her hand to his lips. "Then I will stand with you and do what I can to help."

Jago rose and took her other hand between both of his. "I also," he told her.

Crystal's lower lip trembled and she blinked rapidly.

"Idiot," Raulin said tenderly, and drew her into his arms.

*The centaurs wrought better than they will ever believe,* Sokoji thought. *And I hope I am there when this wizard-child comes to believe it herself.*

Later that day, while Crystal and the giant were deep in discussion, Jago went to his brother and demanded an explanation.

Raulin looked up from the harness he mended—Crystal's method of releasing the buckles had turned them into slag—and raised both brows. "An explanation of what?" he asked.

"Don't give me that, brother, you've never been good at hiding what you feel. Why no response to Crystal's conversation with Lord Death?"

"I gave her the only response I had."

Jago snorted.

Raulin sighed. "Look, Jago, you're a complicated man, I'm not. I'm her lover and her friend, but I've never fooled myself that I'm her love. In a lot of ways, you're closer to her than I am." He shrugged and reached for his dagger. The metal wouldn't pry free, he'd have to cut the leather. "As for this morning, well, I don't see as it changes anything. I'll share her bed for as long as she'll have me and when it's over, I'll thank the Mother-creator that I knew her."

"I thought you loved her . . ."

"Of course I do. So do you. And she loves us both." He grinned and winked. "Although in different ways. But there's too much to her for just you and me. We couldn't hold her and we shouldn't try to. Close your mouth now, and pass me the repair kit."

Jago did as he was bid and then picked up the other harness. "I guess I underestimated you," he said, turning the straps over in his hands.

"I guess you did," Raulin agreed. "You forgot, I've got hidden depths." He looked smug. "It's why I always get the girls."

"They feel sorry for you," corrected Jago, ducking a wild backhand, and more relieved than he could say that when Crystal finally found her own heart she wouldn't be breaking Raulin's.

That evening, just before the sky grew dark enough for stars, the wer came with their answer. Only Beth, Jason, and their daughter actually entered the camp, but it didn't take wizard-sight to spot the rest out under the trees.

Her head high, Beth ignored everyone but Crystal. She walked across the clearing as if she owned it. The baby rode in a sling across her chest and she kept one arm curled protectively around it. The other arm hung by her side, hand resting on Jason's head. She stopped in front of the wizard and gray eyes looked fearlessly into green.

Raulin stepped up to stand behind Crystal's right shoulder, facing the great black wolf.

Jason growled.

Raulin growled back.

From that moment on, they ignored each other.

"Have you come to a decision?" Crystal asked, trying desperately not to laugh.

"We have." Beth's mouth twitched as well. She took a deep breath to steady herself, during which time Crystal also gained control. "Will you heal us, wizard?" she asked simply.

Crystal nodded. "I will."

"There are three other packs . . ."

"Them too."

"They can be here in a quartermoon."

"Then in a quartermoon, no female wer will be at the mercy of the changes again. I will heal all of you then."

The sling wriggled and a tiny fist fell free to flail in the air, turning to a tiny paw as it waved.

"Get down, Jason," Beth admonished as his nose got in her way. She tucked the arm in safely, and looked back to Crystal. "Thank you," she said. *For my life and my daughter's, not what you may, or may not, do in a quartermoon.* Then she turned and they walked away from the camp.

During the week of waiting, Crystal spent a lot of time with Sokoji. The giant's presence calmed the goddesses, lessening the constant struggle to keep them confined. They discussed the healing and once Crystal went into the trees and told the startled sentry she needed to talk with a woman who knew how wer children learned to change.

Beth's grandmother answered the summons, her womanshape so wrapped in leather and fur she could barely walk. She eased herself down by the fire and accepted the offered mug of tea.

"Yes, it'd be damned uncomfortable to change, dressed like this," she said in answer to Crystal's startled expression, "but at my age emotions know their place." Her face creased as she thought of two babies born dead. "Now it no longer matters, I change when I want. You got any honey for this tea?"

"I'm sorry," Jago told her, "we're out."

"I'm sorry too. Tea without honey is an abomination." She sipped, made a face, and decided the warmth made up for the taste. "You wanted to know how the children change?"

As Crystal had suspected, the random changes were necessary in the young, giving the parents a way to teach with stimuli, a sudden cuff snapping the child into the desired form. Only with the female's first heat, did it become dangerous.

Raulin and Jago occupied themselves with butchering a young buck Eli and his hunters dragged into the camp.

"We don't want you hunting on our land," the wer snarled, "and anything you intend to waste, return to us."

"Very gracious," muttered Raulin.

"Very," Jago agreed.

But they were careful to return what they couldn't use to the pack. The weather held, cold and clear, and the quartermoon passed.

Crystal stood, silver and ivory in the moonlight, surrounded by wer. Of the three hundred gathered, less than one hundred were female; Beth and Jason's daughter the only child.

"Is this all of you?" she asked, when they had settled into place and the only movement was the slap of tails on snow.

"No." A young woman stood shivering in the cold. "My sister has reached the time of no changes and could not travel." She looked as though she wanted to add something, then shook her head and flowed back into wolfshape.

*So few,* Crystal thought sadly. If only she had done this sooner. If only they had come to her, asked for her help—but they were too blinded by hate to consider it. As far as the wer were concerned, the wizards were the pain givers and her defeat of Kraydak did not erase the fact that she was a wizard. She sighed, grieving for all the lost ones, then reached for her power and began to sing. Her hair fanned out around her, the moonlight dancing down each strand.

The wer pricked up their ears and waited.

Crystal's eyes began to glow a deep summer's green as she poured power into her voice. She felt Sholah join her, merge with her, and the song changed as the goddess' wisdom gave it form. As it spread, radiating outward, Crystal spread herself with it, becoming a part of the power, becoming, in a way, both the singer and the song.

For an instant, the females listening heard not with their ears but with their hearts, and during that instant Crystal's power touched them and remade the fatal flaw.

The power built until the air thrummed with it and still Crystal sang.

The song changed again. Crystal began to reach. *All* the females of the wer had been her promise, not all but one.

The wer were forced to avert their eyes, so brightly did she reflect the moonlight.

From the sister, she picked up the blood tie and followed it back over the mountains. Back. Back. Her power stretched, thinned; she began to pull from the barriers. There! The thought patterns of the wer were unmistakable. She touched the woman gently. The barriers wavered. She could feel Zarsheiy waiting for them to fall.

The woman started, perhaps sensing the wizard's touch, and the change began.

Crystal stopped the change, held it, and reached for power to complete the healing.

The barriers fell.

*FREE!* Zarsheiy surged forward.

And slammed into a wall of darkness.

*The wer are mine.* Nashawryn's cold voice filled Crystal's head, cutting through Zarsheiy's screams of frustration. *Feared by mortals, hunters in the night; I give them my protection. Finish what you have begun, wizard, I stand by you.*

Crystal reached again for power and found, even still linked with Sholah, that no power remained for her to tap, it was all tied up in the other goddesses. The other goddesses . . .

Keeping a careful hold on the change, Crystal slid into the woman's mind searching for the love she held for the child she carried.

*Clever,* murmured Avreen, and gave up the portion of power she controlled.

The song finished.

Crystal let her body pull her home.

# TEN

From where Lord Death stood, the figures grouped around the sleigh were tiny. Even Sokoji appeared no more than two or three inches high. He watched the giant reach down and lift the sleigh over a rocky ledge and frowned. She was the reason he watched from so far away. Unlike Crystal and the mortal, who could see him only if he wished it—although if one did, they both did—the Elder Races, so close in creation to the Mother, could see him whether he liked it or not. And he did not like it, for Sokoji always drew his presence to Crystals attention. Which meant he had to appear to her as well. . . .

Which meant they talked. . . .

And every conversation seemed to skirt dangerous topics; his feelings, her feelings, their feelings. And every conversation had Jago and the giant listening in, drawing conclusions, trying to bring into the open that which he preferred to have remain hidden.

So now he took the coward's way and watched from a distance.

Crystal laughed at something Jago said, and Lord Death ground his teeth. Once, he remembered with a bitter smile, he'd encouraged her to spend time with mortals. Had, in fact, given her Jago's life and with it Raulin's gratitude. And now, Jago gave her the companionship she used to share with him, and Raulin . . . He looked down at his hands. Raulin gave her the one thing he never could. Even Sokoji placed one more life between them; another living creature, to listen and to help.

"If it was just the two of us again," he murmured at the wizard's distant figure. He could tell her then. If when he finished speaking she didn't have another pair of arms to turn to that were not his nor ever could be.

He no longer wondered what madness had directed him when he said he would answer her call. He had named it the night she'd risked everything and healed the wer because he had asked her to.

"I am Death," he told a passing breeze. *And I am in love. And it hurts.* He sighed and shook his head. "This is your doing, Father," he added aloud. The one true son of the Mother had been fathered by Chaos but never throughout the millennia since his birth had he felt so chaotic.

In midafternoon, between one moment and the next, the world turned gray and almost all the light vanished. Close objects took on a sharp-edged clarity and distant ones disappeared into a merging of snow and sky. For an instant, everything fell completely still, waiting, then the wind came up in strong and random gusts that whipped Crystal's hair about and threatened to knock the mortals off their feet.

"There," Sokoji pointed. "The best I think we have time to find."

There, was a small triangular cut in the mountain, about ten feet deep and almost that across its open end. It offered protection on three sides from the coming storm.

"I think you're right," Raulin agreed, squinting against a sudden flurry of snow. "Let's move, people."

They secured the sleigh across the open end, for only by wizardry could they have fit it inside. By the time they'd wrestled up the shelter, anchoring it firmly within the mountain, the world had turned white and the air was solid with snow.

"Will you be all right out here?" Crystal yelled at Sokoji above the shriek of the wind.

"Of course I will, child." The giant folded her legs and settled herself comfortably against the rock wall. She pulled a hat out of her pocket and tugged it on. It looked like a bright red bird's nest over-turned on her head. "I shall sit here and think." Brushing the already accumulated snow off her lap, she linked her hands and stilled.

Crystal reached out and patted the giant's knee affectionately.

"Hey, come on!" Raulin grabbed Crystal's shoulders and spun her about. "Get inside before you get buried. Or lost."

"Lost?" They took the three steps across the cut, from the giant to the shelter, together. "How could I get lost?"

"Storms are tricky." He pushed her to her knees and held open the outer flap. "Get turned around and the next thing you know you wander off and freeze to death."

Crystal smiled, shook her head, and crawled inside, Raulin close behind. Before he ducked in, he noted that the sleigh, at the very edge of the windbreak provided by the mountain, had become a shapeless white blob and the giant, although as much out of the storm as possible, could barely be seen.

Because they'd brought in most of their gear, the usually snug shelter could only be described as cramped.

"How about cozy?" Crystal asked, when Raulin did just that after contorting himself around various bundles and into a sitting position.

Raulin only growled and tried to discover what was poking him in the back. Enough soft, silver light came from Crystal's hair for him to see her pulling their teapot out of a pack.

She tossed it in his lap. "Fill this with snow, would you, please."

He did, and even though he carefully snaked his arm out between the two flaps, a small eddy of snow found the opening and danced inside. Crystal clicked her tongue and danced it back out.

She slid against Jago, set the full teapot Raulin handed her in front of her on the floor, muttered something at it, and dumped a package of tea in the now boiling water.

"Should you be using your power like that?" asked Jago, twisting around and digging out the mugs.

Crystal ducked his elbow and caught the teapot before it could spill. "I can't see as it'll hurt. Zarsheiy seems happier when her aspect is being used; it's when she gets bored that she tries to make a run for it."

*And she hates being talked about as if she isn't there.*

*Then maybe she shouldn't listen,* Crystal responded to the goddess' complaint.

By rearranging a number of the packs, and intertwining two or three legs, they managed to achieve positions where they could both drink their tea and be reasonably happy doing it. Body heat had warmed the shelter to a satisfying temperature, so damp outer coats were removed and piled against the entrance as an added protection from drafts. Crystal had muted the sound of the storm and, although an occasional gust shook the felt and canvas walls, in their island of comfort and safety, it had become vaguely unreal.

They ate a small meal—more for something to do than from hunger.

"We need more room," groused Raulin as they finished, stretching out long legs and almost kicking Jago in the stomach.

*You'd have more room if you'd lie down,* Avreen suggested. *And more still if you . . .*

*Shut up, Avreen!* But she passed on the suggestion, minus the corollary, to the brothers.

Raulin added the corollary on his own and, with a deep sigh, Jago offered to go sit in the storm until they finished.

Crystal smacked them both.

The amount of squirming necessary to spread out the bedrolls with three adults taking up the space where the bedrolls had to go was impressive but, with only a minor bit of wizardry, they were finally spread.

"I don't know about the rest of you," panted Jago, pulling off his jacket and folding it into a pillow, "but that exhausted me." He collapsed backward, then bounced up again quickly, apologizing for nearly crushing Crystal's elbow.

She only smiled and snuggled her back against Raulin's front, head pillowed on his forearm. Her eyes began to close. Jago lay down more carefully the second time, bending where necessary to fit. Because of the packs, the three of them were close. Very close.

"I hate to disillusion you, Raulin," Jago said dryly, "but that's my wrist you're stroking."

Eventually—being trapped in a small shelter by a storm having limited their options—they all fell asleep, tangled in and around each other like puppies.

Raulin woke, and lay quietly in the darkness listening to Crystal and Jago breathe. He wondered if the storm still raged and decided it didn't matter one way or another—he *had* to go outside. Slowly and carefully, he slid out of Crystal's arms, unwinding a strand of silken hair from around his throat. She murmured in her sleep, but didn't wake. Easing his feet into his boots, he laced them loosely, then pulled his overcoat from the pile of fur by the door—the loops that closed his were cord, Jago's closed with leather—contorted himself into it and backed out into the night.

By both kicking the snow away and compacting it with his body, Raulin got free of the shelter, made sure both flaps had closed securely behind him, and stood. As his head rose above the level of the tent, the wind, snow-laden, struck him full in the face. The storm did, indeed, still rage. And it was cold. Raulin quickly fastened his coat and tried to bury his ears in the collar. He'd come out with neither hat nor mittens. Just to be on the safe side, he bent and tightened his boot laces. By the time he finished, his fingers were already growing stiff.

He plunged around the shelter and began to make his way the length of it to where the sleigh marked the edge of the cut. After the wizard-created warmth inside, the night air felt like knives in his lungs and he was positive the interior of his nose had frozen. Had the wind not been making such a noise, he was sure he'd be able to hear the nose hairs crackling.

"Lucky I'm not going to be out here long," he muttered, stumbling into a drift that reached his thighs. "Any sensible wizard," he added, plowing forward, "would have built her tower farther south."

His foot hit something hard and he tripped, falling against the object and burying his arms up to the elbows.

Righting himself, he shook the snow from his sleeves. "Well, it seems I've found the sleigh." He followed the angle to where the lower, front end butted up against rock, clambered over, and out of the cut.

A solid wall of snow slammed into him and, if not for the rock wall at his back, it would have swept him up and away. Eyes closed against the wind, Raulin kept one hand on the mountain and staggered five paces from the camp.

"Far enough," he decided, and did what he had to. When he finished, he reached out again to use the mountain as his guide. It seemed to have moved. He knew he hadn't. He stepped forward, arms outstretched, expecting to punch his hands into rock. Nothing. His hands were numb with cold, but he thought they should be able to feel a mountain. He took another step. Still nothing. He squinted in the direction he knew he had to go. All he could see was storm. All he could see in any direction was storm.

"Okay," he drew his hands up into his sleeves as far as they would go, "let's just stop and think about this for a moment." Closing his eyes again, for they certainly weren't any help, he took two deliberate steps backward. "Okay, now I turn to the left and go five paces which will take me back to the . . ." He bent and flailed around. Nothing. No sleigh.

"All right," he fought to keep his breathing steady; panic would help the storm, not him. "All right, I could've angled off a little. I turn left again and keep going straight. I'll eventually hit either the sleigh or the mountain."

Eventually didn't happen in six steps, or seven, or eight.

When he tried to open his eyes, he found the lashes had frozen.

"CRYSTAL!"

His scream only added to the wailing of the storm.

Crystal and Jago slept on.


"All right, all right, I'm coming!" Doan stomped out into the storm and stood solidly against the wind. The voice that had imperiously roused him out of sleep had quieted and the Chaos-born storm blocked his sight. His eyes glowed red and a shadowy figure became visible about five body lengths away. He stepped toward it and it moved back.

"Don't play your games with me, Mother's son," he grunted, for only Lord Death could walk unhindered through a blizzard, "I am not in the mood." But he followed anyway, curiosity growing with every step, until the shadow stopped beside a body half buried in the snow. Doan's brow furrowed. The body didn't seem to have a head. He grabbed it and flipped it over. The coat had been pulled up in a turtle attempt at warmth. The man within still lived and he seemed vaguely familiar. Doan searched his memory for a name.

Raulin. That was it. One of the mortals whom the breezes had reported traveling with Crystal. His mouth twitched as he remembered the stories the breezes told. Their descriptions appeared fairly accurate, although Doan couldn't understand the continuous jokes about the man's mustache. When it wasn't frozen solid it was probably quite respectable. But what was he doing out alone in the storm?

And why had Lord Death come to him?

The dwarf bent and hoisted Raulin up on his shoulders. The weight gave him no trouble, but he cursed a little at the length. *Ah well,* he thought, *it can't hurt bits of him to drag. Snow's soft.*

He paused before starting back and cocked his head at the shadow lingering at the edge of sight. "Why didn't you wake Crystal?" he asked.

The shadow that was Lord Death vanished into the storm.

Thinking deeply, Doan carried Raulin to safety.

Once inside, he stripped the heavy outer coat off his burden and checked exposed skin for frostbite. Ears, the end of the nose, a patch on each cheek, and fingertips, he decided, all of them superficial although the ears were a close thing. He tucked Raulin's hands up in his own armpits, and carefully began to warm the mortal's face. Only the ears still showed white when Raulin finally opened his eyes.

*I've been found!* was Raulin's first jubilant thought. *Who or what is that?* was the second. Thick red brown hair, eyes the same color deepset under heavy brows, flat cheekbones, a pronounced nose, and a mustache that made his own look scanty made up the face which bent over him, concern and irritation showing about equally.

"Mom?" he asked for lack of anything better to say.

Doan laughed.

Raulin noted, that the irritation disappeared with the laughter although the man remained ugly—he took another look—and short. "You're a dwarf."

"You have a problem with that?"

Raulin thought of Crystal, Sokoji, a mountain full of wer, and the one-sided conversations his brother had with Lord Death. "No."

"Good. Name's Doan. You're Raulin. Can you sit?"

"I think so." He did and got his first good look around. Blocks of snow arched up over his head, high enough for the dwarf to stand straight. He lay on a low platform; made, he realized, of furs thrown over snow not cut away to form the walls and ceiling. A small camp-stove, much like his and Jago's, burned and kept the place, if not warm, at least comfortable. "Where am I? What is this?"

"Snowhouse," Doan explained, busy at his pack. "I built it when I sensed the storm coming."

"You built this?"

"You think it grew here?" He turned and handed Raulin a small stone flask. "Here, take a sip of this and you'll feel more the thing."

Raulin looked at it and decided it was the kind of container that could hold only one liquid.

"Ah, alcohol and frostbite don't mix."

"You arguing with me, mortal?"

No, Raulin decided, he wasn't. He accepted the flask, pulled free the stopper, and took a cautious sip. The top of his head blew off. Or at least it *felt* like the top of his head blew off. He swallowed again. Someone wrote a name in fire along his spine. The third mouthful turned to edged steel in his throat and cut all the way down. He returned the flask.

"Thank you," he said, surprised at how normal his voice sounded. "I feel much better now." And he probably would, the moment the world stopped bouncing. He definitely no longer felt cold.

Doan nodded, took a healthy swallow himself and stowed the flask away. "Centaurs brew it. They get a few snorts of this stuff in them and they become almost bearable. Now," he shoved his hands behind his belt and rocked back on his heels, "what in Chaos were you doing out in that weather?"

"I was writing my name in the snow."

Doan grimed. "About what I figured. Took one step too far and . . . You know, you're one damned lucky mortal."

"I know," Raulin agreed, shuddering. When he'd fallen that last time, he'd been sure he wouldn't be getting up again. His last thoughts, after he'd cursed the Chaos-born storm with every bit of profanity he knew, had been equally of Crystal and Jago; his one consolation that they would probably find consolation in each other.

"You have any idea why the Mother's son came to me instead of Crystal when he wanted your ass pulled out of the storm?" The tone was only just conversational.

Raulin thought about it for a moment. "Yeah. I can hazard a guess."

"You gonna tell me? Remembering, of course, who pulled your ass out of the storm."

"It's not my story to tell."

"Bullshit. You're in this story up to your eyeballs. Tell."

"He's in love."

"The Mother's son in love? With Crystal?" Doan laughed. Suddenly, Lord Death's actions made sense. Of a sort. "And it confuses him."

"That'd be my guess. I don't imagine love is a usual emotion for Lord Death."

"Is this common knowledge?"

Raulin shrugged. "Everyone seems to know but Crystal." He paused and matched Doan's grin. "And possibly Lord Death."

"Why haven't you told her?"

He shrugged again. "Because I'm not sure how she feels about him and until I am, I'm not going to mess up how she feels about me."

Doan's eyes twinkled and he clapped Raulin on the shoulder,

knocking him into the wall. "I like you," he said, "you think like a dwarf. Come on, let's get you back before the wizard wakes up and brings the mountain down looking for you."

"Okay," Raulin slid to the edge of the platform and began pulling on his coat. "But I've no idea where back is."

"No matter. I do. Dwarves don't get lost. Ever." Doan shrugged into his own heavy fur. "When we get outside, keep both hands on my shoulders and I'll anchor you. We'll move fast enough so you won't freeze up again."

Raulin nodded, then reached out and touched Doan gently on the arm. "Thank you," he said.

Doan snorted. "Thank Crystal. I'd save a hundred mortals if it saved her one tear." His gaze grew distant and strangely sad. "And this doesn't make up for the one I couldn't save."

Outside Doan's snowhouse, the storm had eased a little and by the time they reached the camp, the wind had died. It continued to snow, but softly, the flakes large and gentle.

Raulin turned to thank the dwarf again, but Doan had disappeared and the line of footprints stretching back into the night was filling rapidly. Suddenly, he was exhausted and, barely able to raise his legs, he climbed over the sleigh. He floundered through the drifts to the shelter's entrance and tossing armloads of snow away, dropped to his knees and crawled inside, shedding the snowy overcoat like a skin.

The warm air smelled like sweat and wet fur and safety.

Shifting Crystal's legs, he made enough room to pull off his boots and then he stretched out at her side. She grumbled a little because he was cold, but he whispered reassurances in her ear and she sank back into a deeper sleep. Seconds later, holding Crystal close and with one hand cupped around his brother's shoulder, Raulin joined her.

When Raulin next opened his eyes, Crystal and Jago were discussing shoving snow down his pants to wake him. "Is it morning?" he muttered, rising up on his elbows.

"It is." Crystal bent forward and kissed him briskly. "Jago's been out and the storm's over."

Raulin fell back and tried to drag Crystal with him. When she didn't budge, he yawned instead. "How come Jago never has to get up in the night anymore?" he wondered, remembering his near disaster, what had caused it, and how long it had been since Jago had woken him up by crawling over him to get to the door.

Jago shrugged. "Strength of character?"

*In much the way it healed him, your power takes care of these things as he sleeps.* Sholah sounded amused.

"What?" the brothers asked in unison as Crystal suddenly grinned.

She passed on Sholah's explanation and Raulin threw up his hands.

"Figures. Some guys get all the luck." He meant to tell them then, about the storm and his rescue and Doan, but Jago threw him his coat and the story got lost in the scramble out of the shelter.

Sokoji looked like a massive snow drift, angled up against the mountain.

"Is she okay under there?" Jago reached out and pushed a mitten-print into the unbroken expanse of white.

"I think so. The Elder Races don't worry much about the weather."

Raulin opened his mouth to tell them of the shelter made from blocks of snow, but the emerald of Crystal's eyes grew momentarily brighter and she called the giant's name. In the flurry of Sokoji's awakening—the cut looked for a moment as if the storm had returned—the story got lost again.

During breakfast, he almost mentioned it, reminded of the centaurs' brew by a burning mouthful of too hot tea, but Jago asked him something about the day's route and the story wandered off once more.

He never did tell what happened. He never quite knew why.

"Saving the life of a mortal," Lord Death buried his face in his hands, "I don't believe I did that." In memory, he saw Crystal laughing with Raulin, Crystal holding Raulin, Crystal and Raulin. He groaned. He knew, had Raulin died, Crystal would not have blamed him. But he knew also that every time she looked at him afterward, she'd be looking for Raulin's face, torn between wanting and not wanting to see it on the face of Death.

If only he could touch her. If only he knew how she really felt. Sometimes it seemed her manner held more than friendship and sometimes it seemed not to hold even that.

"Why isn't it this complicated for mortals?" he wondered. He remembered the goddess of love blessing the couples who knelt before her altars, blithely interfering in the lives of her worshipers. Thousands of years ago that had been, and things had certainly not been as simple since. The Mother's son looked down at the shelter where Crystal lay wrapped in Raulin's arms. It would take Avreen to straighten out this tangle, he suspected.

Avreen.

Crystal carried the goddesses within her.

And wasn't sleep a small piece of the oblivion that came with Death?

He would have to be very careful he touched only the part of Crystal that was Avreen, but if he succeeded it would be worth the risk.

The ripe greens of summer swirled around him and Lord Death allowed himself a smile of triumph. He had managed to slip deep into Crystal's sleeping mind, safely past the guardians that would have alerted her to his presence.

"Avreen," he called softly, afraid that if he hesitated in what he'd come to do, he'd lose his nerve. "Avreen, I need you."

"No need to tell me *that,* Mother's son." A throaty chuckle thrummed in the air behind him. "Your yearning is a blazing beacon to me."

Lord Death turned, or perhaps the place turned around him, he couldn't be sure. His jaw dropped and he froze.

Avreen smiled a lazy sort of a smile and pushed silver hair back off her face with a long fingered ivory hand. Thickly lashed lids half closed over emerald eyes. "What did you expect?" she asked, her voice low and teasing. "I wear the face of love and each sees in me what they most desire."

It had taken Lord Death only a second to realize it wasn't Crystal before him, Avreen was more . . . more knowing than Crystal could ever be. Forcing himself to really look at the goddess, he saw physical differences as well. Avreen's features were Crystals ripened; fuller, lusher, inviting just by existing. He found the effect disturbing.

He wondered what, or who, Crystal saw when she looked on Avreen. He wondered, but he didn't ask.

"What is it you want from me, Mother's son?"

"I thought you knew." How could she not know, appearing as she had?

The goddess smiled again and even Lord Death felt the power of it. He gave thanks he had been created more than mortal for he doubted a mortal man could survive Avreen's personal attention.

"The rules state you must petition me. I cannot act without it," she told him. "Although I warn you before you speak," she added dryly, "my range of influence is not great at this time."

"I want . . ." He paused. If he said it, especially here, to her, he made it real. He gathered up his courage. "I want Crystal to love me." The words came out louder than he intended and barely under control.

"And you want me to . . ." Avreen prompted.

"Well, to make her. Love me."

"Are you sure that's what you want?"

"Of course." He tried to bury the confusion. "I'm here."

"Ah."

"You can, can't you?"

"Yes." The goddess' eyes crinkled at the corners and she looked as if she thought about a very pleasant secret. "But why should I?"

"Why?" Lord Death waved his hands about in short jerky motions. *Why?* "Well, because . . ." *Because I love her.* He knew that was the answer Avreen wanted. He couldn't say it. He could barely admit it to himself, he couldn't say it aloud. "Just because. Will you do it?"

"Will she do what?"

Again the voice behind him. Not throaty this time, not low and se-
ductive, but clear and sharp. Ringing. Like a silver bell struck with a
silver hammer. He didn't want to turn, but he did. They were, after all,
in her mind.

"Crystal." He carefully kept all emotion from his voice as he said
her name.

Crystal stood and stared at Lord Death, one hand working in the
loose fabric of her tunic front. He was no construct of her imagination,
no dream—not this time. She took a step toward him, brows drawn
down in puzzlement. "What are you doing here?"

He didn't have a reason he could tell her, so he remained silent.

"Will Avreen do what?"

He shook his head.

"How did you get here?" Crystal heard her voice rising. Why
wouldn't he speak? What did he hide?

"Death and sleep are cousins of a sort," he said, grateful for a question he could finally answer. He felt like a bug, pinned under the hurt
in Crystal's eyes. "As I am the one, I can work with the other."

"So you dropped in for a visit?"

He winced at the sarcasm and countered with a question of his
own. "How did you know I was here? I kept far away from the Crystal
part of you."

"You took a chance." She looked momentarily exasperated, but
not, he thought, at him. "You lost."

"Maybe." The disembodied voice teetered on the edge of laughter.
Maybe not.

Lord Death recognized the source of Crystal's exasperation. He
had dealt with the goddess of chance in the past. "Lady Eegri." He inclined his head. "Why have you interfered?"

"Have I interfered?" She popped into sight and gave him a saucy
wink. "I thought I helped. *She* says you lost the toss, not me." Then
only her giggle remained.

For an instant the wizard and the Mother's son were in complete
accord as they exchanged a puzzled glance and shook their heads.

Mortals had formed the other goddesses out of aspects of the Mother's creation but Eegri, they had called out of themselves.

"So, Crystal, shall I leave you two alone to talk?"

Avreen's words brought Crystal's anger rushing back. She'd trusted Lord Death, had thought him her friend; yet he snuck into her mind like a thief and refused to explain his presence when caught. Friends didn't act like that. What could he be doing? Her head went up and her eyes began to glow.

"I am no more susceptible to your power than you are to mine, wizard." Lord Death began to grow angry as well. How dare she think she had to force him. How dare she try!

The glow faded but the eyes remained hard. "Then why are you here?"

"Can't you trust me?"

Had he spoken more gently Crystal would have responded differently, she knew, because she did trust him. But it sounded like a challenge and she would not be challenged when he was in the wrong.

"The last who so snuck under my defenses was Kraydak."

"Do you compare me to him, then?"

"I do not. Your actions speak for themselves."

That hurt. More so, Lord Death admitted, because it was true. He had done pretty much exactly what Kraydak had done. For other reasons, perhaps, but that could be no excuse. *What am I doing here?* he asked himself, suddenly aghast at what he had been about to do.

"Crystal, I . . ."

"No." Her voice threatened to break and she got it firmly back under control. How could he? "No excuses."

"If you'd only listen . . ."

"Oh, so that's it, you don't think I listen to you." Guilt sharpened her voice; she hadn't been listening to him. As soon as Raulin and Jago had come into her life, she'd all but abandoned the friendship with Lord Death and the realization she could do such a thing twisted like a knife. "You think I should just drop everything and come to your beck and call?"

"My beck and call? When have I ever called you?" Lord Death began to grow angry again. It was easiest. *If I called,* asked his heart, too terrified of the answer to trust the words to his mouth, *would you come?*

Crystal responded to his anger. Of all the emotions beating at her, anger, at least, she understood. "What are you doing in my mind?" And her hair swirled forward to hide the question in her eyes. *Why haven't you ever called me?* She'd needed him so much in the past, but he'd never once shown he needed her.

"I am Death!" It was the last cry of a drowning man. "I go where I choose."

"Tell me why you sought out Avreen!"

"Why should I?"

"Because I . . ."

"What?" He made it a taunt.

"Because I said so!" Crystal almost screamed it.

"Hah!"

Eyes blazing, she stepped forward, placed both hands against his chest and pushed.

Lord Death fell backward and stared up at her from where he lay. He could feel the pressure of her hands, her touch. He wet dry lips and watched her hand reach out again, the way a bird would watch a snake. She would not touch in anger this time, he could see that in her face. And he saw as well, a fear as great as his.

The warmth of her hand caressed his cheek and the hand itself would do so in an instant.

He panicked and threw himself from Crystal's mind.

Avreen's laughter followed his flight.

# INTERLUDE TWO

*After the Mother-creator had formed the world, and walked upon it, and given it life, and after she had shaped the Elder Races, Chaos came out of the void and lay with her and She bore him a son. Their son was Death and from that moment onward, all things created began to die.*

*So terrible was this aspect that Chaos had bestowed upon his son, it was easy to forget Death was also his Mother's child and that nothing died without contributing to life.*

"I hope you're still taking care of business while you're moping around, 'cause things'll sure be in a damned mess if you aren't."

"Go away, dwarf," Lord Death growled, without turning his head. "I want to be alone."

"Oh. Alone." Doan swung out of his pack and leaned it against the wind-scoured rock. Then he clambered up and sat beside the Mother's son. "Tough."

Lord Death sighed, considered going elsewhere—he had a world to choose from, after all—and stayed where he was. It just didn't seem worth the bother. He turned to face the dwarf, allowing the newly dead to parade across his face. Doan grunted—it might have been satisfaction, Lord Death neither knew nor cared—and he let his features fall back into those of the auburn-haired, amber-eyed young man.

They sat in silence for a while, staring into the purple distance.

They sat in silence for a while longer.

"All right!" Lord Death exclaimed at last, throwing up his hands, unable to stand it any more. "What do you want?"

"Me?" Doan shifted his sword so the scabbard strap didn't bind. "I don't want anything. No, I just thought that if you maybe needed to talk to someone . . ."

"I could talk to you?"

Red fires began to glow in Doan's eyes. "You got a problem with that?"

"You're a dwarf!"

"Yeah. So?"

Lord Death's voice got a little shrill as he pointed out the obvious. "You don't even *have* females!"

The red fires faded and Doan grinned. "Oh. Is that the problem." He scratched at the back of his neck and settled into a more comfortable position. "I spent a lot of time with mortals over the years and some women don't care how short a man is, long as everything works."

"But if you don't have female dwarves, how . . . I mean it can't be an urge natural to your kind." *And I can't believe I'm discussing this,* Lord Death added to himself.

"Well, it's kind of an acquired taste." Doan thought about it a minute. "Like eating pickled eggs." His grin broadened into a smile. "'Course, I can't recall any of my brothers having a fondness for pickled eggs either."

"Look, this is fascinating," Lord Death desperately wanted to cut off any reminiscences, he didn't think he could handle them, not in his current state of mind, "but I don't need to talk to anyone!"

"No? 'Course, saving mortals isn't exactly normal behavior for you . . ."

Lord Death whirled on him, lips drawn back. "What do *you* know about normal behavior for me?" he snarled.

Doan remained unimpressed by both the snarl and the implied threat. "You seem to forget, I was around long before the Mother-creator presented you to the world."

"And that gives you the right to judge me?"

"No. But it gives me some grounds for pointing out that you're acting like an ass."

And Doan sat alone on the rock. He smiled and leaned back, soaking up as much warmth as he could from the winter sun. His breathing began to deepen and his eyes began to close and at first he thought the soft voice belonged to a breeze. When he realized whose it was, spotting a bowed head from the corner of one eye, he allowed himself an inward—and smug—pat on the back, but showed no outward sign.

". . . but I guess I started to love her when she faced Kraydak in his own tower, knowing that if she lost not even I could take her from Kraydak's grip. Kraydak had a habit of holding on to my people; he drew power from the dead trapped in his walls and I can't bear to think of what he would have done to her. But she won and I asked the dragon to take her home. I remember that it asked me why, and I said I didn't know. I didn't, then. Or I wouldn't admit it.

"I began to watch her. Curiosity about this lastborn wizard, I thought at the time. Do you know what she went through trying to lift Kraydak's yoke from the Empire? People would run from her in fear, or fall on their faces in terror, or worse still, try to squirm their way into her favor so she would toss them scraps as Kraydak had done. They only saw the wizard, not the child who so desperately wanted to help. She wasn't even twenty when it began. Do you remember what it was like to be that young?"

"Huh? Me?"

Lord Death ignored the interruption and continued in the same quiet, almost singsong tone, but Doan, jolted out of somnolence by the question, saw that the angle of Death's cheek had softened and he looked barely out of his teens. "The young die as well as the old, so I know what it's like at that age. How everything cuts, how easy it is to take up the guilt of something you didn't do. Not even the shields the centaurs had given her could stop all the hurting."

"Shields?" Doan snorted, unable to contain himself. "What shields?"

"Duty and responsibility can be a shield as well as a shackle, dwarf. They've kept her from the path of the ancient ones and, for a while, they

were all that kept her sane. Crystal had been created for one purpose
and one purpose only, and no one gave a thought to how she'd feel
when that was finished, knowing the world held no place for her. Although I'd give anything to stop it, I'm not surprised she's being torn
apart. I'm surprised she's lasted so long.

"Anyway, after she defeated Kraydak, I spent a lot of time watching
her. And when I saw how lonely she'd become, I started talking to her,
getting to know her. I told myself that the mortal part of her heritage
made her my responsibility and so I kept my mind open for other mortals who were worthy of her." He gave a short bark of bitter laughter.
"And we can see how well that worked out." His voice grew melan-
choly. "We're unique, Crystal and I. We belong together. I love her so
much I can't think of anything else."

"So tell her."

"I can't. Not now."

"You're going to let a mortal stand in your way?"

"No, it's not that . . ."

Doan narrowed his eyes. Was the Mother's son blushing? "What
have you done?" he asked, trying not to smile.

Lord Death sat quietly for a moment then the words came out in a
rush. "I asked Avreen to make Crystal love me."

"And Crystal found out?"

"Yes."

"Hmm," Doan nodded his head slowly, "I can see how that might
put a sword through a relationship. Why didn't you start by asking
Avreen what Crystal's feelings were?"

"What?"

Doan sighed. "Read my lips, Mother's son: Crystal's feelings. Why
didn't you ask Avreen what they were?"

Lord Death was definitely blushing. "I didn't want to know," he
mumbled. "I wanted to be sure."

"I am somehow sadly disappointed," Doan remarked to the world
in general, "to find the Mother's son, a divine and immortal being,
acting like a mortal youth whose balls have just dropped."

"Well, I've never been in love before!"

"That's not much of an excuse."

"If you'd ever been in love . . ."

"I was in love once." The uneasy silence this time was Doan's as he remembered Milthra, the Lady of the Grove, and all the long years he'd guarded her child, because that was the only thing she could take from him. "And I suppose," he admitted at last, "it's led me to do some stupid things. But," he added, just in case Lord Death should get ideas, "nothing as stupid as that. Asked Avreen to make her love you, indeed. And am I to understand when Crystal discovered you mucking about in her head you didn't throw yourself on her mercy and declare your undying," Doan snorted, "as it were, love?"

"Not exactly. We fought."

"Brilliant."

"She started it!" Lord Death rested his fingers against his chest where the touch of Crystal's hands still burned. And she'd finished it as well. "What can I do?"

"Stop worrying about what she feels, and tell her what you feel."

"I can't."

"It's the only way to untie the knot you've got yourself in." Doan's voice was matter-of-fact, but not uncaring. "It's the only way to untie the knot you've got her in. Give her a chance."

Lord Death looked desperate. "I don't know how," he whispered, and vanished.

Doan shook his head, suddenly understanding. "No, you wouldn't, would you. You're Death and Death is a surety. There's nothing sure about love." He got to his feet and stretched the kinks out of his legs. Then he faced the place where Lord Death had been.

"You know how," he said, "but you're afraid."

And he thought he heard the breeze sob, "Yes."

# ELEVEN

*B*ut *why won't you tell me what he wanted?*
    *Because it's none of your concern.*
  *None of my concern? What are you talking about, you're a part of*
*ME!*

"Crystal, are you all right?" Raulin grabbed her arm as she stumbled and swung her around to face him. He gave her a little shake for her eyes were unfocused and she'd clearly not been watching the trail.

"Huh? Oh, sorry." Crystal freed enough of her attention from her argument with Avreen to smile sheepishly at Raulin. "I was just, well . . ."

"Talking to yourself?" he finished, maintaining his hold on her shoulders.

She winced a little at his choice of words, for despite what she'd just screamed at Avreen, she didn't consider the goddesses to be a part of her any longer, at least not a part of the *her* that mattered.

"Hey, is everything okay up there?" Jago called from his position at the back of the sleigh. He pushed his snow goggles up on his forehead and peered at Raulin, trying to read his expression. All morning he'd been getting the feeling that Crystal was upset and he hoped it wasn't about something Raulin had done. "Do you guys need to take a break?"

"Crystal?" Raulin asked softly.

"No," she shook her head and her hair made a dance of the motion. "I'm all right, really."

Raulin tightened his fingers for an instant, then let her go, half-turning to face his brother. "We're okay."

Jago looked openly skeptical.

Raulin sighed. "Crystal just lost sight of the trail and tripped."

"You sure?"

"What?" Raulin spread his arms. "You think I tripped her?"

"Wouldn't be the first time." Jago ducked the snowball Raulin lobbed at him and added in a loud aside to Sokoji, "Some guys will do anything to get a woman in their arms."

Sokoji looked interested. "Really?" she asked Raulin.

Raulin flushed a deep red and threw himself forward into the harness. "If we're not taking a break," he muttered, "let's go." He tried to ignore Jago explaining mortal relationships to the giant. Out of the corner of his eye he saw Crystal smile. He knew her hearing was better than his, so he assumed she was listening to his brother. He didn't see the smile freeze and her eyes grow distracted again.

*He wanted something to do with me, didn't he?*

*I'm not going to tell you.* Avreen's voice was irritatingly smug. *The Mother's son asked a boon of the goddess. I don't betray those confidences.*

*You'd betray anything that suited you,* Zarsheiy snorted.

*The wizard does have a point,* Tayja's voice, the voice of reason joined in. *You are, as much as any of us, a part of her.*

Avreen laughed. *Only because I choose to be.*

*Ha!*

*I could leave any time I wanted to.*

*HA!* Zarsheiy said again, louder.

*I stay because I choose to.*

*Maybe,* murmured a quiet voice. *Maybe not.*

*You know nothing.* But the words lacked their previous conviction.

*Stop it! All of you!* Crystal put power into the command and the quarreling goddesses fell silent, but behind the deepest barrier, darkness stirred.

*Careful, little wizard,* Nashawryn sounded amused. *Force our sister to tell you what she knows and you may have to face things you have no desire to.*

"Crystal, what is it?"

Raulin's anxious concern snapped her back to the surface. She took a deep breath and motioned for him to keep walking.

"It's nothing, really."

He looked into her eyes and nodded but wasn't reassured. "It's nothing now," he allowed, "but a moment ago you seemed terrified. What frightened you?"

Crystal's brow furrowed. What had frightened her? She wasn't sure so she gave him the easy answer, hoping he'd dig no further. "Nashawryn."

"Oh." He bent and dragged a protruding branch out of the snow, tossing it clear of the sleigh's path. "Oh," he said again.

"Don't worry," Crystal snagged his hand and brought it to her lips, "she can't get through the barriers." She paused, muttered something unintelligible, and pulled off his mitten.

Raulin laughed, his uneasiness pushed aside by the disgusted way she held the mitten between two fingers and then completely buried by the soft touch of her lips on the back of his hand.

She peered up at him through her lashes and he felt his heart begin to beat faster.

"What do you think you're doing?" he asked, mesmerized by the tip of her tongue as it made a circuit of her mouth.

"I'm using you to chase the bogie-goddess away."

He clutched at his chest with his free hand, and said, "I feel so cheap." With a sudden twist of his fingers, he had his harness undone.

Crystal's eyes widened as he unhooked hers as well and in practically the same motion scooped her up in his arms. She hurriedly adjusted her weight as his snowshoes sank a little deeper in the fine powder.

Moving as quickly as the snowshoes allowed, Raulin carried her off the trail, murmuring into her hair, "She's a pretty powerful goddess. It'll take more than a little hand kissing to chase her away."

"But you'll freeze," Crystal laughed, settling herself more comfortably.

Raulin kissed her on the nose. "You're a wizard, think of something."

"Hey!" Jago yelled. "Where do you two think you're going?"

"Never mind," Raulin called back, neither lessening his pace nor turning his head. "Start lunch."

"You could make better time," Sokoji observed as Raulin and Crystal disappeared behind a boulder, "if those two were not together on the harnesses."

"And if my brother could get a grip on his libido," Jago grumbled, pulling out the campstove and the teapot. But he wasn't really angry, for he could feel the easing of the tensions Crystal had been under all morning.

After lunch, Sokoji stood, stretched, and pointed almost due north, toward a mountain that looked as if its upper third had been sheared off. "That is the way you must go," she said, "if you wish to reach Aryalan's tower. Tonight we can be at the pass and tomorrow cross into her valley."

"Not that I'm saying you're wrong, Elder, but according to frogface's map, we should be heading for the highest peak in the range." Raulin came and stood beside the giant, waving his arm in the direction they'd been traveling. "And the highest mountain in the range is that one there."

"Yes," Sokoji agreed, "now it is. But the demon had not been to the tower for many years, not since before the Doom. The mountain you point to did not exist then. Aryalan drew it out of the earth to stop the dragon, and this mountain . . ." The giant sighed and shook her head as she gazed at the jutting angles of rock that still looked raw even after more than a thousand years. "We called it the Mighty One, and it became as you see it now during the battle."

"Are you sure?" Raulin sounded skeptical.

"Mortal, giants are never unsure. It is a skill we have. And besides, when last I went to the tower, that is the route I took."

"Yeah, a thousand years ago . . ."

Sokoji turned to face him. "No, six winters ago."

"You were at the tower six winters ago?" Jago moved to stand by Raulin and stared up at the giant. "Why didn't you tell us this before?"

"Didn't I?" Her forehead wrinkled as she recalled all the words she'd spoken to the brothers. "Oh. I didn't. How odd. Never mind, I shall tell you of it now." She waved a massive hand toward the sleigh. "Perhaps if we could travel while I speak . . . We have little enough daylight this far north to waste any and it will mean we need not hurry later on."

Raulin and Jago exchanged glances so identically put out that Sokoji smiled. "I have not been keeping knowledge from you. I was quite sure I'd told you."

"I thought you said giants were never unsure," Raulin reminded her.

"I did," Sokoji agreed placidly. "But I did not say we were never mistaken."

There was a long moment of silence, then Jago started to laugh. Raulin glowered for a moment more then, unable to keep the corners of his mouth from twitching back, joined him. Soon they were bent double and swiping at the tears leaking from their eyes.

Staring at them in fascination, Sokoji walked over to where Crystal leaned against the high back of the sleigh. "Are they hysterical?" she asked.

"No. They're mortals." Crystal smiled at the two men who were still laughing but were beginning to regain control. "They tend to be a bit extreme."

The giant cocked one eyebrow in the wizard's direction. "So I noticed this morning."

Crystal had the grace to blush.

When they moved out, the brothers wore the harnesses while Crystal followed behind, the positions shaking down with an even mix of teasing and threats between Raulin and Jago. Sokoji walked by the front of the sleigh where the mortals could hear her unassisted and where she could use her strength to ease the path.

Although Crystal could've heard a leaf fall back in the Sacred Grove in Ardhan, she missed the start of the giant's story absorbed in watching Raulin and Jago walk. They looked like a cross between bears and ducks in their heavy fur coats and snowshoes. She grinned and gave thanks she had no need for the awkward footgear—her feet sank only as far as she allowed them to—then gave her attention to Sokoji's words.

". . . and when the storm calmed, the winds told me that the door had been uncovered. I thought on it for some time . . ."

"One year or two?" Raulin asked, unable to help himself.

"Three. Mortals did not come that way, so I had no need to make a hasty decision. In the end, I admit curiosity alone drew me to the tower for watching would have been sufficient; there was no need to explore. Of old, the tower sat in the midst of a lake, perfectly round and created by Aryalan. Lilies bloomed on its surface, swans glided majestically about, and regardless of the season in the lands surrounding it, the lake remained in perpetual high summer. The tower appeared to be a summerhouse, in the old eastern style, very ornate but not overly large. It rested on an island as perfectly round as the lake. The summerhouse was merely the entrance way, the island itself was the tower."

As Sokoji spoke, her listeners saw the red tiled roofs curving over black lacquer walls, breathed deeply of the exotic flowers, heard the music that played softly from dawn to dusk.

"The Doom destroyed all that, of course, and eventually the wizard as well. Winter, so long denied, moved quickly in to cover both lake and island with ice and snow. When I came at last to view what the storm had uncovered, only memory told me such beauty had ever been."

Jago sighed and Raulin turned to look at him in surprise.

"You grew up in Kraydak's Empire, Jago. You know how evil the ancient wizards were. How can you be sorry Aryalan's tower got trashed?"

"Beauty is neither good nor evil, brother, it just is."

"Well, this was beauty no longer," Sokoji continued as Raulin sputtered. "The lilies, the swans, and the flowers had long since died and of the summerhouse only a single room remained whole. The residue of power echoed strongly and I felt it recognize me as an intruder."

"Trapped," Raulin declared, stepping on the edge of his own snow-shoe and almost tripping himself in his excitement.

"Yes," the giant agreed, reaching out a hand to steady him. "But as I said, only the residue of power remained and it was not enough to hold one of the Elder." Her voice took on a faint shading of pain. "Although it came closer than I care to remember. In the room's floor is a trapdoor and if you seek treasure you need go no farther, for it is made of ebony and ruby. Enough wealth to enjoy ease the rest of your days."

"What? In the gatehouse?" Raulin asked incredulously while Jago looked relieved.

"The ancient wizards were fond of gaudy display."

Crystal remembered the gold-lined room in Kraydak's tower and wondered what his halls had been like when he was at the height of his power.

"Sokoji," she called. "Did you not lift the door?"

"What difference does it make?" Jago broke in before Sokoji had a chance to answer, praying Crystal hadn't put ideas into Raulin's head. "We won't need to go into the tower itself."

Raulin, who had a pretty good idea of his brother's thoughts, caught Crystal's eye and winked. "I'm kind of curious myself," he said blandly. Jago whirled on him, mouth open to deliver a blistering lecture on irresponsibility, when he added, "Not that we'll be entering ourselves. Will we, Jago?"

Jago sputtered in his turn and Raulin punched him gently on the arm.

"Don't worry, little brother, I intend to get rich, not dead."

Sokoji shook her head. Mortals, it would take much thought to understand them, she decided. "Do not think the gatehouse is without dangers," she warned. "Less dangerous than the tower does not mean safe, but, yes, I lifted the door. Below it, a massive staircase spiraled down for a distance over twice my height. It, too, had been trapped but the ancient destruction had fortunately rendered all but one inoperative. That one . . ." She sighed and began again. "That one gave me a small amount of trouble, but in the end I overcame it."

"Why do I get the feeling we don't want to know what went on?"

Sokoji looked down at Raulin, her brown eyes serious. "It doesn't matter. I will tell you no more than I have." She chewed on the edge of her lip—something the others had never seen her do—made a visible effort to banish the memory, and continued. "At the bottom of the stairs there stood another door. I didn't open it although I had paid the price."

"Why not?" Jago asked gently.

"I couldn't pass," she said simply. "In both height and width, it had been built too small."

They traveled in silence after that; Raulin's thoughts on treasure and the battle that would come before he held it, Crystal's moving beyond the second door, and Jago wondering what could be so bad that the giant could not, would not, speak of it.

The next morning they got their first good look at the pass into Aryalan's valley.

"Forget it," Raulin declared emphatically. "There has to be another way."

"Not without going many miles. Another month of traveling perhaps. What's wrong with this path?"

"It's too . . ." Raulin waved his hands about and Jago finished it for him.

"High."

"Yes?"

Jago gripped Raulin's shoulder. "My brother," he explained, "hasn't much of a head for heights. Nor," he added, taking another look at the pass, "are either of us related to goats."

From where they stood they could see the ledge they had to follow dwindling into almost nothing as it curved around the mountain.

"Look, why don't we just follow the gorge," suggested Raulin. "It's going in the right direction. It's an easy walk. When it ends, *then* we can take to the ledge."

Sokoji shook her head. "The gorge ends in a cliff, thirty of your body lengths or more high. If you wish to enter the valley, this is the only way."

Crystal caught both Raulin's hands in hers. "It has to be wider than it appears," she said gently, "or Sokoji would not be able to use it." Her eyes began to glow and she allowed him to sink a little way into their emerald depths. "I would never let you fall." The glow dimmed.

He returned the pressure of her fingers and said, "My heart believes you; I'll see what I can do to convince my feet."

Working quickly, for Sokoji was vague about the length of the pass and none of them wanted to be caught on the ledge after dark, they stripped the sleigh of everything they could carry. Even considering the size of the packs, looming like great misshapen growths on the brother's backs, that seemed a distressingly small amount when compared to what remained on the sleigh.

"It's not as bad as it looks," Jago reassured Crystal after she pointed this out. He settled the rope holding the bedrolls into a more comfortable position on her shoulders. "We always figured we'd have to leave the sleigh at some point. With you and Sokoji helping out, we're taking more than we planned on."

"You planned on being without the shelter?" She shivered in sympathy, warming the fingers he held out to her—knots and lashings needed freedom from mittens.

"It's only for one night," Raulin reminded her. "The next night we'll be in the gatehouse—Sokoji promises it's safe—and the night after, we'll be back at the sleigh. Provided, of course, we haven't all dashed our brains out falling off the mountain."

"Land on your head, you'll bounce."

"I'd land on yours given half a chance."

Jago reached over and chucked him under the chin. "Glad to see you've regained your sunny disposition."

Raulin growled something uncomplimentary and shook his fist at the younger man, but Crystal saw the tightness leave his face for the first time since he'd seen the pass.

Slipping a small bag of oatmeal into her pocket—a pocket Jago was certain already held the teapot—Sokoji shook her head at their bickering and asked, "Are you ready then?"

"As ready as we'll ever be," Raulin sighed.

Crystal and Jago nodded.

The giant turned and led the way up the blasted slope of the Mighty One.

Great chunks of pinkish granite made a straight line impossible, so they wove a serpentine path around and over the destruction, often traveling at an angle where hands were needed as much as feet.

"I don't think," Raulin panted as they rested about halfway between the sleigh and the rock ledge they were aiming for, "I have ever been so tired. This pack weighs two hundred pounds."

"Old and out of shape," gasped Jago, pulling off his hat and fanning himself with the end of one braid. He let a mitten dangle from its string and scratched vigorously at his beard; sweat was running into it and it itched. Maybe it would've been a better idea to let Crystal remove it as she had Raulin's. . . .

"Are your legs sore?" Crystal asked, squatting beside Raulin and studying him with a worried frown. She laid a hand on his thigh and he covered it with one of his.

"Crystal, we've been walking up and down mountains for weeks now. My legs are like rock." He groaned without opening his eyes. "My back, however, is killing me. Thank you," he added as it suddenly stopped. "Now, if you could just transport us to the tower . . ."

"I could make your packs lighter."

"We discussed this already. You use your power for necessities only. Lightening our packs is no necessity." He heaved himself to his feet. His undershirt—living up to its name under four further layers of clothing plus the great fur overcoat—was soaking wet and sticking to his back. Drops of sweat trickled down his sides, and, adding a new sensation to the discomfort, a freezing wind kept trying to sneak into his sleeves, finding the smallest of spaces between mittens and cuffs. "On your feet, junior, we're wasting daylight."

Jago sighed, put his hat on, and tried to stand. The pack remained where it was and, because he was securely attached, so did Jago. "You could quit laughing and help," he pointed out when he'd stopped flailing.

Sokoji reached down and lifted him easily to his feet, her face grave. "Turtles," she said helpfully, "have much the same problem."

"Thank you." He glared at Raulin, daring him to say a word and put out a hand to steady himself. "Chaos!" The corner of granite he'd grabbed had sliced into his outer mitten, almost going through the heavy sheepskin. He studied the slash and then the rock. "That thing's got an edge like a knife." he marveled.

Raulin ran a cautious thumb along it and stuck the thumb in his mouth when it proved not to be cautious enough.

Jago grinned at him. "All right, don't take my word for it . . ." He glanced down as his mitt flared green, but an equal flare in Crystal's eyes decided him against commenting on the necessity of the power use.

"You'd think these edges would've worn smooth by now," Raulin said reflectively. "It's been a long time."

Sokoji's eyes lifted to the shattered peak. "The mountain remembers," she said softly.

"Are you saying this mountain thinks?" asked Raulin.

"It remembers. The mountains are the bones of the Mother."

"Why don't I find that reassuring?" he muttered as they began to climb again.

The ledge was wider than it appeared from the ground and for a little while it edged a slope not much steeper than the one they'd just come up.

Raulin kept his mind on his feet and his gaze firmly locked on Sokoji's broad back. He tried not to notice as the angle of the slope dropped away until the only word for it became cliff. He reminded himself that on level ground he had walked a path much narrower than the width they had here.

Sokoji stopped suddenly and he bumped against her.

"Give me the rope," she said.

Jago took the coil off his shoulder and passed it up to the giant who tied one end about her waist and handed the rest back to Raulin.

"Keep about my body length of slack between us," she instructed. "Then tie it securely and give it to your brother so he can do the same."

"Why so much slack?" Raulin asked, trying to keep his thoughts off all the possible reasons for the rope.

"If you fall, the slack gives those next to you time to anchor themselves." She caught the look on his face and patted his shoulder with a comforting but heavy hand. "You need not continue. At this point we can still easily turn and go back."

"At this point? Does that mean we can't turn later on?"

"Yes."

"I had to ask."

"Could be worse," Jago murmured behind him. "We could be in the snowshoes."

Raulin closed his eyes and leaned against the mountainside, noting absently as he did that it rose up as perpendicular on the right as it fell away on the other side. He heard his brother say they could turn back, that it didn't matter, but on the inside of his lids he saw a great door of ebony and ruby, wealth enough to buy them a secure place in the world. He sighed, opened his eyes, and finished tying the knot about his waist.

Jago took the offered rope without comment, knowing the battle Raulin must be fighting with himself in order to go on. He'd seen his brother shake when he'd had to lean out a third-story window. No words could make it easier, so he offered his silent support.

Crystal felt Raulin's fear, felt Nashawryn twitch in answer, and hoped that if anything happened she would not have to fight the dark goddess for Raulin's life.

"Remember," Sokoji told them when they were all securely tied, "the ledge holds me; you are in little danger."

*Little danger*, Raulin repeated to himself. *Not* no *danger. Little danger. Great.* He shuffled forward as the rope stretching back from the giant grew taut—shuffled, for if he picked up his feet he would be left for an instant precariously balanced on one leg. Inside his mittens, his hands grew clammy. His heart thumped so hard he felt sure the vibrations against his ribs would throw him off the precipice. He tried holding his breath. It didn't help. His focus narrowed to the rope tied around Sokoji's waist. The knot bobbed as she walked and it distracted him enough so that he could keep moving.

Gradually, he began to relax. The combination of the slow and steady pace and Sokoji's bulk—his mind simply refused to acknowledge that the giant could fall—calmed him. Then Sokoji turned to face the mountain, her hands flat against the rock, her feet sliding sideways.

"Hey!" Raulin stopped and as Sokoji felt it through the rope she looked back over her shoulder at him. "What are you doing?"

"There is a narrow place here," she explained. "We must pass carefully. Do as I do. The path will not become less wide than your feet are long."

*Less wide than your feet are long? What kind of a measurement is that?* Raulin wondered. And he looked down.

Down.

A long way down.

He swayed. His head felt heavy, almost more than his neck could support. The world began to tilt.

Suddenly his cheek pressed hard against rock. His arms were outstretched, his fingers trying to dig into the granite. His toes attempted to root. He didn't remember turning. He couldn't make the world stop sliding back and forth. He needed to throw up. His pack. His heavy, heavy pack. It was out over the edge. It would pull him down. He couldn't catch his breath. He couldn't remember how to breathe.

"Raulin!"

Jago's voice slapped against him.

"Take deep breaths. Slow down. Make it last. That's it. In. And out. In. And out."

The world began to still.

"In. And out."

"I'm okay," he managed. The rock near his mouth was wet with drool. His muscles felt like porridge and that weakness brought back the terror. He couldn't stand. He wasn't strong enough to hold his own weight. Before the world began to spin again, Raulin ground his cheek into the rough face of the mountain and drove the fear away with pain.

"I'm okay," he repeated after a moment, and this time he was. "At least, I think this is as good as it gets."

"Can you walk?" Sokoji asked softly.

The laugh he dredged up went beyond strained to just this side of hysteria. "If it'd get me off this mountain I'd dance."

He heard the smile in Sokoji's voice.

"I don't think that will be necessary. If you could just slide your left foot. . . . Yes. Now, the right. . . ."

One sliding step at a time, they crossed into Aryalan's valley.

Safely away from the edge, Raulin took Crystal into his arms and buried his face in her hair.

She held him tightly and whispered. "I wanted to help . . ."

"Why didn't you?"

"Tayja said you needed to make it across on your power, not mine."

He could still feel the fear knotting the muscles of his back. "Yeah," he said, after a moment, "she could be right."

Doan stayed close to the Mighty One as he stomped up into the gully. Unless they looked straight down, the tiny figures on the ledge would not be able to spot him.

At the north end, where a sheer cliff rose up two hundred feet or more, he scanned the rock closely then ran his fingers along a crack invisible to any eye but a dwarf's. A perfectly rectangular door swung open, folding back into the mountain.

Muttering about the dust, he stepped inside and pulled the door shut behind him. His eyes were red lights in the darkness and when they'd adjusted enough he started up the stairs. The watchtower had been destroyed with the mountain, but the lower gate into the valley should still be clear. Dwarves built to last.

*        *        *

Even destroyed by the Wizards' Doom, and with all its majesty hidden under snow and ice, the remains of Aryalan's tower drew the eye. Bits and pieces of half buried buildings jutted up in the center of a perfect circle, the shore of the lake still clearly delineated by a subtle difference in the shading of the snow. From where they stood, distance blurred detail, but the sense of what had once been, the power, the evil, the beauty, was strong.

"I think we have enough light left to get to the lake," Raulin noted, squinting west. "It'll give us less distance to cover tomorrow and we can hit the tower still fresh."

"Sokoji nodded. That would be best."

"There's not much cover down there," Crystal pointed out, scanning the valley with her wizard-sight. She sighed and shifted her gaze to the immediate area. The shattered mountaintop had a greater air of desolation than the land below. "Still, there's not much cover up here either. I suppose we might as well get as close as we can."

"The air feels heavy," Jago said quietly as they started single file down the slope. "It's almost like we're being watched."

Raulin snorted, blowing a great silver cloud into the cold air. "Thank you very much, Jago." He placed his feet carefully in the giant's bootprints—stepping anywhere else left the brothers floundering hip-deep in snow. "All we need is to have spirits haunting this place."

"As to that," Sokoji's voice floated back, sounding thoughtful but unconcerned, "who knows what happens when a wizard dies? My sisters and I spent some time considering it but reached no answer."

"Some time?"

"Ten years and four months."

"And came up with no answers?"

"Perhaps the Mother's son knows, but he keeps the secrets of his people."

Raulin twisted to look at Jago. "I don't suppose he's around?"

Jago shook his head. It didn't seem necessary to mention that Lord

Death hadn't been around for a number of days. Whenever the Mother's son was mentioned, a combination of yearning and fear sang along the link stretching between him and Crystal and as he saw no way to help, he had no desire to add to her burdens.

Behind them, the mountain rumbled.

Slowly, like puppets pulled by a single string, they turned.

A ball of snow, a hand's span wide, smashed against Crystal's legs.

Another followed, then another.

The rumble came not from the mountain, but from the mass of snow beginning to move down it.

Crystal's face paled as the hint of a power she thought she should remember brushed lightly across hers. Not a wizard's power, not quite. Then the memory slipped away in the need of the moment. Her eyes flared and she grabbed Raulin and Jago each by a hand. She could feel their trust in her and it gave her strength.

She met Sokoji's eyes.

The giant nodded. "I can hurry when I must."

The snow beneath their feet began to shift.

"Run," commanded Crystal.

And so they did.

Crystal wrapped the brothers in her power and the three of them almost flew over the snow. Their feet barely touched before lifting again, the packs weighed nothing on their backs, and the wind helped carry them along. In spite of the knowledge that they raced disaster, both men felt a thrill of pleasure in the effortless speed.

Sokoji moved a little ahead, running with great bounding strides.

With a screech, the avalanche finally broke free and surged down the slope, gathering force as it roared toward them.

"Chaos," Raulin swore, risking a glance back over his shoulder.

And Chaos it appeared to be. Boulders ground together along the front edge of the mass of moving snow, a churning wall of destruction rising thirty feet into the air. The screaming rumble grew in volume until it drowned out thought and reason.

They'd covered two thirds, of the distance to the wizard's lake, nearly deafened but unharmed, and Crystal began to feel secure. Even without drawing from the barriers, she had sufficient power left to carry the three of them to flat ground where the beast behind would die of its own weight.

Then Jago stumbled and fell.

By the time she yanked him to his feet, the avalanche was upon them, dragging both brothers from her grip.

"NO!"

She whirled, fingers spread, and threw her power at the enemy.

The wave of snow and stone slammed into a wall of green.

And stopped. And fused.

The green faded.

Ears ringing in the silence, Crystal stared at the white cliff rising above her. She felt whole, complete in a way she hadn't since Kraydak's defeat. *But how?* she wondered and almost cried when the question shattered something fragile within her and the goddesses returned.

She turned as Jago gently touched her arm.

"You were whole," he said softly. "I felt it." That Crystal had saved them seemed of less importance than this.

"Was whole," she agreed and swallowed the lump that had formed in her throat. "Was."

*The whole,* added Tayja's voice, *is greater than the sum of its parts.*

*Not now, Tayja.* The finding—then the losing—of self left a pain too deep for even those goddesses who had proven her friends to be endured.

"Come on," Raulin slipped an arm about her and Crystal rested gratefully against his side, "just a little farther and you can sit down. You'll feel better with a cup of tea inside you and a fire lighting the night."

"Raulin . . ."

"What?"

"Oh, nothing." Jago decided against explaining. He almost wished he had his brother's calm acceptance of the world. He knew that in Raulin's eyes Crystal had merely done what wizards do and now, like a porter who had strained something carrying too heavy a load, she needed taking care of. With one last awe-filled look at the towering pile of snow, he fell into step behind them and wished, for Crystal's sake, it could be that easy.

Sokoji waited for them at the end of the lake. She studied Crystal's face as the wizard approached. Satisfied with whatever it was she saw, she pointed up at the blasted peak of the Mighty One.

Against the pink granite of the mountain, almost glowing in the last of the afternoon sun, lay a great black dragon. The Doom of the ancient wizards.

Crystal's mouth went dry and then she realized the beast was stone.

She reached out with what little power she had left and touched only rock.

The path of the avalanche began at the dragon.

She recalled the power that had brushed against her just before the mountain shook off its load of snow. When she woke Kraydak's Doom—the dragon created in his arrogance from the body of the Mother—she had felt the same type of power.

"What is it?" Raulin asked, squinting in an attempt to make out details. At this distance he saw only black on pink.

"Aryalan's dragon. Aryalan's Doom."

"Is it alive?"

"No, not for years."

The brothers traced the swath of destruction left by the snowslide and exchanged identical glances.

"Are you certain?"

"Yes." She tore her gaze from the graceful line of limb and scale and met first Raulin's then Jago's worried eyes. "Whatever memory of power my presence may have triggered is gone now. There's nothing there but stone." She sighed and added in a small voice, "I thought someone promised me a cup of tea?"

And the marvel of the dragon was banished in making camp.

And if Crystal lay awake that night and wondered what else would be triggered by her presence, no one knew.

# TWELVE

The wind had rippled the surface snow into a parody of the lake it covered and the tiny ridges were all that disturbed the unbroken expanse of white. Staring across from shore to island, the lake appeared wider than it had from up on the mountain. Jago rubbed his eyes and tried to bring the remains of the gatehouse into focus, but the entire area persisted in wavering; one moment sharp and clear, the next no more than a soft gray shadow against the white. He snapped his snow goggles down off his forehead but, although he no longer needed to squint, the scene remained unchanged.

"Crystal," he called without turning, and felt rather than saw her step to his side. "Look toward the island and tell me what you see."

Crystal looked out over the lake, frowned, and shook her head. Her eyes began to glow, living emeralds reflecting the morning sunlight. "I see . . ." She paused and shook her head again. "I don't know what I see, exactly."

"You see one of Aryalan's remaining defenses," Sokoji told them, moving to stand at their backs. "Do not try to puzzle it out for too long."

"Because we can't?" Jago asked.

"Because you'll soon begin to think of nothing else, neither food nor sleep nor drink, and will eventually die still staring across the water." The giant waved a hand at the snow covered ice. "Or what passes for water these days. The full effect may not be working, but I advise you not to risk it."

Jago pointedly turned his back on both lake and tower. "Okay," he said slowly, "if we can't look at the island, how do we cross?"

"Why, by not looking at it."

Raulin grinned at the implied "of course" on the end of Sokoji's answer. "Really, Jago," he teased, bending over the campstove where their breakfast cooked, "use your head."

"Why not use yours? We'll need something solid to test the ice." Jago leaned forward and grimaced at the pale brown mass in the pot that was just beginning to bubble and steam. "And then again, we could just throw that stuff in front of us, let it harden, and we'll have a bridge."

"Ignoring the insult to my cooking," Raulin sighed, "I have to agree with the sentiment. I am definitely tired of oatmeal. Even if Crystal does power out the lumps." He raised the wooden spoon and the sticky clump on the end fell back into the pot with a loud and unappetizing splat.

Clicking her tongue, Crystal dropped a handful of snow into the pot. It turned to water as it hit and began to loosen the gluelike consistency of the porridge. "To begin with, you've got your proportions wrong." She added just a little more snow water and the spoon briskly stirred the liquid in.

"Do mortals usually waste time on trivialities before going into the unknown?" Sokoji asked, her head to one side, her expression both puzzled and faintly amused as she watched the trio gathered around the campstove.

The two mortals and the wizard looked up from the porridge pot, looked at each other, had no need to look out toward the tower, and said simultaneously, "Yes."

Sokoji nodded and sat down on the well-packed patch of snow she'd been using since the night before, her weight having sculpted it into comfortable contours. "That explains your behavior. I had always believed mortals preferred to get danger over with quickly. Perhaps some cinnamon would help." She offered a small bag pulled from one of her many pockets.

"Help to get it over with?" Raulin asked.

"Help the porridge."

"Oh. Right. Do you always carry cinnamon with you?"

Sokoji reviewed the recent contents of her pockets.

"No," she said at last.

Breakfast lasted longer than the oatmeal—even improved by the cinnamon—warranted. No one offered an opinion as to why they were so strangely unwilling to start on this, the last leg of their adventure. Conversations started, stopped, restarted, and sputtered out.

"I'll never forget," Raulin broke into the uncomfortable silence that had fallen after the last abortive attempt to find an acceptable topic, "the look on Crystal's face when she picked herself out of that snowdrift." A laugh hovered around the edges of his voice.

"When?" Crystal shifted around to face him. "After you blithely pitched me off the sleigh?"

"Yeah," he admitted, winking, "then."

And that began a series of reminiscences, as if this were their last evening together and the next day they would all be back in separate and safe lives.

Raulin and Jago traded banter. Raulin and Crystal traded glances almost physical in intensity. Crystal and Jago shared a quiet moment in complete accord.

*We've redefined ourselves,* Jago realized, when talk shifted away from the personal to the dwindling supply of tea. *Reinforced who we are and what we mean to each other.* He glanced in the direction of the tower, not attempting to keep his eyes on it when it slid out of view.

"I've changed my mind," he muttered into his tea. "I don't want to go."

"You never wanted to go," Raulin pointed out.

No, he hadn't. But he couldn't let Raulin go alone, not back in the beginning, not now—and Jago knew Raulin would go on. Not because he didn't feel the menace radiating from the island—menace that kept Jago's mouth dry and his stomach in knots—but because he wouldn't let the fear it caused stop him. An admirable trait, Jago had to admit, remembering the battle his brother had fought and won on the ledge into the valley, but not one likely to allow either of them to die comfortably of old age.

By the time the last cup of tea was finally finished, the pot dried and stowed away, the sun was a pale yellow disc high in the silver sky.

"I'm better at beginnings," Raulin admitted to Jago as they hoisted on their packs. He looked back at Crystal and then forward at the still shifting tower. "I've always been lousy at endings."

"Then think of this as another beginning," Jago told him, yanking a braid free from under the shoulder strap. "Things change, but they don't end."

"Oh, very profound, junior."

Jago tied on his hat, his violet eyes twinkling under the fur edge. "That's why mom liked me best."

Crystal stared up at the distant dragon, her wizard-sight caressing each strong and graceful curve. Life had left it thousands of years before and yet it still had a beauty that caused the breath to catch in her throat. She stood almost perfectly still, mesmerized, only her right hand moving, blindly weaving her hair around the fingers of the left.

"What are you thinking of, child?" Sokoji asked, coming silently up beside her.

"How it must have looked in the air with the sun turning its scales to black fire and its eyes glowing red."

"Its eyes are closed. How do you know they were red?"

"Weren't they?"

The giant nodded. "Yes. But how did you know?"

"Kraydak's colors were gold and blue and so was Kraydak's dragon. Aryalan's colors were black and red and this was Aryalan's dragon."

"Not *her* dragon, child. That is the mistake the ancient ones made, claiming ownership of the Mother's body."

"I wonder," she said dreamily, giving no indication she'd heard Sokoji's last words, "how a dragon would look in silver and green."

"A dangerous thought, wizard."

At the giant's tone, Crystal shook herself free of her fascination with the great beast and turned to face Sokoji. "But only a thought," she said clearly. "I am not like those ancient wizards." Under Sokoji's continuing gaze, she drew herself up, her shoulders went back and her chin rose. Her hair spread out around her, a living silver frame, and her eyes flashed like jewels amidst the ice and snow.

Sokoji, whose memory went back almost to the world's creation, smiled. "No," she conceded, "you are not like the other wizards."

"Hey!" Raulin yelled from the edge of the ice. "You two going to stand and talk all day? These packs are heavy!"

"I will never understand mortals," Sokoji muttered as the two women walked forward. "First they spend the greater part of the morning dawdling and now they must instantly be off."

"An unpredictable race," Crystal agreed, conveniently forgetting for the moment her own mortal heritage.

"Unpredictable." Sokoji turned the word over in her mouth. "Yes, I suppose that's one word for them."

The snow covering the lake was dry and hard packed and it squeaked under boot soles.

"How do we know the ice is thick enough to hold us?" Jago asked, when they were about twenty feet from shore.

"Well," Raulin drawled, "if you're not breathing water, it's thick enough."

"Maybe we should be checking it." After weeks of traveling through the mountains, crossing such a large open area left him feeling exposed and vulnerable. The ice wasn't really the problem, but it would do until something else came along. He could hear Raulin's own nervousness in his flippant answers.

"We are checking it out; we're sending Sokoji out ahead. Anything'll hold her will hold us."

"Don't worry, Jago." Sokoji smiled back over her shoulder at him. "During the second and third winter moons, the ice is as thick as it ever gets. We will not fall through."

Raulin reached out and tugged on a floating strand of Crystal's hair. "You're very quiet." he said. "Copper for your thoughts?"

"I was just thinking that this is really the only time of the year you could get to the tower, when the lake is frozen solid enough to walk across." She waved a hand back at the shore where clumps of stunted trees raised twisted branches barely above the level of the snow. "In the summer you'd need a boat and you certainly couldn't build one from those. Nor could you get one over the pass. In the spring and fall, while the mountains are saturated with water, you couldn't get into the valley at all, the footing would be too treacherous."

She paused and looked up at Raulin. "And if I hadn't gotten to the demon before you, you'd be dead and I'd be . . ." The memory of Nashawryn breaking free tightened her throat around the words. ". . . I'd be . . . well, I wouldn't be, and the map would have never been used. And if Sokoji hadn't met with us, we'd still be heading toward the wrong valley."

"Your point?" Raulin asked.

"Why did you decide to travel in winter? You've got to admit, it isn't when people usually go north."

"In the winter we could use the sleigh and carry a lot more gear. No bugs, few wild animals. It just seemed to make the most sense."

"What about the weather?"

Raulin tucked his chin deeper in his scarf. "The lesser of a number of evils. You were traveling in the winter . . ."

"But seasons don't mean anything to me." She searched for other ways to convince him. "If I hadn't met that brindle, I would never have used enough power for the demon to hear me and call . . ."

*Maybe. Maybe not.*

"Crystal . . ."

". . . and I'm sure Sokoji has a logical reason for being in these mountains as well."

*Maybe, Maybe not.*

"Crystal, what are you getting at?"

She sighed and pushed both her hands up through her hair. "I think someone, or something wants us—you, me, and Jago, possibly Sokoji too—at that tower."

"What!"

"Well, you've got to admit, it's a few too many coincidences to be plausible."

Raulin threw one arm around her shoulders. "I've got to believe nothing of the kind. You're just a little spooked is all." He noticed the giant watching and added, "Right, Sokoji?"

"In the world of the Mother-creator," Sokoji said solemnly, "coincidences are few and far between. Nothing happens without reason."

"Are you telling me you believe what Crystal just said?"

"Maybe. Maybe not."

"Don't you start," Crystal growled.

Sokoji looked puzzled.

"I'm sorry." Crystal hoped she sounded sincere. She couldn't tell over Eegri's giggles.

Jago wondered if he should mention that he'd been mulling over the circumstances that had brought the four of them to this place at this time and had come to much the same conclusion. He opened his mouth to speak, caught sight of the expression on his brother's face—Raulin clearly anticipated what he was going to say—and decided to keep silent.

With the remains of the gatehouse, and the island it stood on, unreliable as a guide, it was difficult to determine both how far they'd walked and how far they still had to go. Judging distance by the shore they'd left helped very little, for the farther they walked over the lake the more the shore took on the same characteristics as the island.

"Look at the bright side," Raulin remarked as they continued, "this is some of the easiest walking we've done for weeks. It's flat, it's clear, we're not plunging through drifts, we're not . . ."

The ice groaned, a long drawn out sound that set teeth on edge and could be felt up through the soles of their feet.

". . . we're not likely to live to see the other side," Raulin finished, white showing all around his eyes. "What, in the name of Chaos, was that?"

"Just the ice settling," Crystal explained, moistening her lips. Knowing the cause barely lessened the sound's chilling effect. "Something to do with thermal patterns in the lake." The centaurs had spent a great deal of time, many years before, teaching her the ways of the world. Knowledge, they reasoned, brought respect. She wished now that she could remember more of it. "We're perfectly safe."

The ice groaned again.

Raulin and Jago went rigid. Even their clothing seemed to stiffen.

"Look," she realized they believed her reassurances and she understood that belief had little to do with their reaction to the sound, "Sokoji hasn't stopped."

The giant had pulled four or five body lengths ahead and continued to walk unhurriedly toward the island.

The brothers glanced at the giant, at each other, and simultaneously stepped forward. The footing remained solid.

Jago sighed deeply and banished thoughts of plummeting down into icy depths, the cold and the water racing to see which could kill first. *I've got to do something about my imagination,* he thought as he kept moving, watching Raulin shrug off even the memory of the fear. Raulin lived wholly in the present and Jago envied him the ability. He grinned as he pictured his brother, resplendent with new wealth, amid the corrupt and fearful aristocrats of the Empire who would, like so many others, take Raulin's bluntness for stupidity. The vision so enthralled him, he didn't notice he'd struck a patch of clear ice until it was brought forcibly to his attention.

"Oof!"

The pack and his many layers of clothing acted as a cushion, but the unexpected fall knocked the breath out of him. He glared up at Raulin and Crystal, who, seeing him unhurt, began to snicker. Even Sokoji's mouth twitched although she, at least, made no sound.

"No need to help," Jago hid his own laughter under an exaggerated sigh—it probably had looked pretty funny—"I can get up by myself." He threw himself over onto his stomach, silently cursing the weight of the pack, got his knees under him, and paused a moment, gathering the strength and balance necessary to stand.

The ice, an arm's length from his nose, was a greenish black. No, he realized with wonder, the ice—ice thick enough to support the giant's passage—was perfectly clear. The water below it was a greenish black.

*If the glassmakers could learn to do this* . . . he thought admiringly.

And then his thoughts froze.

A shadow, darker than the water, solid, and large, passed below the ice.

And the ice became, in comparison, very fragile.

"Hey, Jago, you all right?"

The shadow passed again and Jago knew, beyond any doubt, it was aware of him. Aware of all of them.

A long, trailing something, as thick around as Sokoji's thigh, brushed against the lower surface of the ice.

Panic controlling his arms and legs, Jago scrabbled back onto the nearest patch of snow and sat panting. He could no longer see it and that helped, but he still knew it was there. Knew it waited. Knew it wanted.

"Jago?" Raulin dropped to one knee and took hold of the younger man's shoulders. "What is it?"

"Something . . ." He took a shuddering breath and tried again. "Something under the ice."

"Are you certain?" Sokoji asked.

Jago looked up at the giant and nodded.

"Then perhaps it would be best if we kept walking."

"Good idea," Raulin agreed, standing. "Present a moving target."

"And get *off* the ice," added Crystal, pulling Jago to his feet.

He clung to her hands for a moment, taking comfort in the strength that had all but lifted both him and the extra weight of the pack, feeling the warm pressure of her fingers through his mitts.

"Take a wizard to breach a wizard's tower," he said, a plea for reassurance in his voice.

Crystal met his eyes and, for an instant, openly wore the mantle of her power. Even shattered as it was, held together by the wizard's will alone, it blazed with a painful glory. Then it faded, replaced by the concern of a friend. "I didn't stop an avalanche," she told him with exaggerated pique, "in order to feed you to a fish."

The remaining distance to the island became the longest distance Jago ever walked. With every step, he expected the ice to crack and break and let the hunger that it sheltered out to feed. He didn't doubt Crystal's power. He didn't want to test it.

The others were nervous, he saw it in the way they carried themselves; movements a little jerky, heads cocked to one side and brows drawn down as if to give eyes and ears a better chance to give warning. They all avoided the clear patches of ice.

When he stepped up on land at last, relief hit with such force that if Raulin hadn't grabbed his arm he would've sagged to the ground.

"I'm okay," he protested, embarrassed at his weakness.

"Sure you are," Raulin said noncommittally, and held on until he felt Jago could stand on his own.

As they walked away from the shore, Jago viciously buried the thought that threatened to immobilize him. To get off the island, they would have to recross the ice.

The island looked very little different from the lake; a smaller circle, about a hand's span higher, and covered by that same hard snow. They could see the ruin of the gatehouse clearly now. Here, a wall, still vibrantly red even after centuries, stood alone and unsupported. There, the flip of a tiled roof poked out of the white. From the center of the island rose a small square building, still half buried under drifts.

"But it's only . . ." Raulin raised his hand horizontally to about mid-chest. "We won't be able to stand up."

"I stood in it," Sokoji reminded him. "It was not built level with the surface of the island. There are stairs around the corner."

"Is that where you sprang the trap?" Crystal asked, flexing long fingers, her hair rippling on the still air. She could feel power waiting in this place and it grew stronger as they neared the center.

"One of them. The ancient wizards trusted no one, least of all their fellows. Their towers, their strongholds were built to keep out," the giant paused and searched for the correct word, "visitors."

"Don't you mean intruders?"

She shook her head. "No, their paranoia was never that justified."

Crystal considered what it would mean to trust no one and to have no one trust you. "They must've been very lonely," she said softly.

Sokoji studied the last living wizard, her face thoughtful. "Yes, they must have been."

Indicating Raulin with one hand and Jago with the other, Crystal smiled. Here was her trust. "Don't worry, Sokoji."

Sokoji nodded and half-smiled, understanding what Crystal was telling her, but still looking thoughtful.

"The traps . . ." Raulin prodded. They were still advancing toward the gatehouse and he wanted to know what they'd face before they arrived.

"All the traps I sprang were tied to the life forces of the Elder Races."

"Which means?" Jago asked, although he had a nasty suspicion he knew.

"Others must exist tied to the life forces of mortals and wizards."

"Which we'll have to find?"

"Yes."

"But Aryalan's been dead for thousands of years," Raulin protested. "How much trouble can something this old give us?"

"It almost killed me," Sokoji told them, her voice even slower and weightier than usual. "If Aryalan were still alive and able to feed power and direction to her guardians, I could not have won."

"Lovely."

"Thank you."

Raulin flushed. "No, I didn't mean . . . oh, never mind."

Jago, whose line of sight took in Sokoji's face, smiled in spite of the situation. He simply hadn't been able to convince his brother that the giant possessed a sense of humor.

In the years since Sokoji had been inside the tower, winter had re-filled the stairwell leading down into the gatehouse, leaving only a dimple in the surface of the snow.

Raulin let his pack crash to the ground and straightened up with a groan. "Looks like shoveling," he sighed.

They could see the top lintel of the door, carved with fantastic birds and beasts, but nothing more.

"At least a body length of shoveling if that door's standard size," Jago added, dropping his pack with a little more control but an equal amount of relief. "And if Sokoji went through it, I'm betting we've her body length to clear, not ours."

Crystal stepped into the dimple and spread her hands. The snow flashed green and disappeared. She stood at the top of a broad flight of black marble stairs. At the bottom loomed a door, also black, and large enough for the giant to enter without so much as having to incline her head.

"That may not have been wise," Sokoji said solemnly. "Any power remaining here will now know a wizard has returned."

"Any power remaining knew the moment I entered the valley." Crystal pointed back to where the dragon rested. "That avalanche was no accident."

"What's done is done," Raulin declared philosophically. "And what's done beats shoveling." He slid over the lip of snow and onto the stairs. The small flurry he brought with him melted away as it touched the steps. He shook off a mitten, bent and drew a finger along the slick surface. The luster of the marble made it look wet. It wasn't.

"I destroyed the trap set on the stairs for my kind," Sokoji informed him, "but there may be others set for yours. Shall I come with you, or will you descend alone?"

Raulin looked down the length of black, each step as perfect and sharp edged as the day it had been set. "Alone," he decided. "Less distractions."

"Careful," Jago warned, advancing to the edge but no farther. "Check everything."

"Don't teach grandma to suck eggs, little brother." A memory stirred and he heard his master sergeant screaming orders. *Amazing the things you pick up amid the rape and slaughter,* he thought, inspecting each step before moving onto it. He knew marble could be trapped in the same ways as wood—stairs were stairs, after all—but he suspected he was missing any number of nasty . . .

Stone snapped down on stone.

Raulin froze. Until he saw which way the danger lay, going back could be as deadly as going ahead.

A panel in the base of the door burst open.

Raulin got a vague glimpse of scales and claws and teeth. He had time to shape them into a large and ugly lizard but no time for fear before the thing was on him. He twisted, fell, and slid almost half the remaining distance to the door.

The lizard overshot. Claws scrabbling for purchase on the marble, it whirled to attack.

A piercing noise split the air.

It reared, tail lashing.

Jago whistled again.

It charged.

Jago stood unmoving, smiling slightly.

As it struck, it disappeared.

His heart loud in his ears, Raulin levered himself up onto his knees and yanked his scarf away from his mouth. He felt like he couldn't get enough air. "Thanks, Crystal," he panted. "That's another one I owe you."

"I didn't do anything," Crystal told him. "It was Jago."

"Jago?" Raulin twisted around to face his brother. "What did you do?" he demanded.

Jago shrugged. "It was a gowie lizard," he explained. "They live in very hot climates. Coming out into this kind of cold would stop it dead." They all watched—as if noticing for the first time—while he huffed out a white plume of breath illustrating the temperature. "In fact, the cold would probably kill it."

"Fascinating," Raulin growled. "But what did you do?"

Jago shrugged again. "I disbelieved it."

"An illusion?"

"Seems that way."

Raulin flushed. "I feel like an idiot." He got to his feet. "That was a mortal trap?" he asked Sokoji.

The giant spread her hands. "I saw nothing."

"Illusion!" Raulin spat out the word. "I should've known. Kraydak used illusion all the time. I've seen them before. Chaos, I've fought with them."

"Well, I've created them and I didn't identify it until it disappeared." Crystal's self-mocking tones lifted Raulin out of the guilt he seemed ready to fall into. "Next time you'll know."

"Next time," Sokoji put in, standing on the top step, "it will be real and you'll die. A wizard's tower holds stranger things than gowie lizards."

"That's not very encouraging." Crystal frowned at the giant.

Sokoji thought about it for a moment.

"No," she agreed. "It isn't."

"Do you want me to come down?" Crystal asked, eyeing Raulin with concern.

He shook his head and rubbed an elbow that had slammed into the marble. "I'm okay, just bruised. Anyway," he measured the distance he'd fallen and the distance he still had to go, "I'm almost there."

The next seven steps were clear. He reached the door safely, turned and grinned. "If that was her attempt at keeping mortals out, I can't say as I'm very impressed." He pulled off his hat and wiped beads of sweat off his forehead. "It's warmer down here."

"And warmer still inside," Sokoji said.

Inside.

Raulin turned back to the door, feeling dwarfed. It rose taller than the giant and spread almost twice Sokoji's not inconsiderable width. Its six lacquered panels were carved with marvelously detailed scenes of wild animals nearly impossible to see at more than a few inches away, for the black absorbed all the light that fell upon it. The ruin of a large brass lock dominated the middle right side.

"What a mess." He ran his fingers over the broken metal. "Looks like Sokoji put her fist through this on that last visit." Peering back over one shoulder, he raised an eyebrow in the giant's direction. Sokoji inclined her head, admitting the action.

"Okay, there's no sense putting all our eggs in one basket. You three stay there until I check this out."

Crystal began a protest, but Jago gripped her arm and shook his head.

"He wants us out of the way when he opens the door."

"But what about him?"

"He knows what he's doing."

But both of them realized that if something came out the door, knowledge would do little good.

"It swings in," he called, placing his hand against the shattered lock. He took a deep breath, pushed, and dove to one side in the same motion.

Silently, the great door swung open.

Soft golden light spilled out over the threshold.

"Anything?" he asked as Crystal and Jago dropped to their knees and even Sokoji bent to get a better line of sight.

"Nothing." Jago said. Crystal and Sokoji nodded agreement.

"Nothing?" Raulin repeated, shrugged, pushed away from the wall, and stepped inside.

The gatehouse appeared the same size on the inside as on the outside. Based on what Crystal had told him, Raulin knew that wasn't always a given in wizard-created buildings. The soft golden light radiated down from all but one corner of the ceiling where the tiles were broken, dull, and gray. A great diagonal gouge marked one wall; the others were smooth and all four were bright red. They reminded him of raw meat. Not a particularity comforting analogy.

The floor was the same black marble as the stairs and in the center was a massive slab of ebony. It took Raulin a moment to understand why the ebony appeared to have been splashed liberally with blood and then he remembered what Sokoji had said. Rubies; stones ranging in size from tiny flecks to ovals too large to completely fit on his palm.

Their beauty as much as the wealth they represented tugged at him, drew him forward. So many and so red. Burning . . .

He caught himself in midstride, shook his head like a dog coming out of water or a man out of a dream, and put the foot back where he had lifted it from. Slowly and methodically, keeping his eyes off the gems, he searched the room for less obvious traps. At the spot beside the ebony slab where feet would have to be braced to raise it, he grunted and stopped a careful arm's length away.

"Never a rock around when you need one," he sighed, unlacing his boot. He unwound his scarf and wrapped the boot in the center of it. Holding both ends in one hand, he swung the whole thing around like a flexible hammer and slammed it down on the pressure plate.

Sword blades immediately thrust up from the floor at random points throughout the room.

"Raulin!" Through the open door, Jago saw the flash of steel and flung himself down the stairs.

Crystal tried to follow, but Sokoji held her.

"Wait," said the giant, "until you know he needs you."

Jago reached the door and clutched at the frame to stop his head-long rush.

"I'm okay," Raulin reassured him, stepping back. The razor edge had only parted the hairs of his heavy coat and not even cut the hide beneath. "Dumb luck strikes again." He glared. "And who told you you could come down here?"

"Just seeing if you'd fallen asleep, you were taking so long."

"You always were lousy at waiting for things."

Both men wore expressions much gentler than their words.

Raulin rapped the boot he held against the flat of a blade. "You might as well come in, this is as secure as it gets. Call Sokoji and Crystal."

Sokoji reacted to the call by lifting both abandoned packs. With one dangling from each hand, she turned to Crystal.

"Go," Crystal told her. "We know it's safe for you. I'll wait until you're off the stairs."

The giant nodded and descended.

Crystal waited, readying her power, trying to remain calm. Doubt would only rouse the goddesses and leave her less able to deal with whatever traps Aryalan had left. *I dealt with a living Kraydak,* she reminded herself. *This should be nothing in comparison.*

Sokoji reached the bottom and Crystal started down.

And it was nothing. Nothing at all.

Standing safely in the doorway, Crystal forced herself to relax. Apparently Aryalan had set no traps for her fellow wizards on the stairs. Or the traps that had been set had faded over the years. Or the trap was too subtle to be immediately obvious. The litany tightened her stomach back into knots and she sighed.

"Hey, Crystal," Raulin's voice came muffled around the finger he'd stuck in his mouth, "Could you do something about these?" He waved at the blades with his free hand. "They're a little in the way."

"Are you all right?" she demanded.

"He's fine," Jago said, grinning like an idiot. "Just clumsy."

Raulin's grin grew just as wide. "You're the one who suddenly wanted to dance."

"Dance?" Crystal frowned, then caught sight of the rubies. "Ah, dance."

The blades glowed briefly green and slumped to the floor.

"The use of power may set off other traps," Sokoji pointed out.

Crystal shrugged. "It didn't. And I don't think it matters."

"She's right, Sokoji," Raulin enthused, stripping off his overcoat and dropping the heavy fur to the floor by his hat and mittens and scarf. "It doesn't matter. There's more than enough treasure here. We don't have to go into the tower. *This* is as bad as it gets."

Only Jago saw Crystal's face at that moment. It was so carefully blank he grew suspicious.

"Are we still in danger?" he asked.

"I think not," Sokoji answered. She stretched back her arm and pushed the door shut. "As your brother said, you have no need to go into the tower."

Shrugging out of his coat, Jago allowed himself to be convinced. Crystal could have any number of reasons for hiding what she thought, any number.

"Sokoji," Raulin sat down to pull his boot on and prodded one of the now flaccid swords, "why didn't you set off this trap? Didn't you try to lift the slab?"

"I saw the plate—I think it is meant to be seen—and leaned over from the other side. A position only one of my kind would be both tall and strong enough to use." She paused, remembering. "I loosed something else."

All eyes turned to the gouged wall and the dark corner of ceiling, then back to the giant.

"I won," she said, and fell silent.

Then the silence lengthened.

Raulin rose to his knees and pulled his dagger. "Well, come on," he waved the point at Jago, "our future isn't going to pop out of that door unaided."

"Are you sure it's safe?" Jago asked, tossing his braids back behind his shoulders as he knelt beside his brothers.

"The gems will not be trapped."

All three, Raulin, Jago, and Crystal, turned to look at Sokoji, who paused in pulling the teapot from a pocket to return their multiple stare.

"To you this is a fortune," she explained. "To Aryalan it was merely a decoration. Wizards have no use for wealth."

Raulin nodded, accepting the statement at face value. He slipped his dagger point beneath a small rectangular jewel and began to pry it loose.

Jago watched Crystal's face for a moment, wishing their link was stronger. He'd heard a double meaning in Sokoji's words and didn't understand what it was. Crystal knew, he'd bet his share of these "decorations" on it. Then it hit him. Wizards *have* no use for wealth. Not had. Have.

"Crystal."

When she turned to face him, he knew the answer.

"You're going into the tower, aren't you?"

"Yes."

Metal rang on ebony as Raulin's blade fell from his hand.

# Thirteen

"We're going with you and that's that."

"No, you aren't." Crystal thrust both hands up through her hair and paced the length of the room. At the far end she turned, marshaled her arguments for what seemed like the thousandth time, took a deep breath, and sighed. "What can I say to convince you two to stay here?" she asked plaintively, leaning against the bright red wall and sliding down it to the floor.

Raulin came over and sat beside her, wrapping one arm around her shoulders. "If you go down there, so do we."

She twisted to face him. "I *have* to go down there. The tower is too dangerous to just leave. If even a small fraction of Aryalan's power remains . . . You know the sorts of weapons a wizard wields."

"We know."

"I'm the only one who can destroy the threat and I've got to do it now, before someone else stumbles on it, learns to use it, and tries to start the madness all over again."

"We understand that."

"If you go with me, I'll be too busy taking care of you to look out for myself. You'll be putting me in danger."

Raulin caught Crystal's flailing hand and held it. "And what if you need taking care of? Who's there for you?"

Crystal looked across to where the giant sat by the door. "Sokoji?" she pleaded.

"He is right," Sokoji said placidly. "If you are not like the ancient wizards, prove it now. In their pride, they denied friendship and thought only they were capable. They refused to admit others could stand beside them; saw no strengths but their own."

Crystal winced, but Raulin flashed a triumphant grin at his brother.

"Crystal," Jago dropped to one knee before her. "Could you watch a friend you loved go into danger while you stayed safely behind?"

"No," she murmured, and then louder, "no."

"Then don't ask it of us. Please."

She rubbed her cheek against Raulin's arm where it rested on her shoulder. "You two are crazy. You know that, don't you?"

Recognizing capitulation, Raulin smiled in agreement and Jago laid his hands on both of theirs. "We know," he said softly.

Later that night, Sokoji watched the two mortals and the wizard sleep, a tangle of arms and legs, and gold and silver hair. One of Jago's braids had come undone and his hair and Crystal's had wound in and about each other until they were so completely entwined only power would be able to get them apart. She looked from them to the ebony door, now plucked clean of its rubies. The tower did need to be dealt with and the last living wizard was the only one who could do it; the giants had long since come to that conclusion.

That the last living wizard was also the only one who could fully use the mysteries of Aryalan's tower, the giants were well aware. Nor had they, like Doan, dismissed the centaurs' fears out of hand. If they had not felt there was some basis for those fears, they would not have offered to watch; the wizard was at the time an unknown and unknowns should be investigated.

It hadn't taken much watching for Sokoji to decide that the centaurs had no real knowledge of the child they'd raised and the wizard they'd trained. If Crystal broke, it would be duty that struck the blow, not license. Duty the centaurs had taught her. In Sokoji's opinion, Crystal's greatest fault was her self-doubt, her fear that a very normal and healthy self-interest would lead her down the paths of the ancient wizards.

Raulin muttered in his sleep and tugged at the cover. Jago snorted and hung on. Neither woke.

Sokoji wondered if the brothers suspected how much they had re-molded the shattered bits of Crystal between them.

"Are you ready?"

Raulin and Jago clutched at their daggers, Crystal wrapped her power about her, all three nodded.

Planting her feet firmly, Sokoji leaned across the width of the trap-door, slipped two fingers beneath the ebony bar, and lifted.

Smoothly and quietly, the door rose.

Another black marble staircase, broad and wide enough for the gi-ant to descend, spiraled down into Aryalan's tower. The walls were a familiar red. The air drifting up into the gatehouse smelled strongly of roses. The soft, golden wizard-light continued down the stairs, al-though they saw no visible source.

"Okay," Raulin transferred his dagger to his left hand and wiped the palm of his right on his pants. Like Jago, he wore his jacket but left the fur overcoat behind with the packs. Besides the dagger, he carried a waterskin and the belt pouch that held the rubies. He didn't know why he brought the rubies. He supposed the answer he'd given Jago, *If I'm going to die, I might as well die rich,* was as good a reason as any. "Okay," he said again. "I go first, then Crystal, then Jago. Keep one step apart, no more, and sing out if anything seems the slightest bit suspicious."

He put his right foot down on the first step and slowly shifted his weight onto it. Nothing. Then the next step . . . then the next. . . . When his head dipped below the level of the trapdoor, he suddenly felt as if his ears had been stuffed with lamb's wool. Slowly, he reached up and touched Crystal's leg. Rubbing his fingers against the rough cloth of her pants made no sound.

"Crystal?" He felt her hand wrap around his. As far as he could tell, that was his only answer. Holding on to her tightly, he backed up until his head was once more in the gatehouse. The ambient noise seemed very loud.

"Did you hear me call?" he asked.

Crystal shook her head and looked worried. "No."

Raulin chewed on one end of his mustache. "I think it's just soundproofing. Crystal, keep hold of my hand, and Jago, take her other one. Don't follow her down until she tugs twice. If we can't talk to each other down there . . ." He shrugged. "Well, only one way to find out."

He backed down the stairs, not taking his eyes off Crystal's face. Her expression told him when she hit the effect. "Can you hear me?" he asked.

She smiled in relief, her hair lifting out a little from her ears. "Perfectly."

"We'd better test it." He kissed her fingers. The kisses made no noise, but the words were clear. "You're the most beautiful woman in the world."

"You haven't met my mother." She flicked a fingertip against the end of his nose. "We'd better let Jago know everything is all right."

"I suppose so." Raulin sighed dramatically—and, he was pleased to note, audibly.

Crystal grinned and drew his hand up to her lips. She kissed his palm and closed the fingers over it. "For later," she pledged.

He laid the hand against his heart and waggled his brows in his best lecherous manner. Then he turned and started carefully down the rest of the stairs.

Jago, upon entering the soundproofing, merely murmured, "Interesting," and continued to place his feet precisely where Raulin and Crystal had stepped. He wished he had the comforting bulk of Sokoji at his back, but the giant had remained in the gatehouse. No one had asked her why, and Jago suspected it was because they hadn't wanted to hear the reason.

Crystal kept both arms tight to her sides so they wouldn't brush against the walls accidentally. Perhaps Kraydak had been unique in mortaring his tower with the trapped souls of the dead. Perhaps not. She didn't want to find out.

*Why not? If they're there; they'll call their Lord, and he'll have to come.* Avreen's voice slid like silk through her mind.

Crystal gritted mental teeth but made no answer and Avreen's mocking laughter accompanied her down the next few steps.

Raulin squinted but couldn't see into the gloom that hid the bottom of the stairs. Although their immediate area remained brightly lit, the wizard-light staying with them as they descended, he'd have preferred a little less light where they were and a little more where they were going. He weighed the danger of Crystal sending light ahead against the probable consequences of her depleting her power and decided the gloom would lift eventually on its own. But Chaos, he hated not knowing what he was walking into.

Sokoji watched Jago's golden head disappear around the first turn in the spiral staircase. She could've gone with them to the stair's end but didn't see the point as she could go no farther whether she wished to or not. Nor, she admitted to herself, did she want to take a chance that what had waited for her at the bottom waited there still. It was no danger to the others, but she didn't think she could defeat it again.

She smiled as she heard a faint sound outside the gatehouse door.

"Come in, Doan," she called.

The door swung open and the dwarf stood on the threshold, his sword drawn and a crescent shaped slice of black marble lying at his feet. "Damned step tried to fold up on me," he explained when he saw the direction of Sokoji's gaze. He kicked the piece of stone out of his way and stepped into the room, his brows rising at the limp blades scattered about on the floor. "Had a bit of trouble?"

She shrugged. "Not really."

Doan shoved the door closed and slammed his sword back into its sheath. "When did you know I was following you?" he demanded.

"I never thought you wouldn't. Taking another's word for something is not your way."

He jerked his chin at the hole in the floor. "They gone down?"

"Yes."

"All three of them?"

"Yes."

"And I should stay right where I am?"

"This is her chance to prove herself to herself. Don't ruin it by up-setting the balance she had achieved."

"Pah!" He thrust his hands behind his belt and snarled, "So what do we do now?"

Sokoji's expression saddened. "We wait."

Doan snorted. He hated waiting. "And we think, no doubt," he added sarcastically.

"No. We try not to."


They reached the bottom of the stairs without incident Crystal couldn't understand why. Surely Aryalan would've trapped the only entrance to her tower. Raulin paused on the last step and Crystal watched anxiously as he lowered one foot carefully to the floor. And then the other. He walked three paces away and then it was her turn. Nothing.

The room they stood in had been done in the same combination of red and black.

*Enough is enough,* sighed a voice Crystal thought was Sholah's and she had to agree with the sentiment. The vibrant colors only added to the tension.

She heard Jago step off the stairs behind her, then she heard Raulin gasp.

"What . . ." she began to ask, then fell silent.

Out of the shadows that hid the corners of the room, stepped a woman. Strands of gold wove through the thick chestnut of her hair, flecks of gold brightened the soft brown of her eyes, and a sprinkle of gold danced across the cream of her cheeks. She stood almost as tall as the wizard and almost as slender. Her smile, although touched with sadness, brought such beauty to her face that beauty seemed a word completely inadequate to describe it.

"Mother?"

Tayer, the Queen of Ardhan, held out her hands. "Have you no welcome for me, Crystal? I traveled far to speak with you."

"Mother?" Crystal cursed the break in her voice and reached out with power. This had to be of Aryalan's making. But it felt like the memory she held of her mother. "You can't be here."

The sadness on Tayer's face deepened. "The dead can be anywhere," she said softly.

"Dead?" Crystal's mouth went dry. "You can't be dead. I'd know." She turned her probe into a spear and drove it into the heart of whatever it was that stood before her. Nothing blocked the blow. Not a woman with a life of her own. Not a creature created by wizardry.

"Your power can't affect the dead." Tayer shook her head and sighed. "I've never lied to you, child, why should I start now?"

"But I'd know," Crystal repeated, suddenly unsure if she would. "If you were dead, I'd know."

"Perhaps not. We've grown apart lately, you and I. I blame myself for that."

"No, Mother. I . . ." With a shock, Crystal realized this—this something—had more than half convinced her it—she—spoke the truth.

"You were a miracle, Crystal, and I was never sure of how to treat you. I suppose if I'd treated you like my daughter, and that alone, things would have been better between us." Tayer gazed sadly into emerald eyes. "But that's behind us now. I've come for another reason. Your father needs you. I'm afraid for him."

"Father needs . . ." The words wrapped around her and made it difficult to think. Something was wrong. Something was missing.

"Mother . . ." *No!* she told herself. *This is not my mother.* "How did you die?"

A blush stained Tayer's perfect cheek, the expression making her appear absurdly young. "I thought it was only a cold; that it would go away . . ."

"Oh, mother." Crystal took a step forward, turned away, then turned back. Tayer had always argued with the Royal Physicians, insisting she was perfectly healthy long before they thought she should be up. This was exactly the sort of thing Crystal had always been afraid would happen one day. Her heart caught in her throat. "Mother?"

Tayer nodded. "Yes, my darling. I'm sorry."

Crystal reached out a trembling hand. It passed through Tayer's shoulder. Not even a wizard could touch the dead.

"Crystal, you must go to your father. Now."

"I, I can't."

"I never asked you for anything when I was alive, my child."

"But I can't!" Crystal wailed. "I can't."

"Is it because . . . because he isn't your father by blood?"

"No!" Forgetting she couldn't touch, Crystal reached out in shock. "I never . . ."

"He always loved you as if you were his own."

"Mother, I . . ."

"Please," Tayer pleaded, her eyes filling with tears. "Your brothers are too young and hurt too badly themselves to help. Your father is so alone now. If you should die in this place, I'm afraid he wouldn't survive the loss of us both. Go to him, please, prove to him you still love him. He took my death so hard."

Death. Lord Death. Where the dead were, so was he.

And he wasn't.

Still speaking, the image of Tayer faded away.

*Built on a memory,* Crystal realized as the mists cleared from her mind. *And as real as my memories are.* And hard on that thought came another. *I would know if mother had died I would. We haven't grown apart. And father knows I love him.* She gained a new respect for Aryalan's powers then, for, even defeated, the trap left guilt behind to slow the intruder.

"No . . ."

Jago, his hands raised in supplication, backed toward the stairs. His eyes were fogged and the expression on his face was that of a man torn between duty and desire.

Gently, Crystal reached along the link they shared, found the place where Aryalan's power had lodged, and twisted Jago free. She caught just a glimpse of a brown-haired woman, weeping, and she touched betrayal.

Jago cried out, a strangled sound of loss and pain, and then his eyes began to focus. His hands fell to his sides and clenched into fists, the knuckles white against his tan.

"Not really there," he said huskily. "I should've known." He scrubbed the back of his wrist across his eyes. "A trap?"

"Yes."

"Emotional blackmail?" At Crystal's nod, his mouth curved into something not quite a smile. "Nasty lady, Aryalan, glad I didn't know her when she was alive. Everybody's got something they . . ." He paled. "Oh, Chaos, Raulin."

Raulin, who had served as a soldier with Kraydak's Horde.

Blood trickled down his chin from where he had bitten through his lip. His cheeks were wet with tears. Gray eyes stared at nothing visible, and, although his shoulder blades were hard against a wall, Raulin's feet kept moving, trying to back away.

"Raulin?" Crystal touched his arm. The muscles felt like rock. Without a ready pathway into Raulin's mind, she had to go slowly and carefully, balancing her need to get him free against the damage she could do if she hurried.

Gradually, she became aware of an unending parade of the dead. Not the dead as Lord Death presented them, ready to be received back into the arms of the Mother, but bodies, mortally wounded, risen up from their graves. Every one of them—men, women, and children— named Raulin their slayer, demanded justice, and advanced on him to claim it. And Raulin was almost at the point where their justice would be a small price to pay.

Crystal knew the focus had to be here, somewhere. Desperately, she searched among the bodies, trying not to acknowledge them as real in any way lest Raulin's guilt absorb her as well. She could feel Raulin's will weaken with every second.

There!

A surge of power, green enveloped the dull red glow, and the victims of the Horde were gone.

Under Crystal's hand, Raulin's muscles went suddenly slack. He swayed, Jago grabbed him, and they both sagged to the floor. With Jago's arms tight around him and his head against his brother's chest, Raulin sobbed once, then lay shaking.

While Jago held him, Crystal stroked his back, her power smoothing away the sharp edges of his pain. She didn't care if her power attracted something. In fact, she hoped it would. The last time she'd wanted to hit back this badly, she'd leveled a mountain.

Finally, Raulin pushed himself up into a sitting position. He nodded at Jago, who looked relieved, and met Crystal's eyes.

"I never killed any children," he said.

Crystal leaned forward and kissed him, putting all her trust and all her understanding into the action. When their lips parted, she murmured, "I know," against his mouth. And he had to believe her where he might not have believed words alone.

The three of them stood together, Crystal positioned within the circle of Raulin's arms and both of them feeling better for the contact. Eyes were carefully averted from the shadows in the corners.

"Well?" Jago asked. "Do we go on?"

"Why not? It can't get any worse," Raulin declared, but his usual jauntiness sounded forced.

Crystal didn't mention that it very well could. There didn't seem much point.

The door leading into the tower was locked.

Raulin eyed it speculatively, his color beginning to return. "Two traps tied to the lock that I can see. Figure on at least two more I can't. Jago?"

"Two anyway," Jago agreed. "Well, I've got the steadier hand, so . . ." He slipped a small leather case out of his jacket pocket.

"You pick locks? Both of you?"

The brothers exchanged speaking glances.

"Growing up in the Empire," Jago began.

"Gives you an excuse to develop a wide variety of skills," Crystal finished, shaking her head. "But I'd rather neither of you risk this when there's a better way." She reached up and pulled free a hair which changed to a slender silver rod in her hand.

"You're going to do it?"

"No. Tayja is."

"The goddess?" Raulin's voice rose almost an octave. "Crystal, have you gone crazy."

"I trust her, Raulin. She took control once before and gave it back."

"I'd rather take my chances with the traps."

"I'd rather you didn't!"

They glared at each other.

Jago cleared his throat. "If you're sure . . ."

Crystal tossed her head. "I'm sure."

Raulin transferred his glare to Jago.

A surge of joy, that could have only come from the goddess, accompanied Tayja as she moved up from the depths of Crystal's mind.

Crystal watched as once again her hands took on a life of their own, manipulating the silver probe with amazing dexterity. This time, however, she wasted no energy fighting the possession. Raulin and Jago peered over her shoulders and counted off the traps.

"Four!" Raulin advanced on the door, hands raised.

"Wait." Crystal's mouth formed the word, but it wasn't Crystal's voice. She shoved the probe into the lock and twisted it violently to the left. A sharp crack sounded deep inside the mechanism. "Five!" declared the same voice, smugly. "That is all of them and that one had to be last or it would set off all the others."

Still under Tayja's control, Crystal's hands turned gracefully in the air. *You take a great chance allowing me this much freedom, child. The* long, pale fingers flexed. *I am a goddess, after all, and as proud and arrogant as my sisters.*

*But I know you,* Crystal reminded her. *And I know you are more honorable than some.*

In her mind's eye, Crystal saw Tayja smile. *Yes,* she admitted. *More honorable than some.*

*As you come to know me, you better know a part of yourself.* But the words were so faint, Crystal couldn't be sure if they came from memory or if Tayja had actually said them as she retreated.

Then Crystal's hands were her own again. She stared down at them and frowned, remembering the goddess' joy as she rose to help. She'd felt it herself, back when Dorses had seen her power as a tool rather than an abomination to be feared. This was important; important to her perception of herself and her perception of the goddesses. She reached for the word that would pull it all together.

"She got them all." Raulin pulled the door open a finger's width. Nothing; no steel plates, no poisoned darts, no cascade of acid, and nothing tried to get through the crack. "I'm impressed."

*Chaos!* Crystal swore. Raulin's voice drove the word she reached for from her mind.

"I think your goddess must've hung around with a number of less than holy characters." Raulin readied to open the door wider. "She never learned how to pick locks like that in a temple."

*I taught how to pick locks in a temple.*

Crystal laughed and passed on Tayja's message, ignoring Sholah's indignant, *You did nothing of the sort.*

The door, when fully opened, revealed nothing more threatening than a long red and black expanse of corridor fanning to a half circle into which were set three more black lacquered doors.

"This wizard liked her doors small," Jago observed. "Sokoji might have made it through this one, but she'd never have got through those."

"Surely it's just the distance," Raulin protested. "They can't be as narrow as they seem."

"Well, there's only one way to find out." Crystal lifted a foot to step over the threshold, but Raulin jerked her back.

"Not until we check the corridor for traps." Only when he knew for certain that the first section was safe did he allow her to advance, followed closely by Jago.

Behind them, unseen, dull red runes crawled for an instant along the edges of the doorframe, then faded, leaving no sign of their existence.

They found no traps in the corridor.

"Maybe this is the easy part," Raulin suggested as they reached the wider area and paused to study the three doors. Not only were they unlocked and un-trapped, but they had no locks to trap.

"Maybe." Jago sounded dubious as he measured his shoulders against their width. "We'll have to go sideways to go through."

"And which one do we go through?" Crystal wondered. "They're identical."

Claws dragged against the marble floor. The prevailing smell of roses changed abruptly to rot.

As one, they turned.

The creature advancing toward them supported its weight on its knuckles as much as on its feet. Scimitar-shaped talons scraped as it swung each arm forward.

"Where did it come from?" Jago gasped.

"Does it matter?"

Their daggers looked pitifully small next to the creature's natural armament.

Its eyes showed black from lid to lid, it had no nose that they could see, and its mouth, a lipless gash across the width of its face, bristled with a double row of triangular teeth. No neck separated the head from the powerful torso.

Crystal threw up her hands. An arching green bolt struck the creature full in the barrel chest.

It hissed, staggered back a step, then continued forward, moving surprisingly quickly on its squat legs. It was on them before they had time to consider flight.

"Get in close!" Raulin yelled, dropping to avoid a wild swing.

Jago hit the floor and rolled. Talons gouged the marble near him.

Raulin grabbed an arm on its next attack—the gray skin felt like wet cork—and used the momentum to slam himself and his dagger point into the creature's body. He yanked the weapon free, raised it to strike again, and realized his first blow had left no wound.

"Chaos!"

The smell of rot grew overpowering and Raulin found himself staring between four rows of teeth.

Silver hair wrapped around his head and snatched him back just as the massive jaw crashed shut not a finger's width from the end of his nose. A blaze of green, bright enough to leave spots dancing before his eyes, slashed downward.

The creature screamed. A line opened along its jaw, oily black liquid beading the length.

Crystal appeared to be wielding a dagger formed of power.

"Got another one of those?" Raulin yelled, scrambling backward, slicing into a massive arm and again doing no damage. "Plain steel ain't worth spit!"

An elbow drove into Jago's stomach and slammed him up against a wall. He slid to the floor gasping for breath.

Throwing herself between Jago and the creature's next blow, Crystal caught a talon on the shaft of green she held. The talon smoked and snapped off. She reached behind her with her free hand and dragged Jago to his feet.

"Distract it!" she shouted. "Let me get close enough to use this." A sword of power, she realized belatedly, would've been more practical. She tossed bands of green around the creature, slowing it by the smallest of margins.

Raulin and Jago agreed on strategy with a glance and raced to opposite walls of the corridor.

Crystal swung at the creature twice more.

"You're cutting it," Raulin told her, panting. "But I don't think you're hurting it much." The effort of keeping himself alive was beginning to tell. He'd taken only glancing blows so far and suspected a solid hit would break bones at the very least.

The creature ignored both its gaping wounds and the fluid dripping from them.

Rocking with the force of a blow that clipped his shoulder, Jago kicked with all his strength at the rear of a bony knee.

Taking advantage of the resulting lurch, Crystal opened a diagonal gash across its chest.

*Free me,* Zarsheiy demanded. *Free me and it will burn!* The fire goddess beat at the barriers containing her.

Suddenly, the creature concentrated its attack on Crystal. Both huge, taloned hands reached for her, curved around the shield she threw up, and began to compress it.

The power dagger faded as Crystal reinforced the shield. It lasted maybe three heartbeats longer.

She heard Jago scream her name as she went down.

*We're dead,* she thought, and prepared to pull power from the barriers.

*Yes!* Zarsheiy shrieked.

"Mustn't, mustn't, mustn't!" caroled a high-pitched voice.

The sound of a strangely muffled explosion echoed off the walls of the corridor. Something wet dropped onto her cheek.

As she could feel her power repairing shattered ribs, she didn't try to move. Lying motionless hurt sufficiently.

An iridescent face poked into her field of vision. "Are you mashed?" it asked brightly. "Pulped? Crushed? Scrunched?"

"Yes," Crystal answered.

"Oh." It looked concerned and withdrew.

"Crystal?" Raulin's face was smudged with black and his mustache was caked with blood. "Can I do anything?'"

She shook her head, carefully. "Just let me lie here for a moment and tell me what happened."

"The creature blew up."

One eyebrow rose slowly. "Just like that?"

Raulin grinned. "Pretty much."

"Is Jago all right?"

"I'm not sure the solution wasn't worse than the problem," Jago answered, off to one side, "but yeah, I'm fine."

"Jago was closest to the center of the blast," Raulin explained, smiling strangely "and the whole thing was kind of . . . messy."

"Oh, I see." She didn't, but Jago *sounded* all right. "If you'll help, I think I can sit up now."

He slid one arm behind her shoulders and lifted gently until her back rested against his chest.

The corridor—walls, ceiling, and floor—was awash with black ichor and fist-sized bits of steaming flesh. She noted with disgust that Jago—especially Jago—Raulin and herself were covered with the stuff. Surprisingly—fortunately—it smelled no worse than it had when alive. The demon she'd freed from Aryalan's cave sat cross-legged in midair, about the only place it could sit and stay clean. Its resemblance to the larger creature was illuminating.

"One of yours?" she asked, prodding at a misshapen lump with the toe of one boot.

"Was," the demon agreed. "Warned you not to come here. Told you it was dangerous." It looked down at her, as close to a serious expression on its face as its features were capable of. "No more debt between us," it said. "All debts are paid."

Crystal nodded. "All debts are paid," she repeated.

The demon nodded as well, a motion that set it bobbing in the air. It spun about once, and vanished.

Jago pulled a sodden sleeve out from his arm and summed up the situation with an emphatic, "Blech!"

"Could be worse," Raulin reminded him. "You could be dead."

"I think I'd prefer it," Jago muttered, flipping a braid back and wincing when the movement jarred his shoulder. Using the wall for support, he stood and stripped off jacket, shirt, and undershirt. Where his torso wasn't black with ichor, purple bruises were already beginning to show.

Crystal pushed power across their link and left it to sort out what needed healing. Then she turned to Raulin and drew her finger along the shallow gash that ran the length of his thigh. Behind the finger's path, only a fine white scar remained. "Anything else," she asked.

"Well, I've got a lump the size of an apple on the back of my head, but I can live with that." He brushed her hair back off her face. Not a single drop of ichor clung to the silver strands. "Save your power for when you need it."

"It's not as bad as that," Crystal protested. She reached into her pocket and pulled out a handful of crumbled horse-cake, wishing she'd landed on her other side when she'd fallen. "Sokoji planned for this; I'll eat and I'll be fine."

"Fine," Raulin repeated. "When you're not putting yourself at risk, you can heal whatever you want but now you've got to be close to drawing on the barriers."

Crystal stared at him in astonishment. "How did you know?"

He pinched her chin. "I'm smarter than I look."

*He'd have to be,* Zarsheiy snarled.

"In the meantime," he continued, unaware of Zarsheiy's remark, "let's get out of this mess." He took a step and had to windmill both arms to keep his balance.

"Careful," Jago pointed out mildly, "It's slippery."

Raulin glared at his brother, then turned his attention to the doors. As Crystal had mentioned earlier, they were identical; which one then to open first? Ready to slam it shut at the first sign of danger, he broached the door on the left.

Nothing.

He picked up Jago's discarded jacket and slapped it over the threshold, both breaking the line of the door and spraying the room beyond with black.

Nothing.

He peered into the room and blinked at the red and black checkerboard on walls and floor and ceiling. Both side walls and the one opposite held archways but from where he stood he couldn't tell if the openings led to rooms or corridors. Turning his head, he could see the backs of the other two doors. He examined the floor carefully.

Nothing.

Moving next to the central door and then to the right he repeated the process with the same results.

"Okay," he said at last. "It seems safe. Shall we go on?"

"Which door?" Jago asked.

Raulin shrugged. "Why not all of them? I don't like the idea of one of us being in there while the other two are still out here; those doors are too narrow if someone gets into trouble. If we go through at the same time, at least we'll be together. Are you going to get dressed?"

Jago clawed congealing ichor out of his beard. "No," he growled, "I'm not." Even his undershirt had been soaked through and he didn't want it touching his skin.

"Good thing your legs didn't get hit," Raulin muttered shaking his head, "or you'd be wandering around bare-assed."

Jago ignored him and turned to Crystal. "Your decision," he said graciously.

Crystal hid a smile. "We'll go through together like Raulin suggested." She waved Jago to the right and Raulin to the left while she took the center.

"All right." She drew a deep breath. "On three, open the door and step through. Freeze on the other side until we're sure of what to do next. Ready?"

Jago gave her a thumbs-up and Raulin blew her a kiss.

"One, two, three!"

In unison, they pulled the doors open, turned sideways, and stepped through.

Crystal found herself alone in a room with an open archway cutting through the checkerboard wall opposite her.

She spun around.

No door.

"RAULIN! JAGO!"

No answer.

# FOURTEEN

"CRYSTAL! JAGO!"

The answering silence seemed to mock him and Raulin lost his temper.

"Chaos' balls and the Mother's tits!" he screamed and threw himself against the wall that should've held a door but didn't. He kicked it, he pounded on it, and he slammed his shoulder into it all along its length. When he finally calmed down, he had a sore foot, aching hands, and a bruised shoulder but no better idea of what had become of his companions.

"This can't be happening," he muttered, and slumped against the offending wall. Drumming his fingers on his thighs, he reviewed everything he'd done to check for traps. His memory held no clue to what had happened.

He'd seen a room with three archways and three doors.

He stood in a room with an archway in the left wall and no door.

The red and black checkerboard pattern was the same, and so was the size as near as he could tell. The remaining archway had neither moved nor changed.

He hoped Crystal and Jago were together, but he very much doubted it.

"Okay," he said to the silence, "I have two options. I can stay where I am and maybe Crystal or Jago will find me. Or I can go looking for them myself." He picked at the torn hide where the demon's talon had ripped through his heavy pants, then, squaring his shoulders, pushed himself off the wall. "Right I go looking." Every second that he delayed increased the chance he would arrive too late to help either lover or brother or both survive.

Of the sixteen red and black tiles in the floor, he'd already effectively tested four by his mad race up and down the wall. Hugging the walls, therefore, seemed the least hazardous path to take as it gave him only one more tile to risk. This proved out as he reached the arch safely and sighed in relief at seeing the plain gray stone beyond the opening. The red and black motif was apparently at an end.

Giving the single stone of the threshold a quick inspection, he stepped completely over it. The fine crack surrounding it might have been the result of ancient mortar crumbling away to dust, but he didn't think so.

The hall he now stood in had a high vaulted ceiling and about half the width and twice the length of the room he'd just left. A clear white light banished shadows from even the farthest corners. An archway, identical to the one behind him, cut through the far wall. At equal intervals along each side of a central aisle, were statues of strange and impossible creatures.

"Well, maybe not so impossible," Raulin muttered, staring up at the first, "considering what else is wandering around down here." He scraped a bit of caked ichor off his sleeve. The statue appeared to be a demented combination of snake and bear. He peered closer. Each scale had been intricately carved. He lifted a hand to touch the stone; and stopped, suddenly remembering nursery tales of carvings coming to life.

Hands shoved deep into his pockets, he headed toward the exit, carefully keeping his eyes straight ahead.

Just on the edge of his vision, he thought he saw a giant cat with too many heads twitch slightly. He walked faster.

". . . thirteen, fourteen," he counted as he reached the arch, teeth clenched from the effort of not breaking into a run, "and each one uglier than the last. Interesting taste this Aryalan had."

Although the hall behind him sent icy chills up and down his spine and he wanted nothing more than to be out and gone, he bent and examined this second threshold. The same fine crack ran around it. Satisfied, he straightened and lifted a leg to step over.

The first tile on the other side protruded slightly higher than the others.

Raulin jerked his stride short and brought his foot solidly down on the stone of the threshold. It settled and he felt, rather than heard, the mechanism it controlled click into place.

The first tile now lay level with the rest of the floor and Raulin advanced into one end of a long corridor leading off to his right. Opposite him was a large, wooden, brass-bound door. *Just the sort of door you'd expect to find in a wizard's tower,* he thought, *not like those little lacquer things.* Looking to his right he counted twelve more doors, as far as he could tell, all exact copies.

The door he faced led father away from Jago and Crystal, so Raulin ignored it. He turned and walked to the first in the right-hand wall. His only plan was to circle back until he passed the checkerboard chamber. If the trap that got them into this followed any sort of logical pattern when it split them apart, his chamber would've been the farthest left. Using their initial orientation, he had to go right.

The lock on the door was huge and ornate and had, he saw, a keyhole large enough to look through.

So he looked.

Something looked back. Its eye was large and yellow and bore no resemblance to the eyes of either of the two Raulin searched for—or for that matter, to anything Raulin had ever heard of.

"Jago can't be in there, he hasn't had time to get this far." But a small, illogical part of him kept insisting he go back and check as he walked away; kept supplying him with visions of his brother lying wounded and helpless in the creature's den.

Nothing looked back through a second, similar keyhole but the line of sight was too limited for Raulin to see much of the room beyond.

"It's going in the right direction," he muttered, sliding out a lockpick. "Good enough."

A few moments of careful examination identified the trap and a few moments more was all he needed to spring it. When the dart flew out of the frame, his hand was nowhere near its path. Satisfied, he pulled open the door.

"Empty," he grunted. "Good." Through an archway directly opposite, he could see another small room. It appeared empty as well but he decided he'd better check. The door that led back to his brother might be just out of sight.

He stepped into the room and paused. Both side walls had peculiar scratches running diagonally from the near corner to the ceiling. Under normal circumstances, Raulin preferred to stay near the walls, but those scratches didn't look like normal circumstances so he started across the middle of the room.

About three-quarters to the other side, the entire floor tipped suddenly down like an unbalanced teeter-totter, dropping Raulin with it.

Raulin threw himself at the archway.

The threshold hit him in mid-chest. He clawed at the stone, feet scrabbling against the wall below, and managed to stop his fall.

Then he remembered to breathe.

Bracing his elbows, he levered himself up and flopped the top half of his body over into the second room.

The floor moved.

He jerked away, almost overbalanced, and spent the next few seconds stabilizing again.

The side walls of this room bore scratches as well, running diagonally from the far corner to the ceiling.

"Chaos. Chaos! CHAOS!" Raulin swore, blinking sweat from his eyes. His dangling lower body had never felt so exposed and vulnerable. He could feel his balls drawing up into safer territory. He didn't blame them.

He risked a glance back over his shoulder.

All he could see was a gray stone wall, slightly angled away from him.

"Wonderful," he muttered, steeled himself, and looked down.

The bottom appeared to be no more than two body lengths away.

He snapped his head back and tried to calm the pounding of his heart. It wasn't very far. Next to no distance at all if he lowered himself on his arms before he dropped. He swallowed and wet his lips. His chest hurt where he'd slammed it into the stone. His choices seemed to have narrowed to staying where he was or taking a chance down below.

Slowly he began to inch back, taking his weight on his forearms and then on his hands alone.

Kicking out a little from the wall, he let go.

One leg twisted under him when he landed. He fell heavily, then lay for a moment while he writhed in time to the waves of pain pulsating out from the injured joint. When the demon had slashed his leg during the battle, the blow had wrenched his knee as well, a minor ache in the wake of the other and until this moment he'd forgotten about it. He had a feeling he wouldn't forget about it again for a while.

Finally, the pain began to ebb. He straightened his arms, pushing his body into a sitting position, and dragged himself around until the floor/wall supported his back. Yanking his waterskin forward, he managed to remove the stopper. Although the water had the slightly brackish taste of melted snow, the action of getting the drink helped to calm him.

"What I wouldn't give," he sighed, taking another mouthful, "for even a mediocre brandy." He looked up. " 'Course, it could be worse. If I'd followed the wall like I usually do, I'd have been near nothing I could grab, would've fallen the whole distance, probably broken my leg, at the very least, and lain here until I rotted. Which raises the question," keeping much of his weight on the wall at his back, he stood, "how in Chaos do I get out?"

The area he found himself in was about twelve feet long, about twelve feet wide, and about twice that high. He bent, ignoring as well as he could the protest from his bruised ribs, and prodded at the bottom of the floor/wall. Although there wasn't much space, he found he could grip it with his fingertips. To his surprise, the massive block of stone rose easily when he tugged at it. When it reached his shoulder height, he ducked beneath the rising edge and shoved it hard enough to level it out.

The wizard-light stayed with him, he was happy to discover. He'd half anticipated exploring this lower level in the dark. Looking up, he could see the pivot mechanism and the ledge that supported the one end of the floor; supported it until some Chaos-born fool walked too far.

The new room had the same dimensions as the one above and had a single door in the long wall to Raulin's right.

"Right angles to the way I should be going. Still," Raulin sucked on his mustache, "I haven't much of a choice."

He limped to the door exercising more than his usual caution. The lock was untrapped and, even allowing for the painful distraction from his knee, it gave him no trouble. He stepped into the middle of a long corridor, a T-junction at each end with nothing to choose between them except his need to find Jago and Crystal. He turned to the right and began walking. At the corner he hesitated, his way no longer clear.

He shifted his weight off his bad leg and sighed, his chin sinking down on his chest. Then he blinked. In the wall in front of him was the faint but unmistakable outline of a door. He raised his head. It vanished. He lowered his head. It reappeared. With his chin tucked in, he ran his dagger around the edge, found the catch, and freed it. A rectangular section of the wall swung silently outward.

"Now this has got to be an illusion." He closed his eyes, disbelieved as hard as he could, and opened them again. "Still there." Stepping forward, pushing a gem encrusted goblet away with his foot, Raulin stared at more wealth than he'd ever suspected existed. Gold and silver coins, jewels, both loose and in ornate settings, ropes of pearls, beautiful and gleaming things he couldn't identify; all of it heaped and piled and thrown about the room.

"We could live like kings on this." He bumped into a chest and the lid snapped shut on the bolts of silk and cloth of gold. Bemused, he sat down, his eyes wide with trying to take in the glittering display.

He scooped up a handful of coin and poured it from one palm to the other . . .

. . . from one palm to the other . . .

The clinking of the metal sounded almost like music . . .

. . . almost like music . . .

He'd never noticed before that gold had a texture. That pearls felt like satin. That diamonds could never be mistaken for anything but what they were. That weapons could be beautiful.

He stroked a dagger, its hilt set with emeralds, and thought how well the stones would match Crystal's eyes.

Crystal.

The dagger fell from lax fingers.

Crystal. And Jago.

He had to find them. Suddenly the glitter was only that, and unimportant. He stood and the pain in his knee drove the last thoughts of the treasure from his mind.

"Why in Chaos couldn't they gild a walking stick?" he grumbled, limping out the door.


"RAULIN! CRYSTAL!"

Jago called until he was hoarse and then slumped against the wall in despair. The tiles were warm against his bare back, perversely comforting as those tiles should've been the door he'd entered through. He glanced at the archway to his right, now the only way of exiting the room, and wondered if he should use it. Raulin, he knew, would not sit quietly waiting for rescue. Raulin had never been very good at waiting for anything.

The logical thing to do was to stay right where he was, assume Crystal would find both Raulin and himself, and then the three of them would go on together.

But there was nothing to say that Crystal would even be able to look for them. That Raulin wasn't lying hurt or confined or both. Nothing to say that he, Jago, wasn't the only one able to move about and find the other two.

Logic argued against it, but logic had no proof and logic was no comfort and Jago found himself standing at the archway almost before he'd consciously decided to leave.

The cool, gray stone of the adjoining room soothed his raw nerves and he bent to examine the threshold in a less frantic frame of mind. Nothing, so he straightened and looked up. Not quite touching it, he ran his finger along the crack that split the lintel and continued half-way down the supports on both sides. He couldn't identify it as a trap, but that, he knew, didn't mean a Chaos-inspired thing.

Preferring embarrassment to dismemberment, he squatted and waddled through the opening, careful to keep his head lower than the bottom edge of the crack.

The hall he entered stretched long and narrow to an identical arch-way at the opposite end. Tapestries, brilliantly colored and glittering with gold, hung at equal intervals along each wall.

They had to have been created by power, Jago realized, standing before the first and gazing at it in wonder. No mortal hand could have done so perfect a job for the terror that twisted the man's features was as extreme as the beauty it twisted.

He moved to the next and although it was a different man, it was the same expression.

And then he realized that these men, so perfect of face and form, all stared in terror across the hall, and he turned.

And recognized the tapestry he now faced.

Red-gold hair, sapphire eyes, and a mocking smile; Jago had grown up in Kraydak's Empire and once he'd seen its lord. The blue eyes of the tapestry seemed to glow and Jago felt his palms grow damp. Fight-ing over half a lifetime of fear and oppression that threatened to drop him to his knees, he raised his head and met the wizard's eyes. And saw they were nothing but bright blue thread.

He wiped his hands and swept his gaze along the rest of the wall. The tiny woman with the ebony hair and eyes, with the lips as red as rubies and the smile as cold, had to be Aryalan. He didn't need to put names to the rest.

He turned again to the wall he'd first examined and saw the terror repeated seven times as the seven gods stared out at their wizard-children who had killed them.

Curious, Jago looked more closely at Kraydak's sire. His shoulder-length hair and full beard had been picked out in gold thread and pieces of amethyst had been worked into the color of his eyes. Falling from one limp hand was a scale and from the other a sword. Kraydak had murdered justice.

"And he continued to destroy you, all the rest of his days," Jago said softly to the god. "But for what peace it gives, he too was destroyed in the end."

He looked at no more tapestries as he walked to the archway that would take him out of the hall.

It took him some time to find the trap—his mind kept drifting back to gods and wizards—and he'd almost decided no trap existed when he spotted the false lintel. But the trigger eluded him still. Finally he gave up, put the point of his dagger between the stone and the overlapping masonry, and threw his weight against the hilt. The blade bowed but held and the lintel sprang free, slamming down to shatter against the floor.

Jago waited until the dust had settled and the echoes of the noise had died and then he stepped over the rubble and looked left down a corridor that held twelve huge, wooden, brass-bound doors.

"Twelve," he mused, pushing a chunk of stone back toward the archway. "And fourteen tapestries. And, if I'm not mistaken, sixteen tiles in each wall and in the floor of the checkerboard room." He smiled grimly and began searching for the next number in sequence. At one of the not-quite-identical doors he stopped; ten rivets held the lock to the wood. The door opened a route to the left as Jago suspected it would. He had to go left to find Crystal and Raulin.

Pulling out his lock-picks, he dropped to one knee and set to work. When the eighth tumbler fell, the door swung open.

The room was empty, and, as far as he could tell, untrapped. In the center, a flight of stairs led down to a lower level. There were no other exits.

Jago paused in the doorway and frowned. He'd either solved the riddle, and the rest of his way was clear, or he'd solved the riddle and was walking into a major setup.

"How in Chaos do I out-think a wizard dead for centuries?" he wondered, decided not to try and headed for the stairs.

He reached the bottom in a small anteroom, with padded leather benches against the side walls and a dark red carpet on the floor. A smell he recognized drifted through the open door that faced the stairs; dust and leather and . . .

"Books?" Jago ran forward into the largest room he'd seen inside the tower and rocked to a stunned halt. The room was filled with books—books on shelves, books on tables, books stacked haphazardly on the floor.

"These can't be real," he murmured as his feet, under no conscious control, carried him farther into the canyons between the cases. His disbelief had no effect on either the books or the room in general.

He bumped up against a table, picked a book at random off a pile, and opened it. The lettering remained as clear and sharp as on the day the Scholar had put pen to paper. Jago drew his fingers lightly over the page and began to read. A while later he put it down and picked up another and, later still, he began to wander—scanning titles, dipping occasionally into the pages, marveling at the knowledge stored away.

In a corner, he found a rack of scrolls and carefully unrolled the uppermost. The crackling parchment gave the first indication that time did, indeed, operate on the objects within the room but then, the scroll had been written before the Age of Wizards. He read over half of it before he realized he shouldn't be able to read it at all. None of the words looked familiar, but he knew what they meant.

Thinking back, Jago remembered other books in other languages but never any book he hadn't understood. Aryalan had obviously taken steps to ensure all parts of her library were accessible.

". . . and the Lady of Grove," he read aloud, his voice touched with wonder, "came from the heart of her tree. Greatly daring were the bards who sang of her beauty for she walked in beauty beyond words.

Tall she stood, and slender, with silver hair, and ivory skin, and eyes the green of sunlight through summer leaves." Tossing a braid back over his shoulder, he smiled. "Sounds like the spitting image of Crystal." Then he paused, one arm outstretched to grasp a black leather tome. What had he just said? Parchment rustled under his other hand and he looked down.

The scroll.

Silver hair, and ivory skin, and eyes the green of sunlight through leaves.

Crystal.

And Raulin.

He wet lips suddenly dry.

"Mother-creator, I'd forgotten about Crystal and Raulin."

Close to panic, Jago backed away from the scroll and began to search frantically for another door. There had to be another way out. He found it at last, tucked back behind a shelf of geographies, half buried behind stacks of maps. It had no lock, only a brass hook, and he was afraid, until he opened it, that it was just a closet. He checked the way for traps, moving faster than he knew was safe, and stepped through, pulling the door shut behind him.

The air in the narrow stone tunnel seemed cleaner somehow and he stood for a moment just breathing it in.

"So," he said to the silence, "were the books a trap of Aryalan's making or my own?"

The silence made no answer.

"Did she cause me to forget? Or did I do it to myself?"

He pulled the stopper from his waterskin and took a long drink. He didn't really think he wanted to know.

The tunnel ran, by his best guess, parallel to the hall of tapestries, although a level lower. He started down it, back toward his companions, leaving his questions by the door. He hadn't gone far when the walls began to close in and the ceiling lowered. For the first time since he'd entered the tower, he remembered that it was not only underground, but underwater.

He touched the stone. Was it damp?

And then the wizard-light went out.

It was more than Jago, nerves already frayed, could endure.

"Not alone," he begged. "Not in the dark."

He could feel the weight of rock all around him.

Closing his eyes helped only a little, just enough for him to force his feet to move. With his shoulders pushing against the walls and one hand running along the ceiling to protect his head, he inched forward. It was never so bad when Raulin was with him and he used that as a goad. If he couldn't make it through this, Raulin might never be with him again.

He had no way to tell if time was passing until the blackness against his lids turned gray. And then orange. He opened his eyes and could see the end of the tunnel.

With his whole mind on the open area ahead, he stumbled forward and out.

He thought of traps one step too late, felt the stone give under his foot, saw the steel plate begin to drop. He had no idea what the steel was to close him in with—fire, flood, or wild beast—nor did he care. He dove forward, rolled, and the plate crashed down behind him.

When his ears stopped ringing, he tried to stand and found he hadn't rolled quite far enough. One braid had been caught between the metal and the floor.

Laughter seemed the only appropriate response . . . until he felt a touch against his boot sole and looked up into the tiny black eyes of a male brindle.


Raulin stood and stared at the narrow stone bridge, his back pressed so hard against the wall he was sure his shoulder blades would leave imprints. Mentally, he retraced his route and decided he'd head back to the last cross corridor and try the other direction; just as soon as he could get his feet to move. He'd caught only a glimpse of the depths the bridge spanned, but that had been enough to send him staggering back to safety and freeze him there.

"Just as soon as the memory fades a bit," he told himself, the wall under his palms growing damp, "I'm out of here."

And then he heard Jago scream on the other side.

He was across the bridge before he knew it and running as fast as his bad knee would allow toward the sound.

"Chaos!" Skidding around a corner he only just managed to avoid slamming into the hind end of a brindle. A brindle that appeared to have his brother pinned. Well, he'd dealt with *that* once before.

He pulled his dagger and leaped at the animal's back, aiming for a pale patch of fur at the top of its spine.

A pale patch of fur . . .

Jago watched mesmerized as the brindle swayed above him, both his legs held easily beneath massive paws. He remembered claws and teeth tearing his flesh from the bone. He remembered pain. He waited for it to begin again.

The brindle bent its head to feed. Jago forced himself to look away.

"Jago! Chaos blast it, Jago, look at me!" Raulin grabbed Jago's chin and yanked his head around. "It isn't real! It's illusion!"

To Jago, caught up in the memory of old torment, Raulin's voice seemed to come from very far away. But Raulin's voice shouldn't have been there at all, so he listened and dragged himself free of the words. When he finally managed to focus, Raulin crouched where the brindle had been.

Raulin saw reason return to his brother's eyes, and started to breathe again. "If you believed in that thing so strongly," he growled, "why didn't you run?"

Jago jerked his head to the limit of the trapped hair.

Raulin's gaze ran along the golden braid and back and Jago tensed for the roar that was sure to come. Raulin didn't disappoint him.

"I TOLD YOU TO GET YOUR HAIR CUT!"

With a half-smile, Jago pulled his dagger and handed it over. "Be my guest."

"Serve you right if I shaved half your head," Raulin muttered, bending to the task. "I told you this would get you into trouble one day, but you wouldn't listen. You can sit up now."

Jago sat and tried not to wince as the other braid was cut to match. "What are you doing?" he asked as Raulin coiled the length of hair and crammed it into his belt pouch.

"What does it look like," Raulin snapped. "I can't see how you managed with two. This thing weighs a ton."

"I am feeling a little light-headed." The ragged ends just touched his shoulders.

"That's because there's nothing between your ears." And in a much softer tone he asked, "You okay?"

"Yeah. You?"

"Yeah."

They held each other then, and everything was all right.

"Tested . . ." Raulin nodded. "It makes sense."

"It's the only thing that does. If Aryalan wanted to keep people out of her tower, she wouldn't have bothered with false floors and falling walls and the rest of this nonsense, she'd have thrown up a power barrier or made the tower invisible."

"So what are we being tested for?"

"I don't know."

Raulin sighed. "Great. Lost in a dead wizard's tower, being tested for reasons that probably died with her, and we know what happens if we fail."

Jago stood and offered Raulin his hand. "Frankly, I'm more worried about what happens if we pass. Come on, let's find Crystal."

"RAULIN! JAGO!"

Crystal let the echoes of her voice fade and reached out with power. Nothing. She could feel the link with Jago, but she couldn't use it to track him. She couldn't touch Raulin at all.

"I told them this was going to happen. I told them!"

Feeling better after that short burst of pettiness, she started across the checkerboard room to the archway. Raulin would not stay put, that went without question. Jago might, but she rather doubted it as he had no way of knowing if either of his companions still lived. She had to find them before they found something they couldn't handle. Or something found them.

*Raulin could be dead,* Avreen pointed out. *Why don't you call the Mother's son and find out? He did say he'd come if you called.*

*Raulin isn't dead.* Crystal's voice was edged.

*You could know for sure. What is it about Lord Death that frightens you lately?*

Crystal slammed a barrier down so hard she felt her other shields tremble. She couldn't keep Avreen locked away for long, but she'd enjoy the peace while it lasted. Afraid of Lord Death, indeed. He was her oldest friend. Why didn't she call him?

The center four tiles of the sixteen in the floor dropped out from under her.

Her power caught her just before she hit the spikes. She drifted up and out of the pit, furious at herself for being distracted.

"What a stupid way for a wizard to die," she muttered. "I keep this up and someone's going to have to rescue me."

When she reached the arch she paused and pushed a wave of power through before her.

Glyphs flared up both sides and the opening pulsed red then black then red again. A binding, similar to the one that had imprisoned the demon. With nothing to hold, the binding faded and the way was clear.

She stepped into a long hall, the archway in the middle of one side. Fourteen windows stretched black and featureless almost floor to ceiling across from her. The ends of the hall held identical doors.

As she approached the nearest window, the glass glowed green. When it cleared, she looked out into a snow covered garden where three children were building a fort. One of the children turned to yell instructions and Crystal recognized her half-brother, the Heir of Ardhan. The two smaller children had to be the twins. She laughed as a disagreement turned into a wrestling match, the twins, as usual, ganging up on the older boy but never quite managing to pin him down.

*Maybe,* she thought, leaning against the window frame, *when I'm finished here, I'll go . . .*

Zarsheiy tried to force her barriers and Crystal suddenly realized what powered the window.

She threw herself back and the scene faded.

"Clever," she acknowledged. She hadn't felt it draining her.

*Idiot,* snorted Zarsheiy.

Staying a careful distance from the rest of the windows, Crystal made her way to the door in the left end of the hall. Finding Raulin first seemed the only choice; Jago, at least, she knew was alive.

On the other side of the door were twelve steps, leading down.

Crystal slammed the door.

"Games!" she snarled. "Twelve, fourteen, sixteen, this isn't a tower, it's a puzzle board."

Boredom had been the greatest enemy of the ancient wizards. The world had fallen at their feet and left them nothing to do.

"This *isn't* a tower," Crystal repeated. "And yet the tower must be close or Aryalan wouldn't have been able to watch her games played. Watch and influence the outcome." She pushed her hair back off her face and thought.

After a moment, she smiled.

With lines of power, she drew a door in the air, opened it, and stepped through . . .

. . . into the center of a circular room, its seven walls made up of seven mirrors.

She turned slowly, hoping to catch sight of Raulin or Jago but saw only Crystal. She touched one mirror with power and let it reflect onto all the others. Nothing. If Aryalan had watched from this place perhaps it was tuned only to her, or there was a trick to activating it that Crystal hadn't yet discovered.

Or Aryalan might have anticipated Crystal's move and the room was itself a part of the game.

*Idiot.*
*Trust your instincts.*
*Reason must be the key.*
*She should follow her heart.*
*Maybe, maybe not.*

"Be quiet!" Crystal snapped. "All of you." she buried her face in her hands, trying to think, and when that didn't help, began to spin slowly on the ball of one foot.

"The ancient wizards were not only bored," she said, seeing herself surrounded by herself, "but vain."

The reflections wavered, and changed.

Eegri laughed out at her, tossing brown curls.

Tayja smiled and spread a mahogany hand against the glass.

Zarsheiy's eyes burned with fire contained but far from under control.

Sholah opened wide her arms, offering refuge.

Nashawryn, stars caught in midnight hair, only stared, her silver eyes impossible to read.

One mirror showed a graceful line of shoulder and back, as Geta, still grieving for her brother, continued to hide her face.

And Avreen. The goddess of love pushed auburn hair away from amber eyes.

"Have I no reflection left at all?" Crystal whispered.

Avreen shook her head, and sighed. *All the reflections are you . . .*

*. . . you . . .*
*. . . you . . .*
*. . . you . . .*
*. . . you . . .*
*. . . you . . .*

Red light played over the lowest level of the tower as the most powerful of its guardians stirred. While not exactly aware, it was capable of independent thought and actions within the boundaries Aryalan had set for it centuries before. Until she created her dragon, the ancient wizard had considered it her greatest achievement and it had given her many hours of amusement.

The Wizards' Doom had not affected it, nor had the centuries it had lain dormant.

It had watched the intruders and now it knew them; knew their strengths and knew their weaknesses; followed the lines that joined them and knew how to tie them in place.

It judged them worthy of its attention.

It gathered together the power still at its disposal and prepared to use the knowledge it had gleaned; prepared to place all three pieces in the final configuration.

Had Aryalan been there to watch, she would have been very amused indeed.

—WIZARD—

The mirrors faded and Crystal found herself suspended in blackness. Red lines, sullenly pulsating, held her securely and where they touched they brought torment. Hurriedly, she threw shields up against the pain and found it left her no power to get free.

—YOU HAVE A MOVE STILL REMAINING IN THE GAME—

Fury banished fear.

She bit off each word and spat it out. "I'm not playing."

Lines of red flashed out from those that bound her, wrapped about and illuminated two bodies; Raulin to her left, Jago to her right. They had no protection from the pain and screamed wordlessly and continuously, thrashing and fighting as the light spun out between them and completed the triangle.

The voice sounded clearly over the brothers' cries.

—TO FREE YOURSELF, WIZARD, BREAK THE BALANCE—

Raulin shrieked her name and she spun toward him. The motion caused the lines about Jago to flicker and brighten. He threw back his head and his screams grew shrill. When she turned to Jago, Raulin writhed in new agony.

—ONE MUST BE SACRIFICED, WIZARD, IT IS THE ONLY WAY—

To free herself.

"No." Her chin went up. "I am not like the ancient wizards," she said. "I don't play games."

She dropped all barriers and threw wide her power. This time, she didn't fight. The word she'd searched for, the word that pulled it all together, was acceptance.

*All the reflections are you. . . .*

The pain hit first, from the lines of red, then Zarsheiy burned and the pain was lost in fire. She felt Sholah and Tayja give themselves joyously to the new matrix and she felt Eegri dance through the flame. She acknowledged Avreen, acknowledged the face the goddess wore and added to the reforging the sorrow of love admitted too late. Darkness surged forth with the eldest goddess. But there came no answer from the light.

Only the threat of Kraydak had convinced Geta to help in Crystal's creation. Kraydak, like Getan his father, had died. Geta mourned her twin and would not be moved.

Then Jago screamed and chance alone made the words the last that Getan had cried.

"Mother, it hurts!"

And the goddess looked to the image of her brother writhing in pain.

*No!*

Freedom rose to stand against the darkness.

Crystal looked to Raulin, now hanging limp in his bonds and remembered the strength in his arms and the pleasure they had shared, the warmth that had banished winter's nights. She looked to Jago, who still twisted and fought, and gently touched the place where his life touched hers, savoring the knowledge that, for a time, she had not been alone. Gathering up the memories, she placed them where she hoped they would survive what was to come, for friendship was too rare a thing to lose. All this in less than a heartbeat . . .

. . . then Crystal let go of self.

The red lines disappeared, for the wizard they had held was no more.

\*　　\*　　\*

"Mortal! Mortal, wake, or you will go to my Mother by my hand!"

"Bet you wish you could shake him."

Lord Death whirled and glared at the dwarf. "Do not mock me, Elder, lest I misuse the power I wield. You can be killed and I am Death."

Doan spread his hands, his face unwontedly serious. "I do not mock you, Mother's son. I spoke without thinking. Forgive me." He dropped his eyes to the two men crumpled on the ground. "The mortals live?"

"They live. But I cannot get them to wake."

"Perhaps I can help." Sokoji pushed passed the dwarf, her arms full of fur. She wrapped both bodies in the overcoats, then bent over Raulin. After a moment, she shook her head. "If he wakes at all," she said sadly, "it will not be for some time." She moved to Jago and her expression grew more helpful. "This one has something in him that fights what was done and is almost healed." Lifting Jago's head onto her lap, she held out her hand to Doan. "Give me your flask."

"There's not much left," Doan warned her as he passed it over.

"It won't take much." Sokoji waved the open flask under Jago's nose.

Jago coughed and opened his eyes. "What . . . what happened?"

Doan snorted. "We hoped you'd tell us."

With the giant's arm a firm support across his back, Jago sat up and looked around. The tower, the island, and the lake were gone. In their place, a perfectly circular bowl of bare rock curved up around him, Sokoji, the dwarf, Lord Death, and the still body of his brother.

"Raulin!" He twisted out of Sokoji's grasp. "Raulin?"

"He lives," Sokoji told him, "but he needs help I cannot give."

She paused, and in the silence, Doan prodded: "Perhaps Crystal . . ."

Jago shook his head, spattering the rock with tears. "Crystal is . . . she . . ."

"She what, mortal?"

Jago met Lord Death's eyes. "I don't know," he whispered. He laid his hand against Raulin's cheek, comforted by the feather touch of breath, and tried to describe what he'd seen in the instant between pain and oblivion.

"Her face was perfectly still and her arms were open. It sounds crazy, you couldn't see through her or anything, but she looked clear," his mouth twisted, "like crystal. She'd been wearing clothes she'd borrowed from us—from Raulin and me—they were gone. Silver light began to pour out from her hair, then from her eyes, then from her skin, then there was only light so brilliant it burned. That's all."

He couldn't describe what he'd felt when Crystal had dissolved into light, the searing glory that had burned along the life-link and threatened for an instant to consume him too. He didn't have the words for it. He doubted the words existed.

He wanted to turn away from the expression on Lord Death's face. He didn't.

"She called me," Lord Death told him. "I heard her."

"I'm sorry." And Jago cried for more than just Crystal and his brother.

Sokoji stood and scanned the sky. "From out of darkness came the Mother, but in what fire was she forged?" She glanced down at Doan who stared at her in puzzlement. "It is a question my sisters and I often think on."

"Yeah, so?"

The giant smiled. "And now it has been answered. There will be new worlds born from this day."

"Let me get this straight," Doan shoved his hands behind his belt, "you think that Crystal just became a new . . ." His mouth opened and closed unable to get around the concept.

"A new creator?" Sokoji nodded. "Yes."

"No." Lord Death's hands curled into fists and he staggered forward, fell to his knees and howled. "NO! Crystal, come back! I love you!"

The words hung in the air for a long moment and then they faded.

A silver spark danced along the path of a wandering breeze. And then another. And then another. And then the breeze danced in silver hair and Crystal opened her arms to Lord Death.

"I can touch you now." Her words were a promise.

Lord Death laid a trembling hand in hers and let her pull him to his feet.

"I heard you call," he told her. "I heard you say you loved me."

*Back before the remaking, when love had been separate, and love had worn his face. . . .* "Yes," she said, drawing him close, "I called."

"I came."

Her lips parted.

Then his arms were around her and the glory enfolded them both. The silver light grew brighter, and brighter still, and then, abruptly, it was gone.

Except for one small spark that settled gently on the very tip of Raulin's nose and flared, wrapping his body for an instant in light.

When it faded, Raulin blinked and yawned. "S'it over?"

"Yeah." Jago managed to get the word out past the lump in his throat.

"Then why are you crying? Didn't things work out?"

Jago glanced from Sokoji to Doan. The giant only smiled, the dwarf rocked back on his heels and shrugged, so Jago came to his own decision.

"It's okay," he said, and wiped his eyes. "Everything worked out."

# END

Raulin tossed the purse on the table and grinned at the way the clerk's jaw dropped.

"Go on, man," he prodded, "open it; this *is* the day the Council admits new members."

The clerk glanced nervously over his shoulder at the six councilors and with trembling fingers untied the purse strings. Twice a year, in the spring and in the fall, the Council opened its doors, allowing new members to buy their way in. This was the first time anyone had tried for the seats that cost more than most citizens of the crumbling Empire saw in a lifetime and the price had to be paid in gold. Twice a year the four men and two women who ruled the city ranged themselves at one end of the council chamber and waited while curious citizenry ranged themselves at the other. And also waited.

When Kraydak had fallen, many of the weak and corrupt he had put in power hung on.

". . . 28, 29, 30." The clerk looked back again, and waved one hand over the stack of freshly minted coins. "It's, it's all there, milords." He obviously had no idea of what to do next.

One of the councilors stepped forward, glared first at the coins, and then at Raulin.

"Where did you get this?" she demanded.

Raulin winked at her. "It used to be my brother's." In fact, it used to be Jago's braid, but he had no intention of telling her that.

"It must be tested."

"Go ahead." Nor did he intend to tell her of how, on the long trip back, Doan had melted down the soft pure strands of gold Raulin had found in his pouch and doubled their volume by reforging them into a metal less pure but more acceptable.

The clerk was sent to find a goldsmith and the councilor withdrew back to her fellows where they muttered and fretted and planned. A rustling noise came from the crowd as something very like hope drifted through their ranks.

Although Jago had gone that morning to the Scholar's Hall, Raulin could feel his brother at his back, and knowledge, he'd learned, was as formidable a weapon as wealth or steel. He touched the jewel he wore on a silver chain about his neck—one of the two emeralds inexplicably mixed in with the rubies; Jago wore the other—and thought of the patch of light in the center of his palm. The kiss Crystal had given him, for later. If Jago had been changed by their journey—and there was no denying the younger man had picked up a number of interesting abilities, not the least of which was self-healing—Raulin had only had something he'd always believed reinforced.

Anything is possible.

He smiled at the row of councilors. One by one, they tried to stare him down. One by one, they dropped their gazes.

*That's right,* he said silently, *squirm. 'Cause there's going to be some changes made.*


Other places might look gray and depressing in early spring, but the Sacred Grove, Tayer felt, bore a promise for the renewal that lay ahead. Delicate new growth already touched the ground with green and, even with their branches bare, the ancient silver birches ringed the Grove in beauty.

"Majesty."

Tayer started and stared at the squat, broad-shouldered man who had so suddenly appeared. Her brow furrowed. "Do I know you?' "

Doan bowed. "We met once, many, many years ago."

"Here?"

"No, in the wood. But you had just come from the Grove." His eyes moved for an instant to the space in the circle where a tree no longer stood.

Tayer smiled sadly. "I don't remember much of those days." She remembered light and love and not much more.

"Uh, yes." Doan's gaze dropped to his feet, for he remembered those days very well; back when he'd guarded the Grove and the hope it had contained. "Best that you don't."

"Have you come then to renew our old acquaintance?" Tayer asked, brows raised.

"No." He took a deep breath. Sokoji had offered to bring the news to Tayer but Doan, having been in on the beginning, felt he should see it through to the end. "I've come about your daughter."

"Tell me." The Queen of Ardhan squared her shoulders and waited for the blow. "Has she been killed?"

"No!" In his rush to wipe the pain from Tayer's face, Doan snapped out the word so hard she winced. "No," he repeated, more gently, "she isn't dead." He saw again the glory that Crystal had become wrapped in the arms of Lord Death and added, "Exactly."

"Exactly?" Tayer repeated, looking both relieved and confused.

Doan snorted. "It's a long story."

"Well . . ." Tayer crossed the Grove and sat down on a protruding root. Both her council and her children would have recognized her tone of voice. "Why don't you start at the beginning."

So he did.

When he finished, Tayer sat quietly for a long time.

"Is she happy?" she asked at last.

"Yes. I believe so."

Tayer felt the tug of a baby's lips upon her breast. Smelled the soft scent of sunlight on silver hair as a child snuggled on her lap in the garden. Saw a girl stand to face an ancient evil, green eyes blazing defiance. Heard the voice of a young woman who shared her heart.

Her lower lip trembled. "I shall miss her."

Doan nodded and reached out to wipe a tear away.

"And I," he said softly. "And I."